THE LIFE
OF
ROSE BRAMBLES

Book 3

———— ∼ ————

By

Lesley Tréville

CONTENTS

ACKNOWLEDGMENTS

Thanks to all my wonderful friends who have knowingly or unknowingly given me ideas for the various stories in this book.

As in Book 2, thank you to some of the French places of interest, who gave me permission to include them in the book.

CHAPTER 1

JP and Rose were attending a Christmas Eve ball at Séra's, when a woman shocked and accosted JP. Back in the room, after visiting the toilets to compose himself, he went straight into surveillance mode, and looked around for a pregnant Isabella. Alas, there were quite a few ladies who were expecting. The next hour or so, nothing happened and JP thought there was no way Isabella would be here, and it must have been a genuine mistake. Perhaps the woman thought he was somebody else, and so he relaxed. Rose suggested they went and got something to eat. As they walked into the room with the buffet, a loud voice suddenly said, "Well, well, look, it's my baby's papa." Rose and JP froze, as the whole room went silent. Isabella walked over to them and looking at the guests said, "Everyone, let me introduce my lover. This is JP and the papa of my baby, but he has spurned me for the little English whore."

Without warning, Rose stood in front of Isabella and said with venom, "If it's the last thing I do I will see you in prison. Now leave us alone."

A female voice then said, "Isabella, what's going on?"

Rose knew that voice and turned to see Katriane, who was now stood at the side of Isabella. Rose said annoyed, "You know this two-faced bitch, Katriane? Please, everyone excuse my language, but she has caused great distress to my fiancé and myself."

Katriane replied, "Isabella is my daughter."

Rose's eyes went wide, and she couldn't believe what Katriane had said. Rose asked questioningly, "She's your daughter?" JP now faintly recognised Katriane. Séra and Mathieu had walked in to see the confrontation.

"What is the meaning of this? How dare you spoil my party?" said Séra.

Katriane replied bitchily, "It seems Rose's fiancé is the father of Isabella's baby."

JP said, "I am not the father of Isabella's child, and as Isabella knows, I have proof. May I suggest we take this somewhere else?"

Rose then spotted her uncle, who had paled. Séra apologised to her guests and guided Rose, JP, Katriane, Isabella and Hugh to the study. "Now will someone tell me what the hell this is all about?" said Séra, extremely annoyed.

Rose went to explain, but Katriane stopped her. "This man violated my daughter and you can see the result."

"Oh no he didn't," snapped Rose.

"Môn amour, I will explain," said JP, and he did.

Katriane and Séra were stunned by what JP told them, and also felt his embarrassment.

"Maman, he's lying," said Isabella, crying. "It was him who raped me, and anyone could have written that letter." Hugh went and stood by JP and Rose.

"Do you have a piece of paper and a pen?" asked JP. Séra nodded and got the paper and pen for him. "Please phone this number, but I'm not sure he will be home. He is the President's physician. Ask him what you want to know and tell him you have my permission. This is his name."

Séra took the piece of paper and made the phone call. When she came back, she was as white as a sheet. Séra turned on Isabella and said, "You nasty, conniving bitch. As of now you are no longer my niece. Get her out of here, Katriane."

Rose said, "Niece? So you two are sisters? Now I understand all the questions, Katriane."

Isabella went to leave, but Katriane stopped her. "I think we need an explanation, don't you?"

Isabella looked at them all and said, "I had been estranged from my maman, since my parents decided to get divorced. I went to Italy with my father, who I loved deeply, and was having a great time, until he passed away a couple of months ago, and I miss him terribly. I met my maman again at his funeral. I had been going out with the local gigolo and found out I was pregnant. He didn't want to know. I decided to come back, and when I made enquiries about JP, I found out he was engaged. I was absolutely furious and decided to get my revenge. He had always been mine. If I could get him to love me, then I was pregnant, and he'd have to marry me. My gigolo and I had tried a sex stimulant drug one night. It was the greatest sex we'd ever had, so I knew it worked. I got a friend in Italy to send me some, but it went wrong and I gave JP too much. I still want you as my husband, JP, and the sex between us would be better than with that," she said, pointing at Rose.

JP put his arm around Rose and held her close. Katriane rounded on Isabella and said, "So you decide to come home with some sob story, about how you couldn't live in Italy anymore now your papa had died, and how much you had missed having your maman around, and then you have the gall to make me feel sorry for you because of your so-called rape ordeal. Well, what a complete and utter bloody fool I was. So how pregnant are you?"

"Just over five months," replied Isabella.

Rose frowned at Isabella and said, "You can't be. You seduced my fiancé towards the end of June. You just said you were already pregnant, so you have to be over seven months."

Katriane replied, "Don't insult my daughter, here, look for yourself," and with that pulled down the elasticated skirt Isabella was wearing. They all stared at Isabella. "What in the world have you got on?" asked Katriane. Isabella explained it was a girdle to make her look smaller than what she was. "Undo it NOW." Isabella unlaced it and when it fell away, her stomach rounded out to the correct size. "Again, I will ask. How pregnant are you?"

Isabella replied, "Nearly eight months."

"Môn amour, I think we should leave."

Séra put her hand on JP's arm and said, "I really would like you to stay. I want to tell all my guests what a great photographer I've got, and introduce her to some very influential people." Turning to Katriane and Isabella, she said, "You, however, can leave, and I don't want to see either of you ever again."

Katriane turned to Hugh and said, "Would you take us home please, Hugh?"

Hugh replied, "I'm sorry Katriane, but I'm staying with Rose and JP. I will ring you in a couple of days."

Katriane snapped, "Don't bother. You come with me," and grabbed Isabella by the wrist and dragged her out of the study.

"I'm sorry, Uncle," said Rose.

Hugh kissed her cheek, and told her not to worry.

"Come, we have a party to attend," said Séra.

Rose could feel JP was a little anxious, especially after having his private details exposed. "I think we should leave, Séra. It's going to be quite embarrassing to walk back in there. If I still have a job with you, I will see you in the New Year."

"Of course you still have a job with me. It's my sister and niece I'm disgusted at, not you. I'm sorry, JP, things came out that I'm sure you would rather have kept quiet." JP sort of smiled. He had never been so embarrassed discussing his private life.

Séra then positioned herself between Rose and JP, and with her arms in theirs, they walked backed in. "Everyone, a moment of your time please," said Séra. The room went quiet. "Apologies about what happened earlier, but it turns out my niece is not a very nice person and an accomplished liar. She damned this gentleman in front of you all, and the accusations were completely untrue. Families, who'd have them? So, please, I would like to introduce my talented photographer Rose and her fiancé, JP." Léon, Lil and Cat were the first ones to go to Rose and JP. Within half an hour, the party was in full swing again, and Rose, JP and Hugh were enjoying themselves.

A couple of minutes before midnight, Séra called everyone out in the garden. "Let's go," she said. As the clock struck midnight, the snow fan started up and the fireworks went off, and champagne was served. JP held Rose close and kissed her. "Merry Christmas, môn amour. Je t'aime." Rose replied that she loved him too. Then Rose kissed and hugged her uncle, whilst JP shook his hand. The snow was falling everywhere and everyone was dancing in it, with some trying to throw snowballs. When it was time to go, Rose and JP thanked Séra and Mathieu for a wonderful time. They also took Hugh home, as he had come in Katriane's car.

Back at the flat, JP said, "Well that was embarrassing. Let's hope that is now the end of Isabella."

Rose wrapped her arms around him and said, "Then let me help you forget. I have something special for you," and with that, went into the spare bedroom. JP got undressed and got into bed, and put a box under his pillow. Rose came in wearing a Santa Claus dress. "Would you like to unwrap your present?" she said. JP took her in his arms and kissed her. Rose then straddled him and pulled the dress open where it was done up with Velcro tape. Underneath she had red and white tassels on her nipples, and her briefs had a heart on them flashing "Merry Christmas."

JP smiled and said, "You always amaze me. Now shake those tassels." Rose obliged and soon the tassels and briefs were off, and JP loved her. Afterwards JP put his hand under the pillow and said, "For you, mòn amour. Merry Christmas and Happy Birthday."

Rose sat up and opened the box, and inside was a gorgeous diamond bracelet. "Oh my love, it's beautiful. Put it on for me." JP put it on her wrist. "I have something for you too, my love." She opened the bedside cabinet and took out a box as well. JP opened it and found a lovely watch, with tiepin and matching cuff links. "Oh mòn amour, they're wonderful. Come here." After removing her bracelet, soon they were loving each other again, and then they slept in each other's arms.

The President usually went away over the Christmas and New Year, but this year there was a change of plan. Again his son wasn't well, but it was nothing serious. He did however give JP and his men Christmas and Boxing Day off to spend with their families. Other bodyguards filled in. The New Year's Eve ball was also unusual. Bodyguards were not invited to such an occasion, but the President decided this ball would have none of the high-browed dignitaries. He decided to ask influential people, like bank managers, solicitors, judges, and other professions. On Christmas Day, Ruby, Monica and George, and Hugh all phoned Rose to wish her happy birthday and Merry Christmas. The rest of the day JP and Rose just lazed around, loved each other, and totally relaxed.

On Boxing Day, all his men along with their wives and children descended on them. JP had been cooking from early morning to get everything ready. Rose naturally helped him, but he was keeping quiet about what he was actually cooking. Soon the flat was buzzing with people. JP had brought a small table home so the children could sit round it. He had also penned off an area where the children could play with all the toys they brought. "I think you need a bigger flat, JP," said Antoine, who Rose could see was missing Ruby.

She went and cuddled him and said, "Ruby will be here next week for the ball."

Antoine kissed her cheek and said, "I really do miss her, Rose. Do you think, like you, she will move to Paris?"

Rose replied, "Her decision is more difficult than mine was. Even though I call them Mum and Dad, as you know, they are Ruby's parents, and she loves them dearly. It would be a wrench for her to leave them, but I know they wouldn't stand in her way. She loves you as much as I love JP."

Antoine was kissing Rose's cheek when a small voice said, "Uncle JP, he's kissing Aunt Rose. Yuk." It was Andre's son. Everyone burst out laughing.

At last the meal was ready, and everyone was told to sit at the tables, except Antoine. Antoine brought in large bowls containing roast potatoes, various vegetables, pots of gravy and a huge chicken. JP then brought in sausages, stuffing and Yorkshire puddings. Rose's eyes lit up. "What are these?" asked Emilie, and so Rose explained it was a typical Lancashire/Yorkshire Christmas meal. The mamans sorted out the food for the children, and then they all tucked in with JP carving the chicken. Donatien opened the bottles of wine and poured it into the glasses. Apart from half of the chicken, everything else was eaten.

"I really enjoyed that," said Pierre, "something different. Love the Yorkshire puddings and stuffing." Everyone else agreed and then toasted the chef. JP took a bow.

After a rest and the dishes had been cleared away, JP then put pudding bowls out, and brought in a huge Christmas pudding, which he then poured brandy over and lit it. "Oh goodness me," said

Gabrielle. Once the flames went out, JP put a little bit in the bowls for the children and Céleste gave it to them. There were also jugs of cream and custard.

"Maman, don't like," said one of Céleste's daughters.

"Why is there always one?" asked Céleste.

Donatien got up and put the pudding in his own bowl, and then put some custard and cream in the other bowl. Their daughter liked that. Afterwards Rose made juice drinks for the children and pots of coffee for the adults.

"Well JP, yet again, you have surpassed us with another sumptuous meal. I don't think I will eat for at least a fortnight. Thank you so much," said Emilie.

Pierre laughed and said, "Wait and see, shall we?"

A couple of hours later, all the children were firm asleep. JP had put the television on quietly just for background noise. They all chatted about their Christmases and then JP told them about Séra's party. Gabrielle said, "I would so like to meet this Isabella."

Andre put his arm round her shoulder and said, "And what would you do if you did?"

Gabrielle replied, "I can't tell you because little ears have big ears," she said, looking at the children. Not all of them were asleep. Andre kissed her cheek.

"I have an idea, JP," said Andre dryly. "Why don't you invite Isabella over here, and then let our ladies tackle her?"

JP replied, "No. I don't want blood up the walls."

Rose slapped him and said, "We are not bullies. Words can be more devastating. Right, my sisters?"

"Nice one, Andre, now you've started something," said Pierre.

Andre replied, "Who, me? I was actually joking." Gabrielle slapped the back of Andre's head. "Ouch, that hurt."

"Tough," replied Gabrielle, and then everyone laughed.

After watching a couple of films on the television, JP and Rose vanished into the kitchen and then came out with chicken, ham, and pork sandwiches, along with a Christmas cake. Pierre said, "Should have had a bet, shouldn't I?" Everyone looked at him. "Well my lovely wife said she wouldn't be able to eat another thing for at least two weeks. Yet here she is eating sandwiches and cake." That earned Pierre a slap around his head. "Tell me, my sisters, is this head slapping normal?"

"Oh yes," replied Céleste. "It's the one thing, along with stopping night frolics, they understand."

Rose glanced at JP, who raised his eyebrow and said, "Don't go getting any ideas." They all burst out into fits of laughter.

Soon it was time for them all to go. The children had totally worn themselves out and were now firm asleep, but they had been as good as gold. They would all meet again, along with Ruby, at the President's New Year's Eve ball.

CHAPTER 2

Rose had been so busy, she hadn't had time to get a new gown. She went back to the shop where JP had bought her gown the year before. The assistant recognised her at once. "Mademoiselle, lovely to see you again. How may we help you?" Rose explained. "Just one moment, I think I have just the thing." The assistant went out the back and came back with a lovely grey dress, and some silver lace. The bodice was shaped like a basque, and the skirt flowed down softly.

Rose was a bit disappointed, and said, "Lovely as this is, I'm going to a ball at the President's palace, and need something...."

"Excuse me, Mademoiselle, I have a suggestion. Do you like this lace?" Rose thought it was beautiful. It was light silver, but covered in delicate leaves and roses, in a darker silver, but not all over. "Try and imagine this done as a bodice over the top with sleeves. This would be stitched into the band of the bodice. The rest of the fabric will then go over the top of the long skirt." As the assistant was describing it, she was also drawing it. Rose was over the moon, and said it needed to be done in a couple of days. The assistant said they would start straight away, but first Rose needed to try the dress on. It fitted her perfectly. Before Rose left, the assistant said, "Would you want bra and briefs in this fabric as well?" Rose said she would.

Two days later Rose went back and was totally blown away by the dress. "Oh my, it's absolutely gorgeous," said Rose. At the back was a very delicate zip, and the sleeves slightly billowed out from the elbow, and gathered at the wrist. The bra and brief set were also lovely.

Looking round, she picked out some silver-grey shoes, and a clutch bag. Then she spotted some small silver roses for her hair and bought those as well. The only problem she was going to have was somebody to zip her up. Ruby was due later that night, but naturally was staying at Antoine's. Donatien was picking her up from the airport. Neither of them would see their men until the night of the ball. In the morning Rose phoned Ruby, and Ruby suggested she got a taxi to Rose's, see to her zip and then leave for the ball. Rose said it sounded a good plan.

Later on she went to the beauty salon and had her hair, nails, toes and other things done. Her hair was put up in swirls, so all she had to do was clip the silver roses into the swirls. She made sure she had a good lunch, even though it was late afternoon, and a couple of hours later started to get ready. JP had given Rose the combination to the safe, so she got her diamond earrings, necklace and bracelet out. Carefully she put the clips in her hair, and turned this way and that and was pleased. Her matching bra and briefs were like a bikini, but the fabric was so soft. As she was still tanned, she decided against any makeup, apart from a little lipstick.

Carefully she unzipped the back of the dress, and then stepped into it. Putting her arms into the sleeves, she carefully pulled the rest over her shoulders. It fitted beautifully. She put on her jewellery, and shoes, and then looked in the mirror. The image that she looked at was a tall, graceful, elegant woman, and she smiled. The doorbell ringing brought her back down to earth.

Ruby's mouth opened when she saw Rose. "Oh wow, you look absolutely fantastic. Turn round and let me do your zip up."

Rose said, "Let me see your dress." Ruby looked absolutely gorgeous. She wore a blue fitted dress, with thin straps, and the bodice was covered in tiny gold sequins. The skirt, like Rose's, flared out softly, again with gold sequins here and there. She had matching ruby earrings and necklace on. Her shoes matched her dress along with a clutch bag.

"Well sister, you ready for the ball?" asked Ruby. Rose grabbed her coat and both of them went down to the waiting taxi.

The queue at the palace was long, and so Rose directed the driver to another entrance. The guard recognised Rose immediately and rang through to JP's office. JP naturally gave his permission. Antoine met them at the entrance. He took Ruby in his arms and kissed her passionately. "I'll just go to JP's office, shall I Antoine?" asked Rose, tongue-in-cheek and smiling. Antoine said he was expecting her, and carried on kissing Ruby.

As Rose walked into JP's office, she saw him trying to tie his bow tie. "Would you like me to do that for you, my love?" JP turned and his smile lit his whole face up. Rose put her clutch bag on his desk and tied it for him. Then he took her in his arms and kissed her with a passion. "Now I'll have to re-do my lipstick," said Rose, smiling and taking her bag, went into JP's bathroom. When she came out JP had his jacket on, and was ready to go, but his back was towards her. She quietly put her coat on the chair, and said, "I hope I haven't let you down? Finding a gown was a nightmare."

JP turned and took every bit of Rose in. "You look absolutely exquisite, môn amour. My belle of the ball. Shall we?" Rose gave him a quick kiss and they walked arm in arm down the corridor, towards the ballroom. JP still couldn't get over what a beautiful fiancée he had on his arm. The ballroom was packed, with an orchestra playing soft music in the background, but JP soon saw his men and their wives, along with Ruby, all looking gorgeous. Then he spotted Hugh. First of all though, they had to be greeted by the President and his wife. Rose had never met her before, but straight away knew she was the backbone of his life, and was a stunning-looking woman. JP bowed to both of them and Rose curtsied.

"Rose, you look absolutely divine. May I introduce my wife, Alicía Jacquéline."

"It is a pleasure to meet you, Madame," replied Rose.

"So you are the exquisite beauty who has captured JP's heart? I feel like I know you already, so maybe we could talk later?"

Rose replied she would be honoured.

JP and Rose joined the others, and hugs and kisses were given all round. Hugh came up to them and everyone greeted him. He had a lovely lady with him, and introduced her as Chantelle. They stayed for a short while and then left to mingle. The others chatted, ate, danced and thoroughly enjoyed themselves. The President's wife had been watching them and said to her husband, "Now I understand what JP means when he says he has his family. Look how happy he is with Rose and the others."

The President replied, "If anyone deserves happiness, it's those two with everything they've been through. And no, I'm not going to speak about it, as it was in confidence. Now how about we have a dance?"

Everyone stood to one side as the President and his wife walked to the dance floor. Once on the floor everyone applauded them, and then joined in. Later the President asked Rose for a dance, and so JP danced with Alicía. "You have a lovely fiancée, JP, and in all the years I've known you, I have never seen you so blissfully happy. When is the wedding?" JP replied it was on his birthday, the 30th June. "Well if that isn't romantic, I don't know what is. May I ask a personal question?" JP nodded. "Once you and Rose are married, please tell me you're not going to leave us?"

JP replied, "The only time I will leave the palace is when the President asks me to, or until a new President has to take over, which I hope won't be for many years yet."

After the dance, Alicía asked Rose if she could have a word. They left the ballroom and went into another room. "I know it's not the appropriate time, Rose, but I wanted to ask you if you would do some special photos of my family. It's coming up to our wedding anniversary next year, and I want to surprise my husband. Would you be interested?"

Rose smiled and replied, "It would be my honour to do them, Madame. Will you let JP know when you require me?" Alicía replied she would. They chatted about things in general and then made their way back into the ballroom. Both the President and JP raised their eyebrows.

"If I know my wife," said the President, "and believe me, JP, I know her better than what she thinks, I think she has been vetting Rose." Rose curtsied to Alicía and then went to JP.

"Alright, môn amour?"

Rose replied she was fine and told him about the photos. JP told her what the President had said. "Shows how wrong he was," said Rose, laughing. "Let's dance, my love, as I want you in my arms." JP whispered something in her ear and Rose blushed. "Behave, my love, until later."

As they waltzed round the ballroom, so JP's men kept swapping their partners, so they all danced with each other. Rose loved it. Soon the orchestra stopped playing, and the President said, "Well, another year is about to leave us, and a new one to enter. I wish all of you health, wealth and happiness. Let the countdown begin."

The waiters and waitresses made sure everyone had a glass of champagne, and then the clock struck midnight. Everyone cheered and said, "Happy New Year," the champagne was drunk and then the orchestra started playing.

As Rose and JP danced, JP said, "Happy New Year, môn amour, and now it's only six months to our wedding, and I can't wait. I love you so very much." Tears sprang to Rose's eyes and she replied by kissing him tenderly. Then all his men and their wives hugged and kissed each other. The party carried on until about 2am, when people then started to drift home.

"Boss, don't forget we're not on duty," said Andre, who had noticed JP was surveying the goings on. JP smiled. "Are you staying here or going home?"

"Home," replied JP.

Fifteen minutes later they were all saying goodbye to each other. "See you the day after tomorrow," said JP. "Oh and Antoine – don't be late."

Everyone burst out laughing, but not to be outdone, Antoine replied, "I won't, boss, if you're not."

JP and Rose went back to his office to collect Rose's coat, and then they made their way home. Once in the flat Rose hung her coat up in the wardrobe in the spare room. "Môn amour, it's about time we sorted our bedroom out. At the end of the month we must go furniture buying."

Rose walked into the bedroom smiling and said, "I need your help, my love. Can you carefully unzip the back of my dress for me? But first, let me give you my jewellery." JP took the jewellery and placed it in the safe, and then undid the zip, placing featherlike kisses down her back. Carefully Rose took her dress off and went and hung it in the wardrobe in the other room. As she walked back in, JP was just removing his trousers, and hanging his suit up. Rose sat on the bed and started to remove the rose clips in her hair, while admiring JP's backside. "Anybody tell you what sexy buttocks you've got?"

JP turned and smiled at her. "Now who is this gorgeous creature sitting on the end of the bed?" He took her hair clips and put them on the cabinet, and then held his hands out for her to stand up. He took her in his arms and kissed her with passion.

Rose linked her arms around his neck and said, "Umm, I think my angel wants to play." He picked her up in his arms and gently laid her on the bed. He trailed kisses down her neck and down to her breasts. Then he placed kisses over her stomach, but made no attempt to remove her bra or briefs.

His kisses came back up to her lips. Rose rolled him over and did the same to him, but her hand went nowhere near her angel. They just kissed and cuddled and held each other tight. "Love me, my love," said Rose huskily. JP unclipped the back of her bra and removed it, freeing her breasts. He covered them with kisses and gently took her nipples in his mouth and nipped and sucked them. His hand went under her briefs and cupped her mound. Rose's hand stroked his back up and down and then she cupped his buttocks. There was no rush with their lovemaking, so they just enjoyed exploring each other's bodies. Soon they were naked and JP got on top of Rose and gently pushed his manhood up into her. Rose moaned and said, "That feels better," and started to move her hips. JP carried on kissing her lips, neck and breasts. Then Rose wrapped her legs round him, and putting her hands on his buttocks started kneading them. Her hips started rotating quicker and JP started thrusting quicker. Soon they both went into oblivion and then curled up together and sank into a deep contented sleep.

It was after midday when they woke. Rose stretched like she always did, and took JP in her arms and kissed him gently. She felt him responding, and lifted her leg over his hip and guided him into her. Like the night before it was slow and sensual. Afterwards Rose got up and looking out of the window, said, "My love, come look, everything is white. It must have snowed after we got in."

JP got up and linked his arms round her waist. "Looks like Séra has been out with the snow fan. You hungry?"

"Ravenous," replied Rose.

After they had a quick bath, JP started cooking.

The phone rang and it was Hugh wishing them both a Happy New Year. Rose asked him if he had enjoyed the ball, and who was the mysterious Chantelle. Hugh replied, "I had a lovely time, especially meeting other bankers. As to Chantelle, I'm rather embarrassed to say she was an escort. Please don't say anything, Rose. I just couldn't go on my own."

Rose replied, "I don't think you need to be embarrassed, Uncle, as I'm sure lots of people do it. She was a lovely lady anyway. I'm sorry about Katriane, but now I know why she kept grilling me about JP, Séra and Mathieu."

Hugh replied, "She was getting to be rather possessive, and like you, asking me questions regarding my work and personal life as well. Naturally I never answered her." They talked for a bit and then they promised to meet up for lunch on Tuesday.

CHAPTER 3

"Môn amour, a very late breakfast is served." Rose and JP sat down to bacon, sausages, eggs, fried bread (which Rose loved), tomatoes, toast and coffee. "So môn amour, how do you think we should plan out our new bedroom? I think everything should go, and we have brand new. I have had the furniture a long time." They discussed this and that and decided to wait until they got to the store. "When do you go back to work, môn amour?"

"Séra is away for this week, so I will see if Mathieu needs anything doing, see my uncle, and spend time with Ruby before she goes back at the weekend. I know she wants to talk about coming over here to be with Antoine, and she mentioned Mum and Dad."

For the rest of the day Rose and JP relaxed and just enjoyed each other. In the morning JP went back to work. The snow from the day before had now turned to slush, and it was starting to rain. Rose phoned Ruby and then picked her up an hour later. They went to the shopping centre and looked at all the sales, enjoyed a leisurely lunch, and Rose dropped her back about 5pm. Ruby didn't mention about moving over, so Rose didn't bring up the subject, which worried her slightly. That night JP phoned her with some interesting news.

The next day Rose met her uncle and they had lunch in his flat. "Uncle, I have something to tell you about Katriane. We both understand now why she was always asking me questions about Séra being her sister. Many, many years ago, their parents, who were rich, were killed abroad. In the Will, Séra was left most of the fortune. Katriane obviously was furious, but unbeknown to her, her father had found out her secret. Do you remember she asked me if Mathieu from Gilmac News was married?" Hugh replied he did. "Marcus told us when Mathieu came to Paris, he met someone. It turns out it was Katriane, but she was married. Mathieu didn't know, and Katriane carried on the affair, and then once he was established in his business, she left him. What Mathieu didn't know was Katriane was pregnant. Séra found out and threatened to tell her husband, and they fell out and went their own ways. Séra had been married and divorced before and then met and married a wealthy stockbroker named Dïmon Castillé. He owned the château she now lives in, but two years after their wedding he died of a heart attack, and left her his empire. About two years ago she met Mathieu. Meanwhile, going back to Katriane's story, Katriane had devised a plan and went to Italy to have the child. The boy only lived for a week. Somehow Katriane's father found out, but not from Séra. That was why Katriane's first husband left her, and took Isabella to Italy. You know about her second husband. Katriane had always followed her sister's career, but kept her distance, until I came into it, and then she thought she could pump me for information."

Hugh couldn't believe what Rose was telling him. "Good heavens, what a tangled web. I am so pleased she has gone. I assume JP found all this out?" Rose nodded.

Looking at her uncle with a twinkle in her eye, she said, "Just have to find you somebody else. You can't be on your own at the wedding."

Hugh raised his eyebrow, and said, "I think I'll leave women out of the equation for the moment." Rose laughed and leant over and kissed his cheek. Hugh went back to work, and Rose walked leisurely along the Seine, even though it was cold, back to the flat.

Once back, she phoned Ruby to see if she would like to come and stay with her until the weekend. Rose was stunned when Ruby declined. "I'm sorry Rose, but I'm not feeling well. I will get a taxi back to the airport on Friday," and she put the phone down. Rose just looked at the phone totally lost for words. In all the years she'd known Ruby, she had never done that before, and Rose was at a loss as what to do. Had Ruby fallen out with Antoine? How ill was she? Did she need a doctor? About half an hour later the phone rang and it was Ruby. "Sorry Rose, I was about to be sick. I didn't mean to hang up."

Rose was relieved slightly. "Do you need a doctor, Ruby, and is there anything I can do to help?" Ruby said she had eaten some shellfish at lunchtime, and then she felt ill. She was feeling slightly better now. "Ruby, I'm coming over to pick you up and bring you here, where I can look after you, and I will take you to the airport on Friday."

Ruby laughed and replied, "Okay sister, see you in a minute."

When Rose got to Antoine's, Ruby was packing. "You do look a bit under the weather. Let me do that. What else needs to go in?" An hour later both of them were back at Rose's. Rose made Ruby some tea, and told her to relax on the settee. Rose made up the spare bed, and tidied the room up. Later on she made them a soufflé, which was light, and then they cuddled up on the settee and watched a film. The next two days, both of them stayed in and relaxed. Ruby hadn't been sick again, and Rose was pleased.

Friday came and Rose drove Ruby to the airport. Whilst they were waiting for her to go, Rose asked, "When are you coming back again, permanently?"

Ruby replied, "I don't know. Dad, I know, is making some enquiries, but even though it's only two hours from here to home, I can't do it every weekend, like I do at the moment, unless I'm on assignment. I'm worried I won't get a job, and I'm certainly not living off Antoine."

Rose replied, "I can get you a job, either with Mathieu or Séra. I do know one of the journalists is leaving at the end of April, so I can put a word in with Mathieu."

"Oh yes please, that would be brilliant." Rose said to leave it with her. Ruby's flight was called and they hugged and kissed each other. "Hopefully see you soon," said Rose as Ruby went down the ramp. Before she boarded, Ruby ran to the nearest toilet and was sick.

The following week, Rose was back at Séra's, doing a spring shoot. This time she had the children, along with the rest of them. She could see Séra was getting a bit annoyed with the children as they wouldn't stand still long enough. "Séra, do you by any chance have any light-coloured chairs I could use?"

Séra looked at her perplexed and said bluntly, "Why?"

Rose replied she had an idea.

"What about the chairs in the swimming pool area, as they're white?" asked Léon.

Rose gave him the thumbs up. He was soon back with eight folding chairs. Rose placed four of them on the set, and got the children to slouch on them, in various poses. The children loved it, and soon she got the photos she wanted. Séra walked past her and whispered, "Well done." Rose smiled. It took all week to do the photo shoot, but once Jules developed the photos, Séra was delighted. After that Rose always made sure the children always had something to use.

At the end of the month, on the Thursday night, Rose received a phone call from Monica, and knew straight away something was wrong. It was Ruby and she was going into hospital to have a minor operation the following day. "Does Antoine know, as it's their weekend off?"

Monica replied he didn't, but Ruby wanted her. "Mum, would it be alright if JP came with me?"

"Of course. At last we can meet him. You and I can visit Ruby, and Dad can show JP the pub." Rose laughed at that.

Later that night Rose phoned JP, and he said he would make the arrangements. "JP, please don't tell Antoine. Ruby doesn't want to worry him." He promised, but thought it odd.

Rose didn't work at the weekends, unless it was something special, but still advised Séra she would be away. Séra told her to look after her friend and if she needed an extra couple of days off, not to worry. Friday night JP arrived home. "I have arranged to borrow one of the helicopters for the weekend. We can leave tomorrow morning, and I have also rented a car, which will be at the airport. How is Ruby?"

Rose replied, "Mum said she was alright, but wouldn't actually say what was wrong. Oh JP, I hope it's nothing serious." Tears sprang to Rose's eyes.

JP took her in his arms and said softly, "She will be fine, môn amour. She is lucky to have parents who are a doctor and nurse, and she will be in the best place. Now, let me make us a meal, and then I can start to relax. What time do you want to leave in the morning?"

Rose replied it depended on what time they woke up. They loved each other that night, but Rose didn't sleep well, and was tossing and turning, and ended going to the spare bedroom, so as not to wake JP. About 4am, JP got in bed with her, and wrapped his arms around her, and she slept. JP awoke at his normal time of 6am and quietly got out of the bed. He washed, dressed and started breakfast. Rose was now awake, and also got washed and dressed. By 9am they were at the airport.

The trip over was fine until they got over the English coast. It was lashing with rain and extremely windy. JP was a good pilot though and held the helicopter as steady as he could. He saw Rose had paled and was clutching the seat. "Soon be there, môn amour. Think of something nice, and if you can close your eyes." Rose was feeling sick, as with the helicopter going up and down, so was her stomach. "Môn amour, open your eyes. We've landed."

Rose opened her eyes and saw they were on the ground, and in a very large hangar. "How did we…?"

JP told her, with help, he flew in. It was then she saw the men securing everything. JP got out and went round, and helped her down. "Do you need to freshen up, môn amour? The toilets are over there." Rose nodded.

Once she returned, she saw a car had arrived, and their bags were put in the boot. Rose went to the right-hand side, and JP said, smiling, "You might need these. Are you sure you feel alright to drive?" Rose looked at him, and then laughed, realising what she'd done. As JP drove, through torrential rain, he saw the turning for Fracton and turned off. Rose looked but said nothing. Soon he pulled up across from the barracks. Putting his arm around Rose, he said, "This where our journey began, môn amour," and kissed her so tenderly. At that moment a noise made them jump, and they watched as a helicopter landed at the barracks. "Je t'aime, môn amour."

"Je t'aime aussi, my love." And this time they kissed each other deeply and lovingly.

"Heavens, come in both of you, out of this dreadful weather. George, get the umbrella," said Monica as JP stopped outside the front door. Once inside Rose hugged and kissed them both and then taking JP's hand said, "Mum, Dad, this is my fiancé, Jean-Paul Pascal, but everyone calls him JP." Monica gave him a hug and kissed his cheek, and George shook his hand.

"Welcome JP, and apologies for the weather. Now I bet you'd both like a hot drink and something to eat? Come in to the kitchen where it's lovely and warm," said Monica.

Soon the four of them were sat at the kitchen table. "Mum, how's Ruby?" It was very quick, but Rose noticed a glance between her mum and dad.

"She had her operation yesterday, so we can see her this afternoon. She is going to be delighted to see you both. Now JP, would you like tea or coffee?" JP replied coffee. The next minute the table had an assortment of sandwiches and cakes on it, along with pots of tea and coffee. "Help yourself, JP, we don't stand on ceremony here. Just make yourself at home."

JP smiled and said, "Thank you, it looks lovely. Rose and I will need to book into a hotel. Can you suggest one?"

George replied, "Nonsense, you're both staying here. Rose's bed is big enough for you both. Might be different if you weren't engaged." Both Rose and JP blushed.

Monica smiled and said, "Let's go into the sitting room, and then in about an hour we'll go and see Ruby."

Monica and George got to know JP, and both of them liked him very much, but Monica in particular. She could now see how he had helped Rose greatly. An hour later they were on the way to the hospital.

As they entered the hospital, Rose thought they would go up to a ward. Instead they went to a part of the hospital Rose had never been to before. They got the lift to the top floor, and walked down a small corridor. There was only one room at the end, with a couple of chairs outside. "George, could you and JP stay here for a moment? I need to make sure Ruby is presentable." George nodded. Monica and Rose went in.

"Oh Rose, I'm so glad you're here," said Ruby.

Rose went to her and gave her a hug and kissed her cheek. "How are you feeling?"

Ruby replied better. "You didn't tell Antoine or JP, did you?"

Rose replied, "JP is outside as he came over with me, but no, nothing has been told to Antoine. Surely you would want him here?"

Ruby looked at her mum. "Why don't you say hi to JP and then Dad can take him to the canteen, and then we can have a girly chat?" Rose knew something was wrong, but what?

Monica helped Ruby sit up and then George and JP came in. George gave Ruby a kiss, and then JP gave her a gentle hug and kissed her cheek. "How are you, Ruby?" he asked with concern.

Ruby replied, "Lot better now you two are here. I'm sorry I asked you not to tell Antoine, but I didn't want to worry him. All being well I will be home tomorrow."

"Is there anything I can get you?"

At that moment a nurse came in and said, "Apologies, Doctor Smith, as I didn't realise you were here. Hi Monica. I will come back later." George thanked the nurse, and then looked at Ruby's notes.

Ruby said, "Dad, why don't you show JP the hospital and maybe get me some magazines?" George agreed and with JP they left.

"Would one of you like to explain to me now, exactly what's going on?" asked Rose.

Ruby burst into tears and Monica put her arms round her. "I'm so sorry, Rose. I have been really stupid and done something you will never forgive me for."

Rose took Ruby's hand and said, "Surely it can't be that bad."

Ruby looked at her mum and Monica said, "There's no easy way to say this. Ruby had an abortion yesterday."

Rose looked at Ruby and her mum totally stunned. That was the last thing she expected to hear. Looking at Ruby she said, "So that's why didn't you want Antoine to know. Was there a problem or something?"

Ruby blurted out, "It wasn't Antoine's."

CHAPTER 4

Ruby had totally stunned Rose by telling her that the baby wasn't Antoine's. Rose's eyes went wide and she snapped, "WHAT!! I thought you loved Antoine? Why, please tell me why?"

Monica went to Rose and holding her hand, said, "Let her explain. Rose. Both of us were furious with her as well. We are the only people who know, and that's why Ruby is up here. This is a private room and your dad did the operation with me at his side. Ruby, tell Rose."

Ruby replied, "The day I returned after the engagement party, on the way to the airport, Antoine and I had a bit of an argument. Then he brought up what I stupidly did in the back of your car. I told him I was sorry, and in future, I wanted him to watch me to make sure I didn't get drunk again. That's why I was more or less sober at the New Year's Eve ball. Anyway, it got to me and I went out and got drunk. I ended up at somebody's house where a party was going on. Believe it or not, I was kissing a guy called Anthony, and thinking it was Antoine, well, one thing led to another. It wasn't until a couple of days later I remembered no protection had been used. Later on I realised I'd missed a couple of my periods, and so I told Mum, who gave me a pregnancy test. It was positive. Oh Rose, I can't believe it happened. I love Antoine with all my heart, but now I don't know if I can ever face him again." Ruby burst into tears. Rose went to her and held her in her arms.

Once Ruby had calmed Rose said, "Can you honestly keep this to yourself and not tell Antoine? As JP and I have learnt, there should be no secrets between couples. I promise I will keep your secret, but secrets do have a way of coming out." Monica agreed with Rose.

"Would it help if I told Antoine?" Ruby said to leave it for the time being, as she needed to think.

A tap at the door saw George and JP walk back in. JP picked up on the atmosphere straight away, but smiling at Ruby, said, "Your magazines, my lady." Ruby laughed. They all stayed with Ruby for another hour, and then left.

"Fancy going to an old haunt of yours?" asked George.

About thirty minutes later they drew up outside the tavern, which Harold owned. "Rose, how lovely to see you, and you as well, Monsieur. Oh, you are engaged, how wonderful. Please come, I have just the table for you." Rose introduced her mum and dad. "A pleasure to meet you both. Here is the menu. Rose, is it still gammon and pineapple? And you, Monsieur, fish and chips?"

JP smiled and said, "It's JP, and you have a good memory." Harold flushed slightly. Apart from Rose, they all had fish and chips. Harold brought over a bottle of wine, to toast the couple.

When JP went to pay, Harold refused and said, "On the house, JP. Now you look after my young lady. She has a special place in my heart, but don't tell her." JP smiled and promised.

That night as Rose and JP were cuddled up in bed, JP said, "You alright, môn amour? I know something is troubling you, and it's to do with Ruby."

Rose sighed, and sat up looking down at JP. "You're right, there is something and I know you won't say anything." Rose told him. JP then sat up and held Rose in his arms.

"I honestly don't know what to say. If Antoine ever found out it would crush him totally. I've seen Antoine through thick and thin times, but since Ruby came into his life, he's a changed man, and for the better. What worries me is that if every time Antoine argues with her, is she going to run off and do something stupid?"

Rose understood what JP was saying but replied, "She didn't do it on purpose, JP. She was drunk, and I've seen Ruby drunk, and everything goes out the window."

JP frowned and said, "Out of the window?"

Rose kissed his lips and said, "Her logic is gone." JP understood. "Come, it's late. Let's see what tomorrow brings." Both of them slid back down under the duvet and cuddled up to each other. In the morning, about 8am, they awoke to the smell of breakfast.

"Be prepared, my love, Dad's breakfasts are huge."

JP thought Rose was joking until he went in to the kitchen. Bacon, sausages, eggs, fried bread, mushrooms, tomatoes, black pudding, beans, toast, marmalade, jams, along with tea and coffee. "Morning, you two. Sit and tuck in."

"Told you," whispered Rose.

The four of them thoroughly enjoyed their breakfasts and Monica asked when they had to return. JP replied, "I can stay until this afternoon, as I have to be back at the palace tomorrow morning. Rose, are you going to stay? I can make more arrangements for you when I get back." Rose said she would be returning with him. "In that case, môn amour, we will need to be at the airport for 3pm at the latest, which means leaving here about 1pm." Rose nodded.

Just over an hour later, they were back at the hospital. JP had followed George and Monica in his car, with Rose, so they could drive straight to the airport. Ruby looked a lot better and was pleased to see them. Rose explained they only had an hour and then had to leave. "Thank you both for coming to see me. If I know Rose, then she has told you, JP, about my stupidity, and saying sorry is not good enough. I have thought long and hard, most of the night in fact, and you're right, Rose, I can't lie to Antoine. I am going to phone him later and tell him. Would you give him this back for me? And JP, please look after him." Rose took Ruby's engagement ring and looked at JP. He took it and put it in his top pocket for safe keeping.

"Promise me you'll tell him gently, Ruby. He just might surprise you. That's all I can say, and yes, I will look after him," said JP. Ruby held her arms out and JP hugged her and kissed her cheek. "Stay strong Ruby," he whispered, "and you are always welcome at ours." That brought tears to Ruby's eyes. "Môn amour, we must go. Monica, George, it's been a pleasure to meet you and thank you for looking after us. You are always welcome at ours as well, whenever. We have a spare bedroom." Monica hugged and kissed him, and George shook his hand.

Rose hugged and kissed Ruby, Mum and Dad. "Mum, is Ruby going home later?" Monica said she would be. "Then I'll phone you all later." Hugs and kisses went around again, and then JP took Rose's hand as they left. At least it wasn't raining, yet, so the drive back was comfortable. JP had already phoned ahead, and the helicopter was out and waiting. JP did all the checks and just over two hours later they were back in their flat.

Both of them flopped on the settee. "If Ruby is going to tell Antoine tonight, do you think we should go to him?"

JP replied, "About 9pm our doorbell will ring and it will be Antoine."

Rose cuddled into JP and he kissed her, and said, "That gives us about two, two and a half hours." Five minutes later they were naked under the duvet loving each other.

An hour later, Rose got up and phoned Ruby. Back in bed, she told JP that Ruby was phoning Antoine now. "Better get dressed then, môn amour, and when he turns up, leave him to me. I know how to calm him." As JP had said, Antoine turned up an hour later. Rose had never seen Antoine in such a state. It took JP over an hour to calm him down so he could speak rationally to him. Rose had made up the spare bed, and decided it would be wise for her to go to bed. Her heart went out to Antoine, as she knew how badly he was hurting. She couldn't sleep so she sat up and read a book.

"Môn amour," said JP softly.

"Umm," said Rose sleepily.

"Cuddle down, môn amour, so I can cuddle you." Rose slid down and cuddled into JP and fell asleep.

In the morning Rose woke to find JP wasn't next to her. *Antoine*, she thought. Quickly she got up, washed and dressed, and went into the sitting room.

JP went to her and said, kissing her forehead, "Morning môn amour."

Antoine looked at her with bleary eyes and said, "Sorry to mess your evening up, Rose."

Rose gave him a hug and kissed his cheek. "You two are very late for work?"

JP replied, "Change of plan. Antoine has phoned Ruby, and I'm flying him over to see her." Rose looked surprised.

Antoine said, "I need to put this back on her finger. I can't live without her, Rose. I've not been a saint, and I have something to tell Ruby. I've told JP he can tell you."

Rose just smiled and said, "When are you leaving?"

JP told her in about half an hour. "Môn amour, what are you up to today?"

"At the moment nothing."

"Would be nice to have some company, especially on the way back. Antoine is staying for a couple of days."

Late afternoon JP and Rose were back in the flat. JP cooked a meal, and afterwards when they were sat on the settee Rose said, "What was it that Antoine told me you could tell me?"

JP replied, "This happened before either of you came back into our lives. Antoine had been seeing a woman for about nine months when all of a sudden she just up and left him. He tried to find her but it was like she had vanished into thin air. He pined, for want of a better word, for her for months. We all know time heals and it wasn't until a couple of years later that he ran into one of her friends at a nightclub. Her friend was really off with him, and in the end he asked her what her problem was. What she told him had him reeling. Apparently his girlfriend told her friends she left him because when she told Antoine she was pregnant, he spurned her, and said it wasn't his. Antoine was stunned. He had no idea she was pregnant. Eventually her friend believed him. Antoine asked where she was. If he had responsibilities then he had to help. Her friend told him the last she heard of her, she had married and gone to America. So somewhere in America, Antoine has a daughter, who's about ten years old."

Rose was quiet for a moment and then sitting astride JP's lap, said, "Talk about a pair of odd couples." JP frowned. "Antoine gets a lady pregnant, and she clears off. Ruby gets drunk, gets pregnant and has an abortion. Both of them end up with no children. I can't give you children, and you can't give me children."

27

JP liked her logic and kissed her tenderly, and said, "I know we can't have children, but I do like to practise." Rose burst out laughing, and soon they were loving each other.

A couple of days later Ruby phoned. "Ruby, how are you, and how's Antoine?"

Ruby replied, "I'm feeling fine but still getting the odd stomach cramps and it bloody well hurts. Antoine left today and should be back at the palace now. He told me about an old girlfriend and we've had a long talk about everything. He has forgiven me, but I know he doesn't trust me anymore, so I need to show him that he can. The problem is he's over there and I'm over here."

Rose could understand her dilemma, but it was different to her trusting JP. "Have you thought about going away together, and just being with each other, and nobody else? Both JP and myself learnt a lot about each other when we went away. Just a pity it's winter. Still, spring is just around the corner."

Ruby replied, "We thought about that but until the President goes away he can't get the time off."

"Ruby, leave it with me, and I'll see if I can do anything. Now take care and look after yourself." Ruby said goodbye and then hung up. Rose wasn't sure what she could do, but would have a chat with JP, which she did. JP knew the President had lots of meetings to attend in various countries, but would see what could be done.

The following day the President asked JP to come to his office. "I have just been looking at all these meetings, which will start in March. I have to attend meetings in England, Belgium, Spain and Luxembourg so far. They will all probably last a week. Needless to say I will leave all the itineraries etc. with you. At the moment I'm not sure of the order, but I know you will have a lot of ground work to do. Now, how are things between Ruby and Antoine?"

The President knew, as JP had to get his permission to use the helicopter. JP told him what Antoine had told them. The President thought for a moment and then said, "Antoine must be fully committed on these trips. If he's not, you need to replace him. I know that's harsh, but at the end of the day, all of our lives could be affected. Now, if Ruby can get time off, I will gladly let them have one week at the cottage, where you and Rose stayed. I'm serious, JP, sort him or get rid."

"Yes, Monsieur le President, and I agree with you. I will keep you informed." JP bowed and left. As he passed the surveillance room he saw Donatien and Pierre. "Where's Antoine?" he snapped.

Pierre replied, "Checking the grounds with Andre, boss."

"Tell him my office NOW," and he walked off, letting the door slam behind him.

Donatien looked at Pierre and said, "What the hell has he done now?"

Pierre shook his head. "Andre, respond," he said into an ear piece.

"What's up?" asked Andre.

Pierre told him. "Antoine, JP's office NOW."

Antoine paled, but left immediately.

"Boss, you wanted to see me," asked Antoine gingerly.

JP had been pacing up and down and replied sternly, "Sit down, Antoine, and listen to what I've got to tell you. I've got you out of many scrapes over the years, but this with Ruby is causing huge problems. The President has given me an ultimatum. You sort yourself out or you're gone, for good."

The blood drained from Antoine's face. "I can't lose my job, boss, and I really don't want to lose Ruby, but if it comes to a decision, I will choose to keep my job."

JP knew exactly what Antoine would say, and he sort of smiled, and said in a softer voice, "It hasn't come to that yet, Antoine. Now the President has said he will give you and Ruby the cottage, for one week, where Rose and I stayed. Phone Ruby and get it sorted now. If you're not one hundred per cent on the job, when we go away, you'll go. My hands are tied this time, Antoine, so it's up to you."

Antoine replied, "Thanks, boss. I'll ring Ruby now and let you know, and thank you." JP smiled and told him to go. In all his years as Head of Security he had never had to sack any of the bodyguards under his control. He hoped Antoine would not be the first.

CHAPTER 5

The following day, Antoine knocked on JP's door. JP beckoned him in, and told him to sit down. "I spoke with Ruby last night and told her what the President had said. We are both determined not to let the President or you down. She has just phoned to say she has booked a flight for Friday afternoon, and we would like to take up the President's kind offer of the cottage. We are both sorry, boss, to cause you all this trouble. A week on Friday I will let you know what we have decided, if that's alright? I have spoken to Porte, who is happy to stand in for me."

JP raised his eyebrow and said, "Antoine, I'm going to be honest. I don't want to lose you, and I'm sure that goes for the rest as well. However, if you do decide to leave to be with Ruby, I will understand. I will go now and see the President and then let you know. Stay here, I won't be long." JP was back within the half hour. "The President is pleased you have taken him up on his offer. You know, along with Rose, he thinks the world of Ruby, and genuinely hopes you can sort out your problems. I second that. Now, back to your duties and ask Andre to come and see me." Antoine thanked him and left.

"I have had to give Antoine an ultimatum. He has to sort this out or leave," said JP to Andre.

Andre replied dryly, "I assume that was the President, not you?"

JP replied, smiling, "Let's say fifty-fifty. I have had a word with Porte, who is happy to stand in for Antoine. Now to business. I have four of the itineraries for the President, so we need to start planning. Here is a list of them. The President thinks it might be a week at each. In England he will stay with the Duke again. The other three countries will need to be vetted extremely carefully in the usual manner. Can I leave that to you, Pierre and Donatien? At the moment assume Antoine will be with us."

"Will do, boss," replied Andre and left.

JP wanted to talk to Rose, but knew she was busy at Séra's château, as she had been called in. Later that night JP phoned Rose. "As much as Ruby loves Antoine, she would be devastated if he lost his job. I wish you were here, my love. After the day I've had, I could do with one of your hugs."

JP replied, "I'm sending you one, môn amour. I've been thinking, how do you feel about moving?"

"Moving. Moving where?"

JP replied, "I just wondered if somewhere bigger, with a garden, might be better than the flat. It was something Antoine said when everyone was round."

Rose smiled to herself and said, "Why do I get the feeling you've already seen somewhere?" JP chuckled and said he hadn't seen it, but had information on it. It was on the outskirts of Paris, and was a three-bedroomed farmhouse. It had gardens back and front and was detached. "Sounds interesting. Would you like me to go and look?" JP said she would need the key, and gave her the name of the estate agents. Rose said she would go at the weekend.

Rose drove about twenty kilometres outside of Paris, going south, and into the countryside. She had to admit she did prefer the countryside to the city. She missed the first turning, but the estate agent had told her there were two ways into the village. She took the next right and drove up and down winding roads, passing lots of fields of which some had cattle in, and others had horses. She also passed a couple of farms, and went through tiny villages with only five or six cottages. About five kilometres later she saw a large village. As she drove through, she saw lots of cottages either in rows, semi-detached or detached. There was a large pub with a car park at the side, and a large lawn where men were playing boules. A forest and fields surrounded the village. She thought she had missed the farmhouse, and pulled in and looked at the estate agent's directions. Looking down the road she saw a white post box, which was the entrance.

As she drove down the track it reminded her of the President's cottage. *Wonder how Ruby and Antoine are getting on,* she thought. As soon as Rose saw the farmhouse, she fell in love with it. It was two levels, and all the doors, windows and shutters were in white. The building was made of stone, but it looked like old cobbles. Walking down the path, there was a large lawn either side. The path then went to the left and right. In front of the main door was a wrought-iron arch, which had two rose trees that entwined around it. Either side of the door were two small garden patches with various small shrubs and plants. Rose couldn't wait to go inside.

Inside she was surprised to see all the floors were wooden, and every room had the old-fashioned wooden beams. The entrance hall had a small cloakroom with a toilet, and stairs leading up to the bedrooms, at the far end. Between the cloakroom and the stairs was a door that led out to the back garden. The first room she went into was probably the dining room and the next one the sitting room, and both had long, wide, tall windows that opened out on to the small front and large back gardens. At the top end of the sitting room was another door and she went down a couple of steps into a huge kitchen. There were radiators in the rooms, but there were also large fireplaces.

The layout upstairs was unusual but worked. At the top of the stairs there was a small landing, which then led into a corridor that ran the length of the building. Much like a hotel corridor. On one side were two of the bedrooms, again with large windows and shutters, and overlooked the back garden. The other bedroom overlooked the front garden. The bathroom had a lovely large bath, with decorative claw-like legs, a shower, toilet and washbasin. There was another room with a separate toilet. Between the toilet and bathroom was a huge airing cupboard. Again there were radiators in the bedrooms, and two in the corridor. As Rose was walking round she was mentally trying to picture each room furnished and how much it would all cost!! She didn't want JP paying for everything, if they decided to buy it, and now she was earning a good wage, she could help. She went back out the front door, locking it behind her, and took the path to the left, following it around to the back garden, which was fairly large. Walking down to the bottom of it, like most country farmhouses, there was a wide river with trees overhanging it, with nothing but fields on the other side. Looking back up to the farmhouse Rose thought it was like a large chunk of the forest had been cleared and the farmhouse built in the middle. She could see a path going into the forest on one side, but the other side looked to be blocked by trees that had been planted very closely together. It was like a fence, but made of trees.

Back up the path she passed two more buildings, on the left-hand side, which were fair-sized barns. One could be a garage and the other, which had some logs piled up in one corner, Rose thought for a moment, *This would made a brilliant photography studio*. At the side of these barns there was a large field full of wild flowers, but it was fenced off. The other pathway went down to the river, and joined the path into the forest.

Rose went back to her car after a long look at the farmhouse, and the overgrown gardens. As she drove down the main road, she noticed the farmhouse was more or less at the end of the forest. The forest wasn't dense and she could see some of the meandering river, which went round the back of the village.

Soon she was back in Paris and went to the supermarket and did her shopping. That night JP phoned and she told him all about it. JP replied, "That's only the first one, môn amour. I'm sure we will see many more, as there's no rush."

The following week was very busy for Rose and JP, but both were waiting for Ruby and Antoine's decision. About 6pm, on the Friday, Ruby phoned Rose. "How did it go?" asked Rose.

Ruby replied, "It was really good. We really got to know each other and we have talked about everything, past, present and future. Antoine will be staying in Paris."

"And you?" asked Rose hesitantly.

"I'm at the airport now. My flight is in an hour, but I will be back at the end of April... for good. I need to give Marcus plenty of notice."

Rose was delighted. "Oh Ruby, I'm so happy for you both, and now you'll be able to help me sort out the wedding. I want you as a bridesmaid, so we will need to go dress shopping."

They talked until Ruby heard her flight being called and then they said their goodbyes. Rose had just put the phone down when JP phoned. He too, along with his men, were all relieved, as was the President.

Séra knew Rose would be away the first two weeks of July, and most of June would be taken up with wedding preparations, so she needed her to do the autumn shoot before she went. Consequently the time flew by, and the following weekend was the end of April. Rose had looked at more properties, but nothing as good as the farmhouse. Ruby was due to land Friday lunchtime and she was picking her up.

"Welcome to Paris permanently, Ruby," Rose said as she hugged and kissed her cheek. "Did you bring enough bags?" Her trolley had four cases on it.

"Mum and Dad are bringing the rest over when they come for the wedding. You look tired Rose, are you alright?"

"Just working all the hours I can to get the photo shoots done for Séra. Compiling the weddings for Gilmac, along with other articles. Now I've had a word with Mathieu and one of his journalists is leaving at the end of June. He would like to give you an interview, if you're interested?"

Ruby replied, "That's fantastic news, oh thank you Rose. I think I should treat you to lunch."

Rose laughed and replied, "We are going to Gérard's as I need to discuss a menu, so you can help."

Over an hour later they arrived. "Rose, Ruby, lovely to see you both. Come, ladies, I have a treat for you," said Gérard. He took them into a small room, which had various foods laid out on the table. "I remembered you said you might want a buffet, so please eat and tell me what you think. Would you both like a drink?" Both of them went for a soft drink.

"Umm, these are lovely," said Ruby.

"That is a smoked salmon mousse puff pastry tartlet," said Gérard. Rose and Ruby tasted all sorts of food and it was all wonderful. "Has JP booked the town hall?" Rose looked at Gérard, blank. "You do know you have to have a civil ceremony before your church wedding?" Rose shook her head. "It is one of our laws. Until you have had the civil ceremony you will not be lawfully wed. Perhaps JP forgot to tell you. Now, have you decided on a buffet or do you prefer a set meal?" Rose told him she would prefer a buffet.

For the half an hour or so, all three of them went through a menu that would suit everybody, including the children. "Do you know yet how many?" asked Gérard.

"I think it will now be about fifty or sixty."

Gérard replied, "Well I know of one bodyguard who has, let's say, an appreciation of good food, so if I cater for seventy-five, there will plenty for everyone. Now another tradition is, about 4 or 5am, a late-night onion soup is served, before the guests start to make their ways home."

Ruby said, "Isn't that rather late?"

"French weddings go on all afternoon and evening, sometimes until 9am the following day."

Ruby laughed and said, "Now that's what I call a party." Both Rose and Gérard laughed.

"Ruby, I think we had better get back, as it's coming up 5pm, and JP and Antoine will soon be home." Rose thanked Gérard for a wonderful meal, and said she would in touch nearer the day.

"Rose, what about the wedding cake?" asked Ruby.

Gérard explained he would do a croquembouche.

"A what?" asked Rose.

"It is traditional and is cream-filled puffs, filled with vanilla pastry cream, assembled around a cone with caramel, and then decorated with sugar almonds and spun sugar. Here is a photo."

Rose smiled and said, "That looks divine. Will you do it, Gérard?"

"Of course, leave everything to me." Again Rose thanked him and then they left. Rose dropped Ruby off at Antoine's and then drove home.

About 7pm, JP arrived back. "Môn amour, I'm home." Rose went to him and wrapped her arms around him and kissed him, and JP kissed her back. "Did Ruby arrive safely with all her luggage?" asked JP, smiling. Rose told him about their afternoon with Gérard. "I'm sorry, môn amour, I thought I'd told you about the civil ceremony. It's mainly for family and close friends, but two of them must be Témoins, who stand at the side of the bride and groom and then sign the wedding registry."

"Oh, you mean witnesses?" replied Rose. "Well, I will pick my uncle. Who will you pick?" JP replied that at the moment he had no idea.

As Rose wasn't very hungry, JP quickly did a couple of omelettes. Later on whilst they were cuddled up on the settee, Rose suggested they started to make a guest list, as he would only be home one more weekend, and then it was the wedding. Rose was inviting everyone from Séra's company, and those from Gilmac News. JP said obviously all his men, along with their wives and children would attend, along with some of the other bodyguards who weren't on duty. When they'd finished they had eighty people on the list.

"I told Gérard about fifty or sixty. This is going to cost a fortune."

"Môn amour, don't worry about expense. As long as everyone has a good time, that's all that matters. Now I don't know about you, but I want to love my fiancée."

Rose smiled and replied, "Now that is a very good idea."

In the morning Ruby phoned and asked if both of them would like to come over to Antoine's for a meal, any time after 1pm. Rose said they would love to.

"This should be interesting," said JP.

Rose looked and said, "Why?"

"Antoine can't cook."

Rose laughed and said, "Ruby used to be alright, but now she buys pre-packed stuff, and sometimes burns it!!"

When they arrived at Antoine's flat, straight away they could smell burning. Rose rang the doorbell, and Ruby let them in. "Who burnt the meal?" asked JP, grinning.

Antoine came out with a dish in his hand and said, "It was supposed to be Coq au Vin."

"Looks more like Coq au Black if you ask me," replied JP, laughing. "What else have you got?"

About an hour later, JP had cooked a large cheese soufflé, and served it with a salad.

"JP, we asked you over here not to cook this lovely meal, but to thank you and Rose for everything you did for us," said Ruby.

JP smiled and replied, "You just had problems that needed sorting, and it was our pleasure. I'm just relieved it all turned out for the best." Ruby got up and hugged and kissed his cheek.

The rest of the afternoon and early evening the four of them relaxed, and enjoyed each other's company.

CHAPTER 6

All day Sunday, Rose and JP went through the wedding preparations. By late afternoon they had a proper guest list, but it had gone up to ninety. Rose was going to send the invites, sort out the flowers, and converse with Gérard. Both of them had gone through the menu, and made a few adjustments. JP thought it might be nice to have hot potatoes of various choices to go with the buffet. JP would sort out the cars, the champagne and wine with Gérard, confirm the civil and church times, the honeymoon, and the main thing – the rings. JP had already ordered the morning suits for his men and himself, but no top hats. "All you have to do now, môn amour, is find your beautiful wedding dress, and hopefully, sexy lingerie."

Rose cuddled up to him and said, "Will you be wearing sexy underwear?"

JP laughed and replied, "I will do my very best, môn amour." Their arms went round each other and slowly they undressed each other, and then JP picked her up and carried her into the bedroom, where they loved each other slowly and sensually. The following morning, after loving each other again, they both went back to work.

During the week Ruby went to see Mathieu and he offered her the job, and she would start the first week of July. Ruby was delighted. Rose had given her a key to the flat, and she popped round and started writing out the invitations that Rose had bought. By the end of the week all the invitations were done and posted. "When's Mum and Dad coming over?" asked Rose. Ruby told her the end of May, and they were going to stay with her at Antoine's. "That's a long time for them to be away from the hospital isn't it?" asked Rose.

Ruby replied, "I think they have time owing to them, and anyway Mum wanted to be here for you." Rose smiled.

On the Saturday they went to a florist, who told them until she had decided on the colour of her dress it was best to come back later. Rose told them it would be cream. By the time they left, the roses for the buttonholes and her bouquets were ordered. On the Sunday both of them went to Gérard's and arranged the new menu, and the guests went up to a hundred. On the way back Rose asked Ruby if she'd like to see the farmhouse she liked. They drove through the village but as they got to the farmhouse, Rose stopped by the entrance. "Rose, what's wrong?"

Rose replied, "Looks like it's been sold. The pathway and the front gardens were all overgrown, but now everything has been cut down and tidied up."

Ruby, being cheeky, said, "Let's go have a sneak peek."

They got out of the car, and after locking it, walked down the path towards the farmhouse. Rose noticed work was being done on the two barns. "Ruby, come this way, as this path leads to the forest, just in case anyone stops us." As they followed the path, Rose saw two men working on a fence.

The men nodded at them and Ruby said, "Hello. What a lovely farmhouse this is."

One of the men replied, "It is, isn't it? The place was sold some time ago, to a very wealthy family, but being winter, it was the wrong time to start doing it up."

Rose said, "Seems a shame to put this fence up, as surely it would block out the view of the forest."

The other man replied, "It's only a short fence, to give the owner's a bit of privacy, from people walking up from the forest. We're going to put in shrubs either side to cover the fence."

Ruby asked, "Do many people walk round here then?"

The man replied, "The village will start getting busy in the next couple of weeks. We hold boules tournaments, and coaches that stop at the pub so the holidaymakers can stretch their legs and have light snacks. Our village and the surrounding villages hold small fetes and lots of people come to join in."

Rose saw the back garden had also been tidied up and new plants and shrubs planted. She also noticed the shutters and windows were being repainted in a cream colour. Rose's heart sank, but deep down she now knew it would have been beyond their means. Still, there were plenty of other lovely places to see. They thanked the men and carried on walking down the path into the forest and down to the village. It was a lovely walk through the trees. They returned via the road to the car and then drove back to Paris.

Rose knew where she was going to get her wedding dress from, but didn't want anyone to see it, not even Ruby. Ruby had been a godsend, and opened all the return invitations, to which nearly everyone had replied they would be attending. Ruby had also sent a couple of surprise invitations and even they were attending.

The following week Rose had the Thursday free, and went to the gown shop. The assistant again recognised Rose and greeted her. "Mademoiselle, how lovely to see you again. How may I help you?"

Rose replied, "Please call me Rose, and I wondered if you did wedding dresses?"

The assistant smiled and replied, "Then please call me Mía. We don't keep wedding dresses, but we have a book collection I can show you, and then we can do whatever you require. When is the wedding?"

Rose replied, "In six weeks. Is that enough time?" Mía said that would be fine.

Rose sat for nearly an hour looking through the collection, and only one stood out. She showed Mía which one and she replied, "That is exquisite, but may I make a few suggestions?"

When Rose left the shop, her dress, veil, lingerie, along with other accessories had been sorted. She had also decided on Ruby's dress as well. Next she went to the beauty salon and booked Ruby, Mum and herself in for hair etc. to be done at 8am on the day, but booked another appointment for herself the day before to be waxed. She always smiled at that as she knew how much JP liked her "naked." Luckily the civil ceremony wasn't until 1.30pm and the church 2.30pm, so that gave them the morning. Rose started to feel a bit nervous. Time had gone by so quickly and there were still things to be sorted. She wondered how JP was getting on.

At the palace JP had also been busy. All the morning suits would be delivered to the palace at the beginning of the wedding week, just in case any alterations needed to be done. He had spoken with Porte and the chalet in Montpellier was all arranged. Three wedding cars were ordered along with the rental of a soft-top car to drive to Montpellier. He had phoned Gérard who advised what wine and champagne to have, and he would also arrange the entertainment. He suggested an orchestra playing soft music until the evening, and then a DJ for the rest of the evening. JP was happy with that. He had some spare time coming up on the Friday and was going to go to the church and town hall and re-confirm the dates and times. He was also going to go to the jewellers where he got Rose's engagement ring and sort out the wedding rings. As he didn't know which colour Rose's wedding dress was going to be, he also picked out a pearl necklace, bracelet and matching earrings to be delivered to the flat on the day of the wedding. He had no idea what sexy underwear to get. His main concern was who to pick for a witness. To pick one of his men, in a roundabout way, would show favouritism, and he couldn't do that. His men wouldn't be concerned, but in JP's eyes it would be a bit of an insult. Pierre had already mentioned a night out to celebrate his last night as a bachelor, and suggested they went to the restaurant down the road from the palace. That was booked for about sixteen of them, leaving five other bodyguards at the palace.

A couple of weeks later the President noticed JP seemed deep in thought about something, and asked him if he could help. JP told him about his witness problem. The President replied, "I wish I could do it for you, but alas, I cannot. Who is going to the civil ceremony?" JP told him, and then the President saw his dilemma. JP had no family members living. Suddenly the President said, "How would you and Rose feel about having your civil ceremony here at the palace? I can arrange it and then I can be your witness, but not only that, my wife and I will see you and Rose get married. I know my wife wants to see Rose's wedding dress."

JP's face lit up and he said, "It would be a great honour for us to have our ceremony here, Monsieur le President. Thank you from both of us."

The President smiled and replied, "It's my pleasure, JP, and not only that, the bodyguards not attending the celebrations will now also see the ceremony, along with all the staff at the palace. I'm sure you know, Rose is a very special lady here. This is going to be a glorious event. Now one more thing, don't tell Rose. Let it be the first of many surprises." JP agreed and left the President's office with a huge grin on his face.

"Well, something has cheered you up," said Andre, as JP walked into the dining room. JP told them.

"What a brilliant idea," said Donatien. "The President's wife is going to be absolutely delighted."

The weeks were flying by and soon Rose and Ruby were at the airport waiting for Monica and George.

"Mum, Dad," chorused the pair of them, and ran into their open arms. "I can't believe you're both here, and I'm so happy," said Rose.

Monica replied, "And you're nervous as well." Rose nodded.

Rose noticed all the cases. "Heavens, have you packed your wardrobes up?"

George replied dryly, "You women never know what to bring. I think we left the kitchen sink!!" and winked at them all.

"It's coming up lunchtime, so we thought we'd take you to Gérard's, where we are having the reception," said Rose.

Soon they were sitting having lunch, with Gérard making a fuss over them. Monica thought he was lovely. Before they left, Gérard showed Monica and George the menu. Both were impressed, and said they were looking forward to it. Later on Rose dropped Ruby, Mum and Dad, at Antoine's. When she eventually got back, JP was home. "There you are, mon amour," and took her in his arms, and kissed her passionately. "Four weeks tomorrow, mon amour, and we will be married. Are you as nervous as I am?" Rose replied she was. "Did Monica and George arrive safely?" Rose told him they had and where they had been. "On Sunday, why don't we invite everyone round for our last meal as single people?" Rose said she would phone everyone, which she did, as JP cooked them a meal.

Afterwards they watched the television for a bit and then went to bed. As they undressed each other Rose said, "Just think, in four weeks, you will be home every other weekend. What does my angel say about that?"

JP chuckled and replied, "I'm sure he thinks he's looking forward to it, but let's see what he's up for now."

Gently he picked Rose up and laid her on the bed. He kissed her lips and then made his way down to her breasts and nipples. As he sucked and nipped her nipples they went hard. He carried on trailing kisses down to her mound. "Môn amour, let me love you." Rose was feeling the sensations take over her body and was moaning sexily, and then went into oblivion. Afterwards she straddled JP and loved him, until he too climaxed. They both rolled onto their sides and JP pulled Rose's leg over his hip and entered her, and thrusted until they both went over the edge.

"Je t'aime, môn amour."

"I love you, too my love." And then they cuddled up and slept.

In the morning they again made love, then had a bath, dressed, had breakfast, and then went food shopping. JP was going to cook his Boeuf Bourguignon. The rest of the day, they again went through all the wedding arrangements, in case they'd forgotten anything. Suddenly Rose laughed and said, "We've forgotten something."

"What?" asked JP.

Rose replied, "A photographer." They both burst out laughing.

"Môn amour, surely that is your job?"

Rose threw a cushion at him playfully. "Not this time. I will ask Suzette, from Séra's. She has been doing the photo shoots with me and is excellent."

Sunday lunch time arrived along with all their friends. The table had been set and Rose said, "Hope it's not unlucky, as there's thirteen of us."

JP said, "Put out another place for our invisible guest if it worries you," and was surprised when Rose did.

They all hugged and kissed and everyone was introduced to Monica and George. Hugh said it was lovely to see them again.

Pierre said, "Is that smell what I think it is?"

JP replied, "This is my last signature dish as a single man. The next time we do this, I will be a very happily married man," and gave Rose a quick kiss. The salad starters were brought out and everyone tucked in. This was then followed by bowls of vegetables and mashed garlic potatoes, along with the large bowls of Boeuf Bourguignon and baskets of French bread.

"You are a very good cook, JP," said Monica. JP thanked her, and told her he had learnt cooking from his maman, and wine from his papa. Rose had told them his parents had passed away. Andre made sure the wine flowed, but not for him, as he was driving, and they all enjoyed a sumptuous meal and excellent company. Once they had had a break after the main meal, JP brought in a selection of pastries and two large apple tarts, accompanied with jugs of cream and custard. Rose then made pots of tea and coffee.

During the rest of the afternoon they discussed the wedding, and Antoine nearly put his foot in it about the civil ceremony, until Andre coughed and gave him a glare. Rose noticed but thought nothing of it. Gabrielle asked Rose if she was having a party to celebrate her last night of being single. Pierre told them they were taking JP out, and invited George and Hugh as well. Both said they would be pleased to go. Rose said she thought that a nice idea. Gabrielle said she would arrange it and then let everyone know where to meet. She promised it wouldn't be a late night. About 9pm, they all decided it was time to leave, and would see each other soon.

After everything was cleared up and Rose and JP were cuddled up in bed, Rose said, "My love, what about wedding presents? No one has asked."

JP replied, "Andre told me that all the men and wives had arranged something, but I don't know what. Do we actually need anything?" Rose couldn't think of anything. They then made love to each other for the last time as a single couple. Both were sated, and slept blissfully in each other's arms.

CHAPTER 7

The next two weeks went by so quick, that Rose thought her head was spinning. At last all the work was finished for Séra and Mathieu, and she could hopefully relax before the big day. She hadn't seen anyone or done anything about the wedding, and was totally wiped out. On the Saturday she phoned Ruby and Ruby said she and Mum were on their way. When they arrived they were shocked at the sight of Rose. She actually looked ill. Monica said, "I am now staying with you until the day of the wedding, as you need looking after. Have you eaten?" Rose shook her head. "Right, go and sit down. On second thoughts, Ruby draw Rose a bath, as I know she likes to relax in a bubble bath."

Soon Rose was starting to unwind and fell asleep. Ruby gently woke her up. Rose dried herself and then dressed. Monica had done a breakfast special and told both of them to tuck in, which they did. Slowly Rose's colour started to come back. "There is so much to do," said Rose, agitated. "What happens if it all goes wrong?"

Monica took her hand and sat her down on the settee. "Now listen to me, Rose. You have two weeks to sort out whatever needs sorting. You have me, Ruby and Dad to help, so let us. Now this weekend you are going to do nothing but eat, rest and relax. Do I make myself clear?"

Ruby giggled and said, "I think that must be the first time I've heard Mum tell you off." They all started to giggle.

Strangely, JP phoned that night and Monica answered. An hour later he walked into the flat. "Where's Rose?" he asked, full of concern.

Monica replied, "She's asleep JP, so be quiet when you go in."

JP quietly entered the bedroom and saw Rose. She looked so fragile, as if she would break if he touched her. Rose opened her eyes and said, "My love, what are you doing here?"

"Hush, môn amour, go back to sleep and rest. I just wanted to tell you how much I love you," and kissed her lips tenderly.

Rose replied, "I love you too, JP," and closed her eyes. JP and Monica chatted for about fifteen minutes, and after thanking her, he left to go back to the palace.

Ruby and George arrived on Sunday, and they all relaxed at the flat, and Monica cooked. On Monday, Rose was feeling better. She phoned the gown shop and Mía suggested they came in for a fitting. That was arranged for Wednesday. Then she phoned Suzette to confirm the details for the wedding and the times. Suzette said she would be there, with camera and a lot of colour films. George suggested they went out for lunch. Rose said she would drive, but George said he had other ideas. A couple of hours later, the four of them were doing the cruise down the Seine. They laughed, joked and thoroughly enjoyed themselves. It was just what Rose needed.

Tuesday, Rose picked Ruby and George up and they all went to the shopping centre for the day. Wednesday George said he and Monica were going to go off sightseeing, and would see them later. Rose and Ruby went to the gown shop. Mía smiled as they walked in. "First fitting, I think?" she said. "I can't wait to see your dress, Rose."

Rose shook her head and said, "No one, apart from myself and Mía will see it. I'm not even going to see your dress."

Mía showed them to two large changing rooms, away from each other. "Oh wow, it's absolutely gorgeous," Rose heard Ruby say, and smiled. Mía had put a curtain over the mirror in her changing room, and only when Rose was dressed and veiled did Mía pull the curtain away. Rose gasped. Even she had to admit she looked absolutely stunning. Tears came to her eyes, and Mía looked worried. Rose told her they were tears of joy. Mía was relieved. A couple of places needed a pinch and a tuck here and there, but Mía suggested they both came back the following Wednesday for their final fitting.

Before Rose left she gave Mía two wedding invitations. Mía said she would be delighted to attend.

The President had confirmed to JP that the civil ceremony had been moved to the palace, but the time had changed to 1pm, to give them more time to get to the church. JP now needed two cars to pick Rose, Ruby, Monica, George and Hugh up, but would need three to take them all to the church. Porte, Francois and Sérge had volunteered to drive the cars. Pierre had contacted the restaurant and upped the numbers by two. The jewellers had phoned JP, and he was going to collect the rings on the Wednesday. It was all coming together nicely. JP had phoned Rose every night to make sure she was alright, and was pleased when she said she was absolutely fine. JP, like Rose, was making sure everything was up to date before he finished for two weeks. The President had started to give Andre some of JP's work, which pleased Andre greatly – not.

The weekend flashed by and now there were only five days to the wedding day. As agreed the morning suits arrived on the Monday, and luckily they all fitted perfectly. On the Wednesday, JP went and picked the rings up, and he was delighted with Rose's. Rose was also double checking everything. The flowers and bouquet would be delivered on Saturday morning, but about midday. On the Wednesday, both Rose and Ruby went for their final fitting. Everything fitted perfectly, and Mía said the dresses would be delivered Friday afternoon, along with all the accessories. A quick call to Gérard, who also confirmed everything would be ready.

Friday morning, Rose went to the beauty salon. In the afternoon the dresses arrived. They were wrapped so well, nobody could see them. The accessories were in packed boxes. Rose and Ruby's names were on the dresses and boxes. Rose put hers in her bedroom, and Ruby's went in the spare bedroom, but she hung the dresses up in the wardrobes. Ruby and Monica had gone back to Antoine's so they could dress for the evening meal. This gave Rose time to pack her suitcase for the honeymoon. She half packed JP's but he could sort it out on Saturday night/Sunday morning. They weren't leaving until Monday.

About 6pm, Gabrielle, Céleste, Emilie, Ruby and Monica arrived. Gabrielle had ordered a large limousine, so nobody needed to drive. An hour later they arrived at a rooftop restaurant. The table was decorated with good luck balloons, and party poppers. Champagne was served first, which went down nicely. Menus were given out, and everyone chose their courses. Soon they were eating a lovely meal, and the wine glasses were being topped up. Rose looked over at Ruby, who was drinking a soft drink. She really had meant it when she said she would never get drunk again. Rose decided she would go onto a soft drink as well. Last thing she needed was a hangover. They all enjoyed themselves and left at 10pm.

Meanwhile, across the other side of Paris, things were going with a swing. JP and his friends were eating and drinking wine like no tomorrow. JP knew he was getting merry, and stopped drinking. After the meal, unbeknown to him, he was taken to a strip club. Pierre had arranged it all, and a very big-breasted woman did a very seductive strip in front of JP. She pulled his face into her breasts, but JP didn't like it, and pulled away. Then she sat astride his lap and started gyrating. Her hand quickly undid his zip, and she slipped it inside. "Non. Merci Madame, mais non," said JP, and the woman got off him. She kissed his cheek and went to another punter. His men were in hysterics, but Pierre was mortified as that was not what had been agreed. It was just supposed to be a straight forward strip and nothing else. Pierre apologised quickly to JP, who replied it was just fun, and he knew Pierre wouldn't do that to him, but he knew if he'd been drunk, the woman would have had her way with him, and he shuddered. About 1am they made their way back to the palace.

It was the day of the wedding, and both Rose and JP felt nervous. Rose was up early, washed and dressed and then went to get Monica and Ruby. Soon they were at the beauty salon. By 11am their hair was done, nails and toes painted. The salon offered them croissants and coffee, which was accepted gratefully. They all wished Rose a happy marriage. Rose dropped Monica off, and said she would see them later. Rose and Ruby went back to the flat, where they tried to sit and relax. The doorbell went and it was the buttonholes and bouquets. Ruby naturally saw the bouquets, and the buttonholes were red roses. The doorbell went again, and it was Monica and George. "Come on, you two, you've only got three quarters of an hour." Monica went with Ruby. Rose was happy to be on her own. First of all she undid the box and wrapping, and laid everything out in order on the bed. Then she set about her makeup, which wasn't going to be much. Half an hour later she was ready.

"Rose, Ruby is ready and your uncle is here, and this has been delivered for you," said Monica.

Rose opened the door slightly and took the package and then saw Ruby. She looked absolutely beautiful. She had on an off-the-shoulder, long, pale peach dress, which was pinched at the waist, and had silver and gold sparkles on the bodice. She had beige shoes and her jewellery was also in peach. "Ruby you look absolutely beautiful. I will be out in a second." Rose undid the package and saw the pearl necklace, earrings and bracelet. Quickly she put them on.

Rose came out into the sitting room and all four of them gasped. "Oh Rose, I have never seen you looking so… beyond words. You look exquisite," said Hugh, and they all agreed.

Ruby said, "JP is going to be blown away." Rose was pleased.

The two bouquets were of wild colourful flowers. The large one was for her, which was going to go on JP's parents' grave. Ruby would have the smaller one and give it to Rose later. At 12.40pm the doorbell went and it was Porte. All he said was, "Wow." Outside the sun was shining and the sky blue, with no clouds. Once in the cars they set off.

"Porte, you're going the wrong way. We are supposed to be going to the town hall, not the church."

Hugh patted her hand and said, "Don't panic, my dear, there has been a change of venue."

Fifteen minutes later they arrived at the palace.

"Uncle, what's going on? Oh no, is JP alright?"

Hugh replied, "JP is fine and you'll just have to wait and see. Now we'll give Monica a moment, whilst she hands out the buttonholes." Rose noticed a red carpet had been laid out. Porte got out of the car and then with Hugh they helped Rose out. Ruby arranged her dress and train.

"Rose, photo shoot please," said Suzette.

"How did you know?"

Suzette told her she had received a last-minute phone call. Suzette took photos of Rose on her own, and then with Hugh, then with Ruby, and finally all of them. Ruby then led them into the palace. As they walked down the corridor towards the ballroom, all the staff were lined up, all smiling and clapping. Rose smiled and thanked them. She actually felt like royalty. At the entrance to the ballroom, they stopped for a moment and then the music started and Ruby led the way, with Rose on Hugh's arm behind her.

JP and his men, along with the President and his wife Alicía were waiting. JP turned and his breath was taken away. Rose's wedding dress was in cream, with the most exquisite fabric design of lace covering the whole dress. The bodice was pinched at the waist, and had tiny pearls sewn into it, and the long skirt softly billowed out and behind her. The same lace also made the straps of the dress, not too wide and not too narrow. Rose's hair was half up, and had red rosebuds in it. The rest hung down in large curls. Rose had a small tiara from which her veil hung down to her waist, but not over her face. Also attached to the dress at the waist, was a long detachable train, which again was the exquisite lace, but doubled up. JP saw she had his present on, and wore cream shoes. As she walked down the red carpet, it was like the whole dress shimmered in various colours, and he thought his heart would burst.

"You look absolutely exquisite, môn amour," he said when she reached him.

"You look extremely handsome as well, my love," she replied.

Rose then noticed the President and his wife, and went to curtsey, but the President shook his head and said, "I hope you don't mind, but my wife and I thought it would be nice for you to have your civil ceremony here, and may I say you look absolutely beautiful, as do you Ruby." Rose smiled and thanked him. JP's men all gave her a wink. The President stood at JP's side, and Hugh moved to Rose's other side. The ceremony began and fifteen minutes later they were married, and the President and Hugh signed the wedding registry. All the staff and bodyguards cheered and clapped, especially when JP kissed Rose. Everyone was given a glass of champagne and toasted them. JP and Rose then thanked the President, and Alicía said she was delighted to have attended the wedding. She told Rose what a beautiful couple they made. Suzette had been given permission to take photos in the ballroom and photos of Rose and JP with the President and his wife. About twenty minutes later they left for the church. JP and Rose went in the first car with Porte driving. Monica,

Ruby, George and Hugh were in the second car with Sérge driving, and Francois drove JP's men.

Once in the car, JP took Rose carefully in his arms and kissed her passionately. The car behind tooted, and they laughed.

"Well Madame Pascal, how are you feeling?"

Rose replied, "So very, very happy, Monsieur Pascal. Thank you for my beautiful gift."

"It was my pleasure, môn amour. Once we get to the church, I will have to leave you, and we do it all over again, but this time we exchange rings. I hope you'll like it." Rose replied she was sure she would.

Soon they arrived at the church, and it was packed. JP and his men, along with Monica and George went into the church. Mía had come out and arranged Rose's dress, veil and train. "Ready to go again, my dear?" asked Hugh. Rose nodded. The music started up and like before, Ruby led the way. The church looked small, but the altar was at the very bottom, and to Rose it seemed a long walk. She could hear some of the remarks as she walked past.

"Doesn't she look beautiful; oh she looks gorgeous; what a good-looking couple," etc. She had to smile. JP turned to look at her again, but this time it was like she was gliding down the aisle. She just looked so radiant. At last she was at JP's side, and he winked and smiled at her. His four men were stood at the side of him, and Hugh, Ruby, Monica and George stood at the side of Rose.

CHAPTER 8

The priest started the ceremony and asked who was giving Rose away. Hugh replied he was and put Rose's hand in JP's. His men and the rest then went and sat down. When the priest asked Rose if she took JP as her husband, she nearly said, "I do," but remembered and replied, "Je le veux." Both JP and the priest smiled.

When it came to the exchange of rings, George put them on the small cushion. JP put the ring on her finger, and then Rose put JP's ring on his finger. His band was plain gold, as was Rose's, but it had small rosebuds etched all the way round in silver. She loved it. The priest blessed them and announced them husband and wife. Again JP kissed his beautiful bride. When they walked out of the church, Suzette grabbed them for more photos. Soon everyone was out, and after all the photos were done, Rose gathered up her train, and dress, and with JP walked hand in hand to his parents' grave, and Rose laid her bouquet on it. Tears came into her eyes and JP asked her if she was alright. Rose replied, "How I wish they had been here and seen us get married, my love."

JP tipped her face up and gently kissed her lips and said gently, "They have seen us, môn amour." Rose smiled and then they walked back to their guests.

As they walked back the sun caught Rose's dress and it sparkled in colours. Mía had sewn in tiny sequins of various colours, which gave it the effect. The guests couldn't believe their eyes. It was like Rose and JP were walking through a rainbow. Ruby handed Rose the spare bouquet. Suddenly they were showered with rice, grains of wheat and rose petals, which stood for prosperity and fertility. JP and Rose got into the car and waved to everyone as they drove off. "Well, all done now, môn amour. You still happy?"

Rose took JP in her arms and kissed him with such a passion, that even Porte blushed. Both JP and Rose laughed. "Apologies, Porte," said Rose.

Gérard was waiting on the steps for them to arrive. "Come, I have a room where you can have a few private moments," and led them in. "I'll let you know when everyone is here, and by the way, you both look wonderful." Rose kissed his cheek and JP shook his hand.

"Alone at last, môn amour. Come here." JP kissed her passionately and then trailed kisses down her neck towards her breasts.

Rose moaned and said, "We have a reception to go to, so behave, or my angel will be naughty."

"I can't wait to get you into bed tonight, and love you as my wife." Rose kissed him and said she felt the same, but it was going to be a long reception party.

Gérard tapped on the door, and JP opened it. "Everyone has arrived, my friends, and your reception awaits."

Cheers went up as JP and Rose walked in. Rose put her train over her arm so it wouldn't get damaged. Mía tapped her shoulder and said, "'Allow me, Rose," and carefully detached her train, and also took her veil. Gérard showed her where to put them so they would be safe.

"That's better," said Rose.

A waiter gave JP and Rose a glass of champagne and they made their way to the top table, where George, Monica, and Hugh were already seated. A table at the side had his men, wives, children, and Ruby seated. "Ladies and gentlemen," said JP, gently tapping his glass. "May I have a moment of your time? On behalf of Rose and myself, we want to say a huge thank you for you all giving up your precious time and joining us to celebrate."

Pierre replied, "This beats work any day, boss." Everyone laughed and Rose saw Emilie slap him, and giggled.

Rose then said, "There are so many people I would like to thank,

I'd bore you, so thank you to everyone who has made this day so special. I am now going to embarrass my husband," to which everyone cheered, "and would like you all, along with myself, to wish him a very happy birthday." They all sang happy birthday to him, and JP blushed.

"Please everyone help yourself to the buffet, and more than anything enjoy yourselves," said JP.

"To the bride and groom," said Andre, and everyone toasted them.

Six small children ran up to them, shouting, "Uncle JP, Auntie Rose." It was his men's children.

"Hello, you lot. I understand so far you've been very good," said JP. They all nodded and then hugged and kissed them.

Andre's son looked at them and said, "You been kissing?" JP leant over and kissed Rose. "Oh yuk. I'm going back to Papa," and marched off. Rose and JP laughed. The others stayed for about five minutes and then went back to their parents.

Rose and JP walked round talking to everyone. Rose then saw a face she hadn't expected. "Marcus, how lovely to see you. When did you get here?"

Marcus kissed her cheek and said, "Yesterday, and before you ask, yes I have seen Mathieu and met Séra. They make a lovely couple." Rose was pleased and hoped they would make up. After about two hours of mingling, JP took Rose's hand and led her to the buffet. Gérard had done an excellent buffet. The tables were against the length of the wall. It consisted of glasses of prawn cocktail and various mousses; escargots; Coquille St Jacques; Devilled Eggs; a whole salmon; quiches; vol-au-vents filled with different fillings; lots of salad ingredients; various sliced meats and French sausages; bowls of pasta; hot jacket potatoes, roasted potatoes with garlic and thyme, one of Boulangère (with onions), and Dauphinois; chicken wings and drumsticks; Tartes Flambée (bacon and onion tarts); beetroot and cheese crostini; smoked salmon mousse puff pastry tarts; chicken liver parfait with homemade chutney on toasted brioche; mixed breads with butter and olive oil, and various other delights.

Rose watched everyone laughing, joking and enjoying themselves. More than that though she was delighted to see Marcus sitting with

Mathieu and Séra. Both men looked happy. The waiters and waitresses were busy filling up wine glasses, or clearing away dirty dishes. Once Gérard had condensed the main course onto two smaller tables, the desserts were then brought in. Crème brûlées; Tarte tatins; Crème caramels; chocolate fondant; pêche melba; macarons; clafoutis; mendiants; religieuse; crêpes suzette; assortment of petits fours; and other pastries, fresh fruit, to name a few. There were also a huge variety of cheeses and biscuits. Gérard clapped his hands and said, "Madames, monsieurs, mademoiselles et enfants, 'Le Gâteau de Mariage'." A large Croquembouche was wheeled in on a trolley and everyone clapped and stood up. It was placed at the end of Rose and JP's table. Rose and JP stood either side of it.

"This is going to be fun," said JP winking. JP carefully removed one of the puffs and put it between his lips, and then Rose had to bite the other half off, and they did this four times. Both of them were giggling. Once they had finished, everyone clapped and cheered.

"To Rose and JP. May they have a long happy marriage," everyone said.

JP took Rose in his arms and kissed her passionately, to which again everyone was cheering, clapping and some wolf whistles. The Croquembouche was then moved and placed in the centre of the desserts, and soon everyone was helping themselves. Once it looked like everyone had finished, again what was left was put onto a separate table.

Gérard then said, "Now for some fun, non? Here I have a microphone, which is going to be passed between you all, and you must say something lovely about our couple. Let's see, ah yes, I will start with you," and handed the microphone to Pierre!! JP put his hand over his eyes and shook his head, but smiling. Within minutes Pierre had everyone in hysterics about JP. Then it was the turn of Andre, then Donatien and then Antoine. They all had their own funny stories to tell. Hugh made everyone laugh about some of the antics Rose had got up to, and so it went on. Lots of them had no funny stories of Rose and JP, so they told everyone their funny stories. The whole place was in uproar with laughter. Rose was actually crying with laughter, as well as JP.

Time had zoomed along and it was about 9pm. Gérard had had renovations done during the winter months, and now slid back a partition, to reveal another room, which had a dance floor, and a DJ who was raring to go. The music started and the glitter balls whirled round with specific lights shining on them. Hugh took Rose's hand and led her out onto the floor. As she swirled round with her uncle, the lights of the glitter balls picked up the coloured sequins in her dress, and the dress came alive with different colours. "Oh wow, that's fantastic. In fact it's magical," said Ruby. After a couple of minutes, JP came to the floor, and as tradition, Hugh gave him Rose's hand and left them. They swirled round a couple of times, completely immersed in each other, and then the others started to join in. Rose danced with his men, Hugh and George, and JP danced with their wives, Ruby and Monica.

After an hour the disco started properly. Séra had danced alongside Rose and whispered, "I want the name of your dressmaker. I have a proposition for them." Rose said she would introduce her later.

A bit later the DJ said, "I have been asked for a special request, which I believe is a favourite of the bride. It's YMCA, by Village People." The music started and Rose and Ruby jumped for joy. They were in the middle of the dance floor doing the routine, and soon JP, his men and their wives joined in. The DJ stopped the music and said, "Now you all know the routine, let's start again." Rose and Ruby were placed in a circle, with JP and the rest surrounding them. Everyone watched as they did the routine, some even joined in. JP never took his eyes off Rose. She was enjoying herself so much, and then Ruby changed places with him. The pair of them finished the routine together. "I understand this next record is also a favourite. It's 'I Only Want To Be With You', by Dusty Springfield," said the DJ. JP and Rose danced in each other's arms and at the end JP kissed Rose passionately.

"Get a room, you two," said Pierre, and everyone clapped and laughed. The disco was a huge success.

Gérard had come up to JP and whispered something in his ear, and he went with him. A couple of minutes later JP took Rose's hand and led her to a quiet spot. "Môn amour, something has cropped up and my men and I need to leave for a short time. It's nothing to be worried about. We are going to drop the children back to Pierre's and we will be back soon," and kissed her tenderly. Rose watched as they left.

Emilie came up to her and said, "Who'd marry a bodyguard?"

Rose laughed and they went back to the party. Rose danced with so many people, she was starting to feel dizzy.

Monica rescued her. "Come and sit down Rose, and drink this," and gave her a glass of water. Rose sipped the water slowly and her dizziness went away.

JP saw Rose with Monica and went straight to her. "Môn amour, what's wrong?"

Rose smiled at him and said, "Nothing, my love. I've just danced myself out." Monica left them.

"I can't leave you for a second, can I?" he said, smiling.

Rose wrapped her arms round him and whispered, "I want to love you so much, my husband."

JP replied, "And we will soon, môn amour, but not until our guests are leaving." They sat there with their arms around each other.

"Here they are. You two having a rest?" asked Antoine.

"We were," said JP.

"Gérard wants us all outside." Rose asked why. Antoine shrugged his shoulders.

Gérard went and got between the middle of them and said, "My surprise for you." The sky suddenly lit up with a wonderful fireworks display, which lasted a good half hour.

"Oh Gérard, thank you, that was absolutely fantastic," and hugged him and kissed his cheek.

JP gave him a manly hug and thanked him as well. "Now I think it's time for the late-night Soupe à l'oignon, so everyone back inside."

"What time is it?" asked Rose. JP replied 4am. Rose was stunned. Quite a few of the guests had already left, but those left sat at the tables. The soup was served and Rose asked JP what was in it. JP told her it was made with meat stock and onions, served gratinéed with croutons and cheese on top of a large piece of bread. Rose tried it and liked it, but was glad it was in a small ramekin. A couple of hours later, their guests slowly started to leave, and everyone said what a wonderful time they'd had. Rose and JP thanked every one of them. By 7am the restaurant was empty, except for Rose, JP, his men and wives, Ruby, Hugh, George and Monica. Porte, Sérge and Francois arrived with the cars. Hugs and kisses went all round and they all wished Rose and JP a wonderful honeymoon.

"Ruby, good luck starting at Gilmac News on Monday," said Rose.

Ruby replied, "They won't know what's hit them," and everyone laughed.

Gérard brought Rose her train and veil, which had been carefully wrapped in tissue paper. Rose and JP thanked him again for everything he had done for them, and would see him soon. Gérard waved as the cars drove off.

Rose was cuddled into JP and had closed her eyes and nodded off. "Môn amour, we are nearly home," said JP. Rose opened her eyes, but instead of seeing the streets of Paris, she saw they were in the country. Sitting up, she recognised where they were. They had just gone through the village by the farmhouse. Porte turned the car down the track and pulled up by the front door. JP got out first and then helped Rose. "Thank you, Porte, for driving us. See you in two weeks."

Porte replied, "Your car will be delivered tomorrow morning. Enjoy the chalet." They both waved goodbye.

"When did you buy the farmhouse?" JP unlocked the door and picked Rose up and carried her over the threshold.

"I'll tell you later. Right now I have something else on my mind." Rose smiled.

JP took her hand and led her upstairs to their bedroom, where a huge four-poster bed awaited them. Rose put her train and veil on the bed. "JP this is—" JP's lips were on hers and they kissed each other with a passion full of urgency.

"Let's hang our clothes in the wardrobe first," said JP. Rose undressed JP down to his underpants. Well, if you could call them underpants. It was more like a pouch with thin straps. Rose smiled. JP turned Rose round and carefully unzipped her dress, and then pushed it off her shoulders. Rose stepped out of it, and JP picked it up and hung it in the wardrobe. Rose stood there in a cream basque with matching briefs, and a cream suspender belt that held up her stockings. On her right thigh was a rosebud garter.

"You look as exquisite as you did in your wedding dress." Rose kicked off her shoes, and JP picked her up and laid her on the bed.

CHAPTER 9

JP took her in his arms and kissed her tenderly, and as always, because he knew she liked it, trailed kisses down both sides of her neck. Rose was holding him tight and then her hands went down his back and it like was feathers brushing over his skin. JP went further down and spread her legs. Then he kneeled between them. He took one leg and put it on his shoulder, and undid the stocking. Slowly he rolled the stocking down, kissing the inside of her thigh and leg down to her toes. He lowered that leg and then did the same to the other one. Rose had electric shocks flowing through her body, at JP's sensual kisses.

JP looked down at her and saw Rose still had the rosebuds in her hair, and slowly removed them. His lips sought hers again, and their tongues swirled together. Kneeling back up he slowly undid the laces on her basque. He leant down and placed gentle kisses between her breasts down to her stomach. Rose was moaning as he did it. His hand then pushed the basque back away from her breasts, and he gently pulled it out from under her. His hands kneaded her breasts and then he took her nipples in his mouth and swirled his tongue over them. They went hard instantly. Rose was trailing her fingers up and down his back. JP now slid further down the bed to her mound. He gently pulled her briefs down and to his delight saw she was naked. He knew he was rock hard, but he wasn't going to rush. As he took her briefs off he also took her garter off. Rose looked absolutely radiant laying there totally naked. JP's hand went to her mound, which was so naked and soft and as he kissed it he parted her lips, and soon Rose went over the edge and climaxed.

JP kissed her all the way back up to her lips, and Rose quickly rolled him onto his back. Rose then did everything that JP had done to her, including kissing the inside of his thighs. Something felt different. Slowly she peeled his pouch down and his manhood sprung to attention. She took it gently in her hands and said, "You're my husband now my angel," and took him in her mouth, and cupped and fondled his testicles. JP climaxed quickly, but didn't go soft. He rolled Rose back over and pushing her legs up towards her shoulders, he entered her. This time though they both wanted it badly and so JP thrust hard and fast. Soon Rose's muscles were clenching him, and he pushed her legs up further. His thrusts now went deeper into her and Rose was grinding her hips against him. JP knew Rose wasn't far off and thrust quicker. He felt himself coming to his climax as well. Rose was now writhing and calling his name. Without warning she bucked and grabbed his testicles and squeezed them gently. That took both of them over the edge. Both were exhausted and breathless. JP rolled onto his side as did Rose, and he held her like he was never going to let her go. Rose was holding him tight, still in ecstasy.

JP kissed her lips and said, "Good morning, Madame Pascal."

Rose stretched against him, her nipples moving over his, and replied, "Good morning, Monsieur Pascal." Then they slept.

Rose woke first and saw it was 4pm. She stretched her body out and felt so contented. She looked at JP who was still asleep. There was something different about him, but what? She lowered the duvet carefully, and took all of his body in. Then she realised what it was, as she looked at his manhood. He was completely naked – not a hair anywhere on his body. She wanted to touch him, but would wait until later. Quietly she got out of the bed, and put her briefs and JP's shirt on. She was going to look at her new home. Her feet got cold on the wooden floors, so she went back and grabbed JP's socks. It was then she noticed the suitcases they packed to go away were there. How? Rose looked in the other bedrooms and both of them were furnished with the usual bedroom furniture, but rustic. Downstairs she looked in what she thought was the dining room. It was now the sitting room. Three new very large comfy-looking settees and six armchairs were placed in a horseshoe shape, with tables in front of the settees. On the far wall was the large fireplace. In one of the corners was a huge television, and large and small cabinets were against the walls. Rose saw there were pieces from the flat in the cabinets.

Next she went into the dining room. In the middle was a long rustic table and chairs that would seat sixteen people. Small and large cabinets were along the walls, with another large fireplace. Again, pieces from the flat were in the cabinets. This had Rose curious. She went down the steps into the kitchen and was even more curious. All the pots, pans, etc. were there from the flat. There was a new fridge; a freezer; a bigger dishwasher; a washing machine and all the cupboards were new. What caught her eye though was the huge aga cooker. In the middle was a beautiful rustic oak table and chairs. There was even a larder. She went back to the hallway and opened the back door and looked out. The garden had been completely re-done and it looked wonderful with most of the flowers in bloom.

Suddenly a pair of strong arms encircled her waist. "So that's where my shirt and socks went. Very sexy, I must say."

Rose turned and said, "How did you know how much I liked this farmhouse, and when did you buy it? More important, can we afford it? How did the bits and pieces from the flat get here? How...?"

"Môn amour, I have lots to tell you, but first let's get something to eat and drink and I will explain, or would you rather we go back to bed?"

Rose kissed him and replied, "We have two weeks to love each other, my husband, and if it's anything like last night then wow."

JP kissed her back and said, "Well, my beautiful sexy wife, I will explain." In the kitchen JP said, "Wedding presents, môn amour. The aga is from your uncle; the fridge and freezer is from your mum and dad; the washing machine is from Séra and Mathieu, and the biggest dishwasher I have ever seen is from my men and their wives."

"We must send thank you cards when we return." JP said he already thanked everyone, but that would be a nice idea.

Half an hour later they were sitting down to bacon, sausages, eggs, toast and coffee, and ended up feeding each other giggling as they did. Rose then took JP's hand and led him into the sitting room, where they sat down on one of the settees. Rose sat cross-legged facing JP. "Now my love, explain."

JP replied, "Not sure I can concentrate on the view I'm getting." Rose uncrossed her legs and sat on them instead. "Spoilsport," said JP. Rose threw a cushion at him. JP laughed and threw it back, and soon he had his arms round her kissing her. "No. Not until you explain," said Rose.

"This is all going to be a surprise to you, but a lovely surprise, and that's why we all kept quiet, although Antoine nearly put his foot in it once. Once you'd seen this farmhouse, I could tell by your voice how much you loved it, and that started a chain of events. Monica and George came over months ago for interviews at a couple of the Parisian hospitals, and were told a month later they had got the jobs. George phoned Hugh to ask about properties, and how they stood to get a mortgage, if they couldn't get a quick sale. Meanwhile, they had put their house on the market. They were extremely lucky and a buyer more or less snapped it up right away. They now had the funds to pay for something over here. I bumped into Hugh one day and he told me the secret. I then told your uncle about the farmhouse. Hugh arranged for Monica and George to fly over one weekend and the four of us met at his office. The outcome was, Monica and George have bought our flat, and I then bought the farmhouse. Both of us didn't have the full amount, so your uncle drew up the contracts. Another year and we will own our own properties. As to how our stuff got here from the flat, I told you a white lie at the wedding. There was no urgent matter we had to attend to. The five of us drove back to the flat, packed everything up and brought it here. I couldn't leave Monica and George with no furniture so it was included in the price. The rest of Monica and George's stuff is already here in storage. That's why they flew over at the end of May."

Rose was silent for a bit and then said, "So all of you kept me in the dark and then lied to me. Ruby, Mum and Dad are all here to stay for good. Have I got that right?"

JP wasn't sure if Rose was pleased or bloody annoyed. "Yes môn amour, and I'm sorry."

The next thing Rose jumped on him and said, "I'm so happy. All my family are now here. Oh my love what a wonderful surprise, as was this place. I love you so much, and you're forgiven. Now bed." JP didn't need asking twice. "I see you had another wedding surprise for me," and Rose removed his dressing gown. Her hand went to his manhood and testicles. "So smooth, like me. I bet it hurt though."

JP replied, "You could say it bloody well hurt, but if you can do it, so can I."

Soon they were loving each other with a passion. Afterwards Rose sat up and said, "Please tell me your men didn't pack my lingerie." JP assured her he had done it, and everything was in cases and boxes in the large wardrobe, apart from her evening gowns, which he had put on hangers.

Rose looked at the clock on the bedside cabinet, next to her side of the bed, and saw it was 8pm. "What time is the car arriving in the morning?" JP said about 9am. He had decided to drive straight to Montpellier, but it was still going to be a seven/eight hour drive. Rose said she would drive part way, so he wasn't shattered. JP said he'd see how heavy the traffic was on the motorway.

Rose pulled the boxes and cases out of the wardrobe. Luckily the first case had her slippers and dressing gown in, which she put on. An hour later she had all their clothes hung up, in the wardrobe or laid out in a couple of the six drawer tallboys.

"JP, where's all the towels etc.?"

"Either in the bathroom or the airing cupboard."

Rose went to the bathroom to have a look. Everything had been spotlessly cleaned and Rose decided she wanted a quick bath. JP had nodded off and wondered where she was when he woke. He saw the bathroom door was slightly open and put his head round the door. Rose was firm asleep in the bath. Carefully he lifted her out and laid her on a large towel and dried her off. Then he picked her up and put her in the bed. He went back to the bathroom and pulled the plug out of the bath and let the water drain away, and then wiped it round with a flannel. In the bedroom, Rose had snuggled into a pillow, but the duvet had slipped leaving her lovely buttocks bared to the world. JP got into bed himself, turned out the lights, and spooned into her back, wrapping his arms round her.

Rose said sleepily, "JP."

He replied quietly, "Hush, môn amour, go back to sleep," and kissed her shoulder. Soon the pair of them were in a deep contented sleep.

JP woke at 6am and then realised he didn't have to go to work. Rose was still asleep in his arms, and he decided to get another couple of hours. It was going to be a long drive. He woke again at 7.30am. Carefully, so as not to wake Rose, he slid out of the bed and went and had a quick shower. He dressed and went down to the kitchen and looked to see what was left in the fridge. There was enough bacon and sausages, but no eggs. He found a tin of canned tomatoes, and along with the bread he had enough for their breakfast. He laid a tray and was about to take it up to Rose, when she walked into the kitchen. To JP she looked gorgeous. Her hair was tumbling down in all directions, and she just had her dressing gown and slippers on. "Morning, môn amour. I was going to surprise you."

Rose looked at him, still sleepy. "How did I get to bed last night?" JP told her and she was mortified. "I'm so sorry, JP. I just drifted off as I relaxed." JP kissed her and said it wasn't a problem, any excuse to caress her body. Rose rolled her eyes and he laughed.

"Come, eat, before it gets cold."

They tucked in and once Rose had drunk about two mugs of coffee, she was raring to go. She went upstairs and thought what a fright she looked, when she looked in the mirror. Soon she was dressed and presentable. She re-packed her suitcase, and took half of it out. Whilst they were in the chalet they would hardly wear any clothes. It would only be if they went out sightseeing or for meals. JP had also re-packed. At 9am JP saw a soft-top car being driven down the track, with another car behind it. JP went out and signed the rental papers and was given the keys. The men then left.

"Môn amour, you ready to go?" Rose came bounding down the stairs, and said she was. JP put the bags in the boot, put the roof down, and after checking the house was all locked and secured, including closing all the window shutters, he locked the front door.

Rose had vanished, so he tooted the horn. Rose came round from the two outbuildings. "Sorry my love, just wanted to see what they were." One was a garage, and the other had been decorated in cream and left empty. "JP, what about my car?"

"Antoine is going to drive it over, lock it in the garage and put the keys through the letterbox. Donatien will follow and then take him back. Now, Montpellier, here we come."

They made good time and arrived at the chalet at 7pm, after doing a bulk buy at the supermarket. Rose took one look at the sea and looking at JP, said, "Fancy a swim?"

"Last one unpacks and cooks," said JP. They both ran into the sea, naked, at the same time. "That's a draw then, môn amour." They swam, splashed each other, ran along the beach playing tag, and laughed. Neither of them had thought about towels, so they rough dried themselves with their clothes. Soon they were in the chalet, had unpacked, put their slippers and dressing gowns on, and JP was cooking a meal. Rose could see JP was tired. It had been a long drive. She had offered to cook but he wanted her to relax. JP cooked a couple of steaks with chips and a salad.

Afterwards they cuddled up on the settee and watched some television. JP yawned, and Rose said, "My love, time for bed and sleep. Come on." Within half an hour both of them were firm asleep.

CHAPTER 10

The following morning the sun was up and it was going to be hot. "Fancy taking a shower, môn amour?" Rose nodded and soon they were loving each other with the warm water cascading down over them. After they put their dressing gowns and slippers on, Rose went to the shed and JP went to the kitchen. Rose found the sun beds and put them on the beach, along with the sun umbrellas. Just in case, she put the snorkelling gear by the back door of the chalet. She placed two really large towels over the back of the beds. She had also found a small plastic table, which she put between the beds to put drinks on. JP came down the steps with a tray that had two bacon and egg rolls and mugs of coffee on it. They sat on the beds and enjoyed their breakfast.

A bit later, both of them took off their dressing gowns and put cream on each other's bodies. After an hour Rose was getting hot, and decided to go for a swim. Soon she saw all the fish, and looked round to make sure there were no jellyfish. She didn't see any. She floated on her back, feeling the heat on her front, and the cool on her back. Then she would flip over and swim. JP had been watching her and when she was floating on her back, he nipped down the beach, and quietly went underwater. Rose screamed as his hand went between her legs, and for the first time she clipped him round the head. He roared laughing and soon they were kissing and loving each other.

Late afternoon, JP had been watching the skies, which were starting to get darker and darker. "I think we are in for a thunderstorm. Might be an idea to put everything away, môn amour." Rose looked and agreed. They'd just put everything in the shed, and locked it, when the rain started to fall gently. Within ten minutes, it was absolutely pouring straight down. The thunder roared overhead, and the lightning started.

Rose was taking photos of the lightning when suddenly she was blown backwards. JP, who was in the kitchen, heard a thud and went into the sitting room. "Rose, Rose, môn amour are you alright?" Carefully he picked her up and put her on the settee. JP saw the camera in Rose's hand had exploded. Carefully he removed it and saw Rose's hand was burnt. Straight away he knew she'd been struck by the lightning, and knocked out. Another bolt suddenly hit the window, which shattered. He'd never seen a storm like this before. As he was checking Rose, he noticed she was starting to shake and her heart rate had increased. Shock was taking over her body. He went to the bathroom and found a medical kit and treated Rose's hand, and then put a bandage round it.

A couple of minutes later Rose started to come round. "What... what happened?" JP told her. Then she saw the window.

"Rest, môn amour, I will clean the mess up, but first try and take some deep breaths. It will help." As Rose took the deep breaths her heart rate started to go back to normal. JP was relieved. The rain was still coming straight down, but luckily not in through the window. JP had seen some thick polythene in the garage, and so taking his dressing gown off, naked, he ran there, got the polythene and returned. He grabbed the large towel and rough dried himself off, and put his dressing gown back on. Within fifteen minutes the window was covered.

JP went back to Rose and took her in his arms and kissed her gently. Rose told him she was fine, and said, "Thank heavens that wasn't my expensive camera. Well, I can honestly say I've never been blown off my feet before."

The storm was getting worse and now the wind had started to howl. At that moment the phone rang and JP answered it. It was Porte, checking to see if they were alright, as he'd seen the storm on the television. JP told him what had happened. "Mon dieu, is Rose alright?" JP said she'd have a sore hand for a couple of days. Porte told him where the nearest hospital was, in case Rose got worse. He also gave him the phone number of a doctor. He advised JP to keep an eye on the sea. It had only happened once before, but it came right up to the back door.

"JP, in the loft of the garage are the shutters. They fix on the inside of the windows. Don't worry about the shattered window. I will contact Marcel and he will ring you to let you know when he can come and fix it. If you have to move out, I will pay for a hotel for you." JP told him he was sure they would be alright, and thanked him for the call. He went to the garage again and found the shutters, and put them up against the windows. At least that made the chalet feel safer for both of them. The sea was halfway up the beach. He made a meal, but Rose wasn't very hungry. She said she felt slightly dizzy and had a headache. What she didn't tell JP was that the pain in her hand was hurting like hell. JP suggested she went to bed and rested. He was concerned. Within minutes she was asleep. JP stayed up, but checked on Rose every half hour. It was gone midnight before the storm started to abate. JP opened the back door and saw that the sea hadn't got to the back door, but it was still halfway up the beach. A lot of the trees were down.

When he went into the bedroom, he saw Rose was shaking again. He gently woke her, and talked calmly to her. Rose stopped shaking but said she had such a headache. JP got her some painkillers, which she took. He then spooned into her back and held her tight, gently kissing her neck and shoulder.

In the morning Rose said her hand was still hurting. JP took the bandage off and saw Rose's hand was going black. Within an hour they were at the hospital, and Rose underwent various tests. JP was pacing up and down the corridor when the doctor called to him. "Your wife will be fine. All of her tests so far are excellent. As to her hand, it looks bad, but it's actually a superficial burn. She's lucky her camera took the full force of the strike. Within a couple of days the mark will go. She's asking to see you. Once I have the blood results back, if all is fine, you can take her home." JP, greatly relieved, thanked the doctor.

"Sorry to spoil our honeymoon, my love."

JP kissed her and replied, "Môn amour you have spoilt nothing. We still have plenty of days left to do whatever we want."

"Excuse me," said the doctor. "Madame Pascal, you are free to go. Your blood tests were fine."

"Thank you, Doctor, sorry to have been a nuisance," said Rose.

The doctor smiled and said, "Not a nuisance, better to be checked out. Au revoir." Rose dressed and they left.

When they got back to the chalet, JP noticed the window had been fixed. The rest of the day, and the following day, JP made sure Rose just relaxed and rested.

The following day, Rose's hand looked a lot better, and it was no longer painful. The sun was out along with clear blue skies. Even though the sea had covered more than half of the beach, most of the sand remained.

"Môn amour, do you want to go into Montpellier, or sunbathe, if you're up to it?"

Rose said she wanted to swim and sunbathe. "Can I swim with my hand, do you think?"

JP replied, "Your hand is fine, as the skin isn't broken. I could always find a rubber glove for you to put on, and then wrap an elastic band round, so the water stays out."

Rose replied, "I'll chance it without."

JP got the sun beds and umbrellas and set them up. Rose went and got a couple of large towels, and then took off her dressing gown and laid down. JP couldn't take his eyes off her. Soon he too laid down naked on his sun bed. Rose woke about an hour later and rolled over, and went back to sleep. When JP woke, he looked to make sure Rose was alright. She was laid on her front and his eyes went all the way down her back. He saw the curve of her back, going up slightly to her pert rounded buttocks, and then going down into long slender legs. He hadn't loved her for two days, and now his manhood was standing to attention. He decided to go for a swim to cool his ardour. As he entered the water, Rose rolled over and saw him. She also saw his manhood. He had been so gentle with her since the accident, but now she wanted him so badly, and got up and went down to the sea.

JP hadn't seen her get into the sea, as he was floating on his back. Rose swam under the water, until she was under him. Before JP had any idea she was there, she had parted his legs and taken his manhood in her mouth. He nearly went under the water himself. Rose had her arms round each leg, and was relentless. JP could feel his climax coming, and tried to stop her, but Rose wouldn't let go. His body exploded as he climaxed. Then Rose kissed him, after she had rinsed her mouth in the sea.

"I've missed my husband," she said.

JP replied, "And I have missed my wife, so now it's my turn." JP guided her back towards the beach, to the point where he could stand up. "Float time, môn amour," and Rose went onto her back. Like Rose, JP pushed her legs apart and put his hand on her mound, and then caressed her nub. Next he was between her legs, holding her waist, whilst he let his mouth and tongue pleasure her. Rose was thrashing about in the water, and then her climax hit her. As Rose went to stand up, JP picked her up and carried her back to the sun bed. Once he laid her down, he kissed her so tenderly, that Rose had goose bumps. Her nipples went hard, and JP noticed. "Put your legs either side of the bed, môn amour." Rose did and JP rolled his dressing gown up and placed it under her buttocks to raise them up. He then put his legs either side of the bed, and entered her. His hands caressed her breasts and nipples as he slowly slid in and out of her. Rose was on the brink when JP pulled her up to him and kissed her. He was deep inside her and was thrusting quicker, when Rose's climax hit her and then JP's hit him as well. JP held her in his arms kissing her lips, and then her breasts and nipples.

Rose looked into his sparkling blue eyes, full of love for her and said, "Will this bed hold both of us?" JP looked at her and both of them laughed. He got up and reluctantly went and laid on his sun bed.

Later that evening JP did a BBQ, which they ate sitting on their sun beds. "Umm, that was delicious," said Rose.

JP replied, "I aim to please, môn amour."

Rose got up and leant over JP and passionately said, "You always please me, my love, especially in your arms." JP grinned. "Come on, let's tidy up and then I think I'd like to please you some more, but in bed." Now it was Rose's turn to grin.

Over the next five days, all they did was relax, sunbathe, swim, eat and love each other. Now the time had come for them to return to

Paris. Like the year before, both of them were sad to leave. After a very early start, they were back home about 4pm, after they had been to the supermarket to do a very large shop. By the time everything was put away, the fridge and the freezer was full. Antoine had put Rose's car in the garage, and put the keys through the postbox. JP went round and opened all the shutters and windows. After two weeks the farmhouse smelled musty. "I still can't believe this is ours," she said. Suddenly Rose had a thought. "My love, where's my jewellery? And more important where's teddy?" JP took her upstairs to their bedroom and opened his wardrobe. Pushing down the shelf, she saw the safe and JP gave her the combination.

"And here is teddy, keeping watch over us both as he has always done."

Rose smiled at her teddy on the windowsill, but he was sat in a small chair keeping watch. "Thank you, my love. I know it's stupid but I would be so upset if I lost him. He's the only thing of my past."

JP took her in his arms and kissed her gently and said, "As would I. He looked after you when I couldn't." Rose kissed him back. "Now Madame Pascal, time to make us a meal. I don't know about you but I'm starving."

JP cooked, whilst Rose unpacked and put the washing in the laundry box for the morning. They still had two days before they returned to work. Rose had a quick shower and put her dressing gown and slippers on. "Ooh something smells good."

JP smiled and replied, "Salad to start, then steaks with garlic potatoes, and vegetables. For after, fruit salad and ice cream. I'll let you make the coffee."

Rose sat down at the large kitchen table, and both of them enjoyed their meal. They had hardly eaten all day. Afterwards, Rose made a pot of coffee and took it into the sitting room. JP had switched on the television and both of them cuddled up on the settee. Within half an hour both of them were firm asleep. About midnight JP woke up, and for a minute wondered where he was. He saw Rose was still asleep, so carefully he picked her up and put her in the bed, after taking her dressing gown and slippers off. JP walked round and closed the windows, just in case, but left the bedroom windows half open. Locked the front door, switched the television

71

and lights off, and then went upstairs. Quietly he undressed, spooned into Rose's back, after he'd switched the bedside light off. Rose in her sleep turned over and cuddled into JP's chest.

"Night, my love," she said sleepily.

JP kissed her and said, "Night, môn amour."

About ten minutes later, a loud hammering on the front door woke both of them up. JP quickly grabbed his dressing gown and slippers, as did Rose, and putting the lights on, went down to the front door. "Who is it?" he asked abruptly.

"Gendarme," came the reply.

CHAPTER 11

JP looked out of the window and saw a police car. Immediately he unlocked the door. "Is there a problem, Officer?" asked JP. The gendarme asked him who he was and JP told him. "I need identification," replied the gendarme sternly.

"Please come in and I will get my wallet." The gendarme said he would stay where he was. JP went and got his wallet. "Here is my passport and driving licence, along with my wife's."

Rose was stood at the bottom of the stairs. The gendarme checked the documents and replied, "My apologies, Monsieur and Madame Pascal. One of the villagers was passing and saw the lights going off and thought you had been broken into. They understood you weren't arriving until Sunday, and reported it to us."

JP replied, "No apologies needed. It's nice to know that they were looking after the property for us, and thank you for checking."

The gendarme made his way back to his car and then drove away. JP re-locked the front door and taking Rose's hand, they went back to bed. "I think tomorrow, môn amour, we must walk into the village and thank whoever it was."

Rose replied, "We could go to the pub for lunch." They cuddled up and soon drifted off back to sleep.

Lunchtime, hand in hand, they walked down through the forest to the village. A lot of the gardens had lovely sunflowers growing in them. As the entered the village they saw the name – Village de Tournesols (Village of Sunflowers). "Appropriate name," said JP.

"Perhaps we had better grow some as well, my love." JP replied that was easily remedied.

As they entered the pub, they saw it was quite big inside. In front of them was a large bar, which had quite a few people sitting at tables drinking and eating. To the right was a fair-sized restaurant, and to the left another seating area. Everyone went quiet and turned and looked at them. Rose held onto JP's hand tighter. The man behind the bar turned and said, "Well I'll be damned. JP, what on earth are you doing here?"

JP smiled and said, "Raoul, might ask you the same question."

Raoul replied, "This is my pub. Everyone, let me introduce my old boss to you, Jean-Paul Pascal, known as JP, and...?" JP introduced Rose. "And his lovely wife Rose." Everyone greeted them and then they all carried on with what they were doing. Raoul explained they were some of the villagers. "Please, what would you like to drink?"

JP replied, "Two glasses of red wine would be nice. Raoul, and could we look at the menu? To answer your question, we have bought the farmhouse, and came to thank whoever called the gendarmes last night, thinking the house was being burgled."

Raoul tinkled a glass and everyone looked at him. "More good news. This lovely couple have bought the farmhouse, and are our new neighbours." Rose couldn't believe what happened next. One by one the villagers came up and kissed their cheeks, shook their hands, and welcomed them. Rose and JP were overwhelmed. The gentleman who had phoned the gendarmes apologised for inconveniencing them. JP replied he was pleased he had reported it.

Rose and JP eventually sat down and ate their meal. After they'd finished Raoul joined them. "So JP, you still got your four-man family with you?"

JP replied he had, and gave Raoul a quick update. "How come you've got the pub?" he asked Raoul.

"When I left you, my brother invited me down here. I met and married a gorgeous lady called Lémine. Alas, one day she just up and left. Couldn't stand village life anymore. Couple of years later, my brother passed away and left me the pub. So I learnt everything I could about ordering stock, doing the books, and employing staff. Everyone in the village helped as well. Now I have a thriving business, especially when the coaches stop. Rose, if you don't mind me asking, what do you do?" Rose told him. "Nice place to do a photo shoot, maybe?" Rose laughed and said she would mention it to Séra. JP and Rose stayed for another couple of hours, and then said their goodbyes. As they went to go, Raoul said, "Rose, please take this. It's my phone number. If you feel unsafe at any time, or anything else, just ring me, and others and myself will come up to you." Rose thanked him.

Walking back, Rose asked why Raoul wasn't a bodyguard anymore. JP explained that years ago, Raoul was caught up in a fight, and had been stabbed in his back. It was the end of his career, as he didn't pass the fitness test. "Shame, as he was a damn good bodyguard."

When they got home, Rose said she was going to sit in the back garden, as it was such a lovely hot afternoon. JP put out two sun beds he had bought. Rose put a bikini on, and laid out. "Why have you got a bikini on?" asked JP, who was stood there with nothing on.

"JP, put your swimming trunks on. You never know who's going to walk past!"

"Môn amour, believe me, even if anyone does walk by, they cannot see us here. Further down maybe, but this area is totally secluded."

"And what's happens if somebody comes calling and walks round?"

JP replied, "This side they can't. That side as they open the gate a bell will ring."

Rose looked at him and said cheekily, "Thought of everything, haven't you, my bodyguard."

JP walked to her, and bending over, kissed her lips ever so gently. "Of course," he replied.

Rose took her bikini off and they sunbathed and slept for a couple of hours. Later on, they just dressed in their dressing gowns, and JP did a BBQ of steaks, sausages, and salad. Then he did toasted marshmallows, which they dipped in a chocolate sauce, and fed to each other. Rose then sat between JP's legs on the sun bed with her back and head on his chest, and he had his arms around her, and they watched the sun slowly go down.

The following day Rose phoned Séra, to see where she needed to be in the morning. Séra replied, "I'm away tomorrow for the week, so you can rest, unless Mathieu has something for you. I also have great news for you, but I'm not telling you until I see you. Did you have a lovely honeymoon?" Rose replied it had been wonderful. "I will see you at the château a week tomorrow then." Rose then phoned her mum and dad, and Monica answered. Rose said, "Well, you both kept that quiet about moving over. I am so delighted. I want to know all about it. Are you working this week?" Monica replied they weren't starting their jobs until the first week of August, so Rose made arrangements to see them the following day. Then she phoned Ruby.

"Yeah, you're back. Did you both enjoy yourselves?"

Rose replied they did. "How's working at Gilmac News going?"

Ruby replied, "It's only been a couple of weeks, so I'm not doing a lot at the moment. When can I meet up with you?"

Rose replied, "I'm not working this week, unless Mathieu has something for me, so we could do lunch, say Tuesday, as I'm seeing Mum and Dad tomorrow." Ruby said that would be great and she looked forward to seeing her sister.

Lastly Rose phoned Hugh. "My dear, lovely to hear from you. Did you both have a lovely relaxing time?" Rose said she would tell him all about it, and suggested lunch on Thursday. Hugh said he would see her then.

Rose walked into the kitchen where JP was cooking some pies for her, to put in the freezer, in case she had company. "Well that's my week sorted," she said and told him.

"Don't forget, môn amour, I will be home every two weekends now, instead of four."

Rose said, "Oh poor Antoine, he will be on his own now. Hope they soon set a date."

"He will cope, môn amour," and kissed her neck gently.

"My love, do I need to iron any shirts for you for tomorrow?"

JP replied, "No I have plenty at the palace, thank you, môn amour. How do you feel about inviting everyone over at the end of the month? Call it a house warming."

"Oh yes, let's do that. We can do the shopping on the Saturday, unless they're going to come over that day. In that case you'll have to do the shopping on the way home."

JP took her in his arms and said, "I'll let you know, môn amour. Now I'm going to get us a meal, so you go and relax," and kissed her tenderly.

Rose went out the back and sunbathed. JP could see Rose and saw she was naked. His manhood stirred, so he put his mind to cooking the Sunday lunch. About an hour later, he went out, and sitting on the side of her bed, kissed Rose all the way down her back to her buttocks. "Luncheon is served, Madame Pascal." Rose laughed and rolling over, kissed him sensually on his lips. JP held his hand out, which Rose took, and then helped her into her dressing gown.

In the kitchen JP laid out roast beef, Yorkshire puddings, stuffing, vegetables, roast potatoes and a jug of gravy. "Umm, lovely," said Rose, and both of them tucked in. For a sweet he had made a banana split with ice cream. Rose was in food heaven. After they'd cleaned up, they took their coffee outside and laid on the sun beds, both naked.

JP asked Rose if she was going to be alright being on her own in the countryside. Rose assured him she would be fine. Once she was back at work, it would be after 6pm before she got home. Time for a meal, and then either a bath or shower, and bed. The farmhouse was just over an hour away from the centre of Paris, and the main road was only five minutes away. She would be visiting her uncle, mum and dad, and Ruby. JP explained to Rose he had had a sophisticated fire/burglar alarm fitted, just in case. He took her to the cabinet in the hallway. Inside the cabinet he slid a small partition to the right, which then showed the alarm. All she had to do was press ON when she left the farmhouse, and OFF when she returned, and ON when she went to bed. If she forgot and the alarm went off, she had two minutes to put the combination in. On the inside of the cabinet, only if you knew where to look, were four numbers. Inserting the numbers would switch it off.

Rose asked, "Was it on when we were away?"

JP replied, "It was. When we left, and I'd checked everything was locked down, it was the last thing I did before I closed the front door. When I closed it the alarm kicked in. When we came back, I just switched it off."

Rose raised her eyebrow and then said, "And where's the surveillance cameras?" JP laughed and said there weren't any. Rose was pleased about that.

Later on, she made a tag and put ALARM on it, and put it on her key ring. That would remind her. That night they loved each other so tenderly and sensually, as neither of them wanted to be parted. In the morning they loved each other again, and then Rose waved as JP drove off in the rental car, which was going to be picked up at the palace.

Later on, before she drove off, Rose remembered to set the alarm. About 11am she drove into what used to be JP's old garage, as she still had the pass key. There was no car parked in either of the spaces. It seemed strange for her to ring the bell.

"Rose, come in," said Monica, giving her a huge hug and kissing her cheeks.

"Let me look at you. Well you are blooming, marriage agrees with you." Rose laughed.

"Rose," said George, and he too gave her a huge hug and kisses. "Fancy a coffee?" asked George.

Rose replied, "Maybe later, Dad. I think you both have some explaining to do."

Monica and George told Rose, obviously in more detail, about the events of moving to Paris. "We will be working in two different hospitals," said Monica, "but like you we need driving lessons and two cars." Rose still had her driving instructor's name and phone number and gave it to them. (Two weeks later, both of them were driving and bought second-hand cars.)

"I still can't quite believe we are all in Paris together," said Rose. "It's like a dream come true, and I'm so happy. We are having a house warming at the end of the month, either on the Saturday or Sunday. JP is going to let me know, and you must come. I'm sure Ruby and Antoine, or my uncle, will pick you up. I will let you know at the end of the week." George and Monica said they would be delighted to go. Rose asked them what they had planned for the rest of the day. They said, apart from some shopping, nothing. Rose suggested they went to the shopping centre, and could then do their food shopping before they left, and that's what they did. Both of them thought the shopping centre was great, and it was easy to drive to. They did a huge food shop, and Rose spent the entire day with them. When she returned home, after locking the car in the garage, she remembered to switch the alarm off, but put it back on when she went to bed. That made her feel safe and secure. Soon it became a normal thing to do.

Meanwhile at the palace, JP wasn't really in the mood for work, but needs must. His men were delighted to see him back, and were also concerned about Rose being hit by lightning. JP assured them she was fine, and asked them about the weekend, at the end of the month. They all decided on the Saturday, so if it was a late night, they didn't have to get up for work the following morning. Not only that, it was now a longer drive for Andre, Donatien and Pierre. JP asked Andre to bring him up to speed with palace work, which he did.

"I have made the arrangements for the London trip in October, and we will be attending with the President, as it was his wish we went with him."

"How long?" asked JP.

"Three days," replied Andre.

"Very well. Back to your duties, men, and I will go and see the President."

On his way to the President's office, he bumped into the President's wife. "JP, lovely to see you back. I will assume, by your tan, you and Rose had a lovely honeymoon?" JP replied they did. "JP, will you arrange for Rose to come and see me? But don't tell my husband, as it's a surprise for our wedding anniversary. Is she free at all this week?"

"I will phone her tonight. Do you have a specific day in mind?"

"My husband has meetings most of this Friday, so that would be ideal, say about 11am?" JP said he would confirm it with her. He bowed and then went to the President's office and knocked.

"Entre." JP walked in. "Ah JP, good to see you back. How is Rose, as I heard she had an accident?"

"She is fine, thank you Monsieur le President. May I again thank you from both of us for letting us have our wedding ceremony here.

It truly was an honour."

The President smiled and replied, "I'm glad you accepted, and it was a delight to see you both married. Alas, we now have work to contend with," and the President told him everything that was going to happen. JP quickly thought how he wished Rose and himself were still in Montpellier.

CHAPTER 12

That night JP phoned Rose, and told her everyone was happy with the Saturday, and about coming to the palace to see the President's wife on Friday. "That's fine, my love, and I'll be there. Can I come and see you afterwards?" JP replied he would be waiting for her at the back entrance. Rose smiled. "I'm inviting Mum, Dad, and my uncle as well for the Saturday." JP was pleased about that. A real family gathering. They spoke for another half hour and then said their goodnights.

The following day she went to meet Ruby at Gilmac News. Mathieu greeted her, and said he had a list of wedding dates for her. Rose glanced through the dates and nothing clashed, and she put it in her bag. She thought, *I must buy a diary to put all these dates in.* Mathieu told her Ruby would be about another half hour, and so Rose decided to walk to the town hall and pick up the wedding certificate. When she got there she had to wait about fifteen minutes, and was then given the certificate. "Congratulations, Madame Pascal. I hope the civil ceremony at the palace was to your liking?" asked the clerk. Rose replied it had been a huge honour and it had been a wonderful surprise. She thanked the clerk and then popped into a stationer's and got herself a bag sized A4 diary.

Back at Gilmac News, Ruby was still out. Rose looked at the wedding certificate and smiled. "Is that what I think it is?" asked Mathieu. Rose nodded and showed him. Stunned, he said, "You had your civil ceremony at the palace?" Rose told him about the surprise. "Have you got your wedding photos yet, as I would love to put them in the newspaper, as a special, of course?" Rose replied she had yet to phone Suzette.

"Rose, Rose," said Ruby, running towards her. She gave Rose such a hug.

Rose laughed and said, "Missed me then, Ruby?" Mathieu could see the bond between the two of them and told Ruby to have the rest of the day off. She gave Mathieu her pad covering the story she had just done with Vidal. "Fancy going to Gérard's, as we've got plenty of time now?"

Ruby nodded enthusiastically and said, "That would be great, as I need to ask him something." They chatted about this and that until they got there.

"Rose, Ruby, my two special ladies," said Gérard, giving them each a hug and kissing the back of their hands. "Lunch?" he asked.

"If we're not too late," replied Rose.

"Never too late for you two. Come and I will show you to your table."

Soon they were seated, and both ordered salad to start, followed by salmon en croute with vegetables and dauphinois potatoes. "So how's life at Gilmac News? I'm dying to hear," asked Rose.

Ruby replied, "Just the same as being with Marcus, except different people. The journalists are Alain, Hervé, Olivier and myself. The photographers are Quincy, Étienne, Vidal and Símon. The receptionist you know is Marcine. Terrance is the developer and Picárd and Lébron the printers. They were all so welcoming. I have only done small reports so far, but without a car I'm stuck. Do you have the name of the guy who took you?"

Rose wrote it down for her, and within a month Ruby was driving, and George bought her a second-hand car.

"I have also got more news to tell you. Antoine and I have set a date for the wedding. The 31st March, and that's why I need to see Gérard. It won't be a big party like yours, but I don't care. It will still be wonderful."

The waitress asked them if they had enjoyed their main meal and they replied it had been delicious. They decided to have apple and cinnamon tart with ice cream, along with coffees.

"Ruby, have you met Antoine's parents yet?" Ruby told her that when Antoine was six, his parents were killed in a train crash, but he survived. He was brought up by his grand-mére and grand-pére. They passed away after Antoine had joined JP.

Whilst they were drinking their coffee, Gérard came up to them, and asked if everything had been satisfactory. They replied it had. "Gérard, I have a favour to ask, if you can do it? Antoine and I have set a date for our wedding. Can we please, please, have our reception here?"

Gérard went and got his diaries. "This year or next, Ruby?" Ruby told him the date and Gérard said that day was free, and wrote it down. "We also know what we would like. Exactly the same buffet as Rose and JP's, and a disco afterwards. It would only be for about thirty, maybe forty people. It wouldn't be a late night either."

Gérard wrote it all down in the diary and said, "Ruby we can sort it all out in February, but I can do all you ask. Tell Antoine I will give him a good deal." Ruby flung her arms around Gérard and kissed his cheek. Rose told both of them about the honeymoon, but not everything.

Ruby said, "Wow, I can just see the headline, 'Bride blitzed on honeymoon night'."

"Honestly, Ruby," said Rose, shaking her head, and then all three of them laughed. They didn't leave Gérard's until about 6pm. Rose told Ruby about the last weekend of the month, and was going to phone Mum and Dad later when she knew who was going to pick them up. Ruby said Antoine would pick them up and she couldn't wait to see the farmhouse.

Back home, Rose phoned Suzette.

"Rose, you're back. I have all your wedding photos in albums. Do you want to pick them up or shall I bring them over?" Rose asked Suzette if she was free the following day. Suzette said she was, and Rose gave her the directions, and to arrive whenever she wanted.

Suzette arrived about midday, and had four albums with her, and was amazed at the farmhouse. Rose was absolutely thrilled with the photos and asked Suzette what she owed her. Suzette replied,

"Absolutely nothing. I was delighted you asked me, and it was my pleasure."

Rose replied, "Then I'm going to treat you to lunch in the village, if you've got time?"

Both walked into the village, but this time the villagers called out, "Bonjour Rose," and Rose smiled and replied back. In the pub, Raoul greeted them both and gave them a glass of wine on the house. They both decided to have steak and salad, with steak frites. Rose asked Suzette how things were at Séra's, and she replied lots of shoots had been done, but she couldn't capture the models the way Rose did, and Séra had been unhappy. "I will show you when we're next together," replied Rose. Suzette thanked her. A couple of hours later, they made their way back to the farmhouse, after having chatted to Raoul and some of the villagers. Suzette said she would see her soon, and then drove back to Paris.

Rose sat on the settee, with her legs tucked underneath her and slowly went through every photo again. Suzette had done an excellent job. The ones at the palace with the President were exceptional, and she knew the President would want copies. She had all the negatives, and put the ones she wanted to one side. She would get them re-printed whilst she was seeing her uncle the following day, and then give them to the President's wife. Rose then went upstairs and took out her wedding dress. She smiled at the memories of the happiest day of her life so far. As she put it back she noticed JP's suit was hung up with it as well. "You romantic, JP," she said. She wandered through the house, looking in every room. Suddenly she felt sad. This farmhouse was missing one thing – children running round it. She sighed deeply as she walked down the stairs. She would have loved to give JP children, but it wasn't meant to be. She went into the sitting room and turned the television on, anything to make her think of something else. It worked. A comedy film came on, and soon she was laughing. Every night she put the alarm on. Better safe than sorry.

"Rose my dear, you look absolutely blooming. I have missed you," said Hugh as Rose walked into his office at the bank. He went and hugged her tightly, then kissed her cheek. "I have lunch set out in my flat. Shall we go?" Rose linked arms with her uncle as they walked through the bank to the lift. In his flat a lovely buffet was set out.

"Umm, this looks lovely, Uncle. Must have taken you ages?"

Hugh replied, "I didn't do it. One of the ladies from the bank bought it all and laid it out for me."

Rose smiled and said, "Anything I should know about?"

Hugh laughed and replied, "No, Rose, nothing at all. Now tell me about your holiday." Rose told him and he was greatly concerned. "Is your hand alright now?" he asked.

Rose replied, "Yes, look Uncle, it's fine. I'm just glad I didn't take my expensive camera, but that meant no photos. We didn't go sightseeing this time, as we just relaxed on the beach, went swimming, had BBQs and enjoyed each other's company."

Hugh smiled and said, "Did JP tell you about your mum and dad?"

"Oh yes, and it was a lovely surprise. Thank you so much for helping all of us out. Now, the Saturday after next, you are invited to our house warming at lunchtime. Everyone is coming including Mum and Dad. Will you come?"

Hugh replied, "I would be delighted to, my dear. Now do you want me to pick Monica and George up?"

"That would be great. Ruby said Antoine could pick them up, but I thought you'd like company."

Hugh replied, "Then I will phone them and make the arrangements. I haven't seen them since the wedding. Are they settling in alright?" Rose replied they were.

After a couple of hours, Rose kissed her uncle goodbye. On the way back, she went to the camera shop and picked up her re-prints.

After a good night's sleep, Rose woke to the sun streaming through the bedroom windows, which were open, and for the first time, heard the birds singing. This was what she loved about the countryside. Then she spotted two squirrels in one of the trees. Rose felt contented, and she loved her new home. After a rather late breakfast, she had to rush to get to the palace for 11am. She got there five minutes before. The first person she saw was JP, who gave her a huge smile. "I was getting worried, môn amour," and then took her in his arms and kissed her passionately.

"Get a room," said Pierre as he passed them. Both of them looked at him and sighed.

"Come, môn amour, you're going to be late. Pierre we will see you all later, and remind the others to say nothing about Rose being here. The President mustn't know."

"Right, boss," said Pierre.

JP took Rose's hand, but took her down a corridor she hadn't been down before. "It's a short cut to her sitting room," said JP. JP knocked on a door and a female voice replied to enter. Rose walked in, and the President's wife was stood by a huge fireplace.

"Rose, thank you for coming at such short notice."

Rose replied, "It's my honour Madame—"

Alicía put her hand up and smiling, said, "Rose, please call me Alicía. Take a seat and let's see what we can do."

Alicia discussed exactly what she required. It was photos of herself, her son, her husband, herself and her son, her husband and son, herself and her husband, and then all three of them. "I don't know if you can do that, Rose, without my husband being present?" Rose explained there was a way, and she knew somebody she could trust to do them. "Wonderful," said Alicía.

"Have you any photos in particular that you want in the album?" Alicía gave her about twelve photos. "I don't seem to have any of your son." Alicía said her son was very camera shy. Rose asked if he was at the palace. "Yes, he's playing in his bedroom."

"How old is he?"

"Just coming up six," replied Alicía.

Rose told Alicía of an idea she had. They both went to her son's bedroom, who was called Rémi. "Rémi, my darling, I have brought someone to meet you. This is Rose, who recently married JP."

Rémi went to Rose and said, "Hello Rose," and surprised her by kissing her hand.

"Hello Rémi. What are you playing with?" Rémi showed Rose his Lego trains with tracks and other bits. "Oh, I haven't seen Lego for a long time. Can I help?" Rémi nodded and took Rose's hand.

As they were playing Rose said, "Rémi, I'm a photographer, and your maman wants some lovely photos of you to put into an album for your maman and papa's wedding anniversary. Would you let me take some photos of you with your trains?" Rémi nodded. Half an hour later Rose had some great photos of him.

Alicía was amazed. "How did you do that?" Rose explained they had four young children who modelled clothes, but it needed to be fun.

Rose said goodbye to Rémi, who was the spitting image of his father, and walked back with Alicía to her sitting room. Rose then took photos of Alicía. "When is your anniversary?" Alicía told her the middle of August. "The album will done by then, and whilst I remember, these are for you," and gave her an envelope.

Alicía looked at the photos and said, "Oh Rose, these are wonderful. Thank you so much. Now can you give them to JP to give to my husband? Or he will know you have been here." Rose agreed and then Alicía phoned JP. "Thank you Rose, and may I wish you both a very long happy marriage," and then surprised Rose by giving her a hug and kissing her cheek.

JP arrived and bowed, and then took Rose back to his office the way they had come. Closing his door, he took Rose in his arms and kissed her with such a passion. "Umm, that was nice, now behave. I have to give these to you to give to the President. They're some of our wedding photos, and I have picked up our marriage certificate."

JP looked at the photos and said, "These are brilliant. Are the rest as good?"

Rose nodded and said, "Nobody will see them until you come home next weekend, my love." JP locked his door and led Rose into his bedroom. Soon they were loving each other.

A lot later, they made their way down to the house where his men were eating. They all welcomed Rose with open arms. Rose stayed a short while and then said she would see them all a week on Saturday, along with her mum, dad and uncle. Donatien said, "And our family gets bigger and bigger. Great, isn't it?" Everyone agreed.

JP took Rose to her car and told her he would ring at the weekend. Rose had just driven out of the gate, when JP turned and just got in the door, when he saw the President walking towards him. JP thought, *That was close.*

CHAPTER 13

Once Rose was home, she made herself a cheese and ham omelette with chips, and then watched the television until bed time. On the Saturday morning, Rose looked around the farmhouse again, and decided they needed more furnishings. The only room fully furnished was their bedroom. Even though the floors were polished wood, she decided they needed some rugs. Looking around the kitchen, she found JP had left most of the contents at his flat. With everyone coming the following weekend, they would need more crockery, cutlery, pots and pans etc. The spare bedrooms only had beds and wardrobes. With a list, she drove to the large department store. She bought four small bedside cabinets; two dressing tables with mirrors; four bedside lamps; three standard lamps; and eight large rugs. They said they would deliver the following day, which surprised Rose, as it was a Sunday. In the kitchen section, she bought crockery, cutlery, pots, pans, casserole dishes and other things. Next she went to the furnishing section, and bought tea towels, large, medium and small bath towels, more bed sheets, pillows, pillowcases and extra duvets with covers. The assistant told Rose to bring her car around to the back entrance, and two men put everything in her car. Back at the farmhouse, Rose put everything where it had to go, and she was shattered.

On Sunday the delivery van arrived and the men asked her where everything had to go. The four bedside cabinets and lamps went in the two spare bedrooms, along with a dressing table and a large rug. One rug went in their bedroom, and one in the bathroom, by the side of the bath. Three rugs went under the tables in the sitting room, with another by the fireplace. The three standard lamps also went in the sitting room. She was pleased at the excellent service, and gave them a good tip. The farmhouse now looked cosier and lived in. She just hoped JP would like it all. He phoned on the Saturday night, and Rose told him. JP's reply was, "Whatever you need, môn amour, just get it. Let me know what I owe you."

Rose replied, "My love, you owe me nothing. Look at everything you have paid for just lately. The farmhouse, the wedding, the reception, the honeymoon, etc., etc."

JP replied, "And it was my pleasure, môn amour. Je t'aime."

"Je t'aime aussi, my love."

It was soon Monday morning, and Rose drove to Séra's château. Everyone was there and welcomed her back with open arms. "Suzette, can I have a word?" and Rose asked her about helping her do the President's photos.

Suzette said she would love to help. "What's the shoot?"

Léon replied, "Not sure. We're waiting for Séra, as it's a charity shoot."

At that moment Séra arrived. "Rose, you're back. Now today is something different. This is a charity shoot we are doing on behalf of a friend of mine. Rose, here are all the details, so I will leave everything in your capable hands. When you've finished come and see me, as we need to discuss something," and with that she went back to the château. Rose looked concerned at how sharp and cold Séra was towards her. She looked at the list and then gave it to Léon.

After three hours the shoot was all done. Rose thanked everyone and slowly walked towards the château. Séra had seen her coming, and sat behind her desk. Rose knocked on the door and Séra told her to enter. "Rose, please take a seat. Everything go alright?" Rose replied she would get the photos to Jules on her way home. "Now Rose, I have something very important to talk to you about." Rose got quite concerned and wondered what she had done wrong. Séra walked round and looking at Rose smiled and said, "Sorry Rose, I get all strange when I have to keep a secret. You're not in any trouble so relax." Rose did immediately.

Séra said, "I have been given four tickets for... ready... Paris Fashion Week, which will be in eight weeks' time, and will last for eight days. It will be held at various venues in Paris. As of yet I don't have the full itinerary. I want you to photograph the models, she doesn't know it yet, but Ruby is going to do the write-up with my help, and I'm asking Mía to come as well."

Rose was stunned and said, "Wow, that's fantastic. Where does Mía come into it?"

Séra replied, "After you introduced us at your wedding, we had a chat, and I have met her employer Madame Cherrillé. I thought it might be a good idea for them to make an outfit once a month, which would then go in the magazine, and where to buy it. Mía has some excellent ideas. Mía is good at sketching, and can quickly sketch some of the outfits."

Rose said, "I thought the fashion shows were to be secretly done, with no photographs of the models?"

"It used to be," replied Séra, "but nowadays it's totally different. There are four big fashion week shows. The first is in New York, the second in London, the third Milan and lastly Paris. The show starts about 10am until 8.30pm, with the last catwalk about 6pm. This will be the Spring/Summer collections. In February, the Autumn/Winter collections are shown. It's known as Semaine de la mode de Paris. No children are allowed to model.

"Sometimes there can be as many as five hundred journalists, and two hundred photographers, who hug the catwalk."

Rose asked how the show was conducted.

Séra replied, "You know what a catwalk looks like? Well I'll explain anyway. A catwalk or runway is a narrow flat platform, raised up, that runs into an auditorium, or it can be between rows of seats, where a great many celebrities will be attending. The models walk up and down showing off the collection to the audience. Usually it's daytime and evening wear. It's rare you will see a model smile. They're usually stone faced and sour, but behind the scenes they are lovely people. At the end of the show, the designer will come out on to the stage with his models. People will then stand and applause. Each collection lasts between twenty and thirty minutes, and most of the models have to change three or four times. Believe me, backstage it's manic. There will be a section called 'Prêt-à-porter' which is 'ready to wear'. There is also something called a Look Book. We will do our own. These are your photos of the models wearing a designer or manufacturing clothing that we can then show to clients and special customers. This is where Mía will come into the equation. If anyone requires some of the clothing to be made, it will be made at Madame Cherrillé's." Rose got her diary and marked the days off. "Heavens, are you that busy you need a diary?" Rose explained about all the weddings for Mathieu. Séra smiled and said, "Isn't it wonderful to be in such demand?" Rose just smiled. "Rose, go home, as you look shattered, and I will see you tomorrow." Séra sort of gave her a hug and kissed her cheek and said gently, "It's nice to have you back." Rose said her goodbye and left. It was gone 7pm when she got home.

The rest of the week flew by, but on the Friday, Séra and Rose went to Gilmac News. There they met Ruby and Mía. Séra then explained to them about Paris Fashion Week. Ruby was delighted and said, "Thank you for giving me the chance to show you what I can do, Séra. I promise I won't let you down." Mía also thanked Séra, and then, as it was lunch time, Rose, Ruby and Mía went to eat at a café, and talked about the show.

Saturday morning, Suzette turned up and Rose showed her the photos for the President's album. "Heavens, doesn't his son look like him?" said Suzette. Rose nodded. They discussed how to do the photos and Suzette took them away, and said she would have them ready the first week of August. Rose said that would be fine. It would then give her time to check them and put them in the album. Rose then went shopping and on Sunday just relaxed, sun bathing in the back garden, but she had her bikini on.

The following week also flew by, and soon it was Friday and JP was home, but early. Rose didn't get back until an hour later. "There you are, môn amour. Another long day for you?"

Rose replied, "Extremely frustrating day. The children wouldn't behave. Séra lost her temper, and snapped at everyone. Suzette was in tears. So yes, a very, very, long day, but now you're home, can I persuade you to have a relaxing shower with me?" JP took her hand, and soon they were in the shower. He massaged her shoulders, which felt wonderful to Rose. He planted tiny kisses on her neck and down her back. Rose turned and kissed him on his lips, and their arms went around each other, and soon Rose had her legs round JP's waist, and they loved each other until their climaxes took over.

"Umm, now I feel really relaxed. Thank you, my handsome husband."

JP smiled and replied, "That's both of us relaxed then. You hungry?" Rose nodded, and JP kissed her on the tip of her nose.

Later on they looked through the wedding photos. JP was well impressed with Suzette.

Early Saturday morning Rose and JP went shopping. "It's another sunny day, so I'm going to do a buffet outside," said JP.

"We haven't got tables and chairs to go outside," said Rose.

"We will in a moment, môn amour." By the time they got back, they had four large plastic fold-up tables and sixteen fold-up chairs, some small tables, along with a large food shop. Rose assembled the tables and chairs, whilst JP got on with the cooking. Rose washed down the tables and chairs, so they were clean. Then she helped JP do all the salads and whatever else he needed help with. By midday, everything was more or less done. On two of the tables, Rose put out all the bowls of lettuce, tomatoes, peppers, celery, cucumber, onions raw and spring, plates with various meats, sausage rolls, various quiches, devilled eggs, a salmon, pasta, and the condiments. On one of the other tables, the crockery and cutlery were placed, along with serviettes, and glasses for the wine. The other table had the desserts consisting of various mousses, various tarts large and small, various pastries, cheeses and biscuits. Rose covered all the tables with tin foil. Rose and JP had a quick wash and changed their clothes.

About 1pm, Antoine, Ruby, Hugh, Monica and George all arrived in one car, with Hugh driving. Next Andre and Gabrielle arrived with their boy, then Donatien and Céleste with their two girls, and lastly Pierre and Emilie with their two girls and one boy.

Everyone absolutely loved the farmhouse. Rose gave them the guided tour.

"Two spare bedrooms," said Pierre. "Women in one, men in the other." Rose raised her eyebrow at that. The men and the children all went out into the back garden, where the children ran round to their hearts' content. The women went to the kitchen.

"Oh Rose, what a lovely large kitchen," said Gabrielle.

JP replied cheekily, "Out of my kitchen, women." They all laughed and went out to the back garden. About fifteen minutes later, JP called Rose. "Môn amour, you can take the foil off now, and I will bring out the hot food." Rose did that and then went back to help JP. There were chicken breasts, Coquille St Jacques, jacket potatoes, garlic potatoes, and Rose cut up the French loaves and put them in baskets, along with butter and olive oil.

"As usual, JP, you have done us proud. Thank you," said Céleste.

"Please help yourselves," said JP.

Antoine said, "Uh boss, haven't you forgotten something – the wine?"

JP said cheekily, "I was leaving that for you to do, Antoine, but I will get them." JP came back with bottles of red and white, and Antoine took them and gave everyone a glass of what they wanted. JP had also got various bottles of juices for the children. Gabrielle, Emilie and Céleste sorted out the children with their food first, made sure they were settled, and then got their own meals. About an hour later, JP asked if anyone was getting too warm, as he did have a couple of sun umbrellas. Both Emilie and Gabrielle, who were fair, said they could do with one. No sooner said than done.

The children were having a great time running round and playing. Rose noticed how they all looked after each other, even though they were different ages. The wine and the conversation flowed, and all of them relaxed. Before they all got too tipsy, Rose showed them the wedding photos.

"Oh Rose, these are fantastic," said Monica.

"Do you think Suzette could do our wedding?" asked Ruby. Rose said she would ask her.

Some time later, they all decided to go to the sitting room, but not before carrying in the food, and putting it all on the kitchen table, not that much was left, along with the dishes etc. Rose made teas and coffees. The children were happy enough to sit on the floor, and so JP put the television on, but the sound was low. A short while later, all the children were asleep. "Do you want to put the children in the spare bedrooms?" asked Rose.

Andre looked at his watch and saw it was coming up 10pm. "I think we will need to make a move soon, as it's an hour's car journey back home."

"You can stay, if you want to?" replied JP. Andre thanked them and said maybe another time.

By midnight everyone had left after a great evening. Rose promised she would phone them, when she had any free time. JP put all the dishes in the dishwasher, and the leftover food in the fridge. "Môn amour, the rest can wait until the morning. Come to bed with me. I want to love you slowly." And that's what they did.

Sunday morning, both of them cleared everything up, and then just relaxed for the rest of the day. Suzette phoned in the afternoon to tell Rose she had done the photos. Rose invited her over. "Suzette, these are excellent. How do you put the photos together?" Suzette explained it was complicated. She had to get the photos just right, to re-photograph them, and then on the negative, she had to blur the lines out, and do other things, and then re-print them. JP was very impressed. "The President and his wife are going to be delighted with these. You have an extraordinary talent."

Suzette thanked him and said, "I just wish I could photograph the models like Rose does."

Rose said, "Have you told Séra about this? I think she would be very interested. Why don't you take photos of the models and then put them into one photo?"

"Really?" said Suzette. "Then I'll give it a go. I will leave you two to enjoy the rest of the day, and thanks for the advice."

Rose hugged Suzette and said she would see her in the morning. "My love, can you ask the President's wife when would it be convenient for me to see her?" JP said he would and ring her tomorrow night. Taking her in his arms, he started to gently kiss her neck. Soon they were naked, and Rose straddled JP and they enjoyed their lovemaking.

CHAPTER 14

JP phoned Rose, and said the President's wife would see her at 4pm on Friday. The week flew by and soon Rose was at the palace.

"Oh Rose, these are wonderful. Thank you so much, and to whoever helped you. My husband is going to be so surprised." Rose was delighted, and then made her way to JP's office.

"Môn amour. Was she pleased?"

"She was delighted," said Rose.

They chatted for about an hour and then JP walked down with her to her car. "See you next weekend, môn amour," and he gently kissed her.

"Can't wait, my love." Alas, JP didn't make it home.

The next three weeks went by in a blur, and now it was the Paris Fashion Show. Séra met Rose, Ruby and Mía at the Palais du Louvre. "Heavens, this place is massive," said Ruby.

Séra replied, "I understand it would take nearly eighty days to see everything there is to see, and believe me, they have some beautiful paintings and objects. Now according to the itinerary, the show is at the back of the palace in the gardens." They soon found it by the long queues.

Séra showed the passes to the guards, and they were allowed to proceed. A long catwalk left the back of the palace, and there were seats at either side of it. Already lots and lots of photographers were there, propping up the catwalk. Rose had a look around, and saw just the right spot. "Séra, I'm going to go up there. With the zoom on my camera, I don't need to be by the catwalk. Is that alright?"

Séra replied, "Wherever you think is best, Rose, is fine by me. Now you see those four seats over there, they are ours. Ruby, as the models come down, I will tell you who the designer is, with the name of the collection, and anything else I think appropriate. Listen carefully, Ruby, as it will get noisy."

"Yes Séra," replied Ruby.

"Mía, you are more than welcome to just watch, but if you want to sketch, sketch away." Mía nodded in reply. "We have an hour before it starts, so let's sit," said Séra, and so they did.

Half an hour before the start, Rose went to the ladies', and on the way back, saw some of the models going behind a huge curtain. Being cheeky, Rose peered in. There were hundreds of people, some dressing models, some doing their hair and makeup. Total pandemonium. People were just shouting at each other. Rose took quite a few photos, to finish off the roll already in the camera. Putting a new film roll in, she then left and went and got into position. Looking through her camera, she would get great shots.

Ruby was looking around and saw lots of celebrities, but Séra told her not to be so obvious. Ruby went red with embarrassment. Suddenly music started up, and Séra said, "Ladies, here we go." Rose couldn't believe how quickly the models walked up and down, but she got her shots. Séra had told her there were about thirty models doing each collection, and there would be a very short break between the daytime and eveningwear collections. That was when Rose changed her film rolls, so if she didn't get what she wanted first time, she could take extras. Once the designer had come out on stage with his models, to rapturous applause, there was a fifteen-minute break until the next one. About midday though, there was a two-hour break for people to eat, drink, and use the conveniences.

Rose went back to the others. A young man arrived and Séra said, "This is Sacha. He will take your films to Jules, so he can start developing them."

"Sacha, will you be coming back?" asked Rose. Sacha replied he would be back within the hour. Rose said, "Please can you ask Jules for some more thirty-six film rolls?" Sacha replied he would bring them back with him, and off he went.

"Well ladies, what do you think?" asked Séra.

Rose, Ruby and Mía all looked at each other, so Rose said, "I have to be honest, there are some lovely designs, but some, to me, look hideous. I certainly wouldn't wear them."

Séra replied, "A good honest answer, Rose, and I have to agree. Now according to the itinerary, from 5pm until 6pm it will be one of the prêt-á-porter collections. Rose, get as many shots as you can for Mía."

Again, fifteen minutes before the afternoon start, Rose went back to her position. Sacha arrived, gave her more films and took the ones she had taken.

Four days they went to the Palais du Louvre, the other four days the collections were done in the gardens of an upmarket hotel. By the end of the eighth day, Rose was absolutely shattered and drained, but Séra had been ecstatic about her photos. At least it was the weekend and she could relax.

Saturday morning when she woke, she had a really bad sore throat, and her nose was running like mad. "Typical, now I get a cold," said Rose to herself. She literally had to drag herself out of bed. She managed to eat a little breakfast, but then went back to bed. She slept right through until 5pm. Now she had a wracking cough, which hurt her chest, and gave her a headache. She took some painkillers, which did help her headache, but nothing else. Later on the phone rang and it was JP. "Hello," said Rose with a raspy voice.

"Môn amour, what's wrong?" asked JP, concerned.

Rose replied, "I woke with a sore throat, but now it's turned into a bad cold. I will be alright in a couple of days. Don't worry, my love."

JP said, "Can I get you anything?"

"No my love, and don't come home. I don't want you to catch it. I can't talk anymore. I will ring you in a couple of days."

JP was worried, but promised he wouldn't go home. *That Séra is pushing her too much,* he thought.

Sunday, Rose spent the day in bed, and hardly ate, as it hurt to swallow. Monday she was no better. JP phoned and got no reply, and assumed she'd gone back to work. Tuesday, Antoine knocked on JP's office door. "Sorry to bother you, boss, but Ruby phoned and said Rose hasn't been to work, and she's not answering the phone."

"I knew I should have gone home," said JP. "When I spoke to her, she had a bad cold. Where's Andre?"

"In the surveillance room, boss. Want me to get him?" JP nodded. Andre soon arrived. "Andre, I need to go home. Can you cover for me? The President shouldn't need me, but just in case."

Andre replied, "Of course, boss. Anything we can do?" JP shook his head and more or less ran out of the palace. He drove home like someone possessed. He found Rose at the bottom of the stairs. Immediately he phoned Doctor Michel, who arrived as quickly as he could.

"I would say Rose fainted and she's hit her head, but it's only recently. She has a temperature and maybe she hasn't been eating. Can you carry her back up to your bedroom, JP?"

Gently JP picked Rose up and then laid her on the bed. Rose slowly opened her eyes. Quietly she said, "My love, I told you not to come home."

"Hush, môn amour. Doctor Michel is here and wants to examine you. Were you going down to the kitchen?" Rose said she was and then everything went black.

Doctor Michel examined her and said, "Luckily no broken bones, but you do have flu. JP, do you have any lemons?" JP said he would go and look. "If you do, can you make Rose a hot drink with honey and the juice of a half a lemon in it?"

JP came back a couple of minutes later with the drink. Rose was already sat up and slowly sipped the drink. Doctor Michel had made out a prescription and as JP went to get it, there was a knocking at the door. It was Ruby. "JP is Rose alright? As everyone is concerned." JP told her. "You stay, and I'll go get the prescription."

"Thanks Ruby."

Ruby returned later and went up to see Rose. "Hello Doctor Michel, how are you?" asked Ruby.

"I'm fine, thank you Ruby. Now JP, Rose needs to take two of these tablets every four hours. Try and get her to eat, but soft things like bananas, scrambled eggs, mashed potatoes and vegetables, and not too much. No toast. Again, make her the lemon and honey drink." JP nodded.

Downstairs, Ruby said, "JP, I can stay and look after Rose, if you need to get back to the palace, but I will need to drive home and get some stuff."

JP replied, "I can stay the night, Ruby, but if you could come tomorrow, that would be great."

As Ruby was leaving JP asked her to buy some more lemons, and gave her the money. Ruby gave him the money back, and smiling, said, "I think I can afford some lemons," and then kissed his cheek. Doctor Michel left the same time as Ruby.

JP phoned and spoke to Andre, who told him everything was fine and to give Rose all their love, and get better soon. When he went back upstairs, Rose had fallen asleep. He saw how pale she was. He took his clothes off, and got into bed beside her and took her in his arms. Rose laid her head on his chest, and he kissed her forehead. An hour later and Rose was coughing. "I'll get you another drink, mòn amour," and JP went down to the kitchen, after putting his dressing gown on. He could hear Rose coughing and she sounded dreadful. "Here, mòn amour, drink this. Are you hungry?" Rose nodded, so JP went back to the kitchen and did some scrambled eggs for both of them. "Eat, mòn amour." Rose did and she had the whole lot.

"Thank you my love, that was lovely."

"Good. I intend to make sure you get what you need. Now I have to go back to work tomorrow, but Ruby is coming to stay, and will make sure you have your tablets, honey and lemon drinks, and soft food."

Rose replied, "Honestly JP, I can look after myself, and I promise I will look after myself."

JP kissed her forehead, and replied, "Please, mòn amour, do this... for us?" Rose smiled and nodded. "Move over," said JP. JP got into the bed and sitting up, took Rose in his arms. "Must get another television and put it in here." Rose just looked at him and smiled. She rested her head on his shoulder and closed her eyes.

Four hours later, JP woke Rose for her to take her tablets. "What time is it?" asked Rose sleepily.

"It's midnight, môn amour. Now lay down and we can go to sleep." Both of them snuggled down under the duvet and JP wrapped his arms around her. Within minutes Rose was firm asleep, and didn't wake up until 6am.

JP was already awake and had gone down and had his breakfast. The first he knew of Rose being awake was her coughing. Straight away he made her drink and took it up to her. "Drink and tablets, môn amour, and then I'll do you a couple of boiled eggs." Rose smiled. About ten minutes later, JP gave Rose a tray with two boiled eggs and two slices of bread, which he had cut the crusts off, and spread them with a little butter.

"Where's yours?" asked Rose.

"I've already eaten, môn amour. Now eat before they get cold." Rose did, and ate the eggs and bread. "Ruby should be here soon, and I will leave her a list of what to give you, and the times of your tablets."

"Thank you, my love. I'm sorry to be a nuisance."

"Môn amour, je t'aime and you're not a nuisance," and kissed her gently.

"Now you'll have my cold," scolded Rose.

"I'll be fine," replied JP.

About 8am Ruby arrived, with Monica. "How is she, JP?" asked Monica, concerned.

JP said she was eating and drinking and taking her tablets. "I'm off work for a couple of days, so if it's alright with you, I will stay as well."

JP hugged and kissed them both. "Thank you. I know Rose will be in good hands." JP went upstairs and said goodbye to Rose, and then left for the palace.

Three days later, Rose was more or less back to her normal self. Both Séra and Mathieu told Rose to take the rest of the week off, and to relax, so she did. Monica stayed until the end of the week and then had to go back to work. Ruby stayed until Monday morning.

Soon it was the end of September and JP was home for the weekend. He was so pleased to see Rose back to her normal self. Rose wrapped her arms round him and kissed him with a passion. "Umm, that was nice," said JP. Taking his hand, Rose took him upstairs to the bedroom, where they slowly undressed each other. JP sat up in the bed and Rose straddled him.

"I think, my love, we have some catching up to do, especially as the President made you work on your weekend off." Rose took his manhood in her hand and caressed it so gently, and when he was ready, she lowered herself down onto him. JP kissed her lips, neck, breasts and nipples, as she slowly rotated her hips. JP put his hands on her buttocks and she started going up and down, and then he started thrusting into her quicker, and soon they both went over the edge. JP rolled her over and spooned into her back, and with his arms around her, and they both slept.

In the morning Rose was gently woken up by JP loving her. He trailed kisses down her front and over her mound. Rose moaned. JP kissed her back up to her lips, and Rose put her arms around him and JP lowered himself between her legs and entered her. Her legs went round his waist, and soon they both climaxed into oblivion. Rose snuggled into him, and they slept for another couple of hours. After a shower together, and a late breakfast, JP suggested they drove out further into the countryside. Rose loved it, as all she could see was fields with either wild flowers or sunflowers in them, fields with horses, and not many houses. They passed through a few villages and a couple of taverns. When they went through another village, on the outskirts, there was a huge tavern with lots of cars in the car park. "Hungry?" asked JP. Rose nodded, and he pulled in. As they walked through the door, both were transported back to an era before they were born.

CHAPTER 15

The outside was modern, but inside it went back to the 1600s. It had low dark beams, which JP had to duck sometimes. There were four separate rooms – the bar, the dining area, the kitchens and a separate seating area. The bar was in black wood, with the original stone walls, and looked very olde worlde. The tables and benches were also in black wood. There was a huge old-fashioned fireplace, which had a roaring fire, but surrounding it were various copper and brass pots and pans. Wall light candelabras lit up the rooms, and there was also a modern small chandelier in the middle of each room. Outside were more tables and chairs, but modern, which then led to a lovely large garden. Talking to the owner, he told them it used to be a very old farmhouse that had been left to fall to bits, after the owner passed away. It hadn't been lived in for over five years. His wife fell in love with it and so they bought it. Firstly they renovated the farmhouse, and managed to find some of the same old stones, from ruins around the area. Once the farmhouse was done, a new structure was built around the farmhouse, which gave the outside a more modern look and then built their flat above it. The gardens were brought back to life, and then word spread, and it became popular. It took them two years to rebuild it.

Rose and JP were amazed. They had a lovely meal of freshly caught salmon, along with vegetables and buttered potatoes. "That is the best salmon I have ever tasted," said Rose, and JP agreed. Afterwards they had apple tart with cinnamon and ice cream, followed by coffee. The pub was more or less packed. When they'd finished and JP had paid the bill, hand in hand they walked round the gardens.

"We could bring our family here," said Rose.

JP laughed and said, "If we did it would never be the same again." Rose thumped him playfully and then laughed as well.

Monday morning arrived and JP reminded Rose he wouldn't be home in two weeks, as along with his men, he would be in London with the President. They would be leaving early Thursday morning, and the President would be conducting business over the rest of the Thursday and Friday. Saturday, the Duke and Duchess, from where they were staying, were holding a dinner party in the President's honour. They would all return to Paris sometime Sunday afternoon. "Then I'd better give this to you to last for four weeks then." And she took JP in her arms and gave him a very long lingering kiss. "To be continued," she smiled.

"Most definitely, môn amour." And JP returned her kiss with more passion.

About an hour later, Rose knocked on Séra's office door and was told to enter. "Rose, are you better?" Rose replied she was fine and apologised for being off. "Rose, we all get ill now and then, and Paris Fashion Week drains everyone involved. Now let's go the studio."

When they walked in Rose just stood and looked. Huge boards had been erected, in long lines, and all her photos of the models were pinned to them. Rose walked up and down looking at them all. "Rose, I don't have the gratitude to thank you. These photos are beyond words. Now all I have to do is decide which ones go into this month's magazine," said Séra.

Rose thought for a moment and then said, "It's just an idea, but with this month's edition, why don't you do a pull-out special, just of the prêt-á-porter collections? Over the next couple of months the magazine could just be photos of the collections, and nothing else."

Séra looked at Rose, and then started looking at the photos. "There are so many photos, and it would be months before they were all published."

"Have you spoken to Suzette?" asked Rose.

Séra replied, "Don't take this the wrong way, but Suzette doesn't really have the eye for that sort of thing." Rose then explained about the President's photos. "Suzette did that?" asked Séra surprised. "Is she here?"

"I would think so as the children are here for the shoot."

Séra replied, "Rose, be a darling and go and bring her back. I want you here as well."

A bit later, Rose walked in with Suzette.

"Rose has been telling me about your other photography accolades. I have put twelve photos on the table, so tell me what you'd do." Suzette looked at Rose, who smiled at her and nodded her head.

"How many pages?" asked Suzette.

"Middle spread," replied Séra.

Suzette looked at the photos, and then said, "May I look at the other photos?" Séra nodded. Within half an hour Suzette had married up the photos to do three models in one picture. "Why did you change these photos?" asked Séra.

Suzette replied, "If you look at the lines and flows of the collection, those three photos didn't go, whereas these three emphasise the other two."

Séra raised her eyebrow and looked at Rose and then Suzette. "How quickly can you do ninety-six photos, each print with three models, and four photos to a page, which would make eight pages?"

Suzette's eyes went wide. "If I didn't have the shoots, it would take me two, maybe three weeks."

Séra opened her diary and dragged her finger down over the dates. "No shoots, twelve days?" Suzette nodded. "Go pick your ninety-six photos. Would it be of use if Jules helped you?" Suzette replied that would help her greatly. An hour later Suzette left with her photos, and was on her way to see Jules.

"So now I have a brilliant photographer, and a great, what shall I call her, combination photographer? Thank you, Rose. Right, I had better start picking out the other ninety-two photos, so that will be eight pages from Suzette, ninety-two from me, so that should be the hundred pages for the magazine in total."

"Would you like me to start sorting the ready-to-wear collection?"

"Oh Rose, that would be a huge help."

Within three hours, Rose and Séra had picked out the photos. "All we have to do now is get them ready for publishing, and leave the eight middle pages for Suzette."

With Jules' help, and working long hours, Suzette got the photos done in ten days. Séra was delighted, and immediately told Suzette she would be doing a lot more and she would be rewarded greatly. The following week the magazine hit the shelves, and sold quickly. In fact more copies of the magazine had to be published. As a "thank you" to all the hard work that the whole team had put into it, Séra took them all to the Eiffel Tower Restaurant, for an extremely lavish meal, which lasted until the early hours. Much to Rose and Suzette's delight, they were also given a good pay rise.

Rose now felt she had mastered the art of model photography, and now brought it into photographing Cat, Lil, Théo and Loïc. Instead of them standing still, she got them to walk around and photographed them. The wedding photos for Mathieu, which could be any day of the week, so far she had managed to incorporate within her day. Most nights she was shattered, but as soon as she walked in the front door of the farmhouse, she just totally relaxed. The farmhouse was her comfort haven and she loved it. She loved it even more when JP was there. His trip to London had been and gone, and now two more were planned, before Christmas, and then the President was going away until after the New Year. The next trip was Belgium at the beginning of November, and Luxembourg at the beginning of December.

The weather was now on the turn and it was back inside the studio for the shoots. One day Rose said to Séra, "Do you know an artist by any chance?"

Séra raised her eyebrow and said, "Now why would you want an artist?"

Rose replied, "To paint some different scenes for the shoots. I'll gladly pay."

Séra replied, "We have some over there in the corner, can't you use them?" Rose took Séra over to look at them. They had faded with time, and there were rips in some of them and the canvases were rotting. "Oh, I see what you mean. Yes, of course I know someone, but I will pay, Rose. I will phone her and make arrangements for her to come on Friday morning. We will meet in my office, about 10 ish?" Rose thanked her and said she would be there. Looking at the team, Séra said, "Anyone care to have a bet with me?"

Léon replied, "What sort of bet, Séra?"

"That Rose already has ideas of what she wants painting." Needless to say, none of them took the bet.

Friday morning arrived and Rose was introduced to Georgette. "Please, everyone calls me George. How can I help?" Rose looked at Séra who told her to explain to George what she was after. After an hour George had sketched out six different scenes, asked how big the canvases were to be, and told them it would take her about two weeks, as they were straight forward. George also suggested they were framed in wood and wheels put on the bottom, for ease of moving them around, and would also provide protective covers to be placed over them. Séra said that would be ideal. Rose said goodbye to George and left them to discuss money.

As promised, two weeks later, a huge van arrived with the six canvases, which were then wheeled into the studio. Rose was absolutely delighted. The six scenes were a bedroom, two different country scenes, seaside, airport runway with the side of a plane, and a school yard. The scene of the seaside was left at the far end, and when Séra walked in she looked at Rose and said, "Tell me you're thinking what I'm thinking?"

Together Rose and Séra said, "Catwalk."

Léon scratched his head and said, "What?"

Rose went to him and said, "Cat, can you go and stand in front of the canvas please, and then walk forward?"

Cat did as Rose asked, and as she walked towards Rose and Léon, Léon could see what they meant. "Oh wow, I wondered how they did it. Séra, if it helps, I can build the catwalk for you."

Séra took him upon his offer and two days later Séra's studio had a catwalk. The next shoot, a couple of days later, all of them had fun modelling. The lingerie obviously had the bedroom canvas, the children loved the school yard canvas, and the seaside canvas was used for the rest of the clothes. The clothing company that Séra had used for years was still making most of the clothes, but Madame Cherrillé, Mía and their team were now making "special ones". Both Madame Cherrillé and Mía thanked the day when Rose's husband had brought her to the shop, for her evening ball gown. Gilmac News had published some of Rose's wedding and mentioned where her dress had been made. Madame Cherrillé would soon have to take on more staff.

The rest of October and November went quickly. It was now the beginning of December and JP and his men were off to Luxembourg with the President. Séra had decided to also go away with Mathieu for the Christmas and New Year period. The second Friday of December, and their last working day, Séra took everyone out for a pre-Christmas meal, and to celebrate a brilliant year. Since the Paris Fashion Show, her magazine had hit the best-selling fashion magazine of the year, and Rose's reputation now preceded her. Ruby had settled in well at Gilmac News and was now doing her own stories with photos. George and Monica had also settled into a routine with their jobs, but the good news was that Monica was moving to George's hospital in the New Year.

With everything that had been going on, it had been six weeks since Rose had seen JP. They had spoken briefly on the phone. She needed to know what they were going to do at Christmas, so JP suggested she came to the palace, which she did. On the Monday, as she was walking along the corridor, the President walked out of his office door. "Rose, it's ages since I last saw you. Do you have a moment before you see JP?" Rose replied she would always have time for him. Back in his office, the President asked his guard for some refreshments. "Rose, first of all I would like to thank you for my excellent album from my wife. How on earth did you manage to put the images together?" Rose explained about Suzette. "She has an excellent talent," replied the President. "I must say your own career has taken off. My wife gets Le Monde du Séra every month, and your photos are beautifully done." Rose thanked him. They talked for about half an hour and then the President said he must join his wife to do their packing. A couple of minutes later she was at JP's office.

"Entre," said JP in a rather gruff voice. Rose opened the door and peered round. "Môn amour, you're here," and taking her in his arms kissed her passionately.

"Ah hem, would you like me to leave?" Rose broke the kiss and saw it was Andre.

JP grinned and said, "My apologies, Andre, but it's six weeks since I last saw Rose."

"Six weeks!!" exclaimed Andre. "Why didn't you say something, as I could have covered you for a weekend?"

JP replied, "I think the President had other ideas, and forgets I'm now married, but it's my job at the end of the day."

Andre stood and gave Rose a hug and a kiss on the cheek. "I will leave you to get re-acquainted, but boss, don't forget to lock your door and don't be too noisy." Both Rose and JP were lost for words and then burst out laughing.

"So my love, in just under two weeks it's Christmas Day. I thought it might be nice to have a 'family' Christmas at the farmhouse. What do you think?" JP said he was happy with that, and would ask his men, but he thought they would probably prefer to come Boxing Day. Putting her arms around his neck she kissed him tenderly and said, "So we would have Christmas Day to ourselves then?"

"Yes môn amour, and it's your birthday so I am going to grant you your every wish."

Rose raised her eyebrow and smiling, said, "Every wish?"

JP looked into her eyes and with a very smouldering reply, that left Rose breathless, said, "Every wish, môn amour," and then kissed her with a passion.

"Well my first wish would be for you to be in sexy underwear, so you'd better go shopping my love." JP actually blushed!!

CHAPTER 16

An hour later they had discussed what they had to buy, which this year would include decorations and a Christmas tree. JP gave Rose a list of things for the meal and asked her if she could order everything from the butchers and greengrocer in the shopping centre. Rose said naturally she would. Rose also said she would pick everything up the day before Christmas Eve, as JP was working until Christmas Eve afternoon.

As he walked her back to her car, they called in at the surveillance room, where his men were. They all agreed Boxing Day would be better. Rose told JP she would ring her uncle, mum and dad, and Ruby. When they got to Rose's car a guard called to JP. "Apologies, JP, but we need your wife's car to be returned. It is well overdue for a check."

JP replied, "Do we have a replacement?" The guard replied they did and signalled to another guard. Rose watched as a totally different car was driven towards her. It was a new Renault 9 and in yellow. "Môn amour, this is your early Birthday/Christmas present. I hope you like it. The colour can always be changed." Rose was stunned, but told JP she loved it. JP suggested she drove it round the courtyard to get the feel of it, which she did. The first thing she noticed was that the steering wheel wasn't so heavy, and the car felt easier to drive. She hugged and kissed JP. "Just one thing, môn amour, this car isn't bulletproof, but it can be done." Rose said she liked it as it was, and drove out of the courtyard.

The first thing she did was drive to the shopping centre and order everything from the butchers and greengrocers, which she would then pick up the following Monday. She then went to the kitchen shop where she bought Christmas serviettes, a red tablecloth and boxes of crackers. She got one box of smaller crackers for the children. Next, she noticed a Christmas shop had arrived. There she ordered and paid for a tall Christmas tree that would be delivered. She also bought some table decorations, tinsel, tree decorations, and various other decorations. She decided to take all that back to the car, but couldn't find it, until she remembered her car was now yellow and not a black surveillance car.

Back in the centre, she stopped and had some lunch and people watched, after she had made an appointment at the beauty salon for her hair etc., on the Saturday. Whilst she was eating, she saw Suzette, and called to her. "Rose, you like me, Christmas shopping?" Rose replied she was, and invited Suzette to join her, which she did. They chatted about various things and then Suzette said all she had left to do was buy some presents for her for nephews and nieces.

That gave Rose an idea. "How old are they?" she asked.

Suzette replied, 'Two nieces five and six, and one nephew three."

Rose replied, "Then I need your help. I need presents for, let me think, two girls and a boy aged five and a half, and the girls are twins. One boy of five, and one of two. Lastly one girl aged four and a half."

Suzette replied, "Let's go see what we can find."

In the toy shop, they immediately went to the young children's section. Suzette suggested getting the same things for the twin girls, so they wouldn't fall out. Rose ended up getting Céleste and Donatien's twin girls, Paulette and Michélle, the same reading book and doll; Gabrielle and Andre's son, Dulé, a colouring book and crayons; Emilie and Pierre's girls, Lydie and Aimée, books and dolls, and their son Ouén some building bricks. She just hoped they all would like them. Suzette did ask Rose if she and JP were going to have children. Rose just replied she couldn't. After kissing Suzette's cheek and thanking her for all her help, and wishing each other Merry Christmas and Happy New Year, they parted company. Next stop was to buy something for her uncle, mum and dad, and Ruby. In a newsagent she bought wrapping paper etc. Her very last stop was the lingerie shop.

That night she phoned her uncle, mum and dad, and Ruby. All of them said they would be delighted to come over on Boxing Day. The following day, the Christmas tree was delivered and the men kindly helped Rose to put it in the planter, and then secured it in the corner of the hall. The rest of the day, Rose enjoyed herself decorating the farmhouse. She started with the tree by firstly putting the lights around the branches and making sure they all lit up. Then she followed that with the garlands, silver and gold tinsel, along with pearl strands. Then lastly the decorations went onto the branches, which included small candy canes, silver and gold pine cones, small crackers, bells and balls, pretend red apples and slices of lemon, small toys of Père Noël, angels, reindeers, red and white small stockings, bows of various colours, soldiers and drums, stars of various sizes, small strands of red curled ribbons etc., and lastly placing a large star on the top. Underneath the tree she put boxes of different sizes just covered in Christmas wrapping paper. Standing back she admired her handiwork, making a couple of changes. In the dining room, she put green garlands with bells on them around the cabinets so they went along the top and down the sides. On top of the fireplace, she put a Christmas log, which had various flowers coming out in a spray, along with red candles in small candlesticks. In the fireplace itself, she had bought a huge arrangement of poinsettias, Christmas roses, holly, ivy and twigs with silver and gold pine cones, along with some greenery and mistletoe. She had also bought a long table decoration, which again was a Christmas log and the flowers were all red and the leaves gold and silver. For the time being she put it in the cupboard. She placed a small silver tree with red balls on one of the corner tables. This year the dining room table was long enough for everyone to sit around, including the children.

Next came the sitting room. The smaller Christmas tree, she put on top of a low table, in a corner of the room. Again she decorated it, checking the lights worked properly, but this time put an angel on the top. She wrapped tinsel round the bottom to hide the planter. When she had wrapped them, she was going to put the children's presents under the tree. Like the dining room she decorated the fireplace with a different log decoration, but this time, either side of it, she placed Christmas figures, birds and animals on a thin layer of white cotton wool. If she didn't change the positions of them once, she changed them half a dozen times until she was pleased. JP would lay the fire, and light it before their family arrived. On the front door she put a Christmas garland, and then decorated the front windows with lights and white and red stars. Upstairs in their bedroom she put more lights and stars. That night, after it was dark, she went round and put all the lights on and then went outside. To Rose it looked lovely and Christmassy, and she was pleased at what she'd done. She then turned all the lights off.

Tuesday morning her uncle phoned and asked if she was in town, could she pop in and see him. Rose agreed, but wondered why. She arrived at the bank about midday. The whole of Paris was looking fantastic with all the various Christmas trees and decorations. The bank had a huge Christmas tree, and every bit of the bank was decorated. Robert greeted Rose and phoned her uncle. Hugh asked Robert to tell Rose to go up to the flat. He had already opened the door for her. When Rose walked in, she froze. The flat was decorated in beautiful Christmas decorations. This was unlike her uncle, and Rose knew straight away. "Rose my dear, how are you?"

Rose hugged and kissed her uncle, and looking at him could see he was looking very happy. "So, does this mean I have an extra guest for Boxing Day, Uncle?"

Hugh smiled and said, "Well that depends on you. Come, let's enjoy the food and I'll make us some coffee. I didn't want to talk to you over the phone, and not only that, with you being so busy, I hardly see you these days." Hugh made the coffee and they sat down, to what Rose called a normal meal. A selection of various sandwiches and cakes.

"Who is she, Uncle?" asked Rose, excited.

Hugh replied, "Chantelle."

Rose thought for a moment and then looked wide eyed at her uncle. "Do you mean Chantelle, the escort lady, that you took to the President's New Year's Eve ball?"

"Yes," replied Hugh, "but let me explain. Chantelle has not been an escort for the last three months.

"In February, I literally bumped into her in the street, and we went for a meal. She told me of her past life, which was not very good. She had tried to get employment, but her past let her down. One day she saw an advert for an escort, so she went along and because of her looks she was given the job. It is a very high-class escort agency, and Chantelle, shall we say, was an escort for the more mature gentleman, as an escort only. There was no hidden agenda. I really liked her, and so we started going out for meals, when she wasn't being an escort. Slowly we got to know each other, and in June she told me how lovely it was to be treated like a woman and not a slab of meat on a man's arm. Most of the men would show her off to their friends, and start groping her, which she didn't like. The crunch came in September, when she came to the bank to see me. I could see she was very distressed, and brought her up here. Chantelle told me that just lately the same man had been taking her out. He took her to a very grand ball, but at the end of the evening, she noticed he wasn't taking her home. She asked him where they were going, to which he told her 'his penthouse suite'. Chantelle immediately felt alarm bells ring, and told him she was rather tired and would he please take her home. To her utter horror, the man said he had paid the agency five thousand francs for her to stay with him through the night and he had every intention of, excuse the language, screwing her all night long."

Rose said, disgusted, "Bloody men!!'"

Hugh carried on. "Chantelle told him she had not been told of this, and it was one thing she would not do, and she needed to phone the agency. When the taxi stopped, the man grabbed her and pulled her out. 'You alright, Mademoiselle?' asked the driver, who had been listening to the conversation and watching them in his mirror. Chantelle shook her head.

"As the man pulled her towards the entrance, suddenly a man jumped out of the bushes, with a balaclava on and what looked like a gun in his pocket. 'Don't make a sound or I'll shoot. Now, wallet, jewellery, your watch.' The attacker grabbed what he asked for and then told them to get on the ground and stay down.

"The man with Chantelle immediately went down, but the attacker signalled to Chantelle to remove her shoes and quietly walk backwards. 'Quickly, run to the taxi,' he said quietly. Chantelle did and then realised the attacker was the taxi driver. She thanked him profusely and he drove her home. He returned her jewellery to her, and said he would dispose of the wallet and watch, but not before he had taken the cash out, and gave Chantelle the five thousand francs in it. Chantelle said she couldn't take it, but the driver replied, 'Mademoiselle, he was going to pay this to the agency for you, so now he has paid.' Chantelle took it and thanked the driver again, and then the following morning came to see me as to what to do with the money.

"I asked her if she'd phoned the agency and she said she hadn't. I told her to. The entire agency wanted to know if she was alright, as her escort had phoned and told them they had been robbed, and she had vanished. The man wanted to see her again, but Chantelle said no, and how dare they suggest to any man that she would sleep with them, for five thousand francs. The agency had no idea what she was talking about. The rule was if a client wanted to spend the night with an escort that was a private arrangement and nothing to do with them. There and then she quit the job. She sent the money anonymously to a charity. Luckily as one door closed, another opened. She went to see if she could get in to see the fashion show. She was mistaken for one of the models and shown backstage. One of the designers saw her, and asked who she was with. She explained it had been a big mistake, and she was looking for the way out. He offered her the job as a mature model there and then and she took it. I'm glad to say the designer lives in Paris, and Chantelle has now been a model for two months. There is one other thing. Chantelle is ten years younger than me."

Rose replied, "That's not a problem, Uncle. Would Chantelle like to meet me before you bring her, so at least she sees a friendly face?"

Hugh grinned and replied, "You will both have a lot to talk about, and I hoped you would like to meet her. She should be here..." At that moment the doorbell rang... "about now."

Chantelle walked in with Hugh and straight away she thought what a lovely couple they made. She could also see Chantelle was nervous, so she went to her and kissed both her cheeks and said, "Chantelle, lovely to see you again." She felt Chantelle relax immediately.

A couple of hours later they had been so busy chatting, neither of them had noticed Hugh had gone back to work!! "Thank you, Rose, for accepting me, and I think the world of your uncle. Do you think the rest of your family will be alright with me coming on Boxing Day?"

Rose replied, "They will love you, but I will say nothing. It's up to you if you want to tell them about being an escort. Now I really must go. See you on Boxing Day." Both of them hugged and kissed each other's cheek, and Rose went down to her uncle's office.

"My dear, everything alright?"

"You could have said you were leaving, Uncle."

"What, and interrupt your talk about models and catwalks? I don't think so."

Rose laughed. "See you both on Boxing Day." And after a hug and kiss she left. Rose drove home thinking about Chantelle, and she really liked her; she was just right for her uncle.

CHAPTER 17

On the Friday, Rose went to the beauty salon, and then got some more shopping. Two days later it was Christmas Eve. Rose went to the shopping centre and firstly went to the greengrocers and picked everything up, and then took it back to the car. Next was the butcher's, and a young man helped Rose with everything back to the car. She had just got home and put everything in the fridge or in the vegetable racks, when she saw JP drive in. Quickly she put all the tree lights on. When JP walked in he said, "Môn amour, this is wonderful. Now it feels like Christmas." He took her in his arms and kissed her tenderly. "Let me bring all the wine, etc., in and then you can tell me everything you've been up to." JP brought in twelve bottles of champagne, red wine and white wine, along with a couple of bottles of various juices. After that he put the car in the garage, and found Rose in the sitting room, with a pot of coffee. "Come, môn amour, let me cuddle you." Rose wrapped her arms around him and cuddled into him. "Umm," replied JP contentedly.

"Do you think we have got everything, my love?"

"If we haven't, it's too late now. Now, môn amour, this Boxing Day meal is going to be slightly different. It's going to be a traditional French meal, which means none of our family will be bringing presents or wine. There will be no butter or olive oil with the bread, and the meal will be totally different. Tomorrow I need to start cooking for the cold part of the meal, and there is going to be lots of different things to eat."

Rose said, "Is it wrong to give presents then?"

JP replied, "Why, what have you bought?"

"I've got some books, dolls and building bricks for the children; perfume and brandy for Mum and Dad; earrings for Ruby, and a new pipe and tobacco for Uncle." JP replied that would be fine and what a wonderful thought about the children, and then after kissing Rose, he went to make some dinner.

Afterwards they snuggled together on the settee, watching a film in between kisses and caresses. "One more hour, môn amour, and then it's celebration time."

Rose sat astride him and said sexily, "One more hour and then you're going to fulfil my every wish. I hope you remembered my first wish?" JP replied he had. The clock struck twelve and they wished each other Merry Christmas, and JP wished Rose a Happy Birthday. "Off you go, my love, and get ready. I want you to pleasure me." JP smiled and taking her hand, led her up to the bedroom. "My love, I think I'd like a shower first, but I've had my hair done."

JP got the temperature right and undressed her slowly, and then carefully put a shower cap on to protect her hair. He then undressed himself. As he went to love her in the shower, Rose stopped him. "We have all night, my love." JP washed her whole body, and purposely touched her breasts, nipples and mound. He saw she was naked for him, and wished he had been, but he never had time and it was bloody painful. Once finished he dried every bit of her, and again carefully took the shower cap off. Her hair was dry. He watched as Rose wiggled her hips as she went to the bedroom. He went into one of the spare bedrooms and put his sexy underwear on, and then covered himself with a dressing gown.

Rose was laid seductively on the bed, when JP walked in. "Ooh do I have to unwrap my husband?"

JP replied, "No let me," and dropped his dressing gown. Rose looked absolutely stunned at him, and then broke out into hysterical laughter. JP was stood there in a sexy bra and briefs set. His manhood was poking out of the top of his briefs. Rose couldn't stop laughing. "You asked me to wear sexy underwear, môn amour. Took me ages to find this fetching set." That made Rose laugh even more, as in her imagination she could see JP in a lingerie shop trying to get the right sizes.

"Oh JP, I love you so much. Come here and let me remove your set." JP straddled her on the bed and Rose kissed him, whilst she undid the back of his bra.

"Thank heavens for that," said JP.

"Now the briefs stay, as I want you to love me, but doing something we haven't tried before."

JP had an idea she might ask this, and rather embarrassingly, got a book from the library with various ideas. He unstraddled her, and laid down on the bed. "Mōn amour, you need to kneel either side of my face, with your entrance lips on my lips, and put your hands on the headboard." Rose did as he asked, and JP pulled her down lower so he had access. Gently he parted her lips, and let his tongue flick over her nub. As her nub got harder, JP started sucking it, and could feel Rose responding. His hands were on her waist to keep her from going up. Soon Rose was moaning, and JP sucked harder and harder. "Oh JP, don't stop, don't…" Rose's climax exploded through her body and she was moaning in ecstasy. "Do that again, my love," and JP obliged. "Oh JP, that was incredible," she said as she moved down him and straddled his waist. JP could see her whole body was flushed, and she bent down and kissed him with such a passion.

"Now it's my turn," said Rose, and slowly she unlaced the briefs and pulled them away from his manhood. One hand went round his manhood, and the other cupped his testicles. She only took the top of his manhood in her mouth and swirled her tongue round it. She could feel JP was about to explode and quickly moved and lowered herself down on to him. JP only thrusted a couple of times, and his orgasm exploded, but he wasn't finished yet. He rolled Rose over onto her back and knelt between her legs. He pulled her up so her buttocks were on his thighs and her legs behind him, and then entered her. His hands went to her breasts and nipples and he caressed them so gently. Rose's body was on fire. JP knew she wanted him to thrust faster, but he wasn't going to. He took her over the edge slowly and her orgasm had her writhing on the bed, and he then too climaxed. Both of them collapsed side by side, and they wrapped their arms around each other.

"That was incredible, JP. I love you so much."

JP replied, Je t'aime aussi, mōn amour. Now sleep, and you still have the rest of the day for me to fulfil your wishes." Rose rolled over and JP spooned into her back. Soon they both fell into a deep contented sleep.

In the morning Rose stretched her body out like a cat that had had the cream. JP wasn't in bed, but a minute later he came with a tray. "Breakfast is served, Madame Pascal." Rose sat up and he placed the tray in her lap and smiled. It was her favourite. Two boiled eggs and toasted soldiers, with a mug of coffee. "Thank you, my love. Can I smell cooking?"

JP replied, "You can, môn amour. I wasn't sure what your wishes would be for the day, so I thought I had better start doing the cooking of the food that will be served cold."

Rose replied, "My love, whilst you're cooking for tomorrow, I will put my wishes on hold."

JP bent over and kissed her gently. "I need to get back to the kitchen. Anything else you require, môn amour?"

Rose thought and then smiling, said, "You cook. I help. Deal?"

JP replied, "Deal."

Rose had her breakfast, then washed and dressed. In the kitchen JP had all sorts of things going on. "What can I do to help?" JP said the vegetables needed preparing, along with all the potatoes. Rose set to work. About lunch time Rose looked out the kitchen window. "JP, look, it's snowing."

JP looked and said, "It's thick flakes, and if this keeps up all day, the road outside will be blocked. The snowploughs will keep the main roads open." At that moment the phone rang, and JP answered it.

"Who can't make it?" asked Rose.

"No one yet," replied JP. "That was Raoul from the village pub. Apparently the village has its own snowplough and Raoul will be keeping this part of the road clear, as the other way is too long to the main road. I'll ring everyone and tell them which way to come later on."

Rose replied, "Oh, I forgot to tell you. We have one extra friend coming. My uncle's lady friend." JP raised his eyebrow, and Rose told him about Chantelle. "Well if that had been me, I would have kept the money. What a bloody… well, never mind. Do without men like him. I vaguely remember her, and she will be welcomed with open arms."

Rose kissed him and said, "I knew I married a wonderful man." JP kissed her back.

By late afternoon all the cold food had been cooked, gone cold and was wrapped up and put in the fridge. "Môn amour, what would you like to eat?"

Rose said, "To be honest my love, I would be happy with a selection of sandwiches, and I bought some cakes from the patisserie yesterday. You have a rest. You've done nothing but cook all day. I will do the sandwiches."

JP said, "If that is your wish, môn amour?" Rose smiled and said it was.

JP went and had a quick shower, whilst Rose made the sandwiches. When he came down she had put the sandwiches and cakes on the table in front of the settee. She had also made a pot of coffee. Both of them ate the sandwiches and cakes, whilst watching a film. Rose then cleared and washed up the dishes. JP phoned everyone and told them which way to come. "They've all made contingency plans," said JP. "Antoine and Ruby are picking up your mum and dad, and Hugh and Chantelle in one of the security cars. Better grip on the roads. Pierre and his family are picking up Donatien and his family; Andre and Gabrielle along with their son are going to the palace first and picking up sleeping bags and other things, just in case."

"Thank heavens we have two spare bedrooms," said Rose. "I will make the beds up and then they'll have to decide who takes them. One can accommodate the ladies and girls, the other the men and boys. Two could always sleep on the settee."

JP wrapped his arms around her and said, "Don't worry, môn amour, they will all sort themselves out, if they have to stay. My men have camped out in worst conditions than this. Now do you realise you only have just over an hour left for me to fulfil your wishes?"

"Bedroom now," said Rose.

Looking out of the hall window they could see the snow was

getting deep. Upstairs when JP went to the bathroom, Rose went into one of the spare bedrooms, where she had put her outfit. Once she was ready, she put her dressing gown on. When she went back into the bedroom, JP was sat on the bed. Going up to him, she put her finger under his chin and tilted his face up and kissed him. "My final wish, my love, is for you to undress me very slowly and then take me to heaven more than once." JP was already naked. He stood up and undid Rose's dressing gown and was blown away. Rose stood there in a red and white set of bra, briefs, corset with suspenders, red stockings with white garters, and a red and black plunge-line negligee over the top. Apart from the stockings, garters and negligee, the rest looked like it was moulded over every part of her body. Around her neck was a red choker with a small white bow, and she had black see-through lace elbow-length gloves on.

JP couldn't take his eyes off her, and didn't know where to start first. His manhood was stood to attention and Rose smiled sexily. He took Rose in his arms and kissed her gently on the lips, and then trailed kisses down both sides of her neck. Carefully he gathered up the negligee and pulled it over her head. Then he picked her up and laid her on the bed. He took one arm and kissed it all the way down to her fingertips as he peeled off the glove, and then did the same with the other. His kisses and feather-like touch went back to Rose's neck and then down to the top of her breasts that were spilling out above her bra. He took the choker off and trailed kisses down her throat. He could see Rose's body was already flushing, but she told him he had to be slow, so slow he was. Mind you it wasn't doing his manhood any good, but he had learnt control, and he was going to need it. He moved down the bed, and like he had done on their wedding night, he raised one leg up on his shoulder and undid the suspenders and rolled her stockings down, taking his time to plant kisses on her inner thigh. Then he did the same with the other. The garters were next to go. Then he surprised Rose by kissing her between her legs. Rose's body quivered. JP then had a decision, bra, corset or briefs. His hands went to the laces on the corset, and he undid them one by one, and them unclipped the eyelets. Soon her corset was gone and she was left in bra and briefs.

He trailed kisses all over her stomach, and Rose was wriggling and moaning. Rose suddenly sat up kissing him passionately and said, "I wish you to go quicker, my love."

JP glanced at the clock and said, "Wish denied, môn amour. It's five minutes past midnight." As he embraced Rose, he undid the back of her bra, and literally threw it on the floor. Now her breasts were free, and he caressed and kissed them, and sucked her nipples till they were hard. Just to tease her even more, he went back to her lips and slowly kissed her all the way down to her mound. Now he slowly removed her briefs, and Rose was naked. His hand went to her mound and caressed it, and then started kissing it, but he didn't go near her entrance.

Rose said, "Please JP, I can't take any more. Love me now."

JP put her legs over his shoulders and cupping her buttocks, buried his head between her legs. Rose didn't last long, and her climax exploded through her body. JP then lowered her legs and entered her and he didn't last long either. Rose quickly flipped JP over and started rotating her hips. JP sat up and held her close. He could feel her clenching him and knew she was close, so he thrusted up into her. Rose called out his name as her orgasm hit her again. JP then rolled her back onto her back and took her hard and quick. His orgasm then sent him over the edge. Both sated, they curled into each other arms and slept.

CHAPTER 18

JP woke about 6am, and saw his beautiful wife was firm asleep. Quietly he slipped out of the bed, and went down to the kitchen. Soon various smells were wafting through the farmhouse. Looking out of the window he saw it was still snowing, and was now very thick. He would have to clear the driveway up to the road. He heard a strange noise and saw it was Raoul with the snowplough. On the radio the weather was bad. Snow was expected for the rest of the week. In the sitting room, he lit the fire and soon it was roaring away. He put the guard round it to stop any sparks flying out.

Back in the kitchen he was about to do Rose's breakfast, when a pair of hands grabbed and squeezed his buttocks. "Morning, môn amour. You realise doing that could cause trouble?"

Rose's hands went under his apron and caressed his manhood. "I think you're already in trouble, my love."

JP turned to see Rose stood there naked. Within seconds his apron was off, he picked her up, and carried her into the sitting room, laying her down her on the rug, in front of the fire, where he loved her. Afterwards a very flushed Rose said, "Can we just lay here for the day and love each other?"

JP kissed the tip of her nose and said, "We can, not sure what the others would say, and I'm not into having an audience."

Rose laughed, and then hugging him again said, "Better get ready then."

When everything was going nicely in the kitchen, JP went to the garage and got a shovel and more logs for the fire. He put the logs inside the front door and then started to clear the driveway. A bit later a thump hit his backside. He turned to see Rose was lobbing snowballs at him. "Like that, is it?" he said, smiling, and started throwing snowballs back. Rose grabbed a huge amount of snow and ran up to him and rubbed it all over his face. JP grabbed her and pushed her down onto the soft snow and started tickling her.

Rose was laughing her head off, when a voice said, "You two need a hand there?" Both red faced, they looked to see Raoul. "Thought you might be having company, so I brought the snow shovel up to clear your drive. Apologies if I interrupted anything."

JP replied, "Rose thought it a good idea to rub snow in my face, so I was getting my own back."

Raoul laughed and replied, "Quite right to. Now let me clear your drive for you." Within five minutes it was done.

"Raoul, please come in and raise a glass," said JP. Raoul accepted and they had a coffee with brandy and wished each other Merry Christmas. Raoul told them the pub always had a New Year's Eve do, and they were more than welcome to join them. JP thanked him and said they were probably going somewhere with his men and families, but it depended on the weather.

Raoul replied, "Would love to see them all again, the more the merrier. We do a buffet in the restaurant. Anyway, better get on or the road won't stay clear." JP and Rose thanked him and Raoul went on his way.

Back in the kitchen Rose said, "Has anything been said about New Year's Eve?"

"Not yet. Pierre will tell us today, but this weather is going to cause severe road traffic problems. Now môn amour, I must get on with the meal. I still have lots to do."

Rose kissed him and went to sort the dining room out. "JP, do you think the children would like to have their own table, or be seated with us?"

JP went and looked in the dining room and replied, "We could put another couple of tables at the end of the big table, and that way they'll have their own table and still be with us. We can use the garden tables."

JP brought in three of the tables and some extra chairs and then left Rose to sort it. Luckily she had bought six red tablecloths. She put one table at the top, and the other two at the other end, and then covered all of them with the red tablecloths. Instead of putting the large Christmas decoration down the centre of the table, she now placed it on the top table. Rose then did all the place settings, with crackers on all the plates. With the extra tables nobody would be squashed up now. Rose then placed six red candles in small glasses, down the centre, and would light them later. She put the large serving mats down the middle as well. Seeing as JP hadn't told her the menu, she could only guess. Next she put two sets of glasses by the place settings, but only one for the children. On the top table by the decoration she placed fourteen champagne glasses one side, and coffee cups and saucers the other side. "My love, do you think I need to put anything else out?"

JP came in from the kitchen and said, "Môn amour, that looks wonderful. Nothing else is needed."

Rose replied, "It's coming up midday, what else do you need me to do?"

JP replied, "You, môn amour, can go and make yourself look even more beautiful. I am more or less ready, and will be up in a moment for a quick shower."

"I'll get the shower ready then," said Rose.

About five minutes later, they were both in the shower. "Love your sexy shower cap," said JP, as they washed each other's bodies. Rose slapped his backside.

JP raised his eyebrow and Rose knew that look. "My love, we don't have—" Before Rose could say anything else, JP had slipped inside and was loving her.

They had just dressed and got downstairs when a car horn tooted. It was Antoine. Rose flicked all the lights on, and the Christmas lights lit up the farmhouse. Close behind them, everyone else arrived. Rose and JP greeted each one of them by the front door, and they all said, "Joyeux Noël," and wished Rose Happy Birthday. They all went into the sitting room. The children loved the trees.

"Rose, this is magical," said her mum. Rose introduced Chantelle to the rest, who all greeted her as well.

"Uncle JP, Uncle JP, can we play in the snow, PLEASE?" asked Paulette and Michélle.

"Girls behave, or else," said Donatien.

"Yes Papa," they replied with a pout.

"See what we mean, Chantelle? The men gather in one corner and leave us alone," said Gabrielle. Chantelle smiled.

Andre replied, "You wouldn't have it any other way."

Gabrielle replied, "You live with each other, apart from two weekends a month. What is more important than being with your beautiful wives and girlfriends?"

Andre replied, "Sorry men, I think my wife needs me," and went and sat with Gabrielle. The men all burst out laughing, but then joined the ladies.

JP said, "I have a meal awaiting, so please take your seats."

They all went into the dining room and Ruby said, "Oh wow, this looks fantastic Rose."

Rose explained she had put the children at the end, but it was up to the parents where they sat. They stayed at the end. Rose lit all the candles, and the children went, "Ooohhh." Rose told everyone to pull their crackers, which they did, and all the toys were given to the children, with Emilie keeping a close eye on Ouén. Then they all put their party hats on. JP and Rose brought in the Foie-Gras.

"I have only done small portions as we have a lot to get through."

"That's alright, boss, looks like we might be staying the night," said Pierre, rubbing his hands together.

Whack. Emilie slapped his head and said, "Behave."

Everyone burst out laughing and the children giggled. JP had given Antoine the job of serving the champagne. When the adults had a glass they all stood and said, "A votre santé," and everyone clinked glasses with everyone else. The next course was smoked salmon, followed by oysters and then lobster and crab salad.

"JP, how long have you been in the kitchen?" asked Céleste.

JP replied, "Not long, only two long days and nights."

Rose looked at him and saw a cocky expression on his face, and totally forgetting the children were there said, "Two days, really? So what I thought was you on my birthday night and last night was only a dream then. God, it was so real." Everyone went quiet, JP went scarlet, and then everyone roared with laughter.

Pierre said, "She got you there, boss."

Rose replied, now embarrassed as well, "Apologies, forgot about the children."

Emilie replied, "Oh Rose that was brilliant, and I think they're too busy playing."

JP went to the kitchen, and Rose followed with the empty plates. "Am I in trouble, my sexy husband?"

JP kissed her and said, "I'll keep that one for now."

"JP, why aren't the children eating?"

"They don't just yet. When we take the main meal in, the wives will sort them out. Some of this they can't eat anyway."

The next two courses were escargot and Coquilles Saint Jacques. Antoine was serving either red or white wine. Rose noticed Chantelle was enjoying herself, and her uncle winked at her. The conversation was flowing and plenty of jokes and laughs. JP didn't bring the main courses in for a good half hour to give everyone a breather.

Rose placed bowls of roasted potatoes, garlic potatoes, boiled potatoes, and an assortment of vegetables, with jugs of gravy, in the centre of the table. Rose suggested to JP she moved the table decoration and then he could put the meats on there to carve. JP then placed a turkey with chestnut stuffing, a chicken, and a goose on the mats. Rose brought in warmed plates and JP went round the table asking what everyone would like. He then carved the meat. Céleste, Emilie and Gabrielle told JP what to give the children, and then they put the potatoes and vegetables on the plates with some gravy. The roast potatoes soon went, and JP brought more in. Everyone complimented and then toasted JP for a superb meal. JP thanked them all and raising his glass, said, "To the best family anyone could ask for, and welcome to our family, Chantelle." Chantelle blushed.

His men replied, "To you, boss," and everyone else said, "To JP."

Rose said, "To my wonderful husband," and kissed him. Rose looked at Dulé expecting a "Yuk" but he was quiet. Andre told her that stage was gone now, and he rather enjoyed kissing.

"Just like his papa," said Pierre, which earned him another whack.

After another long gap, the next course was various cheeses, with salad and bread. Then came the very last course, which JP knew the children had been waiting for. Bûche de Noël – the Yule chocolate log. He had actually made six small ones, for each of the children. They all gave him a hug and a kiss. For the adults he had made two large ones.

"I honestly don't think I can move," said Monica.

Rose suggested everyone went into the sitting room, where they could relax more, and she would make pots of tea and coffee. JP had kept his eye on the fire and had been putting more logs on it.

Hugh looked out the window and said, "You're not going to believe this, but the driveway is covered in snow and it's about four inches deep." JP opened the front door and the snow fell in. The children thought it was fun and went to play in it, but JP stopped them. The mess was soon cleared up. Rose took the pots of tea and coffee and placed them on the glass tables.

"JP can we help you clear away?" asked Chantelle. JP said everything would be cleared and to just relax. Within half an hour, the dining room had been cleared, the leftover food stored away, and half of the dishes in the dishwasher.

Whilst Rose was making the drinks, JP let her know there was a strong possibility they would all be staying the night. Rose replied that was fine. Then he took her in his arms and kissed her passionately. "Have I told you lately 'Je t'aime', môn amour?"

Rose took his face in her hands and said, "I love you so much, JP, more than you will ever know," and kissed him tenderly.

Once everyone was settled in the sitting room, Rose whispered to Céleste about the presents for the children, and asked if it would be alright to give them out. Céleste said they would be delighted. Rose whispered to JP, who got up and went to the tree, got the presents and gave them to Rose.

"Does anyone know where I can find some exceptionally behaved boys and girls, so Rose can give them some presents?" asked JP.

The children walked over and said, "Here we are, Uncle JP and Auntie Rose."

Rose said, "This is for you, Paulette, and this one's for you, Michelle. Here's yours, Lydie and Aimée. And these two are for you, Dulé and Ouén." Rose was surprised the children didn't rip their presents open.

"Children, open your presents," said Céleste.

The next minute the wrapping paper was being ripped open. All of them were showing everyone what they had got. Paulette said, "Look, maman and papa, we got twins." Dulé was already colouring in his book with his crayons. Lydie and Aimée were playing with their dolls and Pierre was playing with Ouén's with his building bricks. Rose looked around at everyone and saw how contented they all were, and had never felt happier.

A bit later on, Andre and Donatien went to assess the snow situation. The driveway was about six inches high, but they could see the road was clear. It was coming up 10pm. Andre caught JP's eye and asked if he had any shovels. JP said they could stay, as Rose had got everything ready for them. Andre thanked him, but said the weather was going to be worse tomorrow, and they couldn't stay indefinitely. JP understood, and a bit later on the driveway was clear.

"Sorry everyone to break the party up, but Andre and I are going to make a move, mainly because we have to cross the river, and the weather for tomorrow is not good," said Donatien.

Rose saw Ruby and Antoine chatting to her mum and dad, and uncle and Chantelle. Whatever it was, they all nodded. The children were tired and Ouén had gone to sleep. The families all said goodbye to each other, and told Chantelle they hoped to see her again soon. Céleste, Emilie and Gabrielle, all kissed and hugged Rose and JP. Donatien, Andre and Pierre all gave Rose a kiss and a tight hug, and shook hands with JP and a manly hug, all thanking them for a superb meal and excellent company. Rose and JP waved as they all drove away. The snow had already started to cover the driveway again.

In the sitting room, JP said to Antoine, "If you want to go I suggest you go now as the snow is coming down thick again."

Antoine replied, "We wondered, boss, if we could stay until the morning?" Rose was delighted and said it wasn't a problem, but they would have to sort out the sleeping arrangements. Rose didn't want to embarrass Chantelle and her uncle, as she didn't know how far into their relationship they were and said, "The bedrooms by the way have two single beds in each."

Ruby replied, "Antoine and I can stay down here, as the settees are wide enough." Hugh, Chantelle, Monica and George were happy with that.

CHAPTER 19

"Boss, I need to bring the bags in from the car," said Antoine.

"Bags?" asked JP.

"We all brought overnight bags, just in case."

JP nodded and he went outside with Antoine. Rose was beginning to think they'd got lost when they returned. "We've moved the cars around and got all three of them in the garage," said JP. "The wind is picking up and it's getting really cold. I think the temperatures will drop well below freezing later. Now, anyone want a drink or food?" They all said no to food, but opened another couple of bottles of wine. JP put another log on the fire, and they were all warm and cosy.

"Rose, your dad and I have something for you," said Monica. "Happy Birthday for yesterday." It was a beautiful frame.

"We thought you could put one of your wedding photos in it," said George. Rose loved it and gave her mum and dad a hug and a kiss.

"This is from myself and Chantelle," said Hugh.

It was a Swarovski crystal figurine of a photographer, with her name engraved on the bottom. Rose was stunned, and hugged and kissed her uncle and Chantelle. Lastly Ruby gave her their present. It was three beautifully bound books – Les Trois Mousquetaires; Le Comte de Monte-Cristo, and Fierté et Préjugés (Pride and Prejudice). "Oh Ruby and Antoine, my favourite three books, thank you so much," and hugged and kissed them.

"What happened to your other ones?" asked JP. Rose replied she had no idea, as she hadn't seen them for ages.

Rose went to the Christmas tree and gathered more presents, and gave them one each. Her mum and dad were delighted with the perfume and brandy; her uncle loved his new pipe and tobacco, and Ruby loved her earrings. Antoine had a bottle of his favourite wine, and she had got Chantelle a dainty bracelet. When JP opened his he was stunned. It was a beautiful soft leather wallet, but it had a J and P entwined like leaves, on the front. "Môn amour this is beautiful," and he took her in his arms and kissed her tenderly.

They all chatted for another couple of hours, and relaxed in each other's company. Rose decided to pop upstairs and make sure the spare bedrooms were aired and warm, and was glad to find they were. Thank heavens she had bought all the extra duvets, etc. She brought down two duvets and pillows, with extra towels for the cloakroom, for Ruby and Antoine later on. As she walked through the hall, she saw her reflection with the tree lit up behind her. She went and looked out of the window, and was transported back to her first Christmas with her uncle and aunt. She watched as her face lit up with every present she opened, even though they were all for school. Then aunt gave her a large present, which had her new coat within the wrapping. She watched as the nine-year-old girl looked up at her and walked towards the window and put her hand on it. Rose put her own hand on the cold glass against the girl's small hand. The girl smiled, and Rose smiled back.

A pair of strong arms went round her waist and then a gentle kiss on her neck. "Môn amour, you alright?" Rose saw the past had gone and now she stood there with JP.

Turning in his arms she said, "I'm fine my love. I just saw a happy memory from my past, and you're my present and future." Looking up, Rose had totally forgotten the mistletoe she had put there.

JP looked up and smiling kissed her with a passion, and said, "And you are my past, present and future. Come, you feel cold, especially your hand, or I can warm you up another way?" Rose blushed and he laughed and kissed her.

When they walked back in the sitting room, the rest of them were nodding. "Mum, Dad, time to rest."

"Oh sorry, I totally agree," said Monica. "What time is it?" JP replied it was just after 2am. Shaking her husband gently she said, "George, come on, say goodnight." All of them hugged and kissed each other goodnight, and Monica, George, Hugh and Chantelle made their way to the bedrooms.

"Ruby, are you sure you and Antoine will be comfortable enough on the settees?"

Ruby smiled and said, "We will be fine, and you have three settees. We only need two. Thank you for such a lovely day." Rose went and got the duvets, etc., and put them on one of the settees. Rose and JP said their goodnights. Slowly room by room the lights went out until the farmhouse was in darkness, apart from the glow of the dying fire.

"Well, môn amour, I think everything went smoothly."

"It has been a fabulous day, my love, and thank you for such a sumptuous meal." They wrapped their arms around each other and kissed each other goodnight, and fell into a relaxing, blissful sleep. Meanwhile outside the snow was falling, and falling, and falling.

JP woke first and looked out the window. All he saw was snow everywhere, and icicles hanging down outside of the windows. He couldn't even see the road and he shivered. Quietly he got washed and dressed and went down to the kitchen. He took the last lot of dishes out of the dishwasher and put them away. Looking at the clock he saw it was 10am, and so he turned the radio on for the news and weather, which was pretty grim. The announcer said, "Snow has caused severe disruption in the capital. Many of the surrounding villages have been totally cut off. In some areas power lines have gone down and there is no electricity. Parts of the Seine are totally frozen as temperatures dropped to minus ten last night. Most areas have had a snowfall of between eight and twelve inches. The airports are closed, as are all modes of transport. The head of the gendarme have advised people not to drive, unless it's an absolute emergency. The outlook for the next twenty-four hours is snow, along with icy winds, reaching gusts of force six to seven. Stay home, be safe and be careful everyone."

"That doesn't sound good," said a voice.

JP turned to see it was Hugh. "Morning Hugh, hope you slept well?"

Hugh replied they had. "I'm giving Chantelle a bit of privacy, as we haven't…"

JP replied, "Oh, I hope we didn't cause you a problem?"

Hugh patted JP's shoulder and said they had had their own privacy. "Anything I can do?"

"No thanks," replied JP. "Fancy a coffee?" Hugh nodded, and sat at the kitchen table.

"Is that coffee I can smell?" asked Antoine as he walked in.

"On the table. Help yourself, Antoine," said JP.

"Thanks boss," said Antoine.

Five minutes later George walked in. "So are our beautiful ladies awake then?" The men all nodded.

An hour later and everyone was sitting round the kitchen table tucking into freshly baked croissants, baguettes, and pains-au-chocolat. There were various cereals, fresh orange juice, fruit, butter and jam, and coffee. Monica's eyes went wide as she watched JP spread butter and jam on a long slice of a baguette and then dunk it in his coffee. She noticed Antoine did the same with his croissant. "Is that a tradition, JP?" she asked. JP said it was and to try it, so she did, but pulled a face. JP and Antoine laughed.

The main talk of the conversation was the weather, especially the very long icicles hanging down. JP cleared the dishes, and Rose went and tidied up the sitting room.

"Rose, anything I can do to help?" asked Antoine.

"Thanks Antoine, but I only need to clean out and relay the fire, and all done."

Antoine replied, "Go and join the rest of the family, and I will do the fire. Well, off you go then," he said cheekily. Rose kissed his cheek.

"Where's Antoine gone?" asked Ruby. Rose told her.

"I'll need to get some more logs," said JP.

"Hugh, George, I might need some help."

"Of course," they both said.

Soon the fire in the sitting room was lit and roaring to life.

"Ladies, I'm sure you would be more comfortable in the sitting room, and I can then have the kitchen to myself," said JP, smiling. Rose turned the Christmas tree lights on as they walked through.

Once they were sitting on the settees, Monica said, "Now we have a fashion photographer, a model and a fashion reporter. I've always wanted to know, how do the fashions get into the shops?" Ruby and Chantelle both looked at Rose.

"There are two fashion seasons, spring and autumn," said Rose. "January to June is spring, July to December autumn. Séra sketches out what she thinks will look good, expensive and inexpensive. She then goes to where she gets the clothes manufactured, and gets the sketches cut out into patterns, which are then sewed together on a dummy. She makes any alterations as the article is created, until she's satisfied. Some of the fabrics have to be tested to make sure they hang properly. Once the clothes are ready, she uses her models and I take the photos. The photos go into what is called a 'Look Book'. Séra then takes these photos to her connections and orders are placed. Séra has joined forces with Madame Cherrillé and Mía, and Mía is also doing her own designs, which are featured in the magazine, and their shop is now very popular."

Monica replied, "Well if your evening gowns and wedding dress are anything to go by, she has an exceptional eye for fashion."

Looking around, Rose said, "Where have those four got to?" She went to the kitchen and peered in. They were drinking wine and playing cards!! "So you wanted the kitchen to yourself, did you, or were you worried us ladies would beat you at cards?"

JP replied, "Not at all, môn amour. You were all talking about fashion, which none of us could have joined in, so we decided to leave you to talk and relax."

"Umm," said Rose, and left.

As she went to walk away she overheard Antoine say, "That was neatly done, boss."

JP replied, "As you will learn, Antoine, it's better to placate them." George and Hugh agreed.

Placate thought Rose. *I'll give you placate.* Rose had a plan and told the others. About ten minutes later the men returned with coffee and teas. Monica and George preferred tea to coffee. A couple of hours later JP went to the kitchen and made a soupe à l'oignon, a variety of sandwiches from the meats left over, along with savoury crêpes.

"This looks lovely, JP," said Monica as they went into the dining room.

Ruby had a spoonful of soup and said, "Is it just me, or does this taste a bit funny?"

Everyone looked at her, stunned, especially JP.

"Ruby, it's lovely. What are you talking about?" asked Antoine.

"It's probably that bit of chocolate I had just now. Sorry, JP." Rose watched as JP relaxed.

Everyone tucked into the sandwiches until Monica said, "Ouch." George asked her what was wrong. Monica pulled a tiny chicken bone out of her mouth.

JP was mortified and said, "Monica please forgive me. I thoroughly checked for bones, in fact I never went near the bones. This was the rest of the breast." Monica told him not to worry, as no damage was done.

The rest of the sandwiches and crêpes were eaten without incident. JP went to the kitchen and came back with a variety of soufflés, cheese and biscuits. Chantelle only had a mouthful of soufflé and then pushed it to one side. Hugh asked her if she was alright. Chantelle replied it was too sweet for her, so Hugh ate it instead.

"My love, is this cheese supposed to smell like this?" asked Rose who shoved it under his nose.

"Ah, no it's not, but I've only just unwrapped it. Sorry everyone, don't touch that one. I will dispose of it."

As he went to go towards the kitchen, Rose said with a raised eyebrow, "My love, perhaps you'd like to placate your wife and friends with an apology, and that goes for the four of you."

Suddenly it all slotted into place. "Ladies, my apologies," said JP, but looked at Rose with a look that said, "Just wait." Rose blew him a kiss, and then they all laughed.

"How did you get the bone?" asked George.

Rose explained that whilst JP had his back turned, she snapped a bit of bone off, and then smoothed it down and gave it to Monica.

"The soup?" asked Antoine.

"Absolutely delicious," replied Ruby.

Hugh looked at Chantelle who smiled and said, "Well, I had to join in. The soufflé, JP, was actually the best I've ever tasted."

Rose saw JP sigh a sigh of relief, and went to him and kissing his cheek, said, "The meal, as always my love, was wonderful. Anyone for coffee and liqueurs?" They all nodded at that, and Rose went to the kitchen. JP carried the dishes in, whilst the others went into the sitting room. Quickly he grabbed Rose and put his hand down the front of her trousers, and started caressing her between her legs. "JP, behave," said Rose.

He carried on until he knew Rose was close to her climax and then removed his hand. "To be continued a lot later, môn amour."

Rose was rather flushed when she went back into the sitting room, but no one said a word.

The weather hadn't relented all day, and JP suggested they all stayed another night, which they did.

"Antoine whilst I remember, are we meeting New Year's Eve?"

"Oh, sorry boss, obviously Pierre was going to mention it last night and must have forgotten. This year their wives decided it should be spent with their in-laws. Ruby and I are going to stay home, as it's our first one, but you're more than welcome to join us."

Rose asked, "Mum, Dad, what are you doing?" George replied working. She looked at her uncle who replied they had been invited to a bankers' do.

JP replied, "Well we can't expect to meet up every year, as we all have other commitments. Maybe next year."

The rest of the afternoon they just relaxed. A lot later JP cooked steaks with salad and chips, followed by fresh fruit salad and ice cream. The following morning the sun was shining, and slowly the snow was melting away from the drive. About midday, the six of them said their goodbyes, and Rose and JP waved as they left.

"Alone at last, môn amour. Weather permitting do you fancy

going into the village on New Year's Eve and celebrate with our new neighbours?" Rose said she thought that would be nice.

That evening as Rose and JP snuggled up to each other he said, "The farmhouse seems quiet now that they've all gone, but on the bright side, I now have you all to myself."

Rose smiled and said, putting her arms round his neck, "Fancy a game of cards?"

JP laughed and replied, "Ever played strip poker?" Rose shook her head. "I'll get the cards from the kitchen." Rose flew up the stairs and came back a couple of minutes later. "Shall we start, môn amour?" JP got down to his underpants, when Rose lost her dress. JP looked at her and said, "How many pairs of briefs have you got on?"

Rose replied, "Just twelve."

"Then môn amour, I will peel them off you one by one," which he did. With Rose naked, he removed his underpants. Seconds later Rose was straddling him and they loved each other slowly and gently.

CHAPTER 20

New Year's Eve, Rose and JP walked down to the village pub, hand in hand. All the snow was gone, and the last two days it had rained. At that moment there was a chilly breeze but it was fine. A large watery moon was high in the sky. As they entered the pub, everyone cheered and welcomed them. Raoul came over and gave Rose a hug and kissed her cheeks, and shook hands with JP. "My friends, so glad you could make it. Come, have a glass of wine, and please let me take your coats."

The pub was covered in Christmas decorations, and a large log fire was burning, giving out the smell of pine. Raoul took them into the restaurant, where a huge buffet was being served. "Help yourself, there is plenty." Rose and JP thanked him and then they mingled with the other villagers. Slowly they got to know all of them and listened to their stories of days gone past. Rose was fascinated. One of the villagers told them that many moons ago the farmhouse was part of the village. Over the years, other buildings had collapsed and weren't rebuilt. The forest used to be twice the size, but the trees were cut down for the fires and building materials. The farmhouse was left derelict for many years and then a new owner arrived, who thought he was the lord of the village. He renovated the farmhouse, but treated the villagers badly, and one day he vanished. The next owner was gentler and he named the village after the abundance of sunflowers. To him it was a good omen. The last owners had just decided to leave. "And now we have a lovely couple, and we hope you will stay with us for a long time," said one of the villagers.

Everyone raised their glass to them both. Rose and JP were slightly embarrassed, but thanked them.

Raoul clinked a glass and said, "Ladies and gentlemen, please take a glass of champagne as the New Year is very near." One of the villagers started the countdown and then the clock struck midnight.

The whole pub erupted, and JP took Rose in his arms and kissed her so tenderly, her whole body felt on fire. "Happy New Year, môn amour. Je t'aime."

Rose replied, "Je t'aime aussi, my love."

For the next half hour the villagers all kissed each other's cheeks and said, "Bonne Année." Rose had never been kissed so much, but she smiled at each person.

"Please, outside everyone," said Raoul. The night sky was then lit up with a variety of fireworks and loud banging crackers. "Supposed to ward off demons and evil spirits," said Raoul.

Soon everyone was back inside the pub, and the music and dancing started. About 2am Rose and JP left. They thanked Raoul and the villagers for a wonderful evening. Raoul got their coats and told them not to be strangers. Walking back, Rose cuddled into JP, as the wind was icy. The sky was now clear with a huge brilliant moon, with the stars twinkling around it. "Soon be home, môn amour, and I'll make us a hot drink."

Rose replied, "I think we can find another way to warm each other up." JP smiled. The farmhouse came into view, and soon JP and Rose were inside, in the warmth.

In the bedroom JP took his suit off, and Rose took her black dress off. JP turned to say something and saw Rose stood there in an electric blue all-in-one corset, with stockings and suspenders. His blood rushed to one spot, and Rose noticed. JP had his shirt off in seconds and took Rose in his arms, kissing her lips and neck. "Let me remove these for you, môn amour."

Sitting on the bed, with Rose stood in front of him, he released her stockings from her suspenders, and gently rolled them down. "Foot up," he said and Rose lifted her foot. Carefully he removed both stockings so as not to damage them. "Môn amour, if you don't mind me asking, how do you go to the ladies?"

Rose replied, "That's a secret I'll show you later."

Rose bent over and kissed his lips, and JP gently pulled her down on top of him, and then rolled her over onto her back. Rose wrapped her legs around his waist, and their kisses got more and more passionate. Rose trailed her hands down his back and under his underpants, and squeezed and kneaded his buttocks. She could feel his manhood pressing against her. Rose then rolled JP over and straddled him. JP's hands started to undo the laces on her corset, to free her breasts. The laces only went halfway down the corset and he couldn't see a way to take the rest off her. He put his hands between her breasts and started caressing them. He felt her nipples go hard. "I think these need to go," said Rose and peeled his underpants off, releasing a very hard part of his anatomy. She could feel him trying to find a way to get her corset off, and so she bent over and kissed him. Then he felt her slide down on him.

"How...?" Rose didn't answer, she just started rotating her hips, and soon they went into oblivion. With Rose laying on her back, he saw how she had done it. The piece that went between her legs had poppers on it. Slowly he moved the corset down her body and tossed it on to the chair. He kissed and caressed her mound, until he felt her coming to her peak, and then entered her. Rose put her hand down between her legs and squeezed and caressed his testicles, which took both of them to oblivion.

In the morning, the phone was non-stop as their "family" phoned to say, "Bonne Année." The rest of the day they relaxed and loved each other.

The following morning JP returned to the palace, but Rose had another couple of days and the weekend off. Over the weekend Rose took all the Christmas decorations down, and apart from the fir tree, stored them in the garage. JP had arranged with Raoul that a couple of the villagers would remove the tree, and cut it up for firewood, which they did. The logs were put in the garage. Soon Rose was back at work, and before she knew it, Ruby and Antoine's wedding day was literally round the corner. Ruby's wedding dress was white, with short sleeves, and a V-neck bodice, which then gently gathered at the waist and draped down. It was plain, with no train, but elegant. Her veil was short, and like Rose's, didn't cover her face. Rose's bridesmaid dress was in a pale peach, and in the same design as

Ruby's. Ruby's bouquet was going to be red and white roses.

On the Friday night, both parties went out to celebrate, and Rose stayed with Ruby. In the morning it was the beauty salon for their hair to be done, etc., and Monica joined them. Later on George arrived at the flat, and then the wedding car arrived, to take them to the town hall. Antoine had dressed in a smart navy blue suit, as had the rest of them. Suzette was also there to take the photos. At the town hall, Monica went in and gave them their red rose buttonholes. Ruby walked in on George's arm, with Rose behind her. JP and his men all smiled when they saw Ruby, and JP winked at Rose. Hugh and Chantelle were also there. Soon Ruby and Antoine were married, and then they made their way to a small church near Gérard's restaurant. About thirty people had turned up and Ruby was delighted. After the church service, Ruby threw her bouquet and it was Chantelle who caught it, and she blushed. Then everyone went to Gérard's.

Ruby and Antoine greeted everyone as they arrived, and the waiters and waitresses gave out champagne. JP with Rose and his men were there with their wives; Monica and George; Hugh and Chantelle; nearly everyone from Gilmac News, except Mathieu and Séra who were attending another wedding; and some more of the palace's bodyguards. Ruby and Antoine were delighted with the buffet, and again Gérard had made a Croquembouche as the wedding cake. Speeches were made and there was lots of laughter and jokes. The buffet was nearly demolished, and the wine flowed.

Later on Ruby and Rose went to change in a room Gérard had put aside for them. George had brought up their dresses earlier in the day. "Ruby, I didn't have time to say, but you looked absolutely beautiful, and I hope you and Antoine will be as happy as JP and myself."

Ruby hugged Rose and said, "Who would have thought when we first met them in Fracton, they would end up being our husbands?"

Rose replied, "You and I have come through so much together, Ruby, and now both of us have our fairy-tale ending, and more adventures to look forward to."

Monica came in and said, "You two alright? I think your husbands are missing you."

Rose replied, "We were just having a moment. Ready Ruby to dance the night away?" Ruby nodded, and the three of them went back to the reception.

As the DJ started the music, George took Ruby's hand and did a bit of the dance, and then gave her hand to Antoine. The whole night was a fabulous success, and Gérard also did fireworks for them as well. By 1am most of them had left. JP and Rose, Hugh and Chantelle, and Monica and George went back in one car, dropping Monica and George at their flat, Hugh and Chantelle at Hugh's flat and finally JP and Rose at Ruby and Antoine's as that was where Rose's car was. Ruby and Antoine arrived in the other car.

"Môn amour, we aren't going home, as we are staying at the palace." Rose raised her eyebrow, but just nodded. JP drove to the palace, and soon both of them fell into bed and slept.

In the morning JP took Rose out for breakfast, and they walked hand in hand along the Seine, which they hadn't done since they moved. Rose realised how much she missed doing this. As much as she loved the farmhouse, JP's flat had been ideal and so near to everything. After breakfast they strolled round the streets of Paris, and then JP suggested they went to the Eiffel Tower. For the rest of the day they just became tourists and thoroughly enjoyed their time together.

Back at the palace, JP said he was going to stay to catch up on work. "What, you're not coming home?" asked Rose. "This is the first time I've seen you this month."

JP took Rose in his arms and said, "I know, môn amour, but the next three or four months there are so many crisis meetings for the President, here and away, that they have to be sorted. I hate not coming home to you, as I miss you so much, and a telephone call isn't the same as taking you in my arms. Perhaps once things start to relax, we could go to Montpellier for a two- or three-week holiday." Rose said she would like that, but she missed him as well. JP kissed her tenderly and then walked her down to her car. An hour later Rose was back home – alone.

It was coming up the end of June, when Séra asked Rose if she would like to go to Nantes, just for a couple of days, as there was a new designer showing her collection, and she would like some photos. Naturally Rose agreed. Séra told Rose to let her know how she wanted to get there, by car which would take about four hours, or by train that would take just over two hours. Rose said she was happy to drive, as she could take extra things. Séra said she would arrange everything. Rose couldn't wait for the weekend. It was JP's birthday, on the Sunday, and their first wedding anniversary. She just hoped he liked his present. The day arrived and – nothing. JP had phoned Friday night to say the plans already in place, for the President's visit to Italy, all had to be changed at the last moment. Rose could understand that, and knew JP was probably annoyed, but she did think he might have sent some flowers or something for their anniversary. By Sunday, Rose had had enough. Throwing his present in the front of the car, she drove to the palace, and marched down to his office. The guard told her JP was with the President, so she waited in his office.

"Môn amour, is everything alright?" he asked as he kissed her cheek.

Rose replied, "Happy Birthday my love." JP thanked her and asked her if she'd like some coffee. "Do you not have anything to say to me, my love?" JP looked at her, blank. Rose was getting annoyed. "JP can you please put that bloody work to one side for a moment? It's your birthday and…?"

"Môn amour, can we discuss whatever it is later on? I am really busy."

That was it. Rose went ballistic. She went and closed his office door and rounding on JP, snapped, "Tell me, JP, who are you married to, me or your bloody President? Because from where I'm standing it sure as hell isn't me. It's our first wedding anniversary, JP, but obviously that means nothing to you. We had a lovely flat, here in the centre of Paris, where I could go and walk along the Seine, visit the shops, and see my uncle. Just because I said I loved the farmhouse, didn't mean you had to go out and buy the bloody thing, without asking me first. Yes, I do love the farmhouse, but be honest, it's in the middle of bloody nowhere, and at times I feel totally cut off from the outside world. My family are all here now, in Paris, and I never get to see them anymore. It's over an hour's drive to see my sisters, so they don't come over anymore and I don't go to them. I don't even see Ruby. Do you know how many times you've actually come home so far this year? No, well I'll tell you, four bloody times in six months. Your men all have every other weekend off, why can't you? I understand you're busy, but it's as though I don't exist anymore."

JP said, "Môn amour, I'm so—"

Rose put her hand up and said, "Please don't have the audacity to apologise to me. I should, more or less, be your number one priority. I'm going, but don't bother ringing me, as I am going to Nantes for Séra for a couple of days, and when I get back, no doubt you will have gone to Italy. Do have a good trip." As she walked towards the door, she threw his present on his desk and said, "Happy bloody anniversary, and as far as I'm concerned YOU CAN GO TO BLOODY HELL AND BACK." Rose slammed his door so hard, the coffee cup on his desk rattled. As she walked furiously down the corridor, with tears streaming down her face, little did she know the President's wife had overheard everything, and felt for her.

CHAPTER 21

Back at the farmhouse, Rose curled up into one of the armchairs and literally cried herself to sleep. When she woke she went and made herself some sandwiches and a mug of coffee. Three times the phone had rung and she ignored it. Meanwhile at the palace, after Rose had left, JP swiped his hand over his desk and everything went flying. He told the guard under no circumstances was he to be disturbed. The guard understood, as unfortunately he had overheard the argument. JP locked his door and went into his bedroom and paced up and down. He had seen Rose upset, torn to shreds, vulnerable, but never had he seen her as furious as when she left. He knew she was right, but how could he mend the rift that was now between them? He desperately wanted to go home, but he had phoned Rose three times and got no reply. Maybe she had gone to her parents' or uncle's.

Later on there was a knock at the door. "Boss, it's Andre." JP opened the door and Andre was stunned at the state of JP's office. "Got fed up with the paperwork, did you?"

JP replied, "No, I forgot an important day."

Andre looked at him and said, "Please don't tell me you forgot?" JP nodded. "Boss, how could you forget your wedding anniversary?"

"I've just been so wrapped up in everything else, like my birthday, it just slipped my mind, and now Rose has told me to go to hell and back. I've tried phoning but there's no reply."

Andre patted JP's shoulder and said, "Best leave her tonight, but ring her tomorrow."

JP replied, "I can't as she's going to Nantes for Séra, and she comes back the day we go to Italy."

Andre said, "I forgot my wedding anniversary one year, and it was a week before Gabrielle spoke to me again. I always remember my papa saying, 'Never ever go to sleep on an argument. Always make up.' Now, let's get this mess cleared up." Between them, soon all the paperwork was back neatly on JP's desk. After Andre had left, JP opened his present. It was an album of Rose in different poses and outfits around the house. He smiled at the one of her in the kitchen in his apron. It was a wonderful present, but now he felt wretched. Everything she said had been true, and now he wished himself to hell and back.

The following morning Rose was up early and packed her case. By 7am she was on the road to Nantes. She stopped off at Chartres, where she had some breakfast, and then drove to Nantes via Le Mans and Angers. She found the hotel where Séra had booked her in, and it was also where the fashion show was being held. Once she was checked in, she decided to go and have a look around the town. Some of the streets were narrow, but there were plenty of shops, cafés and restaurants. She had picked up some leaflets, which she now read. Nantes was only fifty kilometres from the Atlantic Coast. Nantes and Bordeaux shared positions at the mouth of the estuary of the Loire River, which was tidal because of the dredging done for the large ships to access the port. There were two tributaries that joined the Loire, the Erdre from the north bank and the Sèvre Nantaise from the south bank. On the Erdre was Versailles Island, which a couple of years before had been changed into a Japanese garden. In Nantes, there were over a hundred parks and gardens, with the oldest created in 1807, and over a hundred and twenty monuments historiques. In the old town of Nantes were the remains of a third-century Roman wall, and a chapel that dated back to 510. On the Loire River was Ile de Nantes. There were also several museums and some lovely looking beaches. Rose decided she might stay an extra couple of days to explore. At least that was better than staying home on her own. She would have to ask Séra.

The next couple of days Rose attended the fashion show. Some of the designs were unbelievable, and she would be very surprised if Séra reproduced them. She certainly wouldn't wear them. Some of the models looked like they were wearing huge triangles or circles in bright bold colours. The evening gowns, however, were spectacular. When it was over, Rose phoned Séra, who told her to stay, if she wanted to, until after the weekend. Rose had a wonderful day exploring the gardens and parks. She drove out of Nantes and found the beaches, and sunbathed the last two days. Rose always felt better when she had a tan.

Early Sunday morning she left Nantes, feeling refreshed and was now ready to sort things out with JP. By midday she was back home. She unpacked her case, put the films on the hall table ready for the morning. She phoned JP but there was no reply. Going into the kitchen she made herself a coffee, and as she was deciding what to eat, she turned the radio on. The announcer said, "This next bit of news is very difficult for me to read. We can now confirm, with the permission from the palace, that the President's plane has crashed somewhere over the mountainous region between Italy and France, on Friday. Rescue planes are already out searching, and the acting President is governing the country. On board with the President were his two aides, and his five bodyguards. This is now an international breaking story and we will keep reports coming to you as we are advised. A very sad day for France." The coffee mug in Rose's hand crashed down on to the floor, and the floor came up to meet Rose as she fainted, just missing hitting her head on the kitchen table.

Rose faintly heard the phone ringing, and got up slowly. The room spun for a few seconds and then her head cleared. She rushed to the phone. "JP, is that you?" she asked.

"Rose, it's Mum. Just to let you know we are on our way over, with Ruby. Hold on, Rose, were coming." Rose dropped the phone and slid down the wall as her heart broke.

"Rose, Rose, come on my dear, come into the sitting room."

Rose looked up to see her uncle helping her up and steadying her as she walked into the sitting room. Her dad was there comforting Ruby. Ruby went to Rose and they clung to each other like they had never done before. Both of them were grief stricken. Monica came in with a tray of tea and coffee, and gave a mug of coffee each to Rose and Ruby laced with brandy.

The phone rang again, and George went to answer it. "That was

Raoul from the village, saying if there's anything any of them can do, you only have to ask."

Rose just nodded and said through her sobs, "This… this is all my fault."

Hugh took her hands and said, "How can it be your fault, my dear?"

Rose replied, "You… you… don't understand. JP… JP and I had a blazing row last Sunday, and I… I told him to go… to go to hell and back. I didn't phone him to say how sorry I was, and now I… I might never be able to."

Monica wrapped her arms around Rose and said, "You can apologise when you see him. It couldn't have been that bad, as you're so close to each other. It's normal to argue. Dad and I have had many."

Rose sniffled and said, "He forgot our first wedding anniversary, and he hardly comes home. I told him I wanted to move back to Paris, as I feel cut off from everyone. I'm so sorry, JP, I'm so sorry." And with that Rose burst into tears again. Monica just held her.

The phone rang quite a few times and either George or Hugh answered it. Mathieu, Séra, Suzette, Gérard all phoned, deeply concerned. Eventually Rose and Ruby fell asleep on the settee cuddled up to each other. Monica found the spare duvets and covered them both. Rose woke in the middle of the night, and quietly walked round the farmhouse. She held JP's kitchen apron close to her, touched his favourite mug. She went up to the bedroom and opened his wardrobe. Taking one of his shirts out, she could still faintly smell his scent on it. She put it on and laid down on the bed. JP immediately appeared before her and she felt his arms go around her, and he kissed her gently.

Quietly he said, "Je t'aimerai toujours, même quand je suis parti. Au revoir, môn amour."

Rose screamed, "No JP, please don't leave me. JP. JP."

Monica came running into the bedroom and said, "It's alright, Rose, you were dreaming."

"No Mum, I wasn't. JP was here and he told me he would always love me, even when he's gone, and then he said his goodbye to me."

Ruby, Hugh and George had entered the bedroom and Rose saw Hugh and said, "Why, Uncle? Why JP and his men?"

Hugh sat on the bed and motioned for Ruby to sit with him. Hugh put his arms round both of them and said, "This is going to sound harsh and unfeeling, but it's not. You must both pull yourselves together. All we know is that the plane has crashed, and no deaths have yet been reported. Look how many planes have crashed and all had survivors. Until the plane is found, you must both believe they are all alive, and will be rescued."

Rose replied, "I know he's gone, Uncle, because I don't feel his heart beating with mine anymore."

Hugh kissed her cheek and said, "Now tomorrow why don't we go to the palace, where everything is being co-ordinated from? Pierre can bring us up to date."

Rose looked at him startled and said, "Pierre? What, our Pierre?"

Monica said, "Yes, our Pierre. It's more sad news to tell you. Emilie was expecting, but they were going to keep quiet until after the three-month scan. Emilie was rushed into hospital last Monday, with dreadful stomach pains and sadly she miscarried. I was glad I was there to be with her. JP told Pierre he had to stay and look after the children until Emilie was better. Poirot went instead."

Ruby said, "They have to live for Pierre, or he will never be the same man again."

Suddenly, Rose's stomach grumbled badly. "Sorry, I haven't eaten since yesterday."

George said, "It's coming up 6am. If I cooked a breakfast, depending on what you've got in, Rose, would it be eaten?" They all nodded. George washed and dressed and went down to the kitchen. Luckily he found bacon and sausages in the deep freeze. There were plenty of eggs and bread. Looking in the larder he found some tomatoes. Half an hour later, everyone had washed and dressed and were sitting round the kitchen table. Rose made the tea and coffees, and did the toast. George then put bacon, sausage, eggs, grilled tomatoes, fried bread and baked beans on the plates. None of them had felt hungry, but the plates looked like they had been licked clean.

About 10am they arrived at the palace. The first person they saw was the President's wife and their son, both consumed with grief. The ladies curtsied and the men bowed. "Rose, I'm so sorry. I pray they will all be found safe and sound and soon."

Rose went to her and taking her hands said, "As do we, and for your husband as well." Bending down she looked at Rémi and said, "Hello Rémi, do you remember me?"

Rémi replied, "Yes, you're Rose. You took my photo."

"That's right. Now I hope you are looking after your maman at this sad time, and if you need anything you only have to ask. I will be in JP's office." Rémi nodded and Rose kissed his tear-stained face.

"Thank you Rose," said Alicía, "and please don't hesitate to come to my private quarters if you need someone to talk to." They all curtsied and bowed as Alicía and Rémi left them.

When Rose walked into JP's office, it was a hive of activity. JP's desk had been cleared and a huge map was laid on it. Around it were four bodyguards discussing various routes. At the back of the office were four more tables with more bodyguards talking over radios. JP's bedroom door was closed. "Rose, Ruby," said Pierre as he walked in the door. Both of them went to him and he hugged them so tight, and kissed their cheeks.

"Sorry about…" said Rose.

"Just one of those things. It's happened before, but we have more important matters to attend to. How dare they have an accident and me not be with them. Just wait until they get back." Rose actually laughed, and the rest of them smiled. They knew Pierre was as heartbroken as they were, but were encouraged by his humour.

"Let me explain what's going on, as I'm standing in for JP at the moment. You've probably gathered by the talk at the back, that they are in communication with the rescue planes, from France and Italy. Other countries have also said they will help with the rescue as well. The map here is the supposed plane route and where we lost contact. As you can see it's a huge area and the last known position of the plane was here," said Pierre, pointing out the spot. "We have no idea where the pilot flew after that. This whole area is full of mountains, forests and rivers. Because of the high mountains, it's very difficult for the rescue planes to fly down to check the lower areas. The good news is Italian helicopters are now assisting. All we can do is pray and hope we find them soon."

Rose asked Pierre, "Can I stay here, in JP's bedroom? I just want to be near him, if that makes sense."

Pierre replied, "Of course you can, but the men will be in here at first light, so they might wake you up, although JP's room is more or less soundproofed. Operations close down once it's dark. I'd like your company as well, and that goes for all of you. You can all stay in the house if you want to."

Hugh, Monica and George thanked him and replied they were only a small drive away, and unfortunately, they had to work. Ruby said she would come every day after work. She needed to keep herself busy.

"Pierre do you remember Raoul, who used to be a bodyguard?" asked Rose. Pierre laughed and said he did, and asked Rose why. "He owns the pub in the village and wanted to know if there was anything any of them could do to help."

Pierre thought for a minute and then said, "Yes there is. He used to be a damn good tracker. Can you ask him to come here?" Rose said she needed to go to the farmhouse to get clothes, etc., and would bring him back with her.

Meanwhile, in an extremely deep ravine, covered by trees and plant life, there was the wreckage of a burnt-out plane, but there were no signs of life.

CHAPTER 22

Four black limousines drove back to the airport. In the first one was the President, along with his two aides, and JP sitting at the side of the driver. The limousine behind had Andre, Donatien, Antoine and Poirot in it. The other two contained Italian police and other bodyguards. Soon the cars drew up at the side of the private jet. JP's men got out and checked the jet, and surrounding area. Everything was secure. Once inside, the President sat in one of the four seats facing each other. The two aides sat with him, and the other seat was for JP. Andre, Donatien, Antoine and Poirot sat behind the President on single seats, either side of the aisle. At the back, were the galley and the toilet. JP went and checked with the pilot, called Benoit, to confirm the weather would be good all the way back to Paris. Benoit replied that everything looked good for flying. JP went back and informed the President. After Benoit had done more checks, he taxied onto the runway, awaiting instructions from air traffic control to take off. Ten minutes later and they were airborne. The President said, "Gentlemen, I would just like to say a huge thank you to you, for giving up your weekends to ensure my safety, and the routes to take. I do understand all the security that goes into these visits. My wife, bless her, had a rather large word in my ear, especially where you are concerned, JP."

JP looked at the President with a blank look. "When we get back, I have decided to take the month of August off, as at the moment, my diary is clear. I need to spend time with my wife and son. Therefore, I hereby agree to the four of you, sorry Poirot, also taking the month off, and that includes Pierre as well." JP and his men thanked him, but JP did say that it was their job to guard and protect him at all times. "Antoine, do we have anything to eat and drink?" asked the President.

Antoine went to look in the galley and came back, saying, "Benoit must have known, Monsieur le President. There is a selection of salads, sandwiches, pastries, wine and a bottle of champagne." JP pulled out the tables from the side panel and unfolded it for each of them.

"Excellent," said the President, and opened the champagne, and poured it into eight glasses. The pilot didn't drink alcohol. "Gentlemen, to many more successful trips," said the President and they all raised their glasses. Antoine then put the food on the individual tables.

About an hour later, JP was looking out of the window, thinking about where to take Rose, if she could get the time off, when he saw a flash, and noticed the clouds had gone from white to grey-black. He went into the cockpit and asked Benoit if a storm was brewing. "When I checked before we left, JP, there were no storms forecasted. Unfortunately we are going over a high mountainous region and as you can see, a storm is about to hit us. The trouble is these storms come from nowhere, with no warning. I have tried to call both air traffic controllers for advice to change the flight path, but I'm getting no reply. If my memory serves me right, between the borders is a ten-kilometre dead zone. I'll try and go above the storm, but can you let everyone know it might be an idea to buckle up, as there will be turbulence." JP went back and made the announcement. Quickly Antoine and Andre cleared all the dishes and glasses, folded the tables and put them back in the side panel, lashed everything down and stowed anything else in the secured lockers. Once they were happy, everyone secured their seatbelts. Suddenly the plane started rocking violently from side to side, and JP noticed Poirot and the two aides had paled. He could see the flashes of lightning were getting closer, and knew Benoit had climbed, but this was a storm that was going to get much worse. The plane dived and then came level again.

Benoit came over the intercom. "Apologies, Monsieur le President, and everyone else. This storm was not forecasted, and I'm trying to avoid the worst of it, hence the plane diving and levelling again. I'm going to release the oxygen masks and suggest you put them on. Hopefully we will be out of it very soon."

There was a small bang, and Andre looked out of the window at the wing, and catching JP's eye mouthed, "Lightning hit," pointing out at the right wing.

JP went and looked, and then looking at Andre shook his head and said quietly, "That's not good." JP then made sure everyone had their oxygen masks on properly, and he also gave words of comfort to the two aides. He had just sat down when there was an almighty bang. JP looked out of the window and could see the problem and knew what was about to happen, and said calmly, "Everyone prepare for a crash landing. Men, you know the procedures. Donatien, can you grab those cushions and hand them to me?" Donatien handed the three cushions to JP. "Monsieur le President, put these two either side of you, and the other put on your knees and rest your head on it." JP went back to a spare seat at the front and buckled up, just as the plane started to spiral downwards. He saw the plane skim the water and then the trees rushing towards them. Just before he put his oxygen mask on he said, "Heads down and crash positions everyone. We're in Gods' hands now." At that moment all the electrics went off, plunging the plane into total darkness. JP's last thoughts were of Rose. *"Je t'aimerai toujours, même quand je suis parti. Au revoir, môn amour."*

Meanwhile, Benoit was doing his best to level out the spiralling plane to an area where he might be able to land better. "Mayday, mayday, mayday. This is flight POF101. Please respond." Benoit was calling for help the whole time, but got no reply. The lightning had hit the fuel tank, which had exploded, and he could see the flames, and now the electrics went out, which included the radio, and the landing gear. All the controls were dead. He was flying blind. The ground was coming up too quickly, but at the last minute he managed to level the plane. He saw a large lake and skimmed the plane over it. All around were trees and that's what he crashed into. The plane bounced as it hit the trees, knocking it from side to side, and up and down. He heard the plane breaking up. Straight ahead the trees were getting denser and denser. The wings of the plane were taking a real battering, and then sheared off. He heard a huge noise and knew the plane had split in two parts. The last thing Benoit saw was the rock straight in front of him, and he prayed.

***

Porte had driven Rose home to pack her cases, and lock the farmhouse up properly, including putting the alarm on. She phoned Raoul, who sorted out who was going to run the pub, and then walked up to the farmhouse. He shook hands with Porte, and hugged Rose, asking her how she was. Rose replied, "Better now I'm staying at the palace."

An hour later and they were back at the palace.

"Well, well, if it isn't me old mate," said Pierre as he saw Raoul. They hugged each other like long-lost brothers.

Rose went off into JP's bedroom and unpacked her cases. His spare suits, shirts, etc., were all hung up. *Come back to me my love, please,* she said quietly to herself, and her tears fell. She wiped them away and went into his office. Pierre was showing Raoul the area, and Rose could see Raoul's mind thinking about everything.

"Rose, you hungry?" asked Pierre. Rose shook her head. "Good, you can come and watch me eat then. Raoul, do you want to stay or come with us?" Raoul said he would eat later. Pierre put Rose's arm through his as they walked back to the bodyguards' house. In the dining room, about six other bodyguards were there, and they all greeted Rose. She had met them at the wedding. A couple of guards brought in the first course of salad, which went down well. This was followed by steaks, mushrooms, tomatoes, steak chips, and onion rings. The dessert was fruit salad with ice cream, followed by cheese and biscuits with pots of coffee. Rose ate as much as she could, and Pierre was pleased. He was her protector now, along with Gabrielle, Celeste and Ruby's, until JP and the rest of them returned. Once the meal was finished, Pierre whispered something to Porte, who smiled and left.

Pierre had the bodyguards laughing at his jokes, trying to keep things as normal as possible. He checked who was on surveillance, and told them to look out for stray journalists, trying to gain entrance. Any trouble and they were to contact him straight away. All the bodyguards had noticed how Pierre had assumed control, and were pleased. He was the one person they needed at the moment, but they were also keeping a close eye on him. With Emilie losing the baby and now his best friends missing, maybe dead, they knew he would crack, but they would be there for him when he did.

Pierre escorted Rose back to JP's office, where they found Raoul studying the map of the area, writing away on a pad. Raoul had lots of questions to ask Pierre, and so Rose went into the bedroom. She was stunned to see a television had arrived. A little later Pierre said, "Thought you might want to watch something to take your mind off the situation. Hopefully it might help." Rose put her arms around Pierre, sort of, and thanked him.

By 10pm the office was clear and all was quiet. Rose walked round the desk looking at the map, and saw there were criss-crossed lines over one part of it. She closed the office door, and went into the bedroom, locking the door behind her. A huge clear moon lit up the room, and standing by the window in the rays of the moonlight, her tears fell down her cheeks wondering if JP and his men, along with the President were alive. She didn't want to think of the consequences if they weren't.

Very early in the morning, Rose heard voices and knew communications had resumed. There was nothing she could do, so she stayed cuddled into one of the pillows. About 8am, she washed and dressed and went out into the office, saying, "Bonjour," to everyone. The men all smiled and acknowledged her. Rose walked down the corridor to go to the house for some breakfast. Raoul and Pierre were there deep in conversation. They both stood and hugged and kissed Rose's cheek, as she did them.

"Gascon, fresh croissants, baguettes etc., and coffee please," asked Pierre.

The smell of the freshly baked croissants made Rose's stomach grumble, and she blushed. Pierre and Raoul smiled. The three of them tucked into the breakfast and then Rose asked, "What happens now, about the rescue?"

Raoul explained. "We have to double check the flight path that Benoit was given. Next we find out when the plane disappeared from the radar, from either the Italian or French air traffic controllers. The plane would disappear from the radar if it fell at extremely high speed. Once that is established it will give us a clearer picture. We also need to check the weather conditions. On board is what is called an emergency locator transmitter. This will send out a transmission, unless it cut out when the plane crashed. We know the aircraft had been checked thoroughly before leaving France and Italy. Benoit is a very experienced pilot, and has been with the President for a long time, and would have made all the plane checks before he taxied to the runway.

"The area it has gone down in is a very mountainous region, with lots of forests, which is going to hamper the location. If, and I say if, the plane caught fire the area is also a little bit like a rain forest, and the fire could have burnt out quickly, leaving only minor damage to the crash site from the air. Forests are strange places. Soon tree branches will close over the wreckage, making it really difficult to locate any debris. When we do get a location, then land rescue teams will be sent out, probably parachuting them in. Rose, please don't give up hope. JP, and all of us, have had extensive training for a situation like this."

Rose replied, "How on earth can you train for a plane crash?"

Raoul looked at Pierre, who said, "Come with me." They went back into the palace, and went down stairs she had never been down before. "This is the Blue Room, where the President has his private meetings with the dignitaries," said Pierre. They walked to the end of the corridor, where there was a lift. They went down another three floors. When Rose walked out of the lift, she had the shock of her life. In front of her was a huge pool, with half a small plane hanging from the ceiling. At the side was a ladder lift that went up to the plane. "This is where we train, Rose," said Pierre. "The plane is a simulator, and we go through all sorts of situations. I would show you, but that would be rather insensitive at the moment. If I press this button the pool is covered and land appears."

Rose was intrigued. "I'd like to go up, Pierre." Pierre nodded and pressed the down button of the ladder lift.

A couple of minutes later they were inside the simulator. "How does it work?" asked Rose.

Pierre replied, "Only JP and Andre know the programmes. We go through bad turbulence, with the plane bouncing all over the places, along with it going up and down. We learn crash positions, and how to help each other. Depending on the situation, we have to jump out of the plane and land on either the land or in the pool. As you can see we have a life raft, and pretend parachutes. Every three months we jump out of a proper plane, over land and sea to make it more realistic. I remember the first time I did it in here, and due to the motion I was as sick as a pig. Long time ago, that was."

Rose heard Pierre's voice crack slightly and looked at Raoul, who said, "Time to get back to reality, you two."

Soon they were back in JP's office. Porte told Pierre they had received the flight route and the last known position of the plane from the Italian air traffic controllers. "We have a problem," said Porte. Pointing at the map, Rose saw two red lines had been drawn. "Between these two points, which is about ten kilometres, due to the mountains, it's known as a dead zone. Once Benoit flew into it, the air traffic controllers lost contact. France would have picked them up once they cleared it, but they never did clear it. We have also been advised that there was a dreadful thunder and lightning storm that came from nowhere."

Pierre replied, "Well at least now we've got an area where they were."

Raoul asked Porte if he could find out how much fuel was on board. Porte already had it, and Raoul started writing figures down. After about an hour, Raoul had circled an area. "Pierre, do we have a much more detailed map just of this area?" Pierre said they didn't. Raoul rushed off saying he'd be back soon.

CHAPTER 23

It was nearly 11am, when two of the kitchen staff arrived with trays of pastries and pots of coffee. Rose could see the men talking to the rescue teams were getting downhearted. Every report was "no sightings". She went and put her hand on each of their shoulders and gave them words of encouragement. Pierre smiled at Rose's strength. Little did he know Rose was broken in two, but was determined not to show it.

It was another hour before Raoul came back with the map he wanted. This map showed the mountains, forests, rivers, lakes and streams in a lot more detail. Raoul was again busy with his figures and measuring things on the map. Eventually he said, "Tell the rescue teams to fly over this area," and gave the coordinates to the four men. "I've worked out that if the storm hit them roughly here, and I'm going to assume lightning hit the plane, which would make it spiral, and if I remember Benoit, he would try his damnedest to level that plane out. Look at the size of this lake. Now if I was the pilot I'd head for that lake. I'm hoping they're around here somewhere. Pierre, helicopters would be better for this terrain."

Pierre went off and came back a short while later. "Helicopters from Hauteville and Beaueville are being sent. They are just over twenty kilometres away from that area." Now it was a waiting game.

The next couple of days came and went with no success. Friday morning, Pierre gathered everyone round, including Rose and said, "I have some bad news. Due to the weather conditions in the area, the search has been called off until it improves. The mountain mist has come down thick and fast, along with storms, making it impossible for the helicopters to fly. I will keep you all informed."

Rose couldn't believe it. "Surely there's something we can do, Pierre?"

Pierre replied, "We could send out scouting parties, but until they find the plane, the teams could be searching in the wrong location's. Rose can I make a suggestion?" Rose nodded. "I understand you want to be here, but what about your job and the farmhouse?"

Rose had been thinking about work, and perhaps Ruby had the best idea. Working would take her mind off the search. "I can't believe it's only a week, as it feels like months. You promise me, even the slightest bit of news, you'll ring me, day or night?" Pierre promised, and Rose went back to the farmhouse that afternoon. Once home she phoned Ruby, Céleste, Gabrielle and Emilie, and arranged for them to come over the following day. She noticed the film rolls on the hall table. They had completely escaped her mind. The farmhouse was very quiet, but Rose found she could relax. Not only that, daft as it sounded, she felt JP was there with her.

In the morning she drove to Jules and dropped the films off, and then she went food shopping. Once back home, she arranged the food on plates, which she put on the kitchen table and covered it over. Rose opened the windows to let the fresh air blow through, as the farmhouse was a bit stuffy. Soon Ruby's car came down the driveway. Rose went out to meet her and was surprised to see Céleste, Gabrielle and Emilie with her. "Saw these three hitch hiking," said Ruby as she hugged Rose.

Rose smiled and greeted each one of them. "I'm so sorry Emilie," and gave her an extra hug. "Coffee everyone?" They all nodded, and Rose said they could either sit in the kitchen, sitting room or garden. They all agreed on the kitchen. "How are you all, and the children?" asked Rose.

Gabrielle replied, "Exactly the same as you, Rose, and the children understand, hard as it is."

"Is there any more news, Rose?" asked Céleste. Rose told them all that she knew.

Gabrielle said, "I'm going to say this, because I can. I know in my heart that they're alive. Benoit maybe not, but with all the training JP puts them through, they are all survivors."

"I'll drink to that," said Ruby and they all toasted with their mugs of coffee.

The rest of the day they all talked about their men, and laughed and cried. They all totally relaxed and ate a lovely meal. About 4pm, Ruby said they had better start getting back. Rose was hoping they might stay, but the children were with Céleste's parents. Rose promised she would stay in touch with them.

Sunday, Rose cleaned the farmhouse top to bottom, did all the washing, which soon dried in the sun, ironed and put everything away. After a sleepless week, that night Rose slept well, dreaming of JP. Monday morning Rose drove to the château. The whole team embraced her and said they were there for her. Rose thanked them. Séra had seen Rose drive up and rushed out. "Rose, have they found them? Please say yes."

Rose shook her head, and brought them up to date. "I don't know what's been said on the television or radio, because I won't have them on," said Rose.

Séra replied, "There's nothing. The acting President has put a total blackout on any reports, until they've been found. If anyone is found reporting on the situation, without his permission, then the gendarme will arrest them immediately." Rose didn't know about that, but she was pleased. "Now Rose, the Paris fashion show, this year, is the first week of September. I am taking Suzette away with me next week to do a fashion show in London, just in case…" Rose understood. "I see what you mean about the fashion show at Nantes. My god, I wouldn't be seen dead in some of those creations."

Séra suddenly realised what she had said. "Oh Rose, my apologies. That was so insensitive." Rose smiled and said it wasn't a problem. Séra said, "Today, the photo shoot is just with the children, and I know they are looking forward to seeing you back."

Suddenly four children came running across the lawns and hugged Rose so tight. "We're sorry about your husband and his friends, but we are praying for them every night."

Rose thanked them and turned her head away as her eyes filled with tears. Séra hugged her and whispered, "Now you know how much all of us love you. You sure you want to work?" Rose nodded.

The photo shoot was out in the château's gardens, and Rose and the children had a wonderful time. It only seemed like she'd just arrived, and now it was time to go home.

Rose had just got home, when the phone rang. It was her mum and dad making sure she was alright. She told them she was fine and back at work. Ruby also phoned later on and then her uncle. She then phoned Pierre, who said everyone was getting frustrated with the weather conditions, but it could go as quickly as it came, they just had to wait. They didn't have to wait long. That Friday, two weeks after the plane had crashed, the sun rose over the mountains, the rain stopped and the mist blew away. At 6am that morning, four helicopters flew to the coordinates given by Raoul. They searched until their fuel was getting low, and then were replaced by four other helicopters, whilst they went back and re-fuelled and rested. This was done until 8pm that night – nothing. This process carried on for the next couple of days – but nothing was visible. Raoul went back to the drawing board and re-calculated his figures. Each time he came back to the same conclusion. Then there was a small, but significant, break through. A month after the plane had crashed, word came in that an eyewitness, who had been climbing one of the mountains, had seen the plane spiralling down. It had taken him all that time to get back to civilisation. He was flown immediately to the palace. He showed Raoul on the map where he had been climbing, and Raoul re-did his calculations. The helicopters were given different coordinates, but again nothing.

Raoul was now convinced that the forest was keeping the plane a closely guarded secret. "Pierre, I want to fly over the area. If we're going to find them, I need to put myself in Benoit's shoes. This is taking too long." Pierre nodded and said he'd be back. Pierre went to see the acting President, Monsieur Bourjôn, who was with the President's wife. They both listened to his request and Monsieur Bourjôn sanctioned it. Within three hours they landed at Hauteville airport. A light aircraft was waiting for them. An hour later they were in the air.

Raoul flew over the mountains to the start of the dead zone, but this time there were two helicopters following. "Pierre you might not like this, but I've got to simulate what the President's plane went through." Pierre nodded, knowing what was coming. Raoul told the helicopter pilots not to be alarmed, as he knew what he was doing. Thank heavens he had kept up flying since he left his job at the palace. Raoul turned the plane, and looked around him. Then he pretended a storm was about to hit. He tilted the plane left and right and dived and levelled. Pierre was watching the path on the instruments and drawing on the map. "Hold on, Pierre, it's spiral time." Raoul put the plane into a dive, but being careful he didn't stall the engine. Then he levelled out and they saw the lake in front of them.

Raoul went as low as he could and Pierre had his eyes everywhere. "This is impossible," he said.

Suddenly one of the helicopter pilots said, "Helicopter 2 to FR333. We have picked something up on the radar, about 2 kilometres east of where you are."

Raoul changed course and flew over the area. The helicopters were below them.

"Helicopter 2 to FR333. We can see the tail of the plane. Heaven knows where the front part is."

"Helicopter 1 to FR333, we can see the front of the plane. If anyone has survived that crash it will be a miracle. Suggest we return to base and make contingency plans."

"FR333 to Helicopters 1 and 2. Great work. Return to base."

Pierre then communicated with the palace. "FR333 to PALACE12. Do you read?"

"Yes Pierre. It's Porte. How's it going?"

Pierre replied, "Plane found. I repeat, plane found. No sign of life though. Can you advise the acting President?"

"Will do FR333, great news. Out."

Raoul landed the plane back at Hauteville, and once out both of them hugged each other. The helicopter pilots did the same. "Now all we have to do is somehow find them," said Raoul, "and that's tricky terrain."

Pierre and Raoul flew back to Paris. When they walked into JP's office, all the wives were there. Emilie went to Pierre and said, "Is it true? Have you found them?"

Pierre replied, "Please, everyone listen. We have only found the plane, nothing else. We need to work out for a start if they are still in the plane."

A voice behind him said, "I can help in that department." It was the acting President, and all the bodyguards bowed. Catching on as to who he was, the ladies went to curtsey. "Ladies, that privilege is for the President. I am the acting President, Monsieur Bourjôn, and I wish we could have met under better circumstances. Tomorrow at 5am, I have enlisted the help of a naval helicopter, which has thermal imaging installed. Pierre, I want you at the helicopter airport at 4.30am.

"You will fly in the helicopter to ensure they have the correct coordinates. Once at the site they will start scanning the area. If they're not in the plane, then the search will be extended around that area."

Rose asked, with a lump in her throat, "Will this thermal thingy show up dead bodies?"

Monsieur Bourjôn looked at her and said softly, "Yes in a roundabout way, but I would rather not go into that at the moment. My apologies, but I do not know who your husbands are." Rose told him, and then introduced the other wives. Looking at Pierre he said to report back to him as soon as he returned, with the images, and to speak to no one. Monsieur Bourjôn then left.

Rose said, "Ladies, seeing as it's Saturday tomorrow, how about we all meet up, have lunch and then come back to the palace, for the news, good or bad?" They all agreed, if they could get babysitters. Rose said she wouldn't leave the farmhouse until just after midday, so they could ring if they couldn't make it. They all left and it was gone 9pm when Rose got back home. She had a quick bite to eat and a drink, and then switched the television on, expecting to see news about the crash, but there was nothing. That night when she was in bed, she cuddled up to JP's pillow. Tomorrow they would all know if their husbands were dead or alive.

Pierre arrived at the helicopter airport at 4am, just as the naval helicopter was landing. The two pilots got out and introduced themselves as Stéphane and Marc. They all went into the airport and grabbed a quick breakfast. 4.45am they were all strapped in the helicopter. Clearance was given and up they went, but then Pierre was surprised at how quickly the helicopter flew. Instead of three hours, they were at Hauteville in two hours. They quickly re-fuelled and took off again. Soon they were over the crash site.

Marc explained to Pierre about the images he could see on the screen. "These two long grey areas are the plane. Now if anyone is inside it will come up in a different colour. The front part of the plane shows a bright image. Sorry Pierre, but that's the body of the pilot. He didn't make it. There is also one more body in the tail of the plane. So we're still looking for seven others. Stéphane, widen the search please." The pilot nodded.

"How do you know those two are dead?" asked Pierre.

"As you can see on the screen the image is orange. When death occurs, insects, mainly blow flies take over, and they generate a higher body temperature." Pierre nodded in understanding. "Marc, we'll need to refuel soon."

"Okay, back to Hauteville," said Marc.

An hour later they were back. "Stéphane can you get any lower in to that small area, the other side of the plane?"

"I'll try, Marc, but there's a wind blowing up. Pierre, make sure you're buckled in safely."

Slowly the helicopter went down. Suddenly Marc said, "Got them. There they are." Marc dragged two bags to the edge of the door, and slowly opened it a little bit. "Stéphane can you get right over them, and I'll drop these bags." Stéphane was right above them and hovered, whilst Marc pushed out the two bags. "They're provisions and two walkie talkies. Once they get them we can talk to them."

"Marc, I need to go up now." Marc nodded.

Pierre watched as the two parachutes on the bags opened and slowly fell towards the survivors. Marc said, "Pierre you need to know two of them are dead, and the other five are severely injured, looking at these images. See these blue areas on their bodies? That's really bad news. We need to get them out of there as soon as possible. Two have lost a lot of blood. When we get back to Hauteville, I'm going to ring my boss and tell him we need a transport plane with parachutists out here immediately. Doctors and nurses will also be on board, with full medical teams." Pierre said he would phone the palace.

"Marc, sorry, we need to leave. Look at that storm coming in."

"Blast," said Marc. "That's the last thing they need. Okay Stéphane, off you go."

CHAPTER 24

Back at Hauteville, the sun was shining, with no sign of a storm. Marc and Pierre went off to make their phone calls. When Pierre got through to the palace, it was Porte who answered. "Porte, I need a secure line to the acting President." Porte put him through.

"Pierre, what news?"

Pierre replied, "Five alive, but Benoit and three others are dead."

"How are they faring?" Pierre replied that the five of them were severely injured and relayed what Marc had told him.

At that moment the other phone rang. "Pierre, stay on the line please." The other phone call was about the transport plane and who would be involved. Monsieur Bourjôn agreed and for the rescue to go ahead as soon as it was safe. "Pierre, I have just given permission for the transport plane etc. Do you know how badly hurt the President is?"

Pierre replied, "No. We couldn't to talk to any of them, so we don't know which five survived."

Rose and the other wives had met for lunch and were joined by Hugh and Chantelle along with Monica and George. They all got to the palace about 4pm. Emilie asked Porte if Pierre was back. Porte replied he wasn't. At that moment Monsieur Bourjôn walked in. Porte and the other men bowed. "Ladies, gentlemen, I have some news. As you know we located the plane, which is in two halves. Alas, the pilot and one other person died on board. After a local search, I can say the other seven were found, but two of them have also died. The other five are severely injured. I'm sorry, but at the moment until the rescue teams get to them, no one knows who has survived." The office fell silent, for some time.

***

JP slowly opened his eyes, and wondered where on earth he was. He was lying face down in the dirt, with something heavy on his back. He tried to move but couldn't and screamed in agony. Then he remembered the crash. Slowly he lifted his head to see he was still strapped in his seat. With his left hand he unbuckled the belt, and pushed the seat away. He went to sit up, but the pain in his right shoulder nearly made him pass out. He knew his shoulder was dislocated, and by the feel of it he had broken ribs. Pain also shot up his left leg – his ankle was broken. Eventually, breathing heavily and sweating profusely, he managed to sit up. Looking round he saw the plane in two parts, and the wings were gone. The front of the plane was totally smashed into a huge rock. JP knew Benoit wouldn't have survived, and felt so sad for his friend. It was Benoit who had urged him to take up flying the helicopter. He felt tears trickle down his face, and wiped them away. He had to get to the tail plane and see how the President, and his men were.

"Can anyone hear me?" he shouted as loudly as he could. Nothing. He dragged himself across the ground, until he got to the tail of the plane. With his left hand he pulled himself inside. He could see none of them were moving. The President was slumped over, but one of the cushions was covered in blood. Antoine's leg was broken, with the bone jutting out. Blood was everywhere. Andre's head was at a strange angle, and Donatien had blood pouring from a head wound. One of the aides was dead. The other one just looked like he was asleep. Poirot was sprawled on the floor. JP dragged himself up to Poirot and checked him over. He was alive.

"Poirot, Poirot, can you hear me?"

A low moan came from Poirot, and he opened his eyes. "Boss, you OK?" JP replied he wasn't. Poirot tried to move and found he could, and sat up. At that moment the aide opened his eyes and moved. "Are we dead or alive?" he asked.

JP replied, "At the moment the three of us are alive. Are you hurt?" The aide said he didn't think anything was broken, just badly bruised. "What's your name?" asked JP. The aide replied it was Paul. "Paul, can you check to see if you're injured anywhere?" Paul stood up and said he was fine. JP then asked him if he could go outside and see if he could find a good sturdy branch for him to use as a crutch. Paul walked slowly off the plane and soon came back with just the thing.

Paul helped JP and Poirot stand up. JP went to the President and examined him. The President had a deep gash above his eye, with blood gushing out. "Poirot, can you see if you can find the first aid box." Poirot searched carefully, in case he disturbed anything that might come down on them. Eventually he spotted it outside the plane and brought it in. "Thanks," said JP. He cleaned up the President's wound and then looked for other injuries. None were visible, so JP wondered if he had internal injuries. Next he went to Antoine. His leg was a mess, and JP was glad he was unconscious, because of what he was going to do next with Poirot's help, but first he needed one of them to put his shoulder back in.

"Poirot, ever put a shoulder back in its socket before?" Poirot said he hadn't, but Paul said he had. "Good, then you know what to do," said JP.

Paul took a deep breath and said, "Ready?" JP nodded. Paul helped JP to lay flat on his back. Taking his hand he moved JP's arm slightly away from his body, and then pulled firmly until he heard a crack. JP screamed in agony, but once the shoulder was put back in, he felt relief. Paul made a sling from the dead aide's shirt. JP thanked him.

"We need to set Antoine's leg next. Paul, I will need splints, so can you make quite a few, as I don't know what other broken bones we've got. Poirot, can you see if there's any alcohol or water still intact." Suddenly Andre started moaning. "Andre, it's JP. Can you hear me?" Andre mumbled something. "Andre, listen to me. Whatever you do, don't move your head. I think your neck may be broken. Squeeze my hand if you understand."

Andre squeezed JP's hand and said, "Gabrielle always says I'm a pain in the neck."

JP laughed and replied, "At least you've still got your humour."

Andre said, "Always, boss. Always. How's everyone else?" JP told him. "Sorry about Benoit…" Andre had passed out.

JP then went to Donatien. Blood was pouring out from a head wound, but he was totally squashed into the side of the plane. JP then noticed something was sticking out of Donatien's leg. Poirot came back and said he'd found bottled water and half a bottle of brandy. "Great. We will need something to strap the splints together. Can you pull some of these cables down, but be careful. Sorry you're having to do all the work."

"Boss, you're injured yourself. I can't believe how you're managing to keep it all together and so calm."

JP smiled and replied, "Believe me, Poirot, I am far from calm, and the pain in my foot is unbearable, but the President and my men come first."

Paul came back with thick branches, which he had cleared of twigs and leaves.

JP went back to Antoine and poured a bit of the brandy over the wound. "Don't like the fact his bone is sticking out. I'll have to try and line it back up. Thank heavens he's unconscious." JP got Paul to straighten Antoine's leg as much as he could. Then he firmly pushed the bone back down. He again poured brandy over it, and then wrapped a shirt around the wound, after first putting some lint over it. With Poirot's help he put a splint both sides and then wrapped the strips of cable around them to keep the leg in place. "Paul, can you gently sit Antoine up so I can see what other injuries he's got?"

JP saw Antoine's right arm was broken, so between them they splinted that. JP was concerned about Antoine as he was feeling cold – he might have internal bleeding. "What's the weather like outside?"

"Sun's hot," replied Paul.

"Can you two lift Antoine out and place him in the sun carefully?" They both nodded. JP got out of the way and watched as they took him out. He dragged himself over to a bag and looked through it. Just what he needed – a pair of trousers. He rolled them up and then gently pulled on one of the dead cables hanging down and wrapped it round the roll, making a neck collar. He went to Andre and carefully wound it round his neck. "Poirot, can you very, very slowly bring Andre's head up?"

As Andre's head came up, JP adjusted the collar to give him the best support for his neck.

Andre opened his eyes and JP said, "Welcome back. How does your neck feel?"

"Sore," replied Andre, "along with my ribs."

"Same as me then," and they both smiled at each other. "Paul, can you help Andre outside, but watch his neck."

JP now had more room to manoeuvre. Poirot and Paul had come back.

"Right, the President's next."

"Monsieur le President, can you hear me?"

Much to JP's relief, the President replied, "Good to hear your voice, JP. How is everyone?"

JP replied, "At the moment I'm more concerned about you. Can you tell me what pain you've got? I've sort of dealt with the gash above your eye."

The President sat up and then said, "Oh, the pain in my hip."

JP unbuckled the President's belt and moved the cushion, and saw the belt had ripped through his side and could see his hip bone. The blood started to pour. "Need to stem this," said JP. "Paul, can you pass me the medical box? Thanks." Like with Antoine, JP poured the brandy over the wound.

"What a waste of good brandy," said the President.

"It's a good antiseptic, Monsieur le President. I'm going to put lint over the wound and I've just found some bandages, but I'll need you to stand up." The President tried but his hip was too painful, so Paul and Poirot helped him. JP wrapped the bandage round, but he knew the President had broken his hip. Again, Paul and Poirot helped him out of the plane. That left Donatien.

JP's shoulder was hurting and he knew he shouldn't have taken the sling off, but it was more a hindrance than a help. The gash on Donatien's head had stopped bleeding. JP could see his arms and legs were okay, but like all of them he was covered in bloody cuts and bruises.

Poirot came back to JP and said, "Boss, Antoine's with us now, and the three of them are talking. How's Donatien?"

JP replied, "What do you think this is?" He showed Poirot the bar sticking out of Donatien's leg.

"Let me look outside." Poirot saw the problem. "Boss, it's from the wing, and I don't think it will be a good idea to pull it out."

JP sighed and said, "Look Poirot, another three, maybe four hours, and it's going to be dark. There's no way in hell we can light a fire here. With the fuel, the whole area will go up, and us with it. We need to move away from the plane, and I'm not leaving Donatien."

"Understand, boss. Paul and I will go and have a look round and see what we can find. What about Donatien?"

JP replied, "I need to feel how far that bar is in his leg, but I need to get rid of some of this debris."

"Paul," shouted Poirot. Paul came rushing in. "Help us move all this, will you? The boss needs to sort out Donatien's leg." Half an hour later and JP had good access, and told them to go look around the area.

JP ripped Donatien's trousers, and gently prodded the area. Luckily the bar wasn't in that far. In the medical kit, JP found a scalpel. He got what was left of the brandy and poured half of it round the area. He then made four incisions round the bar, and then very gently tried to ease the bar out, hoping he didn't hit an artery. He didn't, and slowly the bar came out. Quickly JP poured the rest of the brandy on the wound, and then packed it with the last of the lint, and the last bandage.

"Come on, Donatien, come back to me."

A very faint voice said, "Thanks boss, that bloody well hurt, as much as my back."

JP smiled and said, "Well if you will go getting a bar in your leg, what do you expect?"

Donatien looked round and said, "The others, they're not...?" JP brought him up to speed.

Without thinking JP stood up and put weight on his broken ankle, and shouted out, "Bloody hell that hurt," and immediately fell down, hitting his head.

"Boss, boss, you okay?" called Donatien, greatly concerned. JP was out cold.

When he came round, Paul and Poirot were back, and moving Donatien. "What's going on?" he asked.

Poirot said, "We found a place away from the plane, and we've moved everyone there, and Donatien is the last, apart from you. Andre has got a fire going, and once we get you there, we'll build a shelter."

"I can walk, if you give me my crutch," said JP. Poirot raised his eyebrow, but knew not to argue with his boss.

JP said, "Can you both come back? We need to look round this area and see what, if anything, we can take with us." Whilst JP waited for them he hobbled round, and then spotted the fridge from the plane, along with some of the lockers over by the cockpit. Looking in the cockpit he could see Benoit's body in the tangled mess, and blood was everywhere. JP said a prayer for Benoit. Hobbling over to the fridge he saw the door was smashed open, and inside it were bottles full of water. In the lockers he found some blankets, a couple of pillows and another medical box.

"Boss, where are you?"

"Over here. Bring some bags." Poirot and Paul soon had about eight bags full of stuff.

"Boss, let's take you down first, as there's an incline and you'll need help. Then we'll come back and grab all this."

An hour later everything from the plane and all the men were at the camp. JP gave everyone a bottle of water, which was gratefully accepted. Poirot and Paul had found an excellent sheltered spot, under the trees, but to JP's delight, there was a small stream not far away. "Boss, now you've found another medical box, please can I bandage your ankle?" asked Poirot. JP agreed.

CHAPTER 25

"What's the outlook, JP?" asked the President.

JP replied, "Not good, Monsieur le President. Apart from Poirot and Paul, all of us have severe injuries. We have water, but no food. We are in the mountains and as we all saw, the weather can change dramatically. We need to keep warm and dry, or else dehydration and hypothermia is going to set in. Tomorrow, we can build a shelter from tree branches, which will hopefully keep us dry. Heaven knows how long it will be before we are rescued. I'm going to say it now, but there is a chance we might not be found. This is a very dense forest, but I'm going to do my damnedest to keep us all alive."

The President replied, "That good then?" to which everyone sort of laughed. "I see you found the fridge, did you find any of the cupboards from the galley? Benoit, God rest his soul, always had them packed with food?"

JP replied they hadn't, but he'd go back tomorrow and look.

Paul replied, "May I suggest I go back? You have attended to everyone and now you need to rest, Monsieur JP."

JP smiled and said, "Thank you, Paul, and it's just JP. Now we all need to rest. We found four blankets so as Rose would say, 'It's snuggle up time.'"

Paul and Poirot took it in turns to keep the fire going, and watch over them.

During the night, the forest was quiet and eerie with just the rustling of the trees, and the crackling of the fire. In the morning however, birds chirping awoke them. JP saw Paul had already left. With Poirot's help he stood up and checked the President and his men. What JP was really worried about now was infection setting into the wounds.

Andre collected twigs for the fire, trying not to bend down properly. JP saw Antoine grimacing and went to him. "Antoine, you in pain?" Antoine replied he was, but that wasn't his main concern – he needed to pee. Between JP and Poirot, they helped him up, and carried him to a tree, where he could relieve himself.

JP and Poirot then started breaking branches with long fronds. "Ideal for the roof," said JP. "Andre and Donatien, if we give you some branches, can you strip them of the leaves? You can put them on the fire." Both of them nodded. Within an hour they had more branches than they could cope with, so the President helped as well.

"What's the idea, JP?" asked the President.

"Well Monsieur le President, with those vines, we can tie the branches together and then, with a stone, bash them into the ground, in a semicircle. The branches with the large fronds can be attached to a large pole in the middle. Much like a tent, but with leaves."

At that moment, Paul came running back shouting something.

They all wondered what had got Paul so worked up. "Lots... lots... of..."

JP said, "Paul, calm down. Take deep breaths and then tell us what's wrong."

After a few moments Paul said, calmer, "I've found the cupboards and they are full of food, but even better they're in packets. I've filled up two suitcases and dragged them to the top. I also found the kettle and, wait for it, and yes it's intact... the toilet."

Andre said, "You are joking?"

Paul replied he was deadly serious, but there was no loo paper. Everyone burst out laughing and then regretted it as their ribs hurt.

"Didn't manage to find a shovel, did you, to dig a hole with?" asked Antoine.

"No," replied Paul, "but there's plenty of sharp bits of the plane about."

"Well done, Paul. Where were the cupboards?" asked the President.

Paul told them they were quite a way away from the plane, and that's why he had been so long.

That night, they all sat under a very secure tree tent, with a good fire, drinking hot soup. Paul had found packets of soup, nuts, crisps, rice, coffee, hot chocolate, sugar, biscuits and chocolate, tins of tuna and salmon along with hard plastics mugs, plates and cutlery.

The following morning JP and Poirot walked down to the stream. It was quite a walk and JP was shattered. Poirot made him rest. On the way back JP noticed there were oak and beech trees. "Poirot, any chance you get some bark off those trees for me?" Poirot looked as him quizzically. "That's an oak tree, and the bark and leaves are good for wounds as an antiseptic. The beech bark can be made as a tea, which is good for cleansing the blood. We've got clean water from the stream, so some of us can help the others down and have a wash, but maybe not just yet."

Back at the camp, JP boiled the oak bark and leaves, and then added a bit of the brew to a cup of water. He carefully peeled away the shirt and lint from Antoine's leg, and gently dabbed the wound with a fresh bit of lint. Antoine grimaced, but said nothing.

"Hopefully this will help the wound close and keep any infection away."

"Thanks boss. How's your ankle?" JP just smiled.

JP then checked everyone else and used the remedy. Later on he made a tea from the beech bark, which the President and his men drank, but didn't particularly like. Poirot had found a sharp piece of the plane and dug a very deep hole, and placed the toilet on top of it. He placed it by a tree, so those who had problems standing could lean up against it. Once it started to smell, Poirot would fill the hole in, and dig another one.

Slowly the days turned into weeks, but none of them had any idea how long they had been there. They endured storms and then hot weather. The tent more or less stood up to the storms, with small repairs being done. Poirot and Paul made sets of crutches for the

President, JP, and Donatien. Antoine couldn't use crutches because of his broken arm. Andre was very careful with his neck.

As the days slowly passed by, the food dwindled, until the rations were all gone. They were now drinking boiled water that had gone cold. Paul and Poirot went back to the plane to look for more food, but found nothing. On the way back neither of them saw the snake coiled ready to lunge, and hidden in the undergrowth. It bit Paul's leg first, and he said, "Ouch. What the hell was that?"

Poirot looked and said, "Probably just a bug. Get JP to look at it when we get back."

Poirot didn't realise he put his own foot down next to the snake, which bit his ankle. "Bloody hell, whatever it was just bit me."

When they got back to camp, neither of them said anything, as they felt so tired.

Andre said, "Paul, Poirot, you okay?"

Poirot replied, "Just tired, that's all."

In the morning, neither Paul nor Poirot were in their beds. The rest assumed they'd gone to collect water and firewood. Time went by, and neither of them came back. JP and Andre decided to go and look for them. They found them a short way from the camp, laid against a tree. Andre went over and knelt down. "Boss, don't know what's happened, but they're dead."

JP hobbled over and checked them. "Strange. This doesn't make sense. They were perfectly alright yesterday."

Andre said, "They weren't right when they came back from the plane, and they both crashed out early."

JP just happened to notice Poirot's ankle, and saw the bite. "Snake bite," he said to Andre. Andre rolled Paul's trouser leg up and saw the same marks. "Why the hell didn't they say something? What a waste of two good men. God rest their souls," said JP. They went back to camp with the sad news.

That night there was a terrific thunderstorm. The lightning was hitting the trees and bringing them down, and two were very close to them. The wind was so strong that it totally demolished the camp. The rain was heavy and poured straight down. Within seconds all of them were soaked through to their skins. JP tried to stand up, but slipped in the mud, re-injuring his broken ankle, and swore under his breath. "We need to get under better shelter," he shouted. Without Paul and Poirot to help them, they were stuck. Andre was the only one who didn't have a leg injury. Between Andre, who had to be careful of his neck, and JP, they managed to get the President and Donatien under some thicker trees. Antoine wasn't so easy, but eventually they got him up and took him to the others. Debris was flying everywhere, like air missiles. All of them were struck by various objects, and sustained more injuries. Then there was a huge roar, and they watched in disbelief as a massive landslide started falling down the mountainside. If they had stayed where they were, they would all have been buried alive. The ground was soon becoming a mud bath, and then there were mud slides.

The storm lasted for three days, before the sun came out. None of them now had any strength to do anything and they just laid there. JP noticed Antoine was very pale, and dragged himself across the muddy ground, in agony. Antoine's broken leg was bleeding badly. He also noticed blood was pouring from Donatien's leg. Hypothermia had set into all of them, along with dehydration. JP felt so helpless as there was nothing he could do, and dragged himself back to a tree trunk and put his back to it. Looking at the President and his men, he knew they weren't going to make it. He also knew, like himself, they were all thinking about their wives and families. JP closed his eyes, and said a silent farewell to Rose. Within a short time, every one of them closed their eyes, as the darkness took them down the long path towards death.

***

The following morning, at Hauteville airport, a large transport plane landed. Inside were four helicopters, various equipment that would be needed, and teams of doctors and medical teams, with medical equipment and supplies. There was a medical team for each of the injured men. Another transporter landed at Beaueville with just helicopters on board.

Pierre went over to the transporter and the first two people he saw were Doctor Michel and Doctor Pátrinne. "Good to see you, Doctors," he said.

"Good to see you too, Pierre. We understand five are barely alive and four died."

Pierre told them what he knew, and they asked to see the thermal images. Doctor Pátrinne said, "They've all got hypothermia, so we need to make sure we've got enough foil covers. When do you think we can get to them?"

Pierre replied gently, "You do realise you will need to be parachuted in?" Both the doctors nodded and said it was all arranged. Pierre replied, "Stéphane and Marc have already been up. The storm is still raging, so we can't do anything until it stops."

Doctor Michel said, "We have plenty to do. We are setting up a makeshift hospital here at Hauteville. I understand, once we get the all-clear, all eight helicopters will go up, and drop the men and equipment into the area. Once they're down, and that includes us, some of the men will start clearing an area for the helicopters to land. The men will then be transported back here, where we will take full control."

Pierre smiled and said, "If anyone can save them, it's you two."

Two high-ranking military men made their way over to Pierre and introduced themselves. "This is now a naval/army military operation and we will be taking charge. Any information you can give us will be extremely helpful." Pierre told them everything. The rest of the day was spent by everyone setting up the theatre, recovery room, and a large tent as a command centre, from where the rescue would be coordinated.

Hauteville used to be a large airport, but these days only helicopters and small planes landed. There were four medium-sized barracks, and it was two of these that would be used for rescue headquarters. One would be turned into an operating theatre, and the other a recovery room. When Pierre went to look, he couldn't believe it. Both barracks had thick polythene up against the walls, and then covered in white sterilised fabric. A makeshift floor was laid and again sterilised. In one of the barracks, various equipment was all set up around five separate beds, made ready for the survivors. It was just like the operating room from the hospital had been dropped into the barrack. The other barrack was the same as the other one, but the five beds were in separate cubicles, with screens around them. This was the recovery room. The other two barracks were being used as sleeping quarters.

Two days later, one of the commanders went up in the helicopter with Stéphane and Marc. He radioed to say the storm had abated and the sun was shining, but the landscape had changed dramatically from earlier thermal images. The survivors had moved, but not too far away. Suddenly, there was a hive of activity. Helicopters were being told to take off from both airports, and head towards the area. Pierre was desperate to see who was alive, but he would have to wait until they arrived back at the barracks. He watched as Doctor Michel and Doctor Pátrinne went up in separate helicopters.

Once airborne, they were soon over the area. Both doctors were strapped to an experienced parachutist and down they went. Within an hour everyone was down and making their way towards the survivors. Once they found them, Doctor Michel and Doctor Pátrinne were shocked at the condition of them. "Masks, suits and gloves," shouted Doctor Michel.

Both doctors then examined the men.

"Right," said Doctor Pátrinne, with an air of authority. "Time is of the essence. They are barely alive. Oxygen masks, IV fluids and antibiotic drips up immediately, and someone get the stretchers ready. They all have hypothermia, so use those foil blankets, until we can get them moved and out of their wet clothes. These are their symptoms, as far as I can assess. This is the President and he has a broken pelvis, and an infected gash above his eye. This team see to him please. This is Donatien, and he had a nasty leg wound which is infected, and a head injury. This team please. This is Andre, who as far as I can see has a broken neck. This team please. This is Antoine, who has a severe broken leg, broken arm, and is full of infection. I will be in charge of him and this team with me please. Finally we have JP, known as 'boss'. He has a double fractured ankle, and dislocated shoulder. Doctor Michel and the rest of you to him please. Now they all have broken ribs, cuts that have been infected, and nasty bites. Once they are ready to be airlifted, let me know. To work, everyone."

"Dr Pátrinne, this patient is trying to say something," said one of the medical team.

"Andre, can you hear me?"

"S n a…" said Andre quietly.

"Say again, Andre."

"S S n n a a k k e e."

Dr Pátrinne shouted, "Careful everyone, there are snakes."

Andre had lost consciousness again.

CHAPTER 26

"Rescue One to Command."

"Go ahead, Rescue One."

"Be advised there are snakes in the area. Suggest Rescue Two is advised."

"Will do, Rescue One. Out."

Twelve of the rescuers had branched off and started cutting down trees, and getting rid of debris to make space for the helicopters, which would have to land one by one. The leader received the message about snakes and advised his men. It took some time to clear the area for landing the first helicopter. Antoine would be the first one to go.

"Stretcher over here please. Now very carefully lay him down, but watch his leg and arm," said Doctor Pátrinne. "Careful, people, careful." Antoine was soon on the stretcher. Now they had to wait for the helicopter.

Getting the helicopter down wasn't a problem, but the rotors were. Debris started flying everywhere. "STOP," shouted Doctor Pátrinne, waving his arms. "Rescue Two to Command. Advise helicopter three not to land." The helicopter went back up and hovered. "Quickly everyone, we need to get them away from the landing area. Stretchers, NOW."

Slowly all the men were put on the stretchers and moved well away from the area. The helicopter descended again, and as soon as rotors stopped, Antoine was loaded inside it, and Doctor Pátrinne went with him.

"Rescue Two to Command."

"Go ahead, Rescue Two."

"Helicopter three on way back. One survivor and Doctor Pátrinne. Have medical teams ready. All survivors are near-death situations."

"Will do. Out."

Pierre watched as the first helicopter arrived. "Theatre now," said Doctor Pátrinne. The medical staff were waiting. Pierre saw it was Antoine and he paled. Slowly one by one the helicopters brought the rest back to Hauteville.

"Rescue Two to Command."

"Go ahead, Rescue Two."

"Last survivor on way. Rescue One has two body bags to be picked up. We are making our way to the plane to retrieve the other two bodies, if we can. Out."

"Understood, Rescue Two. Advise when you can. Out."

As the other helicopters landed, Pierre was relieved to see the President, JP, Andre and Donatien, but could see they were all in a bad way. He immediately phoned Monsieur Bourjôn at the palace, and told him the news of who was alive, and he'd been told they were all near death. It was now up to the doctors and the medical teams to save them.

Monsieur Bourjôn thanked him and said he would pass the news on. He went first to see the President's wife, and then to JP's office, and asked Porte to kindly phone the wives and ask them to come to the palace. An hour later they arrived. Monsieur Bourjôn told them the news.

Straight away Rose said, "Can we fly down to them?" Céleste and Gabrielle said they couldn't because of their children.

"I'll take them," said Emilie. "My parents will help and my friends. I promise they will be well looked after. Rose, Ruby, can you get time off work?" They both nodded. Mathieu and Séra had been kept up to date with the reports, as had their mum and dad, and Hugh and Chantelle.

"Very well, ladies, go home and pack what you need, and be back here tomorrow morning at 8am. I will arrange for a helicopter to fly you down." They all thanked him and left.

Back at Hauteville, the President, JP, and his men were now in the operating theatre, and had different medical teams working on them. The men had removed all their soaking wet clothes. Both doctors believed in some things being left private from the nurses. Andre was the first one to regain consciousness.

"Andre, nice to see you back," said Doctor Pátrinne. "Who made your neck brace?" Andre said it was JP. "Made a good job. Apart from your neck and ribs, do you have pain anywhere else?" Andre said he didn't. "Well you're linked up to an oxygen machine, so use it, and you have IV fluid and antibiotic drips. Your blood pressure and heart rate are being monitored every half hour, and like all of you, you have foil and normal blankets covering you to bring your temperature up, so just relax and try to sleep." Andre thanked Doctor Pátrinne, but asked about the others. "Let you know when I know. Now rest."

Next to come round was the President. "Doctor Michel, how is everyone?"

"We are caring for them, Monsieur le President. We have had to pin your hip together, so you are going to be very sore for some time. We have cleaned out the nasty gash above your eyebrow, as infection had set in, and you have some nasty bites. Like all of you, you have an oxygen machine, so please use it, IV fluids and antibiotic drips. You are covered with foil and blankets, to get you warm, along with a blood pressure and heart monitor. Try and rest, Monsieur le President, and I understand your wife has been informed." The President smiled and closed his eyes.

JP underwent surgery for the double break to his ankle, and to adjust a rib that had punctured his lung, but only slightly. His shoulder had also dislocated again when he fell, so that had to be manoeuvred back into place. Donatien also had surgery to his leg, which had also become badly infected. Antoine was the main concern. The break in his leg had sheared to the side, and so they had to re-break it and set it, but only once they had flushed out all the infection. His broken arm also had to be re-set, and he was still unconscious. All of them were covered in nasty cuts, bites and bruises.

Once out of the operating theatre, they were put in the recovery room, so they were all together. Pierre was allowed to visit them and was delighted to know they would all eventually pull through.

"First time I've known you lost for words."

Pierre turned to see Andre looking at him. "That'll teach you leaving me behind. Oh God, Andre, I'm so relieved you are all alright," and the tears fell down his face.

"Been bad, has it?" asked Andre.

Pierre told Andre they had all been missing for thirty-eight days.

Andre was shocked. "Come here, let me give you a man hug, but watch my neck." Pierre bent over and gave him a man hug.

"Are we all getting one of those?" asked Donatien.

Pierre turned and said, "You bet you are," and hugged Donatien. Antoine and JP were still unconscious.

"Where's the President?" asked Donatien.

"They wheeled him out so he could phone his wife," said Pierre.

"Bet we're all in the doghouse with ours?" said Andre.

"Far from it, Andre, far from it. They have been worried sick. They, like me, all assumed the worst."

At that moment the President was wheeled back in, and Pierre bowed. "Monsieur le President, it's good to see you."

"As it is you, Pierre. I understand you took over the whole operations from the palace, and I thank you."

Pierre replied, "Just doing my duty, Monsieur le President."

Doctor Pátrinne walked in and said, "Sorry Pierre, it's time they all got some rest and sleep. You can see them in the morning, when hopefully they'll all be awake." Pierre said goodnight, again giving Andre and Donatien a hug.

The following morning, they were all awake. Antoine was in a great deal of pain, but was glad to see everyone had survived. JP was also delighted to see they had all made it through. When Pierre arrived, he went straight to JP and said, "Good to see you, boss, and you too Antoine." He gave them both a gentle man hug. Pierre asked them what had happened, and each told him a little bit of the events.

Doctor Michel and Doctor Pátrinne came in to check on them all. "Any idea when we can fly back to Paris?" asked the President.

"Not yet, Monsieur le President. None of you are out of the woods, so to speak, yet. That reminds me, your rescuers are all coming in to see how you are before they leave. Now we need to examine you all."

Earlier that morning, helicopter two had returned to the landing area in the forest. Poirot and Paul's bodies had been recovered and put into body bags and taken to Beaueville the evening before. It had got too dark to go to the plane wreckage. Once there, they found the body of the other aide, who was not a pretty sight. Blowflies covered most of his body. Luckily the rescue team had protective clothing on, as when they moved the body the blowflies tried to attack them. They soon got him into a body bag. Next, they made their way to the front of the plane.

"Oh my god, this is horrendous," said the leader.

"Sorry men, but we need to get him out, well, what's left of him."

"Rescue Two to Command."

"Go ahead, Rescue Two."

"Body from back of plane in body bag. Pilot difficult. We need metal-cutting equipment. Can you send helicopter four to drop equipment? Over."

"Rescue Two, will do. Do you need anything else?"

The leader replied, "Rescue Two to Command. A stiff drink."

"Understood, Rescue Two. Look out for snakes. Out."

A short while later, helicopter four hovered over the area, and lowered the cutting equipment. "Helicopter four to Rescue Two."

"Rescue Two. Go ahead, helicopter four."

"Helicopter four to Rescue Two. Will stay in area in case you need extra help."

"Rescue Two to helicopter four. Thanks."

The only way they could get to Benoit was to cut through the side of the plane, as Benoit was totally mangled in the wreckage. Eventually they got to him, and saw one of his legs and arms had been totally sheared off by parts of the plane. He hadn't stood a chance. Like the aide he was covered with blowflies, but he had a snake around his neck, and another coiled round his arm, both hissing nastily. Carefully one of the men unbuckled Benoit's seat straps. Benoit's body slumped to the side, and both snakes lunged for the men, who quickly jumped back. As the men jumped back, two of the others quickly sliced through the heads of the snakes. Very carefully they now lifted Benoit's body out of the plane and put him in the body bag. All the men stood around both bodies and said a silent prayer.

"Rescue Two to Command. Bodies secured. Flying back to Beaueville. Out."

"Command to Rescue Two. Well done, men. Once bodies at Beaueville, clean up and all of you return to Hauteville to see the President. Out."

About midday, the rescuers and medical staff walked into the recovery ward. There were over fifty of them. All of them were thanked for their heroism in rescuing them and bringing them back to reality. They stayed for about an hour. The President said they would not be forgotten, and shook the hands of every one of them, including the two high-ranking military men. Pierre went out to see them off, and also to thank Stéphane and Marc for everything.

Four helicopters flew off towards Beaueville and then the transporter took off, with the other helicopters inside, all the equipment, and most of the medical teams. Doctor Michel and Doctor Pátrinne had brought their own teams, and they were the ones that were staying, mainly because they knew their patients.

As the transporter circled the airfield, Pierre saw two helicopters arriving. He watched as they landed and was surprised when he saw Rose, Gabrielle, Céleste and Ruby climb out of the first helicopter, and the President's wife and son from the second, along with Porte and Sávoire. Pierre bowed to the President's wife and son, who were then escorted to the recovery room. He hugged Porte and Sávoire. Turning his attention to the others, he said, "Ladies, how lovely to see you. I suppose you've come to see those reprobates you call husbands." For that they all slapped him, but playfully.

"How are they, Pierre?" asked Rose, concerned.

Pierre replied, "Well this morning they are all awake, but they are still badly injured and won't be flying home yet. They are in the recovery room, and have all got their own cubicles. Doctor Michel and Doctor Pátrinne and their teams are the only ones left. See that transporter circling, one landed here and another at Beaueville. They brought the helicopters, equipment, medical teams etc. that rescued them."

Rose asked anxiously, "Can we see them, Pierre?" Pierre said he would take them, but they would have to ask one of the doctors first.

Doctor Pátrinne had seen the President's wife and son walking towards the makeshift hospital, followed at a distance by Pierre and the wives. "Looks like we've got company."

Doctor Michel looked and said, "This will cheer them up. Better move the President to somewhere more private." Doctor Pátrinne agreed.

After the President had been moved, on pretence of a scan, Doctor Pátrinne went to greet his wife and son, and bodyguards. "So who have we got here then, Pierre? Hello ladies, come to visit someone?" asked Doctor Michel, smiling. They all raised an eyebrow. "Right, let me run through with you each of your husbands' symptoms, and then I'll take you in. I know it's not ideal, but I can assure you the theatre and recovery rooms are sterilised. We are hoping, maybe the latter end of next week, we can fly them back to the hospital in Paris. Where are you going to stay?"

Ruby replied, "We didn't actually give that a thought, but there must be a hotel or guest house nearby. Pierre, can you help?" Pierre said to leave it with him.

Doctor Michel told them about their husbands and all of them paled significantly, especially Ruby. "Ladies I do need to warn you, there are going to be a lot of emotions running high, just bear with them. Now come with me, and we're both here if you need to talk to us about anything." Doctor Michel told the ladies to wait, whilst he went into the recovery room, to make sure all the men were decent. "Gentlemen, how are we feeling today? Ready for some company?"

Andre replied dryly, "If it's our wives, no." The wives all looked at each other in surprise.

"Come in, ladies, one of the nurses saw you and told us," said Andre.

Gabrielle replied, "I think we just might go home."

Antoine said, "Hey, he doesn't speak for the rest of us."

"Gabrielle, come here. You know how much I love you, woman," said Andre.

The wives walked in, and saw their husbands, and they were all shocked. Ruby rushed to Antoine and kissed him. Gabrielle went to Andre, Céleste went to Donatien, but Rose held back for a moment, until JP held his hand out to her. "Oh my love, I'm so sorry for…"

"Hush, môn amour. I thought I would never see you again. Let me hold you." Carefully Rose sat on the bed at the side of him and kissed him so tenderly.

One of the nurses pulled the curtains round the cubicles to give them all some privacy. "No misbehaving, any of you," said Antoine.

"Ruby, careful, watch my leg. Ow, that was my arm." Everyone was laughing.

Rose looked at JP and said, "Only you could double break your ankle. How's it feeling?"

JP replied, "At the moment not too bad, but when the pain hits I know it. The shoulder is sore, but will soon mend, as will my lung and ribs, so don't worry. Perhaps some kisses would make all the difference." Rose kissed his lips, and then his shoulder. JP whispered, "I must be unwell."

Rose looked at him curiously. "Your little angel isn't responding." Rose looked at him and said, "Are you surprised, my love? Your body has been through a huge trauma. He will come back when he's ready. Now can I get you anything?"

"No, just hold me, môn amour."

Rose saw tears falling down his cheeks and said, "I'm here, my love, I'm here." JP sobbed in Rose's arms, and she held him as tightly as she could, with tears in her own eyes.

CHAPTER 27

"Anyone seen those blasted wives?" asked Pierre, laughing, about an hour later. The cubicle curtains were pulled back and four wives stood there glowering at him. All the husbands were sniggering. "I come in peace, ladies. I have sorted out your accommodation," said Pierre. "I asked at the airport and they said there was a lovely hotel in Aix-L'Abri, which is about two kilometres away. I have booked single rooms and also sorted out a rental car, which will arrive here in about an hour."

Gabrielle replied, "Suppose that'll have to do then." Pierre looked hurt and the wives laughed, and all went and kissed his cheek.

Suddenly Rose said, "Where's the President?"

Donatien told them he had been moved to another room to have a scan. Céleste told them that the President's wife and son had also arrived, with Porte and Sávoire. Then they realised he had been moved to see his wife and son.

"Ladies, we need to check your husbands' vitals," said Doctor Michel, "and I'm sure all the blood pressure readings will be high." Everyone sort of blushed.

"Can we visit the President please, Doctor Michel?" asked Rose.

"Of course, come with me." Doctor Michel took them to the room. "Monsieur le President, I have some guests to see you."

"Ladies, oh how lovely to see you," said the President. "Come in, please come in."

They stayed with the President and his wife and son for half an hour, and then they could see he was getting tired, so they said they would see him in the morning. As they went to go back to their husbands, Doctor Michel stopped them. "It's nothing to worry about, ladies. They have been given their sedatives, which make them sleep. Go and rest yourselves, and we'll see you in the morning."

Céleste said, "Thank you, Doctors, for everything you have done. You saved their lives." Each of them gave each doctor a hug and a kiss on their cheek. The President's wife and son left to go back to Paris, along with Porte and Sávoire, who had quickly seen JP and the rest of them.

"Ladies, your car awaits," said Pierre.

"Where are you staying, Pierre?" asked Ruby.

"Well, I thought it would be a good idea to look after all of you, on behalf of your husbands of course, so I too am staying at the hotel. Hopefully I can go and buy some clothes, as I've only got these."

Gabrielle picked up a bag and said, "With love from Emilie." Pierre smiled and took it.

Soon they were at the hotel, which was lovely. "Ladies, dinner in the restaurant in about an hour?" asked Pierre. They all agreed.

Later on they all enjoyed a relaxed meal and each other's company. Gabrielle, however, noticed later on, Pierre seemed pre-occupied. After everyone had said goodnight, Gabrielle took Pierre's arm and said gently, "Want to talk about it?" They were sitting in a quiet corner of the bar.

"I thought I'd lost them all, Gabrielle, and I was lost. I didn't know what to do," and silently the tears fell down his cheeks. Gabrielle put her arms around him and Pierre sobbed. Rose had come back down to get some water, and saw them. Her heart went out to Pierre, but she didn't intrude.

The following morning, at breakfast, Rose could see a huge burden had been lifted from Pierre's shoulders. He had already been out and bought new clothes, and looked more relaxed.

"Wonder how our men are today?" asked Ruby.

"Let's go find out," said Céleste.

192

Their men were sleeping most of the time, and stayed like that for the next four days. On day five as they were leaving the hotel, an announcement came over the radio. "Ladies and gentlemen. We apologise for interrupting your programme, but this is an important news flash. The Élysée Palace have confirmed that the President's plane has been found. After thirty-eight days of speculation, we can confirm the President is badly injured, but alive. I repeat, the President is alive. Out of the other eight on board, only four survived. Names have not been divulged, and neither has the crash site. We wish all of them a speedy recovery and our thoughts are with them and their families, and also our thoughts and condolences go out to the families and friends of the ones that perished in the crash. Naturally we will keep you informed, as and when we receive any updates. Thank you."

Pierre said, "It's not going to be long before they find out Hauteville and Beaueville have been busy and it won't have gone unnoticed. Damn." Pierre then drove them to their men, but when they got there, Pierre knew something was wrong. Another helicopter was taking off with Doctor Pátrinne on board. Doctor Michel was stood outside taking off a blue medical suit, gloves and mask. "What's happened?" asked Pierre, greatly concerned.

Doctor Michel put his hand up and said calmly, "I'm sorry to say we have a problem. In the early hours of the morning, the nurse on duty noticed they were shivering and were cold and clammy to the touch. Immediately she called for us. A short time later, they started having a high fever, along with sweating and vomiting. We have taken blood tests from all of them, and Doctor Pátrinne has flown back to the lab at the hospital to see what's causing it. We also noticed where they had been bitten, some of the marks have come up into large red lumps. To me it looks like a sort of malaria, but it's different. Until we know what it is, I'm sorry ladies, but none of you can visit them. They are now in quarantine."

Everyone was devastated. "Can't we wear what you had on to see them?" asked Rose.

Doctor Michel explained there was only enough for the team, Doctor Pátrinne and himself. "Every precaution is being taken, ladies, with regards to everything being sterilised, etc. All I can suggest is for you to go back to the hotel, and as stupid as this sounds, try and rest and relax. I don't want all of you becoming ill as well. I will tell them you've all been."

Pierre said, "This is the phone number of the hotel, and it was on the radio this morning they had been found."

"Oh wonderful, now the place will be swarming with news crews and reporters," said Doctor Michel.

Pierre replied, "The palace has not released where we are, but…"

Doctor Michel replied they would sort it out when it happened.

"Please give them all our love and tell them we're thinking of them," said Gabrielle.

Doctor Michel said he would. He watched as the five of them walked back to their car, heads downs and arms around each other, totally dejected. At that moment a nurse popped her head out and said, "Doctor Michel, we need you urgently. JP's ankle has swelled greatly and he's in extreme agony." Doctor Michel put his suit, gloves and mask on, and inside the door the nurse turned the sterilising shower on. Only after that was done, did he enter the recovery room.

JP was writhing in the bed, with two nurses trying to hold him down. His ankle was the size of a balloon. "Operating room," said Doctor Michel. His men were very concerned for him. Once JP had been sedated, Doctor Michel took an x-ray, which showed up an insect inside JP's ankle. "What the…? Scalpel please." Slowly he cut a line into JP's ankle, near to where the insect was. Blood and infection poured out. Once he spread the cut open, he used a pair of tweezers to extract the insect, putting it in a bowl. JP's ankle was full of infection again. Doctor Michel shook his head in disbelief, as this had set in so quickly and JP was on antibiotics. "Bag that insect. It will be vital to find out what it is."

To everyone's surprise, the insect suddenly spread its wings, flew round the room a couple of times, out the door and flew away. "Damn," said Doctor Michel. "Apologies for my language, ladies." The nurses giggled. He then flushed out as much of the infection as he could, and then stitched up the wound. Checking JP's vital signs, they had now stabilised.

Back in the recovery room Antoine said, "How's the boss, Doctor?"

Doctor Michel replied, "Believe it or not, he had one of those insects in his ankle. Strangest thing I've ever seen. Alas, the damn thing flew away."

Early evening Doctor Michel phoned Doctor Pátrinne. "Henri, it's Arnaud, any news?"

Henri replied that various tests had been done, and they all had the same infection. Arnaud told him what had happened with JP. "Can you describe the insect?" asked Henri.

Arnaud replied, "From what I can remember, it had a body that looked like a wasp, with long brown wings folded in over its back. Six long legs and a long proboscis attached to the head. It also looked like it had minute yellow spots on its back."

Henri replied, "That's interesting. Sounds like a tsetse fly, but it's not, and tsetse flies aren't found in France. I'll be in touch, Arnaud. Oh by the way, do we need more IV drips and antibiotics?"

"Yes we do."

"I'll bring some back with me." Both men said goodnight.

The following morning the men were the same, although their temperatures had dropped, but only slightly. They stayed this way for another two days, and then Doctor Pátrinne phoned Doctor Michel. "Arnaud, good news. A specialist has recognised the symptoms and the insect. He said it's along the lines of a tsetse fly, but it's a mutant. He was disappointed it had flown away. The infection is highly contagious, and the recovery period will be about two, maybe three weeks. I'm on my way back, with different antibiotic drips.

"Just to advise you in case the President should ask, the post-mortems have been carried out on the other four. They were taken to a security morgue because of the risk of infection. As we know, Benoit suffered horrific injuries in the crash, and death was instantaneous. Poirot and Paul died from a venomous snake bite, and their deaths were slow and extremely painful. The aide died of a broken neck and serious internal injuries. As none of them had any families, they have already been cremated, and a brief ceremony was held, attended by Monsieur Bourjôn and other bodyguards, whilst their ashes were scattered in the breeze, in the palace gardens. Hopefully I will see you in about four hours." Doctor Michel was greatly relieved.

As soon as Doctor Pátrinne returned, the nurses changed the antibiotic drips, and it did take two weeks for them to recover. The wives had had a huge decision to make. Did they stay or go home? In the end they went home, but Pierre stayed. Pierre now phoned Monsieur Bourjôn and updated him. "Thank heavens for that. I will get Porte to contact the wives. I'm sure they'll fly down again. Thank you, Pierre. I think you should have a rest and I'm giving you the weekend off to spend with your wife and family. Enjoy." Pierre thanked him, and then phoned Emilie, who was pleased he would be home.

The wives arrived on the Saturday morning. Their husbands were delighted, as it had been nearly three weeks since they last saw them. Both doctors had made absolutely sure that all the infections were gone.

"Now," said Céleste, "are you lot going to come down with anything else, or can we get you home to Paris?"

Donatien replied, "We can't wait to get home. Now please can we all have some hugs and kisses?" The wives didn't needed asking twice. The curtains went round the cubicles.

Rose hugged JP so tightly. "Môn amour, not so tight."

"Oh, sorry my love. I've just missed you so much. How's this?" Rose took JP's face in her hands and kissed him so tenderly, that it sent goose bumps through him.

"Do that again," he said huskily, so she did. Much to her surprise JP lifted up his blankets, and smiled. Rose looked under the blankets and smiled as she saw her angel had risen to the occasion. Very quickly she pushed the blankets away and kissed it. That got her angel twitching.

"Now behave, my love, or we might both be very embarrassed. You are getting better, but you still have a long recovery." JP moved his hand under the blankets and put himself back to being limp. Suddenly JP's blood pressure monitor started bleeping like mad.

"Whatever you're doing in there, you've just sent his blood pressure through the roof," said Antoine.

"Shut up," replied JP, laughing. Everybody else then started laughing. The next minute Antoine's machine started bleeping. Rose drew the curtain back, and saw Gabrielle and Céleste had done the same. Rose tiptoed up and quickly pulled the curtain back. Ruby was busy kissing Antoine's tummy!!

"Excuse me, this was a private moment," she said. Antoine was bright red!! The rest all collapsed in hysterics.

"Now ladies, if you're going to send their blood pressures that high, no more curtains will be closed, but it was good to hear," said Doctor Michel.

For the next hour, the wives brought them all up to date about everyone and everything. They were only staying for the weekend.

"So Doctor Michel, when can we fly back? Not that I'm complaining, but our wives do need looking after, if you get my drift?" asked Andre. Gabrielle went to slap his head, but then stopped herself, so she slapped his leg instead. "Look what we have to put up with, Doctor, and you wonder where we get our bruises from. Mind you it's usually our heads, where bruises don't show." Unfortunately Andre had gone just that bit too far, and Gabrielle walked out quite upset. The wives glared at Andre and went after Gabrielle.

JP looked at Andre and said gently, "We know you were joking, Andre, but you've got to remember everything our wives have been through. Rose told me they all thought we were dead, and they actually went through a grieving process."

Andre went to get out of bed, but the nurse stopped him. "Please, I need to apologise to my wife." The nurse went and got Doctor Michel.

"Alright Andre, let me just unhook your machines, but only for a couple of minutes, do you understand?"

Andre said he did. One of the nurses went and got Gabrielle. The rest of the wives went back to their husbands. Andre was just outside the recovery room when Gabrielle came in. "I'm so sorry, Gabrielle. Me and my stupid comments. Come to me, please." Gabrielle went to him and he kissed her tenderly. "You know how much I love you, Gabrielle, and Dulé as well. I really didn't mean to upset you."

Gabrielle kissed him back and said, "Just wait till I get you home. Now back to bed." Andre smiled, and kissed her again.

Even though Andre was the only one who could walk, Gabrielle had to help him back to the bed. Doctor Michel reconnected his drips. "Tell you what," said Andre, "I thought I was alright, but I've never felt so weak."

Doctor Michel replied in a sharp tone, "What all of you men have to remember is your bodies have suffered several serious traumas. You were dehydrated and had hypothermia. Then you came down with the infection. Yes, you might feel like you can get out of bed and run around, but believe me, and especially you three," he said, pointing at JP, Donatien and Antoine, "it will be months before that happens. Not only that, all of you will have to be re-trained again for four weeks, but only when we give you the all-clear. I hope that puts it into perspective for you, and it's no joking matter." The men nodded, feeling thoroughly told off.

CHAPTER 28

In a gentler voice Doctor Michel said, "Now just to advise you that the President is being flown home tomorrow. We are looking at flying all of you back maybe Friday or Saturday. We need to get the hospital ready first."

Rose said, "Can we visit the President? It would be awful not to see him before he goes."

"Of course, you know where he is."

Rose and Ruby went first, followed by Gabrielle and Céleste. The President was delighted to see them, and they all stayed an hour each with him.

Back in the recovery room, Donatien asked, "Where's Pierre?"

Céleste told them he had flown home to Emilie for the weekend, but would be back on Monday. Andre asked how he was. Gabrielle told him that Pierre broke down, but he was alright now. It was coming up 4pm, and Doctor Michel suggested to the wives that they let their men rest. They kissed and hugged their men goodnight and said they would see them in the morning. As they walked back to the car Ruby asked, "Is it only me, or is anyone else starving?" They had no lunch, as the men weren't on solids yet.

They were staying at the same hotel, but when they got there, they saw a news van parked outside. "Oh bloody hell," said Ruby. "How did they get here?"

"Pssst, Pssst." They looked round and saw a porter beckoning to them. "Come this way. The news crew is in the reception, and we have denied any knowledge of you. This is the back way in, and we have got a private room for you, on the same floor, to have your meals in. Just phone reception when you need a meal, or when you need to leave, and we will see you're not bothered or followed."

"Thank you...?" asked Rose.

"Félix," replied the porter. Félix took them up the back stairs.

"Thank you, Félix. Which room are we eating in?" asked Ruby.

Félix showed them. The room was already set up for the evening meal, with menus on the table. "Just phone '0' and we'll take your order."

They thanked him and arranged to meet at 7pm.

"Well, this is all very cloak-and-dagger isn't it?" said Gabrielle.

Ruby replied, "I know what they're like, remember. If they know where we are, they'll be camped outside our bedroom doors."

Céleste said, "We'll be gone tomorrow and hopefully our husbands will be back at the weekend. There's no way the journalists will be admitted to the hospital. I think you, Ruby, should do all the reports, and that way it will be the truth." Ruby blushed and thanked Céleste. Later they met and enjoyed a relaxing meal, with wine.

When they arrived at Hauteville after a very hearty breakfast, and being smuggled out of the hotel, it was to see the President being boarded, on a stretcher, with Doctor Pátrinne, onto a large rescue helicopter. They all promised to visit him soon. They stood back and watched as the helicopter took off.

In the recovery room, JP and his men were talking away, mainly about the crash. The wives stood and listened for a moment. It was good for them to talk about it. When it went quiet, they walked in. Hugs and kisses were given to all of them.

Doctor Michel came in and said, "Good news, ladies. Your husbands are being flown back on Tuesday. Two large rescue helicopters will pick them up, on stretchers, and ambulances will be waiting at the Paris airfield. May I suggest you wait until Wednesday to visit them, as they are going to be tired out." The wives were delighted. At long last their husbands were on their way home.

Tuesday morning, JP and his men were given sedatives to knock them out for the journey back to the private hospital in Paris. JP and Antoine flew back with Doctor Michel and half of the medical team. The rest of the medical team flew with Donatien and Andre. The operating room and recovery room would be stripped by some of the airport staff after they left. Another smaller rescue helicopter had all the equipment. Once they landed at Paris, two ambulances were awaiting them, and soon they arrived at the hospital. This time, however, they all had their own rooms. They were also going to be started on solid food, to get their strength and energy back. The President was already in his private room, and discussing local and foreign affairs with Monsieur Bourjôn, which Doctor Pátrinne wasn't happy about, but the President was the President. He was advised that JP and his men had arrived.

When JP opened his eyes, and looked around, he saw he was in the same room that he had been in after he had been shot. He felt slightly groggy, but that was the sedative. One of the nurses came in and said, "You're awake. How are you feeling, JP?" JP replied he would be fine, but his ankle was hurting. The nurse said she would get Doctor Michel to look at it. She gave him some water to drink, and helped him to sit up more comfortably. "Is everyone else alright?" he asked. She told him they were all coming round, and would let him know.

All he wanted now was to sort things out with Rose, and if that meant selling the farmhouse and moving back to the centre of Paris, then that's what they would do. At least now they could talk privately.

Doctor Michel popped in and checked his ankle, and gave him some more pain relief. A couple of hours later Andre sauntered into JP's room. "Boss, you alright? You look a bit pale."

JP smiled and replied, "You looked in a mirror lately? Sit down, Andre. How's your neck?"

"Thanks to you, it's going to be fine. Thought I'd let you know the rest are awake and are fine. Antoine has to stay in bed and it's annoying him. Donatien has been given crutches and they're going to see how he is tomorrow."

JP was pleased his men were on the road to recovery and said,

"We'll have to meet in Antoine's room then."

Andre looked at JP and said, "Not being intrusive, but did you and Rose sort things out?"

"Not really, but now we've got our own rooms, I'm hoping we can talk when I see her."

A voice said, "Andre Duval, what are you doing out of bed?"

Andre turned and saw his nurse stood there tapping her fingers on her folded arms. "Oops, I'm in trouble. See you later on, boss." JP chuckled as Andre was taken back to his room.

The following morning, they were all given a small dish of scrambled egg to eat. JP thought it tasted delicious.

"Morning JP, how's the pain threshold?" asked Doctor Michel. JP replied it was alright and for the first time he'd slept right through the night. "Excellent. Now I've got you some crutches, and I'd like you to try them. Your ribs have more or less healed, but any pain, tell me straight away." JP nodded. With Doctor Michel and a nurse's help they got him to stand. JP felt slightly dizzy, so they sat him down again. "Nothing to worry about, as that's natural." They got him up again, and he was fine. "Now put your weight on your right leg and the crutches, and lift your bad ankle up." JP did as he was told. "Any pain?" JP shook his head. "Good, now that's it for today. Apart from Antoine and Andre, when you and Donatien want to visit the others we will put you in a wheelchair. Now back in the bed and rest. No doubt you will shortly all be having visitors." That made JP smile.

Lunch time and the wives turned up. They all greeted each of them and then went to their husbands. They had already visited the President.

Rose sat on the side of the bed and kissed JP tenderly. "How are you, my love?"

JP replied, "All the better for seeing you, môn amour. I'm so sorry for everything that you have been through, but heaven knows how, I'm here and I can say, 'Je t'aime, môn amour.'" Rose's eyes filled with tears, and he wrapped his arms round her tightly.

"JP, I'm sorry as well for what I said to you. That crash was all my fault."

JP brushed her tears away and replied, "Of course it wasn't, môn amour. It was lightning that hit the fuel tank." He kissed her gently. "We need to talk. Can you close the door, môn amour?" Rose got up and closed the door, and then sat back down at the side of him. Taking her in his arms, he said, "I've had plenty of time to think about what you said, and you're right. It was unforgivable of me to forget our first anniversary, and I intend to make up for that, if you'll let me. As to the farmhouse, if you want to move back to Paris, then we can sell it and look for something else nearer. The only thing I would ask is, can we have a house instead of a flat? I actually like going upstairs to bed."

Rose took his face in her hands and replied, "I was a bitch that day, and I knew the stress you had been under sorting all the arrangements. The minute I got home I regretted every word I had said, but at the same time, rightly or wrongly, I needed a bit of space, and that's why I went to Nantes. When I heard the news you were missing, the first thing I thought was that we had parted on an argument, and that broke me. I would never, ever have forgiven myself, if you had…" Tears were flowing down Rose's face.

"Hush, môn amour, hush."

Rose carried on. "You don't need to sell the farmhouse, as we are staying, and we have so much to thank Raoul for," and she told him. "The wives and myself got together, at the farmhouse, and had a chat. According to Gabrielle a new road is being built from Paris, going past the village, and it will only take half an hour to get to us. It should be opened at the end of the year. I've seen the roadworks and it's getting done very quickly." Taking hold of his hands, she said sadly, "I had a dream of you holding me and saying how much you loved me and always would, even when you were gone, and then you said your goodbye to me. Oh JP, I couldn't imagine life without you." Now JP had tears in his eyes, and they held each other tight.

One of the machines started bleeping and Doctor Michel rushed in. "Oh, sorry, I didn't mean to intrude, but your blood pressure has gone high, hence the bleeping."

"Sorry Doctor, both of our faults. We were going through an emotional conversation."

Doctor Michel sorted out the machine and apologising again, left them. Ruby had come out of Antoine's room and Doctor Michel called her over. "Ruby I don't mean to interfere, but is everything alright between JP and Rose?" Ruby told him about their argument, and Rose blaming herself. "Thank you Ruby, now I understand. Antoine alright?" Ruby said he had a lot of pain, and so they went to see him.

"Are you absolutely sure you want to stay at the farmhouse, môn amour?"

"Yes I am, my love, and it's our home. Where else can you look out of some of the windows, and see the river and fields of sunflowers and a forest? I saw some squirrels the other day."

JP wrapped his arms round her and kissed her, but this time with a passion. "The door's closed, so we could love each other?"

Rose laughed and said, "That would send all the machines bleeping." JP laughed as well, and then trailed kisses down Rose's neck. His hand went under her blouse and caressed her breast. Rose moaned. He lifted her blouse up and kissed each breast. "That feels nice, my love, but that's enough for today. You need to get your strength back first, and then we can make up for lost time," said Rose.

"Spoilsport," said JP.

"Now what can I bring in for you, apart from myself?"

JP replied, "Whilst I remember, what month is it?"

"Today is the first of September."

"What!!" said JP in disbelief.

Rose was surprised and said, "I thought Pierre had told you. You were missing for thirty-eight days, we were with you for five days, then the infection hit for over two weeks, and then you had to wait to be flown back."

JP replied, "On the way back, before the crash, the President told us he was giving us all the month of August off. Oh well, that's gone. I was going to suggest we went back to Montpellier."

"Ooh that would have been wonderful. Maybe next year, my love. Now next week, it's the Paris Fashion Show, so it will be late when I come in to see you, but we have the rest of this week and the weekend." JP smiled.

At the weekend, the wives arrived with their children, and for a couple of minutes pandemonium broke out. "Children, be quiet," said Emilie. "Now show your mamans and papas how well behaved you can be."

The children were well behaved for the time they were there.

"Hope we're not intruding." Rose turned to see her uncle and Chantelle, and went and hugged and kissed them.

"Good to see you back, JP. You had all of us worried there for some time," said Hugh, shaking JP's hand.

"We were a bit worried as well. Nice to see you Hugh, and you too Chantelle."

Chantelle gave him a gentle hug and a kiss on his cheek, and asked him how he was. JP said he, along with the rest of them, would all be fine. They sat and chatted for a couple of hours.

JP then said, "Why hasn't Pierre been to see us?" Rose chewed her bottom lip. "Rose?"

Rose sighed and replied, "Pierre sort of broke down. Porte found him in your office sobbing his heart out. Emilie has been looking after him, and hopefully he will be here next week. He has been seeing someone to help him overcome what happened." JP was upset at this. He had heard how Pierre had taken charge of operations at the palace. He had to talk to him, but only when Pierre was ready.

As everyone went to leave, once Doctor Michel had asked them, JP called to Emilie. "How is he, Emilie, and be honest?"

Emilie replied, "He will be fine, JP. It just hit him all at once, and that was it. He did say yesterday that you've got to get better quickly, as he's getting Boeuf Bourguignon withdrawal symptoms." JP roared laughing, which made him cough and hurt his ribs.

Rose and Séra attended the Paris Fashion Show week. Séra could see Rose was a lot more relaxed now and she was pleased for her. She had only met JP a couple of times, but she liked him. In fact they made such a lovely couple, it made her think about her own life, and that meant Mathieu. Just for this week, due to the long hours, Rose was staying with Ruby. One night Ruby said, "Mathieu has asked me if I'd like to do the follow-up story on the President, the crash and the survivors. What do you think?"

Rose replied, "At least it will be the truth, Ruby, and not some made-up stories that I've been seeing. I would suggest you ask the President first, but I'm sure he will be more than agreeable."

"Thanks sis," said Ruby.

The next time Ruby was at the hospital, she asked if she could see the President.

"Ruby, come in. What a lovely surprise." Ruby smiled and asked him her question. The President replied, "I can't think of anyone better to do the report, but I would like to see it before it's published. I also think you should get consent from JP, Andre, Donatien and Antoine of course." Ruby said she would. They talked for another fifteen minutes and then Ruby left him. All of the men were happy for Ruby to do the report. The following week, with the President's permission, the report was published in the Gilmac News.

CHAPTER 29

Over the next four weeks, JP and his men underwent stringent physiotherapy, and were back on solid food. September was the month that Ruby turned thirty. With Antoine and the rest of them still in the hospital, Ruby and the wives went out and celebrated at Gérard's. Gérard was delighted to see them and asked after their men. Rose told him how they were. "When they are able, you tell them a table is ready for all of you to have a meal, on me." Rose kissed his cheek and told him she would tell them. Rose had picked all the wives up and stuck to soft drinks. The rest of them got slightly tipsy, but they had a lovely relaxing, enjoyable evening.

Meanwhile at the hospital, the men were now walking round and in and out of each other's rooms. Doctor Michel saw no reason why they couldn't go home at the end of September, for a month's "home" rest. The month of November, JP and his men would be re-trained. Hopefully, they would all be back at work properly in December. The President was already back at the palace, but still using his crutches. Pierre was helping to sort things out, and was in and out seeing JP to make sure he wasn't doing it wrong. JP had had a long chat with Pierre to make sure he was alright. Pierre told him all about Raoul, and other things that had happened. JP thanked him and told him a Boeuf Bourguignon was in order. Pierre was more than happy with that.

The day arrived when it was time for them to go home, and they couldn't wait. Rose picked JP up Friday afternoon, and drove him home. "Now come and sit down on the settee and I'll make us a meal," said Rose.

JP grabbed her hand and said, "I'm feeling a bit tired, so thought I might go and lay down."

Rose told him to go on up and she would bring up some water for him. When she walked in the bedroom JP was sitting up in bed. "Come here, môn amour, I want to kiss you." Rose sat at the side of him and the next thing he had his arms around her and was kissing her passionately.

"My love, I thought you were tired?"

"That just might have been a little bit of a white lie. I want you, môn amour. I want to love you so much." Slowly he kissed her lips and neck as he unbuttoned her blouse. He buried his head between her breasts and as he kissed them he unclipped her bra. As Rose's hand went down his back to his buttocks, she realised JP was naked. Soon Rose was under the duvet totally naked as well. They explored each other's bodies and Rose rolled JP over and straddled him. She felt JP enter her and it felt wonderful to have him back inside her. Slowly and gently they loved each other until their climaxes took over them.

"I've missed you so much, môn amour," said JP.

"As I have you, my love, but now we're together again." Soon they were loving each other again, and then JP spooned into Rose's back and they slept.

Rose awoke to JP gently making love to her. He was caressing and sucking her nipples, whilst his other hand was between her legs. Rose stretched and JP rolled on top of her. "Ahh, that hurt," he said and rolled off her.

"My love, are you alright?"

JP replied, "I just turned my ankle awkwardly. It's just stiff after me being asleep all night."

"Would a nice relaxing bath help?" asked Rose.

"Only if you'll join me, môn amour."

Rose got out of bed and went to the bathroom, where she drew a warm bath. JP walked in and saw Rose bending over the bath. His manhood went hard. He went up behind her and wrapping one of his arms round her waist, his other hand went to her breasts. Kissing the side of her neck, he entered her from behind. Rose put her hands on the side of the bath. Gently JP loved her and soon Rose called out his name as her climax hit her. JP then climaxed as Rose clenched his manhood tight. Afterwards they relaxed in the bath.

Once they had dried each other off, Rose said, "Well seeing as we missed dinner last night, I will cook us a lovely breakfast, or Doctor Michel will be telling me off, for not keeping your energy and strength levels up."

Later on, as they were cuddled up on the settee, discussing various things, there was a knock at the door. Rose answered it, to see Raoul stood there. "Raoul, how lovely to see you. Please come in, come in." She gave him a tight hug and kissed his cheek. "Raoul, thank you for everything you did in finding our men, it will never be forgotten. JP is in the sitting room," and she took him in. "My love, look who's here."

"Raoul, good to see you," said JP, standing and giving him a man hug.

"Raoul would you like a hot drink, or another drink?" asked Rose.

Raoul replied, "Coffee would be nice, thank you Rose." Rose went off to the kitchen.

"Come sit down, Raoul. You and I have a lot to talk about, and thank you for everything you did." Raoul seemed a little bit embarrassed.

Rose returned with a pot of coffee, and mugs, and put them on the table. "My love, I need to go and do some food shopping, so I will leave you two to catch up. Is there anything you want?"

JP smiled and said, "Steak, môn amour." Rose smiled and kissed him, and then left them together.

Rose returned about three hours later, to see Raoul had left. "Did you have a good chat?"

JP replied they had and it had been good to talk to him. He said that Raoul did say he was glad to get back to the pub. "Did you manage to get any steaks?" Rose said they were on offer and so she got four. "Môn amour, I'm going to cook the meal tonight. You know how it relaxes me. What else did you get?" Rose placed everything on the kitchen table, and JP took what he wanted and then put the rest away. Rose put the kettle on, as she was thirsty. A couple of minutes later, JP and Rose curled up on the settee, and watched a film on the television.

"My love, what are you going to do with yourself being home for a month?"

JP looked at her and said, "Now don't get annoyed, but on Monday I'm going in to work, just the mornings only. I have so much work to catch up with, and rotas to sort out. Pierre will be with me, so no doubt I will be watched like a hawk."

Rose raised her eyebrow, but knew it wasn't worth an argument. "If you're sure, but please don't overdo it. At the moment I don't have many photo shoots for Séra, so I can take you and pick you up every day. I know the President will be pleased to see you."

JP took her in his arms and kissed her tenderly. "Well that went better than I thought."

Rose kissed him back and replied, "I can see your mind is made up, and I understand, that's all."

JP ended up cooking the steaks along with steak chips, and vegetables. For a dessert he made an apple pie with cinnamon, and served it with ice cream. As always Rose made the coffee. After they'd finished, they relaxed on the settee, kissing and cuddling each other. The phone went and Rose answered it. It was Monica. "Hello sweetheart. Just checking JP is alright and no setbacks. I'm off this weekend if you need me."

Rose replied, "He's fine, Mum. Just relaxing and taking it easy," and then told her about him going back to work. Monica was a little concerned it was too early, but obviously JP knew best. They chatted for about half an hour and then Monica rang off.

"That was Mum, my love, making sure you were alright." JP said how nice it was of her to think of him.

The next phone call was Ruby. "Nothing to be worried about, but Antoine is back in hospital."

"What happened, Ruby?"

Ruby replied, "Don't laugh, but he fell out of bed. I phoned Doctor Michel straight away, but nothing's broken, just keeping him for the night."

"Give him our love, and let me know when he's home and we'll come and visit." Ruby said she would.

A little bit later JP asked who'd phoned and Rose told him. "Was he pushed, or did he fall? I wonder."

"JP," said Rose, raising her eyebrow.

JP chuckled and said, "I think I remember a certain young lady falling out of bed?" Rose blushed and then smiled. "Talking of bed, I think I'm ready to go up," said JP. "You coming?" Rose said she would put the dishes away and then be up. JP locked the door, and put the house alarm on.

When Rose entered the bedroom, JP was in bed and gently snoring. *And he's thinking of going back to work,* she thought. Quietly she undressed and slipped into bed beside him, and switched the light off. JP automatically rolled over and took her in his arms, without waking up. Rose cuddled into him and they both slept until the morning.

Rose woke first, and so she went down to the kitchen and made some coffee, put some croissants, butter and jam on a tray and took it back upstairs. JP had just opened his eyes and said, "I got cold, môn amour. Come back and warm me up." Rose put the tray on the bedside table and got back into bed. JP wrapped his arms around her and kissed her tenderly, and then trailed kisses down to her breasts, which he caressed and kissed, and then to her nipples, which he sucked until they were hard. "Umm, I'm warming up now," he said. Rose giggled. Slowly his kisses went down over her stomach to her mound. She had been to the beauty salon to get naked when she knew he was coming home. He kissed it all over, and soon brought Rose to her climax. Slowly he kissed her all the way back up again. Rose was flushed and it had been a long time since he had seen the sexy look on her face.

"Now it's my turn," said Rose. Like JP she kissed him all the way down to his manhood, which was standing to attention. Gently she kissed it and cupped his testicles, kissing them also. Then she straddled him. She heard JP moan. Now it was her turn to smile. Slowly and gently she brought JP to climax. Then she kissed his lips. "Oh môn amour, I have missed you so much." JP rolled onto his side and put Rose's leg over his hip and entered her. They took their lovemaking slowly and then both exploded into oblivion.

Afterwards Rose said, "That's a shame."

"What is?" asked JP curiously.

Rose smiled and said, "The coffee and croissants have gone cold." They both burst out laughing, then cuddled into each other and went back to sleep. It was midday when they woke again.

"Shower time I think," said JP. Again they loved each other in the shower. JP told her he was making up for lost time, and Rose giggled.

As they were walking down the stairs, the phone rang, and it was Hugh. "Hello, my dear. Just checking you're both alright, and to ask you both if you would like to have lunch with Chantelle and myself next Sunday."

"Oh Uncle, that would be lovely. Where were you thinking of going?"

Hugh replied, "Here at the flat, and then you can both relax." Rose said they both looked forward to it and would see them about midday. Rose told JP and he said he looked forward to it.

"Now seeing as we skipped breakfast, I'll do us some lunch," said JP.

About an hour later they sat in the kitchen starting with a salad, followed by salmon en croute with vegetables and dauphinois potatoes, followed by fresh fruit salad. Once they'd had a rest from their meal, JP suggested a walk down to the pub. They both wrapped up warm and sauntered down to the village. When they walked into the pub, rapturous applause broke out. Everyone was delighted to see JP was still with them. Raoul gave them a drink, on the house. They stayed for a couple of hours chatting away to the villagers, and then much to his embarrassment, JP yawned. "Please excuse me," he said. Raoul suggested it was the heat from the fire, as the pub was rather cosy. JP and Rose said their goodbyes to everyone and walked back home, arm in arm.

"Now I think you should rest," said Rose, "or no work tomorrow."

JP smiled and said he would rest in the sitting room watching the television. Within ten minutes he was firm asleep, and Rose cuddled into him, and also fell asleep. When she woke JP wasn't there. Curious, she went to look for him. She found him in the kitchen making some sandwiches.

"Happy with sandwiches and pastries for dinner?" he asked. Rose smiled and nodded.

That night when they went to bed, they kissed and cuddled and slept.

In the morning, like clockwork, JP woke at 6am. Quietly he got out of bed, had a shower and dressed, and made Rose breakfast. He was about to take it up when she walked in the kitchen. "Morning, môn amour." Rose replied by putting her arms around him and giving him a long lingering kiss. JP said, "Can we keep that kiss on hold until later on?" Rose laughed, and they had their breakfast. Rose drove JP to the palace and walked with him to his office.

"Good grief. What a mess," he said.

"Boss, nice to see you back," said Porte, who had walked in behind them. 'Hi Rose." Rose smiled. "Sorry boss, we weren't expecting you today, or we would have cleared everything away."

JP had been walking round his office looking at the maps set out. "Are these maps of the area we went down?" he asked. Porte nodded. JP started to study them, and so Rose kissed him goodbye and said she would see him later. "Môn amour, there's no need. My car is here and I can drive home. I promise I'll drive carefully. See you later on?" Rose smiled and left. JP and Porte went over the events.

Rose had a wedding to photograph, and so she made her way to the town hall. The couple didn't look very happy, and Rose had a problem getting them to smile for their photos. In the end she asked one of the bridesmaids what was wrong. "Found out she's pregnant and he's told her it can't be his. She's gone ballistic and her father has made him marry her."

"Oh dear," said Rose. "Not a good start then." The bridesmaid said she'd tell them a daft joke, and hopefully they would laugh. It worked and eventually Rose got some good photos. She wondered how JP was getting on.

CHAPTER 30

At the palace, after Porte had run through everything with JP, he set about getting his office back to normality. A couple of hours later, Pierre walked in.

"Boss, wasn't expecting you. Can I get you anything?"

JP replied, "Some coffee would be good, as my coffee maker seems to have vanished, along with other things."

Pierre replied, "They're in your bedroom, boss." JP opened his bedroom door, to see all sorts of articles on the bed. He soon found the coffee maker, and five minutes later was enjoying a cup, along with Pierre.

"Can you bring me up to date, Pierre?" Pierre went through some of the paperwork, and time flew by. "Oh no, Rose is going to be furious. I promised her I'd only work mornings, and here it is 4pm."

Pierre grinned. "I'll see you in the morning then, boss. You alright to drive back?"

JP replied, "Only one way to find out, but I'm sure I'll be fine. Thanks, Pierre." JP took his time driving home, and arrived just as it started to pour with rain. He put his car in the garage, but smiled when he saw Rose wasn't home yet. Quickly he started cooking a meal.

Rose arrived about an hour later. "No argument, but where have you been? I got really worried, and drove to the palace, for Pierre to tell me you had just left!!"

JP could see Rose was annoyed and concerned so he replied, "Honestly môn amour, you saw the state of my office, but not my bedroom, and you would have been furious. I had to tidy up and the time just flew by. I promise I won't be late again. More important, how was your day?"

Rose raised her eyebrow and knew when he was trying to change the subject. "Good. Séra has persuaded a friend to let us use her castle for a photo shoot. It's near Chartres. We are all going down a week on Friday. Séra said you are more than welcome to join us. Want to come and see how I work?"

JP replied he would like to, and maybe they could stay longer and look around Chartres.

Rose smiled and kissed him tenderly. "Something smells nice."

JP replied, "Cheese soufflé."

"I'll just go and change and be straight down."

Rose came down in her dressing gown, and sat at the table. The cheese soufflé tasted light and delicious. "Hmm, that was lovely, my love. Coffee?" JP nodded. With their coffee they went and sat in the sitting room.

A short while later, JP took Rose in his arms and kissed her gently, whilst undoing the belt of her dressing gown, and saw she was naked. "Umm, dessert," he said as he started kissing her breasts.

The next couple of days, JP got most of his work up to date, and had seen the President, who was still on crutches. As promised he finished about 1pm every day and then went home to wait for Rose. On the Saturday they went and visited Ruby and Antoine.

"So you fell out of bed then?" asked JP. Antoine reddened slightly and looked at Ruby, who was smiling.

"Go on, tell them what you did," said Ruby.

Antoine replied, "I don't know how I did it, but I had totally got myself tangled up in the duvet, and ended up down the bottom of the bed. Ruby called to me, and thinking I was at the top of the bed, I went to roll over, and fell on the floor, leaving my good leg tangled in the duvet, which went up in the air and fell over me." Ruby was trying not to giggle.

JP replied subtly, "Ever heard of two left feet?" That made them all laughed.

"I'm fine, thanks for asking," said Antoine, pouting. Ruby gave him a kiss and then he smiled.

They spent about two hours at the flat, and because Rose and Ruby needed shopping, they drove their cars to the shopping centre, and had a lovely meal at one of the up-market cafés.

That night JP was wriggling under the duvet when Rose walked in. "My love, what on earth are you doing?"

JP popped his head out from under the duvet and said, "Trying to get tangled in the duvet like Antoine, but I can't."

Rose was creasing with laughter watching him. "JP, did you ever think that Antoine might have just strayed on the truth a little bit?"

JP looked at Rose and said, "Have I just tried that for no reason at all?"

Rose nodded. "The truth is they were mucking about and Antoine rolled over onto Ruby and kept rolling, getting tangled in the duvet, and fell out, and hurt himself in a delicate area, along with his leg."

"Ooh ouch," said JP, and then laughed. Looking at Rose sexily he said, "Can I interest you in a duvet roll?" Rose undressed quickly and joined him, and soon they were loving each other.

Afterwards JP cuddled into Rose and said, "At least our duvet roll went better than Antoine's."

Rose replied, "JP, that's not fair. Poor Antoine," but she did giggle.

As arranged, on the Sunday, they went to see Hugh and Chantelle. Rose noticed that Chantelle had moved in, and smiled. Chantelle made some coffees, and sat next to Hugh on the settee. Hugh said, "Rose, my dear, and JP, I have something I need to tell you." Rose had a feeling she knew what he was going to say, but she was wrong. "At the end of the year I will be moving from here, but as of yet, I'm not sure where."

"Why, Uncle?" asked Rose.

"The thing is, my dear, I have now reached an age, where it's time for me to be retired from the bank, and as you know the flat comes with the job."

Rose was stunned and said, "You're still young, Uncle, and what will you do?"

Hugh smiled and replied, "My dear to be honest, it's time for me to have time to live my life. I have, like many other people, worked since I was fourteen years old."

JP replied, "I don't know if it would be too far out, but Raoul told me one of the cottages was up for sale in the village?"

"Oh Uncle, that would be wonderful. You would only just be down the road from us, and we would see more of each other."

Hugh replied, "I would certainly like to take a look."

JP said if he didn't mind him using the phone, he would phone Raoul there and then. Raoul told JP that Hugh could come whenever he liked. The owners hadn't actually put it on the market just yet, so maybe they could do a private sale. Everyone was now excited.

"I hope you don't mind," said Hugh, "but I have done a traditional Sunday roast, with all the trimmings, as Chantelle has never had it."

"Lovely, Uncle," said Rose.

A little while later, they all sat down to roast beef, roast potatoes, a variety of vegetables, Yorkshire puddings and gravy, along with English mustard and horseradish sauce.

"I have done some stuffing, which is normally served with chicken, but I know how much Rose likes it."

Rose asked Chantelle how the modelling was going and Chantelle told her really well. Now she knew everyone, they all helped her. Rose was pleased. The wine flowed along with the conversation. For a dessert, Hugh had done a rice pudding topped with lots of nutmeg. "This is delicious, Uncle. It's a long time since I had rice pudding." JP and Chantelle enjoyed it as well.

Afterwards they sat on the settee and armchairs and had coffee and macarons. Rose and Chantelle talked about photo shoots, and Hugh and JP discussed investments and other things. Later on Hugh made some beef, ham and cheese sandwiches, along with various pastries and tea and coffee. About 8pm, Rose and JP left after hugs and kisses for Hugh and Chantelle.

"Well what a lovely day that was," said Rose. "Do you think Uncle would move to the village, my love?"

JP replied, "I don't know, môn amour, that will be up to your uncle, and I'm assuming Chantelle. They do make a nice couple."

Rose drove down the drive and parked the car in the garage. JP unlocked the front door, turned off the alarm, and set it again once Rose was in. "Do you want a drink, my love?"

"No, môn amour, I'm ready for bed."

Rose smiled and they went up to the bedroom. JP took Rose in his arms and kissed her tenderly, and then said, "It would be good if your uncle moved to the village. At least you'd have one family member close by."

Rose smiled and replied, "Once the road is finished, all our family will be nearer."

JP unzipped the back of Rose's dress and started kissing her back. He saw she had a black bra and brief set on, and pushed her dress down, and Rose stepped out of it. JP quickly undressed and picked Rose up and laid her on the bed. "Je t'aime, môn amour."

Rose replied, "Je t'aime aussi."

Their arms went round each other and their kisses were tender and then became passionate. Rose rolled JP over and straddled him. JP reached round to her back and unclipped her bra, letting her breasts go free. His hands caressed them and then he gently pulled her down and started kissing them. Rose's nipples went hard at his touch. He rolled her over and his hands went to her lacy briefs and undid the laces. At the same time Rose pushed JP's underpants down, and he wriggled out of them. Rose's legs went round his waist and he entered her. Slowly he brought Rose to the brink and then pulled back. He did this three times until both of them reached an ecstatic climax. As always JP then spooned Rose's back, with his arms around her and they slept.

The rest of the week went by quickly and soon it was Friday. JP had asked the permission of the President to spend the weekend at Chartres, and he agreed. Two more weeks and JP and his men would be back at the training academy. JP hadn't seen much of his men, but he phoned them every week to make sure they were alright, and to see if they needed anything. He would spend more than an hour talking to each one of them. Rose and JP packed a suitcase each, and put them in the boot of Rose's car. Rose had all her photography equipment on the back seat. Soon they set off, with JP driving. Séra had given Rose the directions to the castle. Séra and the rest of the team were travelling down in the large trucks, and Séra's car.

Just before they entered the town of Chartres, Rose told JP to follow the road to Bartieux. They could see the castle in the distance, and the nearer they got, the bigger the castle became. Séra and the team more or less arrived at the same time. A huge forest surrounded the castle, which had a large moat going all the way round it, with swans, and various ducks on it. To get into the castle they had to drive over the main wooden drawbridge. Six other drawbridges were around the castle, leading to different areas. Once over the main drawbridge it led into a large courtyard, covered with gravel, and this is where they parked.

A very elegant lady appeared, coming down the steps from the castle. "Séra, you found us then? Welcome to our castle."

Séra gave her air kisses, and then said, "Everyone, I would like to introduce you to the Comtesse Boneaux." Séra introduced everyone, including JP.

"I must say you're a very handsome man for a model," the Comtesse said, looking at JP.

JP replied, "I'm afraid I'm not good enough to be a model, Comtesse. I'm actually the President's Chief of Security."

The Comtesse nodded in understanding, but Rose noticed she never took her eyes off him. "I think you've made a conquest, my love."

JP smiled at Rose and replied, "My only conquest is you, môn amour," and gently kissed her.

"Come on everyone, let's get to work before we lose the light," said Séra.

The Comtesse said, "JP, may I invite you to look round the castle? My husband is away at the moment, and I do so enjoy a gentleman's company, and I'm sure I could show you a good time."

JP, rather taken aback by her comment, politely refused and said he wanted to watch how his wife did a photo shoot. The Comtesse turned her back and walked off.

Séra smirked and said quietly to JP, "She's not use to being refused, and I apologise for her manners."

JP replied, "Not for you to apologise, Séra, I'm here for Rose and to see how all this works." Séra smiled, and taking his arm led him round to the gardens where the photo shoot was taking place.

JP watched as Rose had the models standing in various positions, using the gardens as a backdrop. Sometimes the models were on their own, and other times they were all together. He thought he would be bored, but he was fascinated by all of it. Mind you, he rather enjoyed the lingerie section shoot!! Rose just smiled at him, when he made certain suggestions to her. Once the photo shoot was done, Séra told them on the Sunday, the castle was open to the public, if any of them wanted to stay. Séra was driving back to Paris that evening. Apart from Rose and JP they all decided to return. JP had booked a hotel in Chartres. After helping everyone to clear up, they drove there.

As they approached Chartres, they couldn't miss the massive Cathédrale Notre-Dame. "Tomorrow we could have a look inside if you wanted to, môn amour?" Rose said she would love to.

Once they had checked in, Rose was shattered and decided to have a relaxing bath. She was just nodding off, when JP came in. "Môn amour, I have ordered us room service, so we can just stay here and relax. I hope that was alright?"

Rose replied, "What a good idea. I'll just get dried." Rose stood up, with the water and soap suds running down her glistening body. JP felt himself react, but just held up the large towel and wrapped it round her, and dried her off. Rose then put on a thick luxurious robe. Whilst Rose dried her hair, JP had a quick shower, and put on the other robe.

Their meal arrived, which consisted of a mixed salad to start, followed by chicken casserole, and a bottle of wine. Afterwards they cuddled up on the small settee and watched some television. About an hour later Rose had fallen asleep. JP now understood why Rose was always shattered when she returned from doing a long photo shoot. He thought the models just stood wherever, and Rose took a photo. Definitely not. Poses had to be just so, facial expressions to match the mood, all the changes of clothes and hair and make-up. Even the men had the same treatment. The light had to be just right, if not the artificial lights had to be used. Séra explained to him how the photos were edited, and then the right ones ended up being published. Some pages would just have one model in different poses and clothes, another could have all of them together. In a day he had learnt a lot about fashion photography and how the magazine was published.

Picking Rose up gently, he put her on the bed, and then took her robe off. He took his robe off and got in beside her, and drew the duvet over both of them. Rose snuggled into his chest, and JP turned out the lights.

CHAPTER 31

The following morning, JP woke Rose with gentle kisses. "Good morning, my love," said Rose, wrapping her arms around him.

"Morning, môn amour. Are you well rested?"

Rose replied by kissing him passionately. JP pulled her close and Rose eased her leg over his hip. She felt JP slip into her and moaned. "Umm, that feels good." JP loved Rose sensually and slowly until she went over the edge. Rose rolled JP over and straddled him, moving up and down his manhood slowly. Soon both of them went into oblivion.

After a short sleep, Rose awoke and quietly slipped out of the bed and went to have a shower. She had just got under the shower when JP joined her. They soaped each other's bodies as the hot water cascaded down over them. JP kissed Rose and then let his kisses trail down to her mound. Slowly he brought Rose to another climax. Rose then took JP's manhood in her hand and brought him to his climax. After drying each other off, they dressed and went down and had breakfast.

"So môn amour, shall we explore the delights of Chartres, or…?"

Rose smiled and replied, "The or… can wait until tonight. Let's go explore the cathedral."

The Cathédrale Notre-Dame was massive and dated back to Gothic times. It had two towering spires, flying buttresses, Romanesque sculptures, elaborate rose windows, and a pavement labyrinth. Inside the cathedral there were distinctive blue-tinted stained-glass windows. The windows were financed by merchants and craftsmen and had their names on the bottom of each window. Behind the cathedral was the Musée des Beaux-Arts. It was here that the coronation of Henri IV took place in 1594. Most of the building was renovated in the seventeenth and eighteenth centuries. The town of Chartres had lots of cobbled streets with half-timbered houses. Medieval lanterns were suspended on chains illuminating the streets. Along the River Eure, was an interesting pathway, along with humped-back bridges, public washhouses and water mills. One of the water mills had been renovated into a beautiful restaurant. On the river you could hire a boat or a canoe. In the town there were lots of various shops, and on that day there was a colourful market in the square. JP told Rose that the Rétrodor baguette was a must to be eaten, as they were made from the finest wheat from Beauce. Chartres Pâte was made with game, pheasant or partridge. The macarons were made with a softer texture than those made in Paris. JP bought Rose some Mentchikoffs, which were a praline chocolate sweet, covered with Swiss meringue. Rose loved them.

As they walked round the various streets, and just outside the city centre, they came upon Maison Picassiette. This was a house made from millions of pieces of broken crockery, glass, bottle caps, and compiled into mosaics. Rose and JP could not believe their eyes. Needless to say Rose took plenty of photos. There were told the house was built in 1938. Even the furniture, walls, tables, chairs, and beds were covered in mosaic, but portrayed flowers or animals. They decided to return to the riverside restaurant, where they had a lovely meal of locally caught fish, with a variety of vegetables, and dauphinois potatoes. For a dessert they had peach flan with ice cream and cream. Cheese and biscuits and coffee followed this.

"That was lovely, JP, and I feel so full. Can we walk back to the hotel through some of the parks?" JP had to agree, as he was full as well. Hand in hand they slowly walked back through two different parks, both full of varieties of flowers and trees. One had a large lake, which had swans and ducks on it.

Back in the centre of Chartres, Rose decided to have a look at the fashion shops, and ended up buying some trousers, skirts and blouses. JP went off to look around the gents' clothing, and in his absence Rose bought some sexy lingerie. They had spent the whole day looking round Chartres, and instead of going out for dinner, they ate in the restaurant. Both of them had a salad to start, steak with vegetables and potatoes, but didn't bother with a dessert.

Smiling cheekily Rose said, as she drank her coffee, "Would you like to go back and see your Comtesse tomorrow?"

JP raised his eyebrow and replied, "On one condition. You don't leave my side for a second." Rose laughed and promised. That night they loved each other and then slept.

Once they had checked out of the hotel, they drove to the castle. They had had a leisurely breakfast, as the castle didn't open until 10am. There was already quite a queue when they arrived. They had a guide who told them a brief history of the castle. It dated back to the era of King Louis XII, and had been handed down generation by generation. The castle had nearly two hundred rooms, and also housed a kennels where there were fifty hunting hounds. The hunt usually took place twice a week. It was only open to the public on a Sunday. Quite a lot of the rooms were private and therefore not for public viewing. The guide advised them that they were free to wander round at their leisure, as most of the articles actually had plaques telling them what they were, where they came from etc., etc.

As they entered the reception hall, in front of them was a stone staircase that led to the upstairs rooms. A huge chandelier hung from the ceiling. The first room they visited was the library, which was huge. Rose was in her element, looking at the very old books, which were behind clear glass. Some dated back to the fifteenth and sixteenth centuries, and some of the writing was unreadable. Next was a huge armoury, which JP enjoyed. Knights wore armour from the early centuries, and then more modern ones. Various swords, spears, muskets, and guns adorned the walls. The dining room had a table, which could seat sixteen people, and was already set for a meal. There were bouquets of flowers down the centre of the table, and plates of pretend food at each place setting. Bottles of wine were in wine carriers, along with crusty bread in bread baskets. At the end of the dining room was a small room made up to look like a kitchen. It had all the different size copper saucepans on the shelves, along with various utensils hung on the wall.

Some of the other rooms were a trophy room, with the heads of various animals, a large study, a sitting room, a smaller library, a room full of paintings with some old and some modern, and a music room with a piano and a harp. Huge chandeliers hung down from the ceilings, which all had floral paintings on them, and most of the rooms had large fireplaces, some even had gold surrounds. A red rope looping through gold posts cordoned off the furniture, some of which dated back to Louis XIII. Lots of cabinets held crockery, silverware, various glasses and small statues. Large and small vases were everywhere, along with various clocks.

Once everyone had seen the rooms downstairs, they made their way up the stone staircases to see some of the bedrooms. Pictures of ancestors going way, way back, adorned the whole length of the corridor. Smaller chandeliers hung from a plain ceiling. A lot of the rooms were cordoned off. This was the Comte and Comtesse's private apartments. The bedrooms were ornate to say the least. Huge four-poster beds, with drapes that could be closed around the beds. Paintings and tapestries on the walls, large fireplaces, and very ornate furniture dating way back. Some of the rooms had mannequins dressed up in costumes of various eras. Like all the other rooms, chandeliers hung from the ceilings, some had wall candelabras. The bedroom that had most people talking about was the children's bedroom. There was an old-fashioned crib, two small children's beds, and a rocking horse, that had seen better days. On a table was a small mock-up of the castle, and the detail was very impressive. A newer invention in the room was a couple of the hunting hounds made up from Lego bricks. Rose went to say something to JP, but he was nowhere to be seen.

JP had been looking at some of the paintings in detail, when a hand grabbed him, and thinking it was Rose, followed. The next minute he was in a very exotic bedroom, all in a seductive red colour. Much to his surprise he saw that it was the Comtesse who had grabbed him. She was stood in a very provocative, more or less see-through negligee, and nothing else. Looking him up and down and licking her lips the Comtesse said, "I saw you arrive and have been waiting to show you how a real woman can satisfy, and play, with an extremely handsome man like yourself." JP looked around and saw she had an array of whips, handcuffs, and other sexual objects, laid on the bed. He went to leave, but the Comtesse quickly locked the door and put the key down between her rather large breasts.

"I'm sorry, Comtesse, but I am a happily married man, and I can assure you I have no intentions of letting you seduce me. Now, if you would kindly unlock the door, my wife will be wondering where I am."

The Comtesse laughed and replied, putting her hand on his manhood, "Now I'm sure you're not shy, and you feel like you manhood is rather large, and would fill me up tightly, so why don't you undress and then let me pleasure you in ways that you've never been pleasured in before."

JP's rape came back to him and not wanting to be rude, he pushed her hand away and replied calmly, "Comtesse, I have already been raped by a woman, and I will not let that happen again."

The Comtesse looked at him, stunned. "Believe me, that is not my intention. My husband can't satisfy me these days, and I can see what a virile man you are, and I don't usually get refused. I could seriously damage Séra's reputation. Is that what you want?"

JP sighed and replied, "I feel sorry for you, Comtesse, that you have to stoop so low, to get someone to love you, but as I said I'm not your man. Will you now please unlock the door?"

The Comtesse took JP's hands and placed them on her breasts, saying, "You know where the key is. Help yourself."

JP could see the key wedged between her breasts and had an idea. He gently took her in his arms and shook her. The key fell to the floor. Quickly he picked it up and went and unlocked the door. As he went to leave the Comtesse said, "Sure you want to leave this luscious body to get cold?" JP turned and saw her negligee was gone and she was propped up on the bed, with one hand massaging her breast, and the other between her wide opened legs, stroking herself. JP just raised his eyebrow, went out of the door and relocked it, throwing the key on the floor. He saw Rose walking up and down the corridor.

"JP where have you been? I was getting worried." JP told her. "I have an idea," said Rose. "Quickly unlock the door." JP looked at Rose, but unlocked the door.

"So you do desire me after all," said the Comtesse, still on the bed, baring all to the world, but she now had a vibrator inside her.

"No he doesn't, and don't you ever threaten my husband or my boss again," said Rose, and raised her camera and took photos. "Who knows, one day these might appear in a newspaper article." Rose slammed the door and relocked it. Taking the key, she put it in the waste bin.

JP looked at Rose and said, "Please tell me you're not going to develop those. Ugh."

Rose laughed and kissing his cheek said, "I didn't take any photos, but she doesn't know that. I was about to put a new roll in the camera."

JP chuckled and said, "You're devious, and je t'aime," and taking her in his arms kissed her passionately.

The grounds outside were extensive, and they only walked round a small part of it. There were lots of small pools, with animals or fish spouting out water. There were two large fountains, with water gushing up very high, and when the breeze touched the water, it fanned out over that part of the garden. Going down a narrow pathway, the next garden had them standing there just looking. "Now I see where she gets her ideas from," said Rose. There were twelve large statues of couples, in all various sexual positions, some leaving nothing to the imagination.

"Don't think I would want children to look at these," said JP. "There should be a warning notice." Rose agreed. The gardens were full of various trees, shrubs and flowers, and pathways. "Well my love, I think we should get back to Paris, and leave Comtesse Boneaux to her castle. I for one will not come back here again."

JP replied, "I agree, let's go home to our lovely farmhouse."

Two hours later they were in Paris. Once back Rose phoned her uncle, Ruby, and Monica and George, just to make sure everyone was alright, and they were. JP sorted out a few chores that needed doing in the garden, and then settled down to cook the evening meal.

The next two weeks went by quickly and it was the last weekend before JP and his men went back to the academy for training. On the Saturday, Rose and JP had invited everyone over for a meal. JP cooked his signature meal – Boeuf Bourguignon. Pierre was delighted. Luckily it was a clear, but coolish day, and so the children were running in and out of the garden. Everyone had lots of catching up to do, so over the meal the conversation flowed nicely. Hugh had some good news and said both Chantelle and himself had seen the cottage in the village, and he had made an offer, and was waiting to hear back. Rose was thrilled. Gabrielle told them the new road was opening earlier, at the end of November, so they would only be half an hour's drive away. The men were all now recovered from their injuries and were looking forward to getting back to their duties. Pierre told them the President was also fully recovered and back with a vengeance!! Everyone stayed until about 8pm and then made their ways home. After Rose and JP had cleared everything up, they went to bed and slept. The Sunday, they just relaxed and enjoyed each other's company. Late afternoon Rose decided to go and have a relaxing bath, which she did. JP was sorting out a problem he had with his car.

After a meal, it was soon time to retire and they both went upstairs. JP had a quick shower and Rose was in bed when he returned. Pushing the duvet back he saw Rose had a black sexy lingerie set on. Rose saw his manhood rise to the occasion and giggled. Rose said, holding her arms out to him, "A memory to take with you to remember over the next four weeks." JP sat astride her and slowly peeled her out of her lingerie, kissing every bit of her body. Then they made slow and sensual love to each other, until both of them were totally sated.

CHAPTER 32

Monday morning and Rose and JP made love to each other. After a shower and getting dressed, they sat down to their breakfast. An hour later they arrived at the palace, where his men were waiting for him. JP decided to leave his car at home, so Rose had driven him in, before going to Séra's. Andre brought round the large car, and Rose said her goodbyes to them, and wished them well for their training. She waved as they drove off, and then she drove to Séra's. None of the models were there that day, as Séra was going through the photos that Rose had taken.

"Rose, some of these photos you've taken are wonderful. I was thinking of doing a different spread in the magazine. What do you think of this layout?" Normally one model had one page, but this time Séra had put the same model on the page, but from different angles, in different clothes, along with accessories. Another page had all four of them in various poses. A couple of them had Mía's name under them for people to order.

"It's different," said Rose, "and I like it. Maybe Suzette could do some merging, and have all of them on one page, in different outfits and poses?" Séra liked that idea.

After they had sorted out the photos, Séra asked her how the weekend had gone, and if JP and herself had gone back to the castle. Rose told Séra what had happened. "What!!" she said in disgust. "I can't believe it. I saw she liked JP straight away, and I know she has marriage problems, but never thought she would go that far. I am so sorry, Rose, and please give JP my sincere apologies. I certainly won't go there again." Rose replied she had no need to apologise; if anyone should apologise it should be the Comtesse Boneaux.

The next four weeks flew by, and JP and his men had finished their training. Rose had been busy doing photo shoots, weddings, having lunch with her uncle and sometimes Chantelle, and seeing the other wives, Monica and George, and of course Ruby. Now it was so quick to get into the centre of Paris, Rose and Ruby met up at least three times a week, just for lunch. Ruby was thoroughly enjoying her job with Mathieu, and got on really well with everyone. Mathieu was also pleased with Ruby, and was now sending her off to do her own assignments.

Friday afternoon, Rose went to the palace to pick up JP. He was in his office, and was delighted to see her. "All go well, my love?"

JP replied, "We all passed and are fully fit for work again, thank heavens. Give me five minutes and I will be ready to leave." JP made a phone call to Porte, who came up and picked up the new rotas. JP locked his office door and hand in hand they went back to Rose's car. They drove to the supermarket to do a large shop.

Once home Rose asked JP how it had gone. JP replied, "Honestly, môn amour, it was really hard work. It was like none of us had had the training before. After two days it was all we could do to walk, never mind anything else.

"None of us realised how that crash had taken all our strength and stamina away. I didn't think Antoine was going to complete the course, but he did – just. Every day we were put through our paces, and every night we were too tired to eat, but we did. It must have been week three before we all started getting it together, and then there was no stopping us. We were all declared fit, and are back to work on Monday morning, bright and early. So môn amour, it's back to you seeing me every other weekend."

Rose replied, chuckling, "So I now have a 'fit' husband. Sounds good. You do realise it's only just over three weeks to Christmas?"

JP replied he did, and the President was going away, until the middle of January.

"What are we going to do for Christmas?"

JP replied, "As far as I know, none of my men or their wives have anything planned, so we could have them all over here again. Now this road is open, it won't take them so long."

Rose took JP in her arms and said, kissing him, "Well for now, I think I need to see how 'fit' my husband is." JP smiled and picking her up, carried her up to their bedroom. "Umm JP, can you just give a minute?" JP raised his eyebrow and let her down gently. Five minutes later and Rose was back. JP was stood looking out the window, so Rose went to him and put her arms round his waist. "I thought you'd be undressed by now, my love, so let me help you."

Rose's hand went to his shirt and pulling it out of his trousers, she slowly undid the buttons, and then removed it. JP tried to turn around but Rose wouldn't let him. Next she undid his trousers, and pushed them down with his underpants, which fell to the floor. JP quickly kicked his shoes off, and stood out of his trousers and underpants. "Take your socks off," said Rose in a rather husky voice. JP bent over to remove them and Rose ran her hands all over his back and down between his legs and caressed his testicles and manhood. JP responded immediately.

Rose then let him turn around. JP was blown away. Rose was stood there in a white short negligee and he could see underneath she had on a bra and brief set, with suspenders and stockings all in pure white. Her long hair was tied up in a high ponytail. Rose watched as his manhood stood to attention, and smiled. "You look so sexy, môn amour," and JP took her in his arms and kissed her lips. Picking her up he then laid her on the bed, and then carried on kissing her lips and down the side of her neck. His hand wandered to her negligee and he pulled the four lace ribbons apart and then removed it. He took all of Rose in. Her breasts were pushed up by the bra, making then look so large. The suspender belt was round her trim waist, holding up the white stockings on her long athletic legs. The lacy briefs fitted her snugly and he could see she was naked under them. He could have taken here there and then, but he would have to wait. His manhood was as hard as a rock already. He carried on kissing her all the way down to her mound.

"This is like undressing a virgin, but what a gorgeous virgin you look, môn amour." Rose smiled and let her hair down, making her look even sexier. JP undid the suspenders on one leg, and then carefully rolled the stocking down and slipped it off. He kissed her leg all the way back up her inner thigh to her mound, where he placed gentle kisses. He then did the same with the other leg. He then removed her suspender belt. Rose held her arms out to JP and wrapping her arms round him kissed him passionately. She rolled him over and straddled him. Bending over she took one nipple and sucked, nipped and licked it. It went hard immediately at her touch. She then did the other one. Sliding down the side of him, she kissed his stomach down to his manhood, which she took in her mouth. JP knew he wouldn't last long, and he didn't. Rose smiled, as it made a change for her to bring him first. JP grabbed her gently and drew her up to him, where he kissed her with a passion. His hands soon undid her bra and her breasts were free. He caressed and kissed them and her nipples went hard. He nipped and sucked them. Rose was moaning. "Môn amour, straddle my face and let me take you to heaven." Rose did as he asked, but still had her briefs on. JP saw the laces and pulled them so her briefs fell down and he removed them. Spreading her lips, he licked, kissed and sucked her nub. His hands were on her buttocks and held her tight to him. Rose was holding onto the headboard.

JP carried on until Rose's climax hit her and she called out his name. JP carefully moved Rose down until she was nearly over his manhood, and then rolled them both over, and lifting Rose's legs up to her shoulders, entered her. He thrust deep and deeper and Rose was moaning, as he could feel her coming. His mouth went to her breasts and nipped her nipples. Rose had manoeuvred her hand between them and was caressing his testicles. JP started thrusting quicker and quicker, and Rose caressed him a little bit tighter. Rose was squeezing his manhood so tight with her inner muscles, and then both of them shuddered as their climaxes hit them.

Both sated, they cuddled up to each other, kissing and caressing each other. Rose said breathlessly, "Well, my fit man is back, and that was wonderful." JP smiled and started kissing her neck and breasts again. The next minute Rose's left leg was over JP's hip and he was thrusting into her again, but slowly. Soon they both went over the edge. "I love you so much, JP."

"Je t'aime aussi, môn amour."

Within a couple of minutes both of them had fallen into a deep contented sleep.

In the morning Rose heard the phone ringing and went to answer it. It was her uncle. Hugh wanted to know if they were free for lunch on Sunday. "Oh Uncle, we would love to. What time?"

Hugh replied, "Say about midday, but you know you're both welcome to come whatever time you want to."

They talked for about half an hour and then Rose went back to the bedroom. JP wasn't there, and then she heard him in the shower. Putting her hair up, she went to the bathroom, and stepped into the shower with him. "Good morning, môn amour," he said and kissed her. Rose took the soap from him and lathered it up between her hands and then washed his back, but her hand accidentally slipped between his legs and massaged his manhood, which responded.

"I think my angel wants to play, my love."

JP turned and smiling, picked her up and slipped her down over his manhood, saying, "I think he does." Both of them climaxed under the warm cascading water. As they dried each other JP asked who was on the phone.

"It was Uncle asking us to go over for lunch tomorrow. I said yes. Is that alright?"

"Fine, môn amour, and perhaps he has some news on the cottage."

Once Rose had got back in the bedroom, she put her dressing gown on and then dried her hair.

Later on they both went to the shopping centre but on the way back JP turned off and headed for Gérard's. It had been ages since they had been. In fact that gave JP an idea. "Rose, JP, how wonderful to see you. JP, I hope I find you in good health after the accident?" asked Gérard.

"I'm all the better for seeing you, my friend, and yes, I'm quite recovered as all of us are."

"Come, come, I will take you to your table."

Once they were seated Gérard gave them the menu. Rose went for Cassoulet, whilst JP had Navarin D'Agneau (like Boeuf Bourguignon, but made with lamb). Gérard put a small bowl of Gougères (cheese puffs) on the table. Rose asked JP, "Aren't these what we had in Marseille?" JP nodded. Rose thought they were delicious. JP had also ordered a bottle of red wine.

"I've had an idea, môn amour. What do you think about all of us spending Christmas or New Year here at Gérard's?"

Rose smiled and replied, "I would imagine your men would want to spend Christmas with their families, but you and I, along with my uncle and Chantelle, Ruby and Antoine, and Mum and Dad, if they're not working, could come. It would be lovely if we could all do New Year's Eve together and hope next year will not bring any of us bad news." JP said that he would ask his men.

When Gérard came back, JP asked if he would be able to arrange a table for them. Gérard replied, "Mon ami, I will fit you in any time. You know you are all welcome." JP thanked him.

For a dessert, they had a variety of macarons, with coffee. When JP went to pay the bill, Gérard would not take any payment. "Mon ami, like a lot of us, we thought we had lost you for good. My heart went out to those who didn't make it, especially Benoit. Please accept my gift, JP." JP shook Gérard's hand and was surprised when Gérard gave him a manly hug. "JP, let me know about Christmas or New Year." Gérard hugged and kissed Rose's cheek as they left.

JP told Rose about not paying and Rose replied, "I came here with Ruby, and he did say all of us were to come for a free meal. He had been greatly concerned about you all."

Sunday morning they made their way into Paris to see Hugh and Chantelle.

"Rose, JP lovely to see you. Chantelle, Rose and JP are here." Chantelle walked into the sitting room and greeted both of them with a hug and a kiss on the cheek. "Coffee, everyone?" asked Hugh. They all nodded. Chantelle was concerned about JP, until he reassured her that he and his men were fully recovered. "Well, we have some news," said Hugh. "We have purchased the cottage in the village, and will be moving in over the next three weeks. I had the pleasure of meeting Raoul, who introduced me to the buyers, and we cemented the deal over a glass of brandy."

"Oh, Uncle that's wonderful news," said Rose, hugging her uncle and Chantelle. "If I can help in any way, you only have to ask. Alas, JP is working."

Hugh replied, "As are we. It will have to be weekends I'm afraid, but seeing as the bank furnished this flat, I have to leave it. Chantelle and I have been to the furniture store you suggested, Rose, and most of it is being delivered the weekend after next. Chantelle finishes modelling at the end of the week, until the end of January, and with me retiring, we will have plenty of time to sort the cottage out. It goes without saying both of you will be welcomed at any time. Now I had better get the meal going or else we won't be eating today. Rose can you quickly give me a hand?" Rose and Hugh went into the kitchen, and Hugh pushed the door to.

"What's going on, Uncle?"

Hugh put his finger to his lips, and heard JP and Chantelle laughing about something. "I need your blessing, my dear."

Rose looked at him curiously and replied, "Blessing about what, Uncle?" Putting his hand in his trouser pocket, he pulled out a small box. Rose immediately knew what it was. "Don't show me, Uncle, as I want to be surprised when Chantelle shows me. You certainly don't need my blessing. I am absolutely delighted for both of you. Now I've got to keep it a secret. When are you going to propose?"

Hugh replied, "I was thinking of Christmas Eve at midnight."

Rose hugged and kissed her uncle and said, "Think we had better start cooking something." Both of them smiled.

CHAPTER 33

Rose and JP spent a lovely day with Hugh and Chantelle. On the way back home, Rose told JP about her uncle proposing to Chantelle. "That's great news. They make such a lovely couple, just like us, môn amour." Rose leant over and kissed his cheek. That night they loved each other and then slept.

Monday morning JP drove to the palace and Rose was off photographing a wedding. Once at the palace he met his men and the rest of the bodyguards, who were all delighted to see them back. JP mentioned Christmas and New Year. His men said they would let him know.

About 10am, JP received a call from the President asking to see him and his men. JP phoned Andre and they all met outside the President's office. JP knocked on the door and was told to enter. The President was sitting behind his desk, and they all bowed to him. "Gentlemen, it's good to see you all back and fit for duty again," said the President. "I never had the opportunity to really thank you all, for all your efforts in saving each other, and myself. You are all a credit to being my loyal and trustworthy bodyguards. I still can't believe that Benoit is no longer with us, or Poirot, Paul and my other aide. A new jet is arriving within the next couple of days, and will be piloted by Raoul, on a temporary basis." JP was pleased at that bit of news. "Now, next year we have a very busy year, and I have to warn you, it just might be my last year in office. It will all depend upon the French people when they cast their votes."

That bit of news shook all of them.

"I'm sorry JP, but you are going to have a lot of travelling arrangements to make, and sorting out the rotas."

JP replied, "That will not be a problem, Monsieur le President."

The President smiled and said, "My plans for Christmas and New Year have unfortunately changed. My family and I will now be leaving Paris on 3rd January and return ten days later. I will only require two bodyguards and Porte and Sávoire have already volunteered. Seeing as we will now be here for New Year's Eve, my wife and I wondered if all of you would like to attend a very informal evening with us, along with your wives? That's if you're free of course. No need for your wives to rush out and buy expensive ball gowns. Let JP know and then JP, you can let me know." JP nodded his head in acknowledgement. "Now I'm sure you all have lots of duties to attend to, so I will detain you no longer. JP, if you would stay please."

Andre, Donatien, Pierre and Antoine all bowed and left.

"JP, here is a list of the countries to be visited next year."

JP looked at the list to see there was Italy, England, Belgium, Spain, Luxembourg, and others. "You are going to be busy, Monsieur le President."

The President replied, "I have to make sure that all state affairs are in order in case a new President succeeds me."

JP said, " I'm sure I speak for all my men and myself when I say that you would be a huge loss to us, Monsieur le President. May I ask if Raoul is going to be your permanent pilot?"

The President replied that Raoul was thinking about it. JP and the President discussed affairs for another two hours, and then JP returned to his office.

The first thing he did was make himself some coffee. "Smells good," said Andre as he walked in.

"Help yourself, Andre. How is everything?"

Andre replied they had found a few problems with the security cameras, but were being worked on as they spoke. JP handed Andre the list of countries. "Good grief, that's a gruelling schedule. Some of these countries we have never visited before, so I'll look into them and let you know. Do you think the President will be re-elected?"

JP replied, "I have no idea, but I hope he is. The thought of working from scratch with somebody new doesn't bear thinking about, but it will happen. If not next year, then in five years' time, by legislation, he will be replaced."

Andre nodded and replied, "Whilst you were with the President, we all quickly phoned home. Our wives said they would be delighted to attend on New Year's Eve, but Christmas Day they wanted to spend with their families, unless it was in the evening."

JP saw no problem with that and suggested 6pm. Andre said that would be good. JP would phone Rose later, when she was back home, and then let the President know.

At that minute JP's phone rang, and Andre left. It was the President saying that Hugh and his lady friend, and Rose's mum and dad were also invited, if free. JP said he would contact them. JP already knew that Rose would say, "Yes."

JP phoned Hugh at the bank, who said they would love to attend both. He phoned Monica and George, but there was no reply. Later on he phoned again and Monica answered. "JP, lovely to hear from you. How are you?" JP replied he was fine and then asked what he needed to know. "Oh JP, we would love to come to both of them, especially Rose's 30th birthday. What an honour to be invited by the President."

JP smiled to himself and replied, "You and George are family." JP couldn't see Monica blushing.

"Who will be coming on Christmas Day?"

JP replied all of them would be there, but it would be early evening about 6pm. Monica said they looked forward to it. Afterwards he phoned Rose. "How was your day, mòn amour?" Rose said it had been good but tiring. The wedding had been most of the day, and she hadn't had a drink or anything to eat, as she was only the photographer. JP was not happy about that. He told her about the President's offer and as he thought, Rose agreed. He told her he would phone Gérard and book for Christmas Day for fourteen of them. They chatted for about an hour and then JP phoned Gérard's and made the booking, and then went to join his men for a meal.

On Saturday, Rose was busy sorting out some photos when there was a knock at the door.

"Chantelle, how are you? Come in."

Chantelle replied, "Bonjour Rose. Apologies for bothering you but I wondered if I could borrow some coffee?"

"Are you moving in?" asked Rose. Chantelle said they were. Rose made her two flasks of coffee and grabbed her coat and walked back to the cottage with her. Rose didn't know which cottage it was, but soon did, as there was a huge delivery van outside. "Uncle." Hugh turned to see Rose with Chantelle and went and hugged her. "I thought you weren't moving in yet?" Hugh told her the furniture warehouse had phoned to ask if they could deliver this weekend instead of the next one. "Good job I brought two flasks of coffee then," said Rose.

"Rose," called a male voice. She turned to see Raoul, and went and hugged him. "Raoul, how are you? I haven't seen you since you came to visit JP." Raoul said he was fine and told her about his job offer from the President, and asked what she thought. "I think it's a great job. Just think of all the countries you'll visit."

Raoul replied, "Planes and helicopters I can fly, but not private jets."

"Surely the President will send you for training?" Raoul replied he would, but his first assignment would be in January. Rose said, "I don't know a lot about jets, but surely it must be the same as flying a normal plane."

Raoul replied, "Sort of, but I'm not up to date with the new equipment."

Rose said, "Ask JP if you can see the jet once it's delivered, and then at least you can have a look."

Raoul pondered on that thought and then said, "Ladies, why don't you go into the pub and keep warm, as the wind is getting up. I'll get a couple of the village men to help the delivery men."

Rose and Chantelle went into the pub, and talked about the future. Chantelle was concerned that Hugh might be bored after retiring, but Rose assured her he would always find something to do. Chantelle had finished modelling until the end of January, and was going to enjoy making the cottage cosy.

About an hour later, Hugh and Raoul walked into the pub. "All done, ladies," said Raoul. "Now can I get you all a drink?" Raoul gave them all a brandy. "Are you moving in permanently today?" asked Raoul.

Hugh replied, "No. That will be the last weekend of this month. Chantelle will be popping over to do whatever womanly things need to be done, and myself at the weekends."

Slowly the other villagers sauntered into the pub and Raoul introduced them all to Hugh and Chantelle. Rose apologised and said she had to leave. She had an afternoon wedding to do. She hugged and kissed her uncle and Chantelle, and reminded Raoul to speak to JP. Outside the wind had got up and it had an icy feel to it. Rose made sure to wrap up warm. Unfortunately, at the wedding, the wind got worse and it poured with rain. Rose was absolutely frozen by the time she finished, but not as cold as the bride, who she felt sorry for. Once back home she got into a hot bath and relaxed. The last thing she needed was a cold.

Before any of them realised it, Christmas week arrived. This year there was no snow, just icy winds and torrential rain. Rose had finished work as Séra had gone away until the end of January. She went and did the Christmas shopping as JP was working until Christmas Eve. She had been down to the village and helped her uncle and Chantelle as much as she could. Their cottage was lovely. It was small and compact. Downstairs there was a sitting room, dining room and kitchen. Upstairs had two bedrooms and a bathroom. The whole cottage had central heating, so no fireplaces. Her uncle and Chantelle had bought cottage furniture and it blended in well. There was a small garden at the front and back, with a garage for two cars.

Raoul had phoned JP and had been over and seen the new jet. Luckily for Raoul, the controls were not all that different, and he had been up with an instructor three times and felt more confident.

About mid-afternoon on Christmas Eve, JP arrived home and Rose noticed how tired he was looking and was concerned. "I think you need to rest, my love. Are you alright?" JP replied he had a lot of work at the moment, but once all the travel arrangements had been confirmed, and all the rotas sorted out, so different bodyguards were picked, work would be easier. This year he only had Christmas Day and Boxing Day off, as did his men. He would then be back home for New Year's Eve and New Year's Day.

That night JP cooked a Christmas meal of chicken, roast potatoes, vegetables, stuffing, and gravy. For a dessert he made an apple tart, which they had with ice cream and cream. Later on sitting on the settee, curled up together, Rose said, "It's nearly midnight, my love. I wonder if uncle has proposed to Chantelle yet?"

JP replied, "I think he said he was going to propose when the clock chimed midnight. I wish them all the best. Now talking of midnight, I think it's time we went to bed."

Upstairs in the bedroom, the moon lit up the room. Rose went and stood by the window. JP wrapped his arms round her waist, and moving her hair to one side, started kissing her neck. Rose snuggled into his chest. JP gently turned her and kissed her lips so tenderly. Slowly, in the moonlight, they undressed each other. At that moment the clock struck midnight, and they heard fireworks going off, and knew they were from the pub in the village. JP picked Rose up and sat her down on the bed, and then went over to his wardrobe and took out a small parcel. Turning he saw Rose sitting up, with a pillow behind her, and the rays of the moon covered every bit of her body, and she looked radiant. Straddling her, he said, "Merry Christmas, môn amour and Happy Birthday," and gave her the parcel.

Rose kissed his lips and said, "Thank you my love," and then unwrapped it. She gasped at what was inside the box. It was a gold and silver eternity ring, with the tiniest of diamonds she had ever seen, in a rose pattern. "Oh JP, it's gorgeous. Will you put it on my finger?"

JP said, "There is an inscription on the inside, môn amour."

Rose put the lamp on and read, *"My heart and love for eternity."* JP took her wedding ring finger, but Rose said, "Other hand, my love." JP slipped the ring on her finger, and then Rose took him in her arms and kissed him passionately.

"I have something for you too, my love." Opening her bedside cabinet, she took out a parcel. JP opened it and inside was a leather wallet with the J and P entwined with a rose.

"It's lovely, môn amour, and I will treasure it."

Rose said, "I knew you had lost your other one in the accident, and—" JP was kissing her lips and Rose felt him rising to the occasion. Slowly and tenderly they made love to each other.

In the morning JP woke her up with his head between her legs, and then she loved him. After making love again in the shower, they put their dressing gowns on and went down and had some breakfast. Rose was dying to phone her uncle, but JP said she mustn't, or Chantelle would know. They spent the rest of the day relaxing and loving each other.

"What time are we leaving tonight?" asked Rose.

JP explained he had ordered two limousines to pick everyone up, so they could all have a drink and not worry about driving. Their limousine would pick them up at 5pm, go and collect Hugh and Chantelle, and then into Paris to pick up Ruby and Antoine, and Monica and George. The other limousine would pick up Andre and Gabrielle, Donatien and Céleste, and Pierre and Emilie. JP put on his blue suit with a pale blue shirt, and Rose had her light blue knee-length dress on, which had a sweetheart neckline. Underneath she had her electric blue bra and brief set. JP smiled at that and thought of later.

The limousine arrived and Rose put her coat on as it was very cold outside, but at least it had stopped raining. Rose recognised the driver as one of the other bodyguards and smiled. JP gave him directions to Hugh's. Once Hugh and Chantelle had got in, Rose noticed the glint of Chantelle's ring and grabbed her hand. "Are you and my uncle?"

Chantelle nodded and said, "I hope you approve?"

Rose hugged her and said, "Chantelle, I'm over the moon, and I am so happy for both of you." Rose then hugged and kissed her uncle. Chantelle's ring was an opal, with a diamond surround.

Soon they picked up Ruby, Antoine, Monica and George. Everyone was delighted at Hugh and Chantelle's news. As they reached the restaurant, the other limousine pulled up. Everyone greeted each other and joined in the celebrations of Hugh and Chantelle's engagement. Once inside the first thing they noticed was there were no other diners. Gérard greeted them and Rose said, "Please tell me Gérard you haven't opened just for us?"

"My beautiful Rose," said Gérard, "I can think of no better way to spend Christmas evening, than with all of you." All the ladies hugged and kissed his cheek, and the men gave him a manly hug.

CHAPTER 34

The restaurant was decorated with a Christmas tree, various ornaments and decorations. A large round table was decorated with crackers and floral arrangements in the middle. They all sat down and Gérard took their drinks order. "Now my friends, you can either order off the menu or have the set menu. I will get your drinks while you decide." Seeing as Gérard had opened especially for them, they all decided to go with the set menu.

Rose whispered to JP, "Looks like your meal from last year."

JP smiled and replied, "Yes, but I'm not cooking it." Rose laughed. The menu was: -

Duck Foie Gras

Smoked salmon with a crab and lemon mayonnaise

Oysters and lobsters

Coquille Saint Jacques

A turkey and a chicken, served with chestnut stuffing, various vegetables, roasted, boiled or garlic potatoes, bread sauce and gravy

Cheese and biscuits

Bûche De Noël

Coffee and macarons

The conversation, along with the wine flowed, but Rose had noticed that Céleste, Gabrielle and Emilie were not drinking a lot. Ruby was also being good, but these days she was. Her uncle and Chantelle were in deep conversation with Monica and George. Rose smiled at how happy her uncle looked. Another wedding to attend. Everyone noticed her ring, and said how gorgeous it was.

The start of the meal arrived and the conversation stilled. JP had asked Gérard to join them, but alas he had to decline, but promised he would join them at the end of the meal. Every dish was delicious and slowly they made their way through the courses. After the table had been cleared, but before the coffee was served, Gérard tinkled a glass and everyone went silent. "My beautiful friends, I apologise for the interruption, but I have a couple of announcements to make."

"Please don't tell us you're leaving," said Pierre.

Gérard shook his head and said, "Not yet, Pierre, not yet. Due to certain circumstances, the husbands missed an event, and today is another day of celebration. Rose and Ruby, happy 30th birthday." A waiter pushed a trolley in with two birthday cakes on it. One was iced with Rose and the other Ruby. Champagne corks popped and glasses were filled. "Ladies and gentlemen, please raise your glasses to Rose and Ruby." A couple of musicians had been playing quietly in the background and now played "Happy Birthday." Everyone sang the song and Rose and Ruby both hugged each other.

Gérard continued. "We have another celebration to toast, and that is to Hugh and Chantelle who have just got engaged." Again, glasses were raised to the happy couple. "Lastly, I have an announcement that none of you know about. Next year, around June, more celebrations will take place. Ladies and gentlemen, please raise your glasses to Gabrielle, Emilie and Céleste who I understand are all expecting."

"What, all three of you?" said Rose, absolutely stunned.

Emilie, Gabrielle and Céleste all looked at each other and said together, surprised, "Your expecting as well?" They couldn't believe it and they stood up and hugged each other. Then everyone cheered and was absolutely delighted.

Jokingly JP said, "Now ladies don't forget my birthday is 30th June, so that would be a wonderful birthday present."

Gabrielle replied, "No problem, JP, we will put corks up to keep them in." Everyone burst out laughing.

The coffee and macarons were placed on the table, with the two birthday cakes. Rose and Ruby cut them up and Gérard was given a slice from each cake.

"You alright, boss?" asked Pierre.

JP smiled and replied, "After hours of sorting them out, due to the wonderful news, I just thought I will have to re-arrange the rotas." His men laughed and said they would help him.

Gérard opened the sliding door and the musicians started up a disco. Soon everyone was up dancing. It was 3am before they left. Apart from Gabrielle, Emilie, Céleste, and Ruby, everyone else was quite tipsy, but in a very happy way.

Rose and JP were the last ones to be dropped off, and both of them were still quite tipsy. Once inside the farmhouse Rose said, "Well, what an evening of celebrations. I can't believe Céleste, Emilie and Gabrielle are all pregnant. Our family is getting bigger and bigger. Wonder when Ruby and Antoine will be expecting?"

JP took her hand, and wandering from side to side, led her up the stairs. In the bedroom he said, "At the moment I don't care. Being selfish, all I want to see is you in that sexy bra and brief set, and kiss every bit of your body, especially between your legs."

Rose rolled her eyes and replied, "Umm, I might sleep in the spare room tonight."

JP wrapped his arms round her and undid the zip on the back of her dress. "If you insist, môn amour, but I think you might get cold." His kisses trailed down her neck and Rose felt the electric shocks cursing through her body.

Her hands went to his shirt and she fiddled with his buttons. "Bloody buttons," she said. JP undid them and then threw his shirt on the floor. Rose stepped out of her dress. For a second, JP saw two of her stood there looking absolutely ravishing. He unzipped his trousers, but as he went to step out of them he fell and landed on the bed, face down. Rose burst out laughing. She grabbed his feet and pulled his shoes and socks off, and then his trousers. JP rolled over onto his back, and pulled Rose on top of him. She slid off him, still laughing.

JP looked a bit bewildered for a moment. "How did you get over there? I put you on top of me."

"I slid off. Hang on while I sit on you." Rose climbed over him and then straddled him. JP's hands undid her bra, and threw it on the floor. His hands and lips were on her breasts, caressing and kissing them. His tongue swirled round one of her nipples, which quickly went hard.

"Don't forget the other one," said Rose giggling. JP took the other one and did the same.

Rose started to slide again, but JP caught her, and rolled her over. Rose's hand went to his buttocks, and realised he still had his underpants on, so she started to push them down. Suddenly she said, "JP, I need to go to the loo for a wee." JP rolled off her and Rose went to the loo, leaving her briefs on the bathroom floor. When she came back, JP was on his back with his eyes shut. Rose pulled his underpants off, and then climbed up the bed to him. "Aw, my angel has gone to sleep. Let's see if I can wake him up." Taking his manhood and testicles in her hands she started caressing and kissing them. JP stirred and so did his manhood. "There you are, my angel."

Rose straddled JP, and bent over and started kissing JP's lips. His arms went round her, and his manhood grew between them. JP rolled Rose over, and her legs went round his hips, and her hands caressed his buttocks. Twice JP missed entering Rose, but then he was successful. JP climaxed quickly, and rolled off Rose, and was asleep in seconds, snoring softly. Rose prodded JP and got no response. Her hand went to his manhood that was still hard. She straddled him and slid down on him. She felt herself coming, and slid up and down quicker, and then massaged her nub, which sent her over the edge. She could feel her insides clenching his manhood hard, but slowly his manhood shrunk. Rose collapsed on top of him. JP rolled over and Rose slid off him, and taking some of the duvet with her, ended up on the floor. The next minute the duvet was snatched away from her, and she was left on the floor naked. The cold air hit her and she shivered. Rose wasn't impressed, and after standing up, she saw JP had wrapped the duvet round himself like a sleeping bag. "Well, that's not nice, JP," she said. The only reply she got was a snore.

Walking out of the bedroom, she went to the airing cupboard and pulled out a pillow and duvet, and went into one of the spare bedrooms. The bed was cold, and so she wrapped the duvet round her, put the pillow down and then led down. Quickly she fell firm asleep.

In the morning JP woke up and wondered why he couldn't move. Then he saw he was wrapped up in the duvet. He turned over to find he was on his own. Looking at the clock he saw it was 8am. He went to the bathroom, and saw Rose's briefs on the floor, and then went downstairs. No Rose. He scratched his head, and went back upstairs. It was then he saw the spare bedroom door slightly open. He peered in and saw Rose curled up with her arms around a pillow. To him she looked beautiful, and his manhood stood to attention. He moved the duvet to one side and took in all of her sexy body. Carefully, he got in the bed with her, and cradled her in his arms. His hands roamed over her body, and went down between her legs. Rose stirred and turning looked into JP's blue eyes. "Umm that feels good, but I'd rather have something else in me." Again, carefully, JP held her close whilst he rolled Rose underneath him. He kissed her lips and then made his way down to her mound, and brought her to her climax. Then putting her legs on his shoulders, he entered her. His thrusts were deep and soon Rose was writhing in the bed. "Oh JP, JP," she said, whilst caressing his buttocks with her hands. They both more or less climaxed at the same time.

Rolling onto their sides, Rose grabbed the duvet that had fallen off the bed, and covered them. Rose then sat up and looking round said, "Why are we in the spare bedroom?"

JP replied, "I was hoping you would tell me, môn amour."

"I have no idea, my love." Laying back down she cuddled in to JP, and they slept.

They woke up twice, made love, and went back to sleep. It was 1pm when Rose woke. She wanted a bath, as she was all sweaty. As she got up JP opened his eyes and said, "Where are you going, môn amour? Come back to bed."

Rose replied, "I need a bath, my love, and it's 1pm."

JP was surprised at the time but replied, "Good idea. It's a long time since we had a bath together, and then I will cook us a wonderful meal."

Soon they were loving each other in the bath. They really couldn't get enough of each other. When Rose walked back in the bedroom, she stopped. "That's why I was in the spare room," and told JP.

JP was mortified, and said, "Oh, môn amour, I am so sorry. I have never done that before. That was selfish of me."

Rose took him in her arms and said, "My love, I think you have more than made up for it. We were both pretty tipsy. Look at me leaving my briefs in the bathroom. Thank heavens we didn't have company." Both of them burst out laughing and then kissed each other.

"Food," said JP, and gently tapped Rose's naked buttocks.

Later on they sat down to a meal of salad, followed by steaks with garlic potatoes and vegetables. JP then made a chocolate-chestnut mousse. "Um JP, this is so wonderful." JP smiled. Rose made the coffee, which they took in the sitting room. Cuddled up together, they watched a film on the television.

About 6pm the phone rang. It was Antoine. "Hi Antoine, you want JP?"

Antoine replied, "No, it's… um… you I want to talk to."

"What's wrong, Antoine? Is it Ruby or you?"

Antoine told Rose that Ruby had been really down since she learnt of the wives expecting. "I don't know what to do, Rose, and last night she wouldn't even sleep in our bed." Rose had a good idea what was wrong, but told Antoine she would meet her for lunch and have a chat. Antoine thanked her and rang off.

Rose told JP. "What do you think is wrong?" he asked. Rose said she wondered if it was something to do with Ruby's abortion. "They've only been married nine months, surely they need time?" asked JP.

Rose replied, "If I know Ruby, she's thinking her biological clock is going quickly, and having a baby over thirty years of age, is actually old. I'm sure it can be sorted. Do you think Antoine is ready for a family?" JP smiled and told Rose that Antoine had always wanted children.

That night they just cuddled up and slept in each other's arms. The following morning, JP left for the palace and told Rose he would try and finish the day before New Year's Eve, if he could. Rose phoned Ruby about 11am.

"Hello," said Ruby, sounding rather down.

"Ruby, you alright. You don't sound so good?"

Ruby replied, "I'm fine, sis. Just feeling a bit down, that's all. I'll be fine."

"Right, I'll pick you up in half an hour and we'll go for lunch, and I'm not taking 'no' for an answer. See you soon," and Rose hung up.

An hour later they were sitting in a café in the shopping centre. "What's wrong, Ruby? Tell me?"

Ruby had tears in her eyes and replied, "Why can't I get pregnant, Rose? What's wrong with me? We don't use any contraception, and to be blunt, we are at it like rabbits."

Rose sort of giggled, but then said gently, "Have you spoken to Mum?" Ruby shook her head. "That's the first thing you need to do. I'm no doctor, but I did wonder if it was something to do with the abortion you had."

Ruby looked at her in surprise and said, "I never gave that a thought. Oh Rose, do you think that's what it is?"

"Ruby you need to phone Mum, and I'm sure she'll examine you. Look, there's a phone box over there, so let's ring her."

Luckily Monica was at home. "Ruby, when did you have your last period?" Ruby said it was about ten days ago. "That's good. I'm on duty at the hospital tomorrow, so can you come and see me about 10am, or are you working?" Ruby replied she wasn't working and would be there. Rose said she would go with her.

The next day, both of them turned up at the hospital and were told where to find Monica. "Hello my lovely daughters," said Monica, hugging and kissing them. Rose and Ruby hugged and kissed her back. "Ruby, I have arranged for you to see Doctor Madeleine Beauchene. She will talk you through the procedure. Rose you can come, but won't be able to go in the x-ray room."

Monica took them down to see the doctor. Monica introduced them both.

"Pleased to meet you both. Now Ruby, I understand you are

having problems conceiving. I must ask first, has your husband been tested?" Ruby replied he hadn't. "That's alright. So the procedure is that you will lie down on the table with your legs in the stirrups. I will give you a pelvic examination, and insert a speculum into your vagina. The x-ray machine will be lowered over your abdomen. A swab will be inserted to clean your cervix, and then a plastic catheter called a cannula will be inserted into your cervix, into which I will inject some dye. This will give me a clearer picture of your fallopian tubes. Afterwards I will give you some painkillers to take, and you might have cramps for a day or two. If you're ready, I'll take you in, and Monica will be with you the whole time." Ruby nodded and Rose gave her an encouraging hug.

CHAPTER 35

The procedure took forty-five minutes, and Rose had started to worry, thinking something was badly wrong. Eventually Monica and Ruby came out of the x-ray room. "Doctor Beauchene, as a favour to me, is going to let us know when the results will be available. I suggest we go to the canteen and have a coffee."

About an hour later, they were back in the doctor's office. Rose held Ruby's hand as she was shaking slightly. "Ruby, I've had a thorough look at your x-rays. I see from your notes you had an abortion some years ago. The results are that your fallopian tubes are blocked with scar tissue. You will need an operation to remove the scar tissue, and I would be pleased to do that operation for you. You will be given a general anaesthetic, and I will make a small cut in your abdomen, and put a probe in and eventually remove the scar tissue. Your stitches inside will be absorbable. You will stay in hospital overnight, and can probably return to work in a week. After the procedure, I suggest you wait to have sex until you have had a couple of periods. I do have to point out that it's not a guarantee you will get pregnant."

Ruby replied, "Thank you, Doctor. When would I be able to have the procedure?"

Doctor Beauchene checked her diary and said, "I could do it the second week of January?" Ruby agreed, and the doctor told Monica she would confer with her. They all thanked the doctor and left. Monica apologised and said she must get back to work. She hugged and kissed them both and said she would be in touch.

"Late lunch?" asked Rose. Ruby agreed.

"Thank you, Rose. What would I do without you?" said Ruby.

"As you always say, Ruby, that's what sisters are for. I have to be honest though, it was Antoine."

Ruby replied, "I know. I heard him on the phone to you. Now I've got to tell him I need an operation, and I'll have to ask Mathieu for time off work."

"Ruby, they'll be fine. We can't help being ill."

"Let's eat," said Ruby.

They wandered into a café down by the Seine and had a meal. Afterwards, arm in arm, even though it was cold, they walked up and down the Seine. "I've missed doing this," said Rose.

Ruby looked at her and said, "You've got red cheeks and a red nose, and you miss this?"

Rose laughed and replied, "As have you, and yes I do."

"Let's go home and have a hot drink," said Ruby.

Rose stayed with Ruby for the rest of the afternoon and left her about 4pm, just as it was getting dark. Once home, she had a relaxing hot bath. The following day, the skies opened and it was torrential rain all day. Rose noticed the height of the river was really high, and wondered if it would come over the bank. Rose looked through her wardrobe, trying to decide what to wear on New Year's Eve. Nothing. It had been ages since she saw Mía, and so the next day she went to the shop.

"Rose, how lovely to see you," and Mía kissed her cheek. "What can I do for you?"

Rose told her she was going to an informal dinner, but at the palace, and needed a dress. Whilst Mía looked through her stock, Rose asked how business was.

"Rose, we are so busy, that Madame Cherrillé is looking for bigger premises. Séra has really put us on the market, for which we are very grateful. Ah, here is what I was looking for." Mía brought out a plain silver knee-length dress, which had small capped sleeves and a V-shaped neckline. It didn't look much, but when Rose tried it on, it looked perfect.

"As always Mía, it's beautiful, and I'll take it."

Midday on New Year's Eve, JP arrived home. "Môn amour, where are you?"

"Upstairs, my love."

JP took the stairs two at a time, to find Rose ironing some of his shirts she had washed. "I wasn't sure which one you were going to wear."

JP took the iron out of her hand and placed it upright on the board. "Come here, môn amour," and taking Rose in his arms kissed her with a passion.

Rose giggled and said, "Missed me, have you?"

"I need a shower, môn amour. Join me? And I was going to wear the white shirt with the pleats down the front, which you have ironed."

"Well, in that case, shower here we come, but let me put this away first."

Five minutes later Rose and JP were soaping each other down, telling each other how the last five days had gone.

"What time do we have to be at the palace?"

"Not until 7pm, and I've found out it's not just us either. The President has invited other people, so there's about fifty of us, and it's a buffet"

"Oh, that's better."

"We can also stay in my office, if we don't want to drive home, so suggest we take a change of clothes, just in case." Rose nodded. "What's wrong, môn amour?"

"Has any one told you, you talk too much?" The next minute she was in his arms and they were loving each other.

Once they were dressed, JP made a large cheese soufflé, and served it with salad and French bread. For a dessert they had fresh fruit salad and cream. "Wasn't today, the last day for your uncle at the bank?" asked JP.

Rose replied it was, but his colleagues had taken him for a farewell meal a couple of nights before.

"Do they need a lift?"

"No, my love, they're spending the last night in the flat, and then moving the last of the bits and pieces tomorrow."

About 5.30pm, Rose went upstairs to start getting ready. She had decided to put her hair in long curls, and just a touch of makeup. To keep her dress a surprise, she changed in the spare room.

"Môn amour, why are you in the spare bedroom?"

"You'll see in a minute, my love."

JP put his white shirt on with a black bow tie, his black suit, socks and shoes.

"Does this look alright my love, or is it too much?"

JP turned and he took all of Rose in. "Môn amour, as always, you look stunning. Do you want your diamond earrings, necklace and bracelet?" Rose said she just wanted her small diamond earrings, and heart-shaped necklace. JP got them from the safe for her. Rose put the earrings on, and then JP put her necklace on. "I don't usually say things like this, but looking in the mirror, we do make a stunning couple."

Rose smiled and kissing his lips, said, "And I love you."

"Je t'aime aussi, môn amour." JP held Rose's thick coat out, and wrapped it round her. "Ready?"

"Ready," replied Rose, grabbing her silver purse, which matched her shoes.

Half an hour later they drove into the palace. Quite a few cars were there already. "Does the President know the wives are expecting?" JP replied he did, as he had to change the rotas. Porte greeted them at the door and went to take Rose's coat, but JP said they would put it in his office, along with the two bags he was carrying. Porte nodded.

When they walked in the ballroom, Rose saw quite a few of the ladies were in long evening gowns, with jewels dripping off them. "I thought it was informal?"

JP replied, "It is, but you know how ladies like to impress. There's our friends over there."

They walked over to them and everyone hugged and kissed each other. Pierre had grabbed a large round table, so they could all be together. Waiters walked round with champagne, and JP took two, and gave one to Rose. Rose noticed Céleste, Gabrielle and Emilie were on soft drinks. She had to be honest, that the three of them didn't look pregnant. Ruby was laughing and joking with Hugh and Chantelle, which was good to see.

Pierre said, "You seen that wonderful buffet? I'm getting hungry."

Emilie sort of put her hand round his shoulders and gently slapped the side of his head. "Behave." Everyone laughed.

A voice said, "Ladies and gentlemen, the President and his wife."

Everybody stood up, and JP's men went to bow, but JP shook his head slowly. The President was dressed like most of the men in a black suit and bow tie. His wife was in a gorgeous blue, long, flowing dress, with sapphire earrings and necklace. "Please everyone, sit down and relax," said the President. The pair of them went from table to table talking and joking with everyone.

"So here is the table with the most beautiful ladies sitting at it," said the President. "May we congratulate Gabrielle, Céleste and Emilie on their exciting news. If you need anything, you only have to ask." The three of them thanked him. The President and his wife talked to all of them for about half an hour.

"My dear, I think our guests need refreshments," said Alicía.

"I look forward to dancing with all you lovely ladies later on. Please excuse us for now," said the President.

The President gently tapped a glass, and the room went silent. "Ladies and gentlemen. On behalf of my wife and myself, we would like to welcome you to our evening, and we hope you will all enjoy yourselves. As you know some of my men and myself had a rather nasty crash back in July. I'm pleased to say we are all well recovered, and would like to thank them for taking great care of me, including Doctor Michel and Doctor Pátrinne. However, I would like everyone to raise a glass to the four who passed away." Everyone raised their glasses and drank. "End of speeches, you'll be glad to know." Everyone laughed. "There is a wonderful buffet waiting to be eaten, and there is wine, champagne, water and soft drinks, so just ask the waiters and waitresses. Music will be played in the background, and naturally, there will be a countdown to midnight. Now please enjoy yourselves."

Everyone clapped, and then slowly went up to the buffet. Needless to say, Pierre was the first one and came back with a plate full. Andre raised his eyebrow and said, "Please tell me you've left some for the rest of us?" Pierre just smiled and raised his glass of champagne.

"See you've got your appetite back." They all looked to see Doctor Michel and Pátrinne stood there.

"Doctors, come and join us," said Antoine. They declined as they were with their wives. Rose had never given it a thought that they were married.

As the evening went on, the orchestra started playing louder, and the carpet was rolled back to reveal the dance floor. Rose and JP were the first to get up and dance to a slow song. Then the rest joined in. The ladies all swapped husbands as they danced round for a few minutes. When Rose danced with Antoine he whispered, "Thank you for looking after Ruby. Hopefully, we too will soon become parents." Rose kissed his cheek.

Next it was her uncle. "Well Uncle, how was your last day?"

Hugh replied, "To be honest my dear, it was a relief, but sad as well. Now I have a new life to begin with Chantelle, and a new home. You must come down whenever you want to. You know how much I love to see you, so don't be a stranger." Rose promised. Rose then danced with Pierre, Donatien, Andre, and her dad George.

Back at the table, all the ladies got together and were talking babies. "Time to bring out the frumpy trousers and tops," said Emilie. Rose asked why.

Gabrielle replied, "There's not a lot of choice of maternity wear, and the lovely clothes are expensive." Rose thought for a moment and then had an idea. The rest of the evening was spent eating, drinking and dancing. As promised the President danced, again for a few moments, with each of the wives. JP danced with Alicía, as did his men, even though it felt a little strange. After all, she was the President's wife, who they protected, not danced with.

Soon the orchestra stopped and the President said, "It's nearly midnight everyone, so let the countdown begin." Everyone was given a glass of champagne, and then the clock struck twelve. "Happy New Year to you all, and I hope this year will be better than the last one," said the President.

Everyone raised their glasses and said, "Happy New Year." JP took Rose in his arms, like all the other husbands and wives, and kissed her so tenderly, it gave her goose bumps. Then they all kissed and hugged each other in their family.

The music played on until the early hours of the morning. It must have been about 3am before the guests started to leave. Hugh and Chantelle, and Monica and George, said their goodbyes and went off in a taxi. JP and Rose decided to stay in his office, and his men, were staying at the house. The President and his wife said their goodnights, and JP thanked them both for a wonderful evening on behalf of all of them. The President said, "Alicía and I were just saying what a wonderful 'family' you all are. I've watched you all grow into the best of friends, and I hope all of you have many, many, more years of friendship and love to come." JP thanked him, and wished them both, and their son, a lovely holiday, and would see him on his return.

Taking Rose's hand they went up to his office. Rose went into the bedroom and drew the curtains, and then put the bedside lamp on.

"Come here, môn amour, as I've got you all to myself now." Rose went to him and wrapped her arms round his neck. His arms went round her waist and drew her to him. Their kisses were gentle and sensual.

"I think my love, you had better lock your door."

JP locked his office door and then closed and locked the bedroom door. Rose had removed her jewellery and shoes. "Can you unzip me please, JP?" JP obliged and then Rose dropped her dress. She stood there in a silver bra and briefs set, with silver hold-up stockings. JP's suit, shirt, shoes and socks were off quickly.

"My lady in silver," he said huskily. Picking her up he laid her on the bed, and then taking her in his arms, kissed her passionately. "I need to remove your stockings, môn amour." Rose lifted her leg up and JP rolled the stocking down. Rose lifted her other leg and JP rolled that one down.

"Now, you're not going to roll me out of bed are you?"

JP held her close and unclipping her bra, replied, "Not a chance, môn amour."

Their kisses got more passionate and soon they were loving each other. JP wrapped the duvet round both of them, and Rose laid her head on his chest, playing with his nipple. Soon they were both firm asleep.

JP woke about 9am, and went to the bathroom for a quick shower. Rose was still firm asleep. He had some work to do before they left. About half an hour later Rose woke up. Peering out the door she saw JP working. Rose said cheekily, "I'm feeling neglected, my love."

JP looked up to see her stood by the door totally naked, and his manhood, naturally, reacted. He went to her and kissing her said, "As much as I want to ravish you, I think maybe we should go and eat with the others, and then home to bed for the rest of the day."

"Sounds good to me. I'll just have a quick shower."

They had breakfast with the others, and then went home and spent the rest of the day in bed loving each other.

CHAPTER 36

JP left the following morning to go to the palace. The President would be going away the day after, and everything had to be checked, with regards to security and protocol. The President had told JP he was rather nervous about flying in a jet again. JP assured him he would be fine.

Late morning there was a knock at his door and it was Raoul. "Raoul, come in and Happy New Year to you."

"Thanks JP and the same to you and Rose. Can I have a talk with you, if you're not busy?"

JP beckoned him to sit down. "What's up, Raoul?"

"Nothing really. JP do you think I should pilot this new jet?"

JP looked at him and replied, "I can't think of anyone better. You've flown it three, four times now, so why are you concerned?"

Raoul stood up and looked out the window. "I have the pub to run, and I enjoy it. I don't particularly want to stay away too long."

JP got up and walked to Raoul and putting his hand on his shoulder said, "Raoul, this is called nerves. You will be fine, and you don't have to stay. The President will contact me when he needs to return and I will contact you. It's a great opportunity, Raoul. Look at all the different countries you will visit. In fact, I've just had a thought."

Raoul left JP's office feeling a lot happier. Next JP phoned Rose and asked her advice on something. "I honestly don't know, my love, but I'll find out. Do you think Raoul will be alright?"

JP replied, "I've decided to go with him. The President is nervous, so hopefully I can put them both at their ease. Once we land in Switzerland, Porte and Sávoire will take over, and we should be back mid-afternoon."

Rose went quiet and then said, "Please my love, be careful. Let me know the minute you get back."

"Môn amour, don't worry. We will all be fine. Je t'aime." Rose told him she loved him too, but it didn't stop her worrying.

The President and Raoul were pleased to see JP. The trip there and back went without any hitches, and once back, JP phoned Rose who was delighted he was back.

The days flew by. Rose visited her uncle and Chantelle, and one day took them over to the pub for a meal. Raoul was there, and Rose had a quiet word with him. "Uncle, what are you going to do with all your spare time now?"

Hugh replied, "Relax and enjoy myself, along with my lovely Chantelle."

Rose sort of chewed her bottom lip and said, "Would you not like a little job to occupy you?"

Hugh wasn't stupid and said, "Chantelle, this is my niece in action, when she's had an idea and isn't sure how to say it. Out with it, my dear."

Rose blushed and said, smiling, "Raoul wants to fly for the President, but he needs somebody to look after the pub."

"What, me?" said Hugh, stunned. "Rose, I have no idea how to pour a pint, never mind run a pub."

Raoul laughed and said, "Hugh, it's pull a pint, and I will show you. Come, let's me show you, and we can have a chat about everything." Hugh agreed, and an hour later Raoul told Rose and Chantelle he had a new bar manager. Both were delighted.

The day arrived when Ruby had to go into hospital. It was also the day that JP was flying back to Switzerland with Raoul to bring the President and his family home. Rose picked Ruby up, and they went to the hospital ward. Monica was there to hug them both, and then showed Ruby to her bed. Rose could see Ruby was shaking, and said, "It'll soon be over, Ruby, and then hopefully you and Antoine will get your wish."

Doctor Madeleine Beauchene arrived and smiled at them both. "How are you feeling, Ruby?"

Ruby replied, "Bit scared."

"Oh please don't feel scared, you won't feel a thing. I just need to check your blood pressure and heart rate, which I'm sure will be elevated." It was. "I will see you in the operating room in about five minutes."

In the theatre, Monica said, "Alright Ruby. You'll feel a small prick," and proceeded to put the cannula in the back of her hand.

"Ouch, Mum, that hurt."

Monica just smiled and then injected the anaesthetic into the cannula. "Ruby, count back from twenty for me."

Ruby started counting and soon was firm asleep. When she woke, she was back in the ward, and Rose was holding her hand. "Hello sleepy, how you feeling?" asked Rose.

"Groggy," replied Ruby.

The next minute the doctor and Monica walked in. "The operation went well, Ruby. You will stay in overnight, and then tomorrow go home. Now don't forget, no sex until after your second period, no heavy lifting, just rest and relax, and I will see you in four weeks for your check-up." Ruby thanked her, and then Monica suggested she slept, which she did.

When she woke, Rose was still there talking to Monica. "Mum, can I have a drink please?" Monica turned and went to her with a glass of water. "Sip it slowly Ruby. Do you feel hungry?" Ruby said she did, so Monica went and got her some sandwiches and tea.

"Rose, have you heard from JP?" Rose replied they wouldn't be back until early evening, and Ruby could see she was worried. The weather was far from being kind. Monica came back at that moment and the pair of them had sandwiches and a drink. Rose told Ruby she would leave her to rest and see her in the morning. She had already told Ruby she would stay with her for a couple of days, and Ruby was pleased. Outside the rain was torrential and Rose's windscreen wipers were on full, and only just keeping her windscreen clear. Eventually she got home, but got soaked through just walking from the garage to the front door. After Rose had had a long soak in the bath, she made herself a meal whilst waiting for JP to phone. By 8pm she was really worried, and phoned Andre at the palace.

"They have been delayed, Rose. He has been trying to phone you, but got no reply. The weather is dreadful and Raoul didn't want to fly in it, so they are staying at a hotel until the morning, which is a bodyguard's nightmare. How is Ruby?" Rose replied all had gone well. Andre told her Antoine was at the hospital. Rose was pleased. One thing about her "family" was there were no secrets. All of them had phoned and wished Ruby good luck with her operation. Rose thanked Andre and went and watched the television for a couple of hours and then went to bed.

In the morning, Rose packed a small case to take to Ruby's, and it was still pouring down with rain. The news had said lots of flooding had taken place, and several rivers had burst their banks. There had also been lots of car accidents, with people driving too fast. Rose checked the river at the back of the farmhouse, but at that moment it looked to be alright, but it was very high. Soon she was at the hospital, which was absolutely manic. She saw George and Monica working flat out, and went up to find Ruby. Ruby was pleased to see her and asked if she had heard from JP. Rose told her what had happened.

"You can phone him from the flat," said Ruby.

"What's going on downstairs?" asked Rose.

"There has been a multiple pile-up on the motorway. Mum said about thirty cars were involved. Once the doctor has been to see me, we can go. Mum and Dad said they would phone later. You are still staying with me, aren't you?"

"Of course I am. Who's going to look after you otherwise? At least Antoine will be home at the weekend, but remember, no sex."

Ruby burst out laughing and said, "Ouch, that hurt. Don't make me laugh."

About half an hour later the doctor popped in and gave Ruby the all-clear, and soon both of them were back at Ruby's flat. "Ruby your fridge is empty. I'll need to go shopping, and no, you're not coming with me. Bed now and sleep and rest. I won't be long."

Ruby did as she was told, and soon fell asleep. Rose did enough shopping for three days, as Antoine would be home then. When she got back, Ruby was sitting up in bed, reading a book. "How does a cheese soufflé sound? Nice and light, but it won't be as good as JP's." Ruby replied she couldn't wait.

"Oh Rose, that was lovely. You must show me how to make it." Rose said she would. Ruby had got up and now they sat on the settee. "Do you know, Rose, it's a long time since we did this. Reminds me of the old days." Rose agreed and soon they were reminiscing, laughing and joking. They talked about when they first met JP and Antoine, and how they couldn't wait to see them, and what to wear.

"Isn't it strange," said Ruby, "that now we are both married, we don't do those things anymore."

Rose replied, "When you're better, we will, and with the others as well. We should make arrangements to meet up more often, but now our three sisters are expecting, it just might be you and me."

"That's fine by me," said Ruby.

At that moment the phone rang. "Hello," said Rose.

"It's me, môn amour. Antoine told me where you were and I wanted to let you know we are all back safe and sound. How is Ruby?"

Rose told him she was alright but sore, and was so pleased he was back. They talked for about ten minutes and then JP said he would see her at the weekend.

"That's better, as you've got your smile back now," said Ruby. Rose blushed slightly.

For the next three days, Rose and Ruby had a great time. They looked through old photos, and wedding photos. Talked about all their large family, and it getting larger. Friday evening, Antoine arrived home. "Thank you so much, Rose, for looking after Ruby. I bet the pair of you have had a great time together?"

Rose replied they had. She hugged and kissed both of them, but as she went out the door she shouted, "REMEMBER, NO SEX." She heard both of them laughing.

Back at the farmhouse, JP was cooking. "Môn amour, you're back. Hope you've had a good three days with Ruby?"

Rose replied they'd had a great time, and then wrapped him in her arms and kissed him. "What's for dinner?"

JP replied, "Boeuf Bourguignon."

"Ummm," replied Rose.

As they were eating, they told each other what had happened, and then cuddled up on the settee. JP said, "Raoul told me about your uncle looking after the pub. Good way to get to know the villagers."

"We should have them up for a meal, my love." JP suggested Sunday, so Rose went and phoned them. "They would love to come Sunday, and as you can see, tomorrow we need to go shopping," said Rose.

"Now it's time for bed," said JP.

Soon they were cuddled up together under the duvet after loving each other.

JP drove to the shopping centre the following morning, and after doing the shopping, they went for lunch. "JP, is there any way we can build something from the garage to the front door? I got soaked the other day."

JP said once they were back he would have a look, and he did. "If we put a door, here in the kitchen, then a covered walkway could be built, going into the garage. I'll have to get our builder to come and tell me if it can be done."

"That's sounds good," said Rose.

JP went and made a phone call. "The builder is on his way."

"Heavens, that's quick."

"He owes me a favour," said JP.

The builder arrived, and Rose made some coffee. A couple of hours later he left. "He's going to start on Monday, môn amour, but I told him not too early. You can trust him, if you need to go out. I have known him many years." Rose replied she would be going out, as she needed to see what Mathieu had for her to do.

Sunday lunchtime, Hugh and Chantelle arrived. JP had done a roast for lunch. As they sat round the kitchen table Hugh said, "We have some news. Our wedding is booked for the middle of April. It will just be at the town hall, and of course, we have booked a meal at Gérard's for our large family. The following day, we are also going to celebrate with the villagers in the pub, to which you are both invited. Chantelle is sending the invitations out this week."

"That's wonderful news. Now Chantelle if you need any help, please ask," said Rose.

Chantelle replied, "We do have a favour to ask of you both. Rose will you be my bridesmaid, and JP would you be Hugh's best man?"

Rose replied excitedly, "I would love that, Chantelle."

JP replied, "It would be my honour to be your best man."

Hugh replied, "I'll drink to that," and they raised their wine glasses.

After the meal they went in the sitting room, where a huge log fire was burning. Rose and Chantelle chatted about wedding dresses etc., and JP and Hugh talked about Hugh working at the pub, and other things. JP gave Hugh a rough idea of when Raoul would be away, but some of the journeys they would be away one, maybe two weeks. Hugh raised his eyebrow at that.

"When do these journeys start?" asked Hugh.

JP told him March, but at the moment there was nothing for April, then May, June, August, September and October. "Hugh, you will be fine, and I know the villagers will help you. You and Chantelle are part of the village now." Hugh replied that Raoul had said that, but it didn't stop him worrying about the coaches turning up for snacks and lunches. At least Raoul had plenty of reliable staff.

The rest of the day passed pleasantly, with sandwiches, cakes and coffee later on. Hugh and Chantelle left about 8pm. JP took Rose to bed and loved her passionately, leaving them both sated.

JP was gone early on the Monday morning. The builder and his men turned up about 10am, and Rose left them to it. Firstly she went to see Ruby, to make sure she was alright, and she was. Ruby went with Rose to see Mathieu.

"Weddings are quiet at the moment, Rose, but another couple of months and you'll be running round again. Ruby, I don't want to see you back until the end of next month. You must rest and make sure you're one hundred per cent fit before you come back, but I do have some work you can do on your computer at home." Ruby was happy with that.

When they left, the rain had stopped and the sun was trying to come out. "Fancy a drive?" said Rose. Ruby nodded. Rose decided to drive to Versailles, as Ruby had never been. Even though Rose had seen the palace, she didn't see the town. Rose found a car park right in the centre, so Ruby wouldn't have far to walk, but there were plenty of cafés and brasseries to stop at. You couldn't help but see the baroque cathedral, with its unique dome, which was situated in the centre of the town. It was built in 1754 and had been badly damaged by fire years later, but was restored. By the cathedral were quaint little homes, which Louis XV had built as market stalls, and were never intended to be lived in, but they were now. Hôtel de Ville was another impressive building with its architecture.

Rose and Ruby went into a café and had coffee and a pastry, so Ruby could rest. She saw a leaflet advertising Musée Lambinet, but it was closed. Apparently it had over thirty rooms to explore. There were lots of boutiques and antique shops on the small cobblestone streets. Rose saw it was coming up 1pm. "Time to go somewhere else, if I can find it."

CHAPTER 37

Rose drove down to the Palace of Versailles, so Ruby could see it.

"Wow, it's massive," said Ruby. "Can we go one day, Rose, when we're both free?" Rose said they would have to make a list of places to go, and try and do one a month.

Rose turned at the palace and tried to remember the way she had driven behind Léon. Soon she saw the turning and went down it. There in front of them was the restaurant.

"Rose, this looks wonderful. How did you find it?" Rose explained about coming with Séra's models. Like Rose, when they walked in Ruby said, "Is this it? It looked so impressive from outside." Rose told her to wait. They looked through the menu and both decided on chicken chasseur. The waiter beckoned them and Ruby followed Rose up the couple of steps and through the door. "Oh my, this is fantastic," said Ruby. The waiter had given them a table by the window. Even though the trees were stripped bare of their leaves, and the river was high, the view was still impressive.

"Who lives in that house?" asked Ruby.

"That, my dear sister, is a mystery. Léon told me that no one knows who lives there or how to get there. I meant to ask JP and forgot."

Ruby said she would make some enquiries as well. They enjoyed a great meal and Ruby suggested all of them should come for a meal. Rose and Ruby stayed for most of the afternoon, and then Rose drove her home.

Rose arrived home just after 4pm, to see the builders packing up. "All done, Madame Pascal."

Rose looked stunned. "You've finished already?"

"Yes, with you going out we could make as much noise as we wanted, and with the extra help it's done. Come look, and I hope you like it."

Rose went into the kitchen to see what had been done. The door opened out into a small stoned corridor, with another door at the end into the garage. "JP suggested a glass corridor but I thought it might be rather noisy with the rain hitting it. As you can see you do have a couple of windows, so I hope you like?" Rose replied it looked lovely and blended in well with the farmhouse. She waved the builders off, and then went and made herself a snack and a coffee.

The next couple of weeks flew by. Rose visited Ruby, who was now looking and feeling a lot better. She also visited her uncle and Chantelle. Rose had introduced Chantelle to Mía, for a wedding dress. Monday morning she was back to work, as was Chantelle. Séra was delighted to see her.

"Rose, I have some news for you. This year I have been invited to attend the New York, London, Milan and Paris fashion shows. New York is too far away, but I intend to accept the other three, and I would like you, Ruby and Mía to accompany me. This is going to be very hectic and will all take place next month in March. I understand from Mathieu that Ruby has had an operation. Do you think she will be well enough to travel?"

Rose replied Ruby had had her four-week check-up and was now back at work.

"Excellent," replied Séra. "On Friday, we will all meet here, and I will go through the itinerary."

Rose said, "May I ask you something, Séra?" Séra nodded. "My 'sisters', Gabrielle, Céleste and Emilie are all expecting. Have you ever thought about doing maternity wear?"

Séra looked at Rose, raised her eyebrow and said, "Actually no I haven't. I'm not exactly into children, as you know, but I will give it some thought. Would your sisters be interested in modelling the clothes?" Rose said she would have to ask them, but didn't see any reason why not.

On the Friday, Rose, Ruby and Mía joined Séra at the château. "Thank you for coming, ladies. Rose already knows why I have asked you to come here. I would like both of you, along with Rose and myself, to attend the London, Milan and Paris fashion shows. As I've told Rose this will all take place next month, and is going to be very hectic. Literally we fly from one show to the next, but at least in Paris we will be home. At the end of this month, the first fashion show in New York will take place. Then it's London, Milan and finally Paris. Basically your will be away for the first three weeks of March. Ruby and Mía, I have already spoken to Mathieu and Madame Cherrillé, who are both happy for you to attend. I understand at the moment Mía you are moving to much larger premises?"

Mía replied they were, but everything would be in place before they left, and ready for production when they came back. Séra was pleased about that. Séra gave each of them a copy of the itinerary, which included all the times of the flights. Literally they would fly from Paris to London, London to Milan, and Milan to Paris.

"It will be lovely to see London again," said Ruby.

Séra replied, "Sorry Ruby but you won't be seeing much of any of the cities. This year the shows have been extended. They will start at 10am and finish at 8pm. Lunch, early dinner and other refreshments will be available, but as to sightseeing, sorry no chance."

Ruby smiled and replied, "Leave that for another time then, Séra."

They all stayed for a couple of hours going through various suggestions as how the days would go. Afterwards Rose, Mía and Ruby went for lunch. All three of them were excited about going.

That weekend, JP arrived home. Rose told him about the fashion shows, and JP replied, "That's going to be hectic for all of you. You will take care and make sure you rest properly, môn amour?" Rose replied she would. JP then said, "As it turned out, my men and myself won't be here in March either. Here is a list for you of our itinerary."

March – Switzerland and Luxembourg

May - Spain and Portugal

June – London

August – Belgium

Sept – Greece and Italy

Oct – Denmark, Sweden and Norway

"In November, that is when the elections take place, and then it's a waiting game, to see if the President is re-elected."

Rose asked, "Why nothing for April and July?"

JP replied, "Well môn amour, Hugh and Chantelle get married in April, and hopefully in July, you and I will be spending our two weeks in Montpellier. In June when we go to London, Antoine, Porte and Sávoire, along with two others will be joining me, as I didn't want Donatien, Andre and Pierre away from home. The three of them will probably be away for the months of June, and maybe July to help their wives with the other children. The President, naturally, has agreed all of this."

Rose wrapped her arms around his neck and said, "So we are going back to Montpellier then. I can't wait. Sun, sea, sand, and relaxation."

JP kissed her tenderly and said mischievously, "You missed out nude swimming and incredible lovemaking."

Rose replied, "No I didn't. I knew you'd say that," and kissed him back.

"Talking of incredible lovemaking…" said JP. Within minutes they were upstairs undressing each other. They loved each other slowly and sensually until both of them were sated.

Afterwards JP made a meal of Tartiflette (potatoes, melted cheese, bacon and onions), and served it with a Charcuterie board (a couple of different meats, with cheeses and French bread). A Banana Tartes Tatin followed this. "Oh JP, that was lovely. Don't take this the wrong way, but if you fed me like that every evening, I'd soon be the size of this farmhouse."

JP roared laughing and replied, "You are like me, môn amour, you can eat what you like and not put any weight on."

Cuddled up together on the settee, Rose asked him about the house at Versailles.

"I know the one you mean," said JP, "and I know a little of the history. Not that it looks like it now, but it was built in the seventeenth century, and was once surrounded by a small hamlet. Those buildings have now all gone. It was also situated in the grounds of the Versailles Palace. Over the centuries the lands changed, and lots of the Versailles gardens were sold off, including the old lodge, as it was then. Through the centuries various high-ranking people have lived there. Must be over fifteen years now that a couple bought it, but their names were never disclosed. The first thing done was to renovate the outside of the lodge. Word was the husband liked it, but the wife didn't, so just at the front only, he built a separate wall to make it look more modern. I imagine there is a gap between the original and new walls. The front gardens were totally rebuilt into the terraced gardens with fountains you can see from the restaurant. As to how they get in and out, I remember my papa telling me a story that there were underground tunnels built in war time, which could explain why they're not seen leaving and arriving back. Apart from that, môn amour, I am in the dark."

Rose replied, "Wow, what a story. I would never have known it was that old. Wonder what it's like inside. If I had a house like that, I'd want people to see it in its full glory."

"Instead, môn amour, you got an old farmhouse."

"Hey, I love my old farmhouse, it's home." JP kissed her.

Séra had a word with Madame Cherrillé and Mía about maternity clothes. Mía said she could come up with some drawings and did. Séra liked them, and so Gabrielle, Céleste and Emilie arrived at the château for their first photo shoot. Rose soon put them at ease and they loved every minute of it. Séra said they were naturals. The photos were put in the March issue, which actually appeared in the newsagents late February, and was a huge success. Orders came in to Séra from all over the shops wanting the designs. Madame Cherrillé had taken on extra staff and were soon busy in one part of the new premises. Séra had also sent orders to her own suppliers, who were busy also. Séra rewarded Rose by giving her a substantial pay rise. She blessed the day she took Rose on.

The weeks flew by and soon March was upon them. JP and his men flew to Switzerland and then afterwards to Luxembourg. Séra, Rose, Ruby and Mía flew to London, Milan and back to Paris. The fashion shows had been manic, but they had all survived, but were shattered. Rose took as many photos as she could, whilst Ruby wrote down what Séra told her. Mía went through six sketch books. Some of the fashions they had seen had been unbelievable. There had been bold styles and colours, huge belts, and chains. Most of the models had permed hair, with feathers, scarves or other accessories. Every designer naturally was different. One was devoted to the glam rock look. Another had everything in metallic colours. Some of the ensembles were all in the same colour. The other designers showed: -

Oversized outwear, with huge glasses

Sheer or torn tights

Dresses with huge shoulder pads

Polka dot dresses with bright coloured hats and matching accessories

Puff leopard sleeved coats in different colours

Jumpsuits

Suits with large fur collars

Fur coats and leather boots

Bodysuits, leg warmers, sweat bands for the gym

Baggy trousers that could be ripped off into shorts

Leather and suede miniskirts with shiny tights and boots

Big chunky jumpers with trousers

Spandex leggings, teamed up with baggy t-shirts

Ruffled shoulder gowns with lace gloves

Denim jeans, skirts and jackets

Large oversized blazers, with baggy overalls

Then there was menswear, for women, which consisted of a sports jacket, trousers and a big overcoat. The models even had their hair cut short to look like men.

Some of the men's fashions were: -

Jeans

Bomber jackets

Windbreakers

Turtlenecks under a wild-coloured sweater

Oddly stripped shirts

Skinny neck ties

Hawaiian shirts

Nylon tracksuits in neon colours

Leather pants and jackets

Leg warmers

Frilly puff-sleeved shirts

Mesh tops

Long-sleeved velour shirts

Thick colourful sweaters

Parachute trousers

After the fashion shows had finished, many of the top magazines had photos of celebrities posing in some of the outfits on their covers. Over the month, Rose and everyone else had either seen or met thousands of people. Due to Séra being there, they had invitations to go backstage to meet the models and designers. Quite a few of the designers had seen Rose's work and tried to poach her from Séra. One even offered her twice the wages she was getting. To Rose, the models looked to be a lot skinnier than the year before.

Once back in Paris, Rose had seen Chantelle modelling at the fashion show, but never got chance to talk to her. She needed to see her about the wedding, so would go down at the weekend. That weekend though, all Rose wanted to do was sleep. JP arrived home and was shattered as well. They did venture down to the village on the Sunday, and after having a pub lunch went and saw Hugh and Chantelle. JP was keen to know how Hugh had managed without

Raoul. He had been absolutely fine, and the villagers had all helped him. Hugh was concerned for Rose, who he thought looked totally drained. She told him she would be fine, but had made some notes for when they did it all over again in September. Now Mía was back, Chantelle was going to try and see her the following weekend, and Rose said she would go with her. The wedding was now four weeks away. Hugh had sorted everything out with Gérard, as Chantelle had been busy. When Rose and JP got back home, both of them just wanted to sleep. As much as they wanted to love each other, they were just too tired.

Over the next four weeks, Rose and Séra went through hundreds of photos and sorted out which ones would go into which issues, along with Ruby's write-ups. Rose and Chantelle had been and seen Mía, and the dresses were ready.

The day of the wedding arrived. Hugh had ordered two cars, one for JP and himself, the other for Chantelle and Rose. Hugh had stayed at the farmhouse, and Rose with Chantelle. Just before they were due to leave, JP saw how nervous Hugh was and said, "I think you need a brandy to calm your nerves, Hugh." JP put a small amount into two glasses. "Here's to a lovely day, Hugh."

Chantelle was just as nervous as Hugh was. Rose helped her dress and she looked beautiful. Rose also looked lovely in her dress. The car arrived, and soon they were at the town hall. This time, however, there was only the four of them, as everyone else was driving to Gérard's. Hugh and JP turned to see Chantelle and Rose walking towards them. Chantelle was wearing a long cream dress, which had an intricate embroidered bodice with sequins, with a sheer neckline. It was nipped in at the waist, from which a shimmering skirt flowed down to the ground. The sleeves were capped, and she wore a pearl choker and earrings. Her bouquet was a mixture of wild flowers. Rose's dress was the same design, but came to just above her knee in a very pale yellow colour. Rose wore her small diamond earrings and her heart necklace. They both looked stunning, and that was how Hugh and JP saw them. About twenty minutes later the ceremony was over, and Hugh and Chantelle were man and wife.

CHAPTER 38

As a favour to both of them, Rose was their photographer. When they left the town hall, Rose took quite a few photos, but one of the staff took photos of all four of them. Rose and JP arrived at Gérard's first. When Hugh and Chantelle arrived they were greeted by rapturous applause, as they entered the reception. Hugs and kisses were given to both of them. Rose was busy taking lots of photos. Like Rose and Ruby, they had gone for a buffet, which looked sumptuous. After Hugh and Chantelle had thanked everyone for coming, and everyone raised their glasses in a toast to the happy couple, the buffet was slowly eaten. Gérard had made a small Croquembouche, as there were only thirty guests. Once the tables had been cleared, the music started. JP held his hand out to Chantelle, who accepted it. Then JP gave Chantelle's hand to Hugh. Everyone cheered. The day and evening were a huge success, and everyone thoroughly enjoyed themselves.

By 10pm, apart from Hugh, Chantelle, Rose and JP, everyone else had left. Céleste, Emilie and Gabrielle were now all seven months into their pregnancies. Mía had designed their dresses and each of them felt very feminine, but tired quickly. Once a month, Rose had picked them up for their photo shoot, and as a "thank you", Séra had offered them two free summer or winter dresses from Mía's, after they had got their lovely figures back. Rose and JP waved to Hugh and Chantelle and said they would see them the following day. Rose and JP stayed for another hour and chatted to Gérard. Once they were back at the farmhouse, JP said, "I haven't had time to tell you how beautiful you look, but…"

Rose turned and looked at him and said, "But?"

JP smiled and replied, "But you look sexier out of it."

Rose raised her eyebrow and said, "You too look handsome, but…" JP laughed and took Rose in his arms. Slowly they undressed each other, and then loved each other.

Later the following morning, Rose and JP made their way down to the village. In the pub, which was packed with villagers, Raoul had put up wedding decorations, and a large buffet, with a wedding cake, was laid out in the restaurant. "Rose, JP, lovely to see you. We are awaiting our new bride and groom. Help yourselves to a glass of champagne," said Raoul. Soon Hugh and Chantelle turned up, and the whole pub cheered, hugged and kissed them. Hugh gave a small speech, and then Raoul advised that the buffet was ready to be eaten. Rose, JP, Hugh and Chantelle sat at the same table, and chatted about this and that.

Some time later Raoul said, "Ladies and gentlemen, may I have your attention for a moment? As we all know our distinguished guests were married yesterday, and after only being in the village for a short time, we have been honoured by them to celebrate their wedding with all of us today. Hugh and Chantelle please come up, so you can cut your wedding cake."

Hugh and Chantelle made their way to Raoul and as they cut the cake, everyone toasted them by saying, "To Hugh and Chantelle." To everyone's delight Hugh then kissed Chantelle. The celebrations carried on until about 9pm, and then the villagers started to make their way back to their cottages. Hugh asked Raoul when would he be needed to cover the pub for him. Raoul said it would be in May, when they went to Spain and Portugal, and then a week in June for London.

The trips to Spain and Portugal, followed by London, all went off without a hitch. Celebrations were held as Emilie, Céleste and Gabrielle all gave birth to boys, and all were doing well, over the months of May and June. Andre, Donatien and Pierre were now on leave until August.

"Well môn amour, now it's our time to relax. Montpellier here we come." Rose had been really busy doing wedding photos for Mathieu and photo shoots and couldn't wait to relax.

Soon they were at the chalet, and after unpacking everything, and putting the shopping away, both of them undressed each other and then ran into the inviting sea. "This is so refreshing," said Rose.

JP took her in his arms and nuzzling her ear, said, "And now we'll relax each other," and slowly made love.

Afterwards JP set up the BBQ and they had sausages, steaks, jacket potato, and salad. This was followed by apple pie and ice cream. Rose said, "A belated Happy Birthday, my love," and toasted him with a mug of coffee. Earlier in the year, Porte had been down to the chalet and had bought new sun loungers, and these were sturdy white plastic loungers and quite wide. After drinking their coffee, Rose and JP snuggled up on one of the loungers, in their dressing gowns, and watched as the sun slowly went down. Both of them were so comfy, they didn't really want to move, but eventually they did. JP cleaned and put away the BBQ and loungers, whilst Rose washed up, and then they went to bed and loved each other.

A couple of days later the weather was overcast, and JP said, "Porte told me of a couple of places to visit, which he thought we might like. One is called Saint-Guillem-Le Desert, and the other one is Séte. Both are about a forty-five-minute drive away. What do you think?"

Rose replied, "Sounds good to me. We should look around the area more. Let's do Saint-Guillem first."

Just over an hour later they arrived, and managed to find a large shady car park.

"Oh JP, what a beautiful place this is." They walked into the main square, which had a small market. First of all they went and sat at one of the café's terraced tables and ordered coffee and a pastry. "Look up there, JP." JP looked up and saw a rocky peak, which looked like it overlooked the whole village, and had the ruins of an old fortress. In the square was one of the biggest trees Rose had ever seen, and so she asked the waiter about it. He told her it was dated back to 1865 and was a Plane tree, and roughly six metres high. The building on the opposite side was the abbey, which dated back to 804. It was closed that day, which sadden Rose, as she would have loved to look round it. After their refreshments, they walked up some steep steps, which led into the long village street, which had various names. The street was cobbled, and not that wide, and had lots of plants on ledges in the stone walls of the buildings. Every now and then they saw a drink fountain, but they were very old.

There were lots of shops, including art boutiques selling paintings, pottery and other various items. Rose went into one of the dress boutiques, and had to go down a few steps. The only way she could describe it, was like going into a small underground cave. She was fascinated.

As they walked in the upper part of the village, they saw a stone bridge that used to have a small river running under it. This had now dried up and had grass and plants adorning it. They saw a plaque, which told them that the village followed the line of a small river, which flowed steeply down to the Hérault River. The village was small, but was very busy. As they walked back to the square, a cat strolled across in front of them, and started purring. Rose knelt down and the cat started to rub itself up against her leg, and Rose stroked it. Then it rolled over on the ground, but Rose made no attempt to tickle its tummy. A plate rattled behind them and the cat was gone as quick as a flash. Little did they know, they had strolled round the village and shops for nearly two hours. Rose had taken lots of photos as usual. The sun was now out and so they decided to go back to Montpellier.

Once back at the chalet, JP made a variety of sandwiches, and some fresh orange juice, and said he would cook later on. He then got the sun loungers out, and the pair of them went for a cooling swim. They swam quite a way out, and then raced each other back. Needless to say JP won, because Rose had seen the various fishes swimming with them, and stopped to watch them by treading the water slowly. JP turned and wondered why Rose had stopped and went back to her. "I might have known it was the fish," he said. Rose linked her arms round his neck and kissed him gently. "Come, môn amour, let's go eat."

After they had eaten, both of them drifted off to sleep for a couple of hours. After another swim, they then put the loungers away, and loved each other under a warm shower. Rose had just finished drying her hair, when the phone rang. "Môn amour, it's Ruby."

"Hi Ruby. You're WHAT!! Oh Ruby I'm so happy for you and Antoine. Be back next weekend and then we'll meet up." Rose was jumping for joy.

"Môn amour, what's going on?"

"Oh JP, it's Ruby – she's pregnant – with twins. She has just had her three-month scan with Mum."

JP was stunned and then realised why Antoine had been quieter than his normal self. "That's why Antoine has been quiet. I have never known him keep a secret for so long," he said.

"I am delighted for both of them." As they ate their dinner, they both toasted Ruby and Antoine. In bed, they loved each other slowly and sensually.

The following week, they decided to spend a day at Séte. When they got there, they saw it was a major port, and two cruise ships were anchored in the harbour. JP drove around and eventually found a parking space. JP had read up on the town and told Rose it was built in the 1660s, as the Mediterranean terminus of the Canal du Midi, and was bordered by a biodiverse saltwater lagoon. As they walked around they saw lots of activity on the waterways, and Rose managed to find a map. The town had gridded streets, canals and bridges.

"I wonder if this is what Venice looks like?" asked Rose.

JP replied, "Perhaps one day, we might go."

Rose then spotted an information stand and took a guide. "It says here that lots of cherished French artists, poets and musicians were born in Séte. There is a museum that covers the history. Oh, look at all those painted houses." As usual Rose was taking photos of everything they saw. As they walked along the harbour, they watched as fishing trawlers brought in the fresh catches for the restaurants, and pleasure crafts sailing in and out. Soon they found the museum and went in. Inside were historical documents covering the history of the city and fine arts. There were in-depth accounts of famous jousts, with results going back to 1666. Another room had a display of antique shields and lances.

"My love, are we going to lunch here in Séte?"

"I think that would be a great idea. We can sample the local dishes."

Rose then said, "Before we do, can we walk down to the lighthouse? It says here there are a hundred and twenty-six steps, but at the top are great views of the city, harbour, port and sea."

"Come on then," said JP, taking her hand. When they eventually got to the top, it was worth it. The views were brilliant.

"Look at the length of the beaches," said Rose.

Back down in the town, they found a restaurant, which was quite busy. They were greeted and shown to a table by the window. The waiter gave them the menu and whilst they decided, Rose was looking at what everyone else was eating. JP said, "I think we should try the Fruits de Mer for two. Or would you prefer something else?" Rose decided to go with JP's suggestion.

"May I suggest a white wine, Monsieur, which will compliment your meal?" asked the waiter. JP thanked him.

The Fruits de Mer arrived on a large bed of ice. The waiter poured a small amount of wine in a glass, which JP tasted. "Excellent wine," replied JP. The waiter smiled in acknowledgement and filled their glasses. Rose was looking at what they had got. There were oysters, lobster, crab, shrimps, prawns, scallops, clams and mussels. "Môn amour, don't add lemon or vinegar to the shellfish, the wine will do the job. You do know they say oysters are an aphrodisiac."

Rose laughed and replied, "I don't think you need oysters in that department, my love. You always 'rise' to the occasion." JP giggled. Rose wasn't actually a lover of oysters and only had a couple, but tucked into the rest. For a dessert they both had fresh fruit and ice cream.

The waiter asked them if the meal had been up to their expectations and both said it had been excellent. "I see you're a photographer," said the waiter, nodding towards Rose's bag. She replied she was a professional photographer. "If you're not in a hurry, may I suggest you visit Mont Saint-Clair? The summit is one hundred and seventy metres high, and the views are spectacular." They both thanked him, and JP gave him a good tip.

Rose and JP strolled round the shops, and at the large open market, JP did some shopping. Hand in hand they walked back to the car, and JP put the shopping in the boot of the car. Then they drove to the top of Mont Saint-Clair. The first thing they saw was a huge statue of Our Lady of La Salette, in the middle of a rockery. As the waiter said, the views were stunning. The chapel was built on the site of the Montmorencette fortress, which was built by Louis XIII, and still had a piece of the Bastion in its design. Fishermen use to go and pray before going out to sea. Inside, the stained glass windows were in brilliant colours depicting various scenes of a religious theme. On the walls were various frescos of all different kinds of religious pictures and messages of thanks. Statues in white were in alcoves, and a large table had lighted candles in glass pots. A lady told them that it now attracted pilgrims from all over the world, all year round, but especially on the 19th September. Rose asked why the date was special. The lady replied, "On the 19th September 1846, two children who had been tending to the cows, saw a beautiful lady. They went to her and she was sitting down with her elbows on her knees and her face buried in her hands, and she was weeping badly. She wore a white robe, with pearls sewn in here and there, and a gold-coloured apron. Her shoes were white, and there were roses by her feet and in her high headdress. A crucifix on a small chain was around her neck. She told each of the children a secret, and then got up and walked up the hill and vanished. Five years later, in 1851, and after lengthy investigations, a bishop decreed that it had been The Holy Virgin. If you go outside and round the back, you will see a statue of her sitting down crying, and another one of her standing with the two children."

Rose and JP thanked the lady. After taking some more photos, they then made their way back to Montpellier.

CHAPTER 39

Rose and JP still had four days of their holiday left, and they spent it relaxing, swimming, sunbathing, enjoying each other's company, and loving each other. Soon it was back to reality and work. At the weekend, Rose went and visited her sisters, and cradled the newborns in her arms. Deep down she still wished that JP and herself could have had a family, but fate had intervened. When she saw Ruby, she hugged her so tightly. Ruby had waited so long to become a maman, and now she was going to have twins.

"Oh Ruby, I'm so excited for you and Antoine. Your wishes have come true at last."

Ruby laughed and replied, "Yes and we are so happy, although I didn't expect twins."

When the fashion shows came round in September, Séra decided not to invite Ruby, as she was now six months, and rather large. "I'm waddling like a duck!!" said Ruby to Rose one day. Rose laughed and told her it would be worth it when the twins arrived. Ruby had also finished at work, and Mathieu had been sorry to see her go. Rose and Mía attended the fashion shows, and it was just as hectic as it was back in March. JP and his men had flown to Belgium in August, and in September, it was Italy and Greece. They only had one more country to visit and that was Denmark in October, and then it was the Presidential elections. By the end of October, the President had done all he could. Now all they could do was wait and see which way the people of France voted. There were three candidates standing, and on the day the voting took place, it was very, very close between the three of them. JP thought the President would wear out the carpet in the Presidential office. At last, all three candidates were called to attend in the palace ballroom. The atmosphere was tense. Between second and third there was a difference of fifty votes, but between first and second the difference was fifteen votes. The President had succeeded and would be serving his last term of five years. To JP and his men, it was a massive relief, and the rest of the evening they celebrated.

This year, the President, his wife and his son, flew to a secret destination to totally relax. Raoul flew them out of Paris on the fifteenth of December, along with four other bodyguards, and would return on the fourth of January to pick them up. Mathieu and Séra had flown to Italy for the Christmas and New Year, so Rose had also finished work. She had decorated the farmhouse, and was also spending a lot of time with Ruby.

"I really wish these two would hurry up and come out, I'm so bloody big, and I feel like an elephant. I'm so tired as well," said Ruby.

"Antoine will be on leave in a couple of days, until after the twins are born, and he will be with you, Ruby."

Ruby replied, "Fat lot of good he'll be. It's not like he's going to give birth, is it? My figure will take ages to get back to its normal size. Oh Rose, I'm sorry, I'm just so fed up."

Rose tried to hug Ruby, but it was rather difficult. "Ruby Gille, you just pull yourself together. Antoine loves you and is so excited about the twins as we all are. Mum and I will be with you at the births, so come on, snap out of it. Where's my sister Ruby gone?"

Ruby smiled and replied, "It's a long time since you told me off, sister," and they both laughed.

The day before Christmas Eve, JP and his men finished until the fourth of January, but the end of February for Antoine.

Due to all the new babies, who were now more or less six months old, and Ruby due any time, it was decided that they wouldn't meet up for a family Christmas celebration. When Rose got home to the farmhouse, JP was cooking a meal for them. "Môn amour, how is Ruby?"

"Honestly, exasperating, bless her. At least Antoine is home with her now. Something smells good. What is it?" JP told her it was Hachis Parmentier. Rose looked at him, blank. JP replied, "In English, it's um… how do you say meat with mashed potato on top?"

Rose thought and then said, "Do you mean shepherd's pie?" JP nodded. "Have I got time for a quick shower?"

JP replied, "We do." Rose smiled.

After their shower they sat in the kitchen discussing Ruby, and what to do for Christmas and New Year. "We could always invite Uncle and Chantelle, as I think they will be on their own. I'll phone uncle a bit later on," said Rose. Alas, Hugh was taking Chantelle down to Monte Carlo for a belated honeymoon for a week.

"Just you and me then, môn amour. We can hibernate from everyone, under the duvet."

Rose laughed and taking JP in her arms, said, "I like that idea, but I still want my Christmas dinner."

"But of course, môn amour. Tomorrow we will need to go shopping, and then, maybe go to Gérard's for lunch?" Rose nodded in approval.

As they left the following morning, JP saw the van, but Rose didn't, and he smiled to himself. Rose knew JP wasn't a lover of walking round the shops, but today, he more or less went into every shop. He even ended up buying a new suit!! They arrived at Gérard's just after 1pm. Gérard was delighted to see them, and once they had eaten their meal, they chatted for a couple of hours. Rose was quite relaxed, as she had drunk quite a few red wines.

"JP, do you know it's 5pm?"

JP smiled and said, "What, already!! Time flies, môn amour, when we're enjoying ourselves. Better get back home then, before the mad rush starts." They thanked Gérard, with Rose giving him a hug and kissing his cheek, as he did her, and JP shook his hand, and they wished each other Merry Christmas. Luckily for JP, Rose had nodded off as he drove back, so she didn't see the van pulling out from the farmhouse.

"Môn amour, we're back," he said gently.

Rose opened her eyes and said, "Sorry, my love, it must have been the wine," and together they took the shopping in. Rose started putting everything away, whilst JP took his suit upstairs. When he came back Rose said, "Did you nod off up there?" JP replied he'd tried his suit on again, as he wasn't sure, but decided he liked it after all.

Rose raised her eyebrow. *He must be tired,* she thought, *as it's not like him to be indecisive.* Rose made some coffee and they cuddled up on the settee. Both of them nodded off, and were awoken by the fireworks in the village. Sleepily Rose said, "Merry Christmas my love."

JP replied, "Merry Christmas, môn amour, and happy birthday. I think we should go to bed."

In the morning, JP woke Rose gently by caressing and kissing her body. "Umm, that's nice," replied Rose, as she cuddled into him.

"Got to celebrate your birthday, môn amour. Now lay back and let me pleasure you." Rose rolled over on to her back, and JP started with her lips, then her neck and very slowly made his way down to her mound. Rose's body was on fire, and she started moving her hips. JP knew she was on the brink and soon brought Rose to her climax. JP kissed his way all the back up to her lips, and Rose wrapped her arms round him, and pushed him over onto his back. She straddled him, and after kissing her angel, lowered herself down. JP slid inside of her easily, and Rose rode him, bending down to nibble his nipples, and kiss him. She could feel JP hard inside her, and moved quicker. JP was also thrusting up into her, and they both climaxed.

After a short while JP said, "Now môn amour, I'm going to get you breakfast in bed, so keep my side warm as well."

Fifteen minutes later JP was back with boiled eggs and toasted soldiers, and a pot of coffee. "My favourite breakfast. Thank you my love," said Rose.

JP replied, "Afterwards, I suggest we have a shower, put our dressing gowns on, and then I will give you your joint present." Rose was intrigued.

As they went to the bathroom Rose stopped outside one of the spare bedrooms and said, "JP, when did we have another door put here?"

JP replied, "Later, môn amour, later."

Once they had showered and dried each other off and put on their dressing gowns, JP took Rose's hand and said, "Your surprise, môn amour."

JP opened the door Rose had seen, and they walked in. Rose stood there not believing what she was seeing. It was an office. Standing behind her with his arms round her waist he said, "I hope it's to your liking. You have said quite often you have nowhere to put your photos, paperwork etc., so I had this done yesterday whilst we were out."

Rose looked around. There was a desk, which had a set of drawers either end. On the top of the desk was a computer with a printer, and a telephone. On one wall there were three tall cabinets, and a coffee-making machine. On the other wall was a long table. Rose went and sat down in the rather comfortable typist chair, and she had a view of the front garden. "Oh JP, this is wonderful. I can save all my reports in one place now. I can use this long table to spread my photos on, and so much more." She went to him and hugged and kissed him. JP was pleased and could see the excitement in her eyes. "So that's why you dragged me round all the shops yesterday. You needed me out of the way?"

"Yes môn amour, I confess. I also have this for you," and handed her a plaque. On it said, "Rose's Office." Rose laughed and this time kissed him so sensually, her angel stood to attention. Seconds later, in the bedroom, Rose was making love to JP.

Afterwards, JP went down to the kitchen and started cooking a meal. After about an hour, he wondered where Rose was. He went upstairs to see her in her office, putting all her paperwork, etc., in files, and sorting her desk out. "Môn amour, lunch will be ready soon."

Rose had been so engrossed in what she was doing, she actually jumped. "Sorry my love. I didn't hear you come in."

JP took her in his arms and kissed her. "I am so pleased you like it."

Rose took his hand and they went down to the sitting room. "I have to be honest, I had no idea what to get you, but I remembered something you said when we were in Montpellier. Your present is under the tree, my love." JP got the present and opened it. It was a

VHS recorder. "Now you can buy and watch films you like, my love."

JP was delighted with his present, and couldn't wait to buy some films. "Thank you, môn amour. Now we had better eat." JP had cooked a turkey with vegetables, sausages, stuffing, and gravy. A Christmas pudding and custard followed this. Rose made the coffee, and they had just got comfortable on the settee when the phone started ringing. It was JP's men, Ruby, Monica and George, and Hugh, all wishing them Merry Christmas and happy birthday to Rose.

About 6pm the phone rang again and this time it was Antoine. "Rose, Rose, Ruby is in labour. We are at the hospital. She needs you."

Rose replied, "On our way, Antoine." Both Rose and JP rushed upstairs and dressed and after breaking a few speed limits, they arrived at the hospital.

George met them and took them to where Ruby was. Even though George and Monica worked at the hospital, they paid for Ruby to be in a private room. Rose could hear Ruby in pain, and Antoine was pacing up and down outside. "Bloody men," she heard Ruby holler, and smiled.

Antoine saw them and rushed to Rose. "Oh thank heavens you're here, Rose. Please go to her. I didn't know what to do. Your mum is with her."

Rose kissed Antoine's cheek and said, "Antoine, for a start, relax. She'll be fine, but the babies will only come when they want too. We could be in for a long night."

As Rose opened the door, Ruby shouted, "Why can't men give bloody birth?"

Monica went and hugged Rose, and whispered, "You ready for all the obscenities she's going to call Antoine?" Rose giggled.

The doctor arrived, who examined Ruby, and told her everything was looking good, and left. Rose was given a gown and mask to put on, the same as Monica. Rose went and held Ruby's hand, and told her about her new office. Ruby said she couldn't wait to see it. "I think Antoine and I will have to look for somewhere else soon. The flat isn't big enough now."

"Plenty of time for that Ruby," said Rose.

"Oh bloody hell, here we go again," said Ruby who let out a painful cry. Each time Ruby had a contraction she squeezed Rose's hand so tight, Rose thought she was going to break it. "I bloody hate you, Antoine Gille, for putting me through this. No, I don't really, it's just…" Another contraction had her in agony.

"Ruby, use the gas and air, that's what it's for," said Monica.

Ruby took a huge gulp and then laughed. "I like this, can I have it on tap?" Both Rose and Monica looked at each other and rolled their eyes.

"Where's Antoine?" asked Ruby.

Rose told her he was outside with JP and dad.

"Ruby, you do know Antoine can be in here with you, don't you? He just might want to see the babies born," said Monica.

Ruby pulled a face and said, "Yuk, no. I don't want him seeing what will happen down there."

Rose and Monica laughed and Monica replied, "My lovely daughter, I think Antoine knows what's down there, after all it did take the two of you."

Ruby actually went scarlet. "Mum, I want him here. I'd rather break his fingers than Rose's. Sorry Rose, didn't mean to hurt you."

Rose replied she hadn't. Monica went out and brought Antoine in, all gowned and masked. "I'll give you some space," said Rose.

"Rose, you will be with me when I give birth? Please." Rose smiled and said she would be.

Rose went and joined JP and Antoine. The doctor and a midwife, along with Monica, were keeping checks on Ruby. They could hear Ruby calling Antoine all the names he didn't want to hear. A nurse went in, and Monica came out and said, "It's like World War Three in there. I need a coffee." George asked how long, and Monica said it would be hours. They all went to the canteen and had a drink and relaxed slightly.

About an hour later, they went back to Ruby, and Monica re-gowned and went in. "You're bloody useless," they heard Ruby say.

The other nurse came out and said, "I hope her husband doesn't take to heart everything she's saying to him."

"Oh dear," said Rose, and all three of them giggled.

The hours ticked away, and it was soon midnight. "No birthday babies, môn amour," said JP. Rose smiled and cuddled up to him.

About 4am, Monica gently shook Rose awake. "The babies are on their way."

CHAPTER 40

Rose gowned and masked up and went into the room. The doctor, two midwives and two other nurses were in the room. Rose noticed Ruby looked totally exhausted, as did Antoine. The doctor said, "You're near now, Ruby, so do what I tell you. Only when I say 'push' do you push. Understand?"

Ruby nodded, followed by, "Bloody hell it hurts."

Antoine said "Ouch," as Ruby squeezed his hand so hard.

Monica took Ruby's other hand and said, firm but gentle, "I didn't raise you to swear every five minutes, so stop it."

"Sorry Mum, it's just so blo… painful." Monica told her it would soon be over.

At 4.30am the first baby was born. Rose had never seen anything so incredible, and had tears in her eyes. About forty-five minutes later the other baby arrived. Both babies were crying and that brought tears to Ruby and Antoine's eyes. Antoine kissed Ruby and said, "I love you so much, and thank you for our babies."

Monica said, "Congratulations to you both, you have two healthy babies, a boy and a girl. We just need to make them presentable, weigh them etc., and then you can hold them."

Meanwhile the doctor had been seeing to Ruby, and checking everything that needed to be removed had. Rose had left the room and looking at George, said, "Congratulations Granddad. A boy and a girl."

JP hugged and patted George's back and congratulated him. Then he hugged and kissed Rose. "You alright, môn amour?"

"Oh JP, I have never seen a baby born before. It was incredible, and Ruby was so brave." Tears fell down Rose's face, in joy, and JP held her close, knowing what she was feeling, although he knew she wouldn't mention it.

An hour later, the doctors, midwives and nurses left. Monica told them they could come in. Ruby was now sitting up with one baby, and Antoine had the other. Rose wished she had her camera. The look of joy on both of their faces was wonderful. They all kissed Ruby and the men patted Antoine's shoulder. "Oh Ruby, they are so beautiful," said Rose.

Ruby smiled and said, "Well, they do have two good-looking parents. Rose, do you want to hold him?" Rose nodded. Monica made her sit down in the chair and then gently laid the baby in Rose's arms. At that moment JP's heart broke for what they had both wanted and couldn't have. He quickly blinked his tears away, but not before Rose had seen him. Rose smiled at him, and he smiled and winked back at her.

"Boss, you want to hold our little girl?" JP was used to holding babies and took her. Now Rose's heart broke. When Rose looked round, all of them had tears in their eyes.

JP looked at George and Monica and said, "Grand-pére and Grand-mére's turn." Rose and JP handed the babies over to them.

The door opened and a nurse came in. "Sorry everyone, another five minutes and then we must take the babies to the nursery, as Maman needs to rest. Ruby, you will be staying in hospital for at least a week, but when babies need feeding we will come and get you. Have they taken to your breasts?" Ruby replied, after a bit of juggling around, they had. The nurse smiled and left. Monica and George gave both babies to Ruby, who kissed their foreheads, and Antoine bent over and did the same. The nurse returned with another nurse and two incubators. They put the babies in each one and then wheeled them out to the nursery, which was at the end of the corridor.

"I think we will leave you to rest now. Antoine, I can drive you home?" asked George. Antoine thanked him. Rose and JP also left, but Monica was staying the night with Ruby.

Back at the farmhouse, JP made some breakfast, and then both of them decided to go to bed, where they snuggled into each other and slept. Rose woke just after midday and went and had a shower. A pair of strong arms went round her and JP nuzzled the back of her neck, whilst his hands caressed her body. Rose turned and kissed him gently. As the water rained down in them, they made love slowly and sensually. It was what they both needed. Once they had dried each other, JP said he would phone his men to tell them the news. Rose phoned her uncle and Chantelle. Everyone was delighted and glad to hear Maman and babies were well. Rose and JP spent the rest of Boxing Day just relaxing, eating, and watching the television.

In bed that night, after they had loved each other, Rose sat up and looking at JP said, "I saw your heart break when I held the baby, and I felt the same when I saw you. Are we going to be alright?"

JP now sat up and wrapping his arms round her said gently, "Fate decided that, môn amour, not us. I have you and that's all I need. You are my life and my world."

Rose took his face in her hands and kissed him so gently. "And you are mine, my love." They both snuggled back down under the duvet, kissing and caressing each other, and then slept.

Over the following week, Rose went to the hospital every day, and JP helped Antoine set up a nursery for the twins at the flat. Rose watched as Ruby was shown how to hold her babies, wash, feed and dress them. Rose, however, was pleased she didn't have to do the nappy changes!! "How can something so small make a smell like that?" said Ruby, holding a soiled nappy at arm's length. Antoine visited every afternoon and stayed as long as he could, and soon it was time for Ruby and the twins to go home. Rose and JP went to help them.

"Boss, can I ask you something?" asked Antoine. JP nodded. "Ruby and I wondered if you and Rose would be godparents to the twins?"

Tears came to Rose's eyes, and JP replied, "We would love to be godparents, to him and her. Just hurry up and name them." All of them laughed, and left the hospital.

Whilst Ruby had been in hospital, she had a constant stream of visitors. JP's men and their wives visited, along with Hugh and Chantelle, George and Monica popped in when time permitted, and even Gérard made an appearance. Ruby had no idea how Mathieu had found out, but a huge bouquet of flowers was sent from himself and Séra. Ruby and Antoine thanked all the nurses and midwives who had helped and taught her so much.

Back at the flat, Ruby was amazed at the spare bedroom. Between Antoine and JP they had turned it into a wonderful nursery. The babies had a cot each, with whirly things above for them to watch. Lots of toys had appeared. The lighting was soft and one wall was painted a light blue, and the other a pale pink. There were also two small cribs to place at the side of their bed for night time. "Oh Antoine, I love it. Thank you, and thank you JP." She gave both of them a kiss on the cheek.

"That's not all," said Antoine. Opening one cupboard he said, "These are from our family." Inside were bags of nappies, baby clothes for both, a changing mat, a steriliser with bottles for formula feeds, and a bag to put everything in. In another cupboard was a double fold-up stroller, two car seats, and a double pram. Ruby was stunned and for once lost for words. She just stood still and cried. Antoine took her in his arms and hugged her.

A baby's cry told Ruby it was feeding time. "You two look after your twins, and Rose and I will cook you a lunch. How hungry are you, Ruby?" asked JP.

"Starving," came back the reply. JP, with Rose's help, made a salad starter, followed by steaks with various vegetables, and steak-frites. For a dessert he made chocolate soufflés. "JP that beats hospital food any time," said Ruby. JP smiled.

"What did you two do for New Year's Eve?" asked Ruby. Rose told them they had a lovely quiet evening in together. "Romantic," said Ruby.

"Ruby, Antoine, is there anything you need or we can do?" asked Rose.

Antoine replied, "You have both done more than enough. Ruby and I need to get into a routine, and we need to discuss if we will need help, especially once I'm back at work."

Rose said, "Don't forget Mum and Dad have arranged for a nurse to come and see you every day for the next couple of weeks." Ruby had forgotten.

"Antoine, whatever you need, just let me know," said JP.

"Thanks boss, from both of us."

JP replied, "We'll leave you now, but remember, both of you, we are only a phone call away." They all kissed and hugged each other and very carefully, so as not to wake them, Rose and JP kissed the foreheads of the twins.

A couple of days later Ruby phoned Rose. "You and JP will be pleased to know we have decided on the twins' names. Armand and Rachel."

Rose replied, "The names suit them. How are you? I'm frightened to phone in case I wake them up."

Ruby said, "So far so good. I'm doing the day shift and Antoine the night shift. The nurse is lovely and stays with us for at least a couple of hours. She's shown us how to bathe them, and dress them in layers, so they don't get too hot, and all sorts of other stuff. I know JP goes back to the palace tomorrow, so do you want to come over?" Rose said she would love to.

"They alright, môn amour?"

"Yes my love, they are fine, and I'm going over tomorrow, whilst I can. You're back to work tomorrow, and I'm back on Monday. Then it's all go for the fashion shows in February, but we are only doing London and Paris, so it won't be so tiring."

JP held Rose close to him and said, "These fashion shows wear you out, môn amour. Please take care."

Rose looked into his beautiful blue eyes, and said, "I will take care, if you take care on all these Presidential trips."

JP promised and kissed her passionately. "Time for bed?"

Rose, who was already halfway up the stairs replied, "Last one in bed sleeps in the spare bedroom. Don't forget to turn all the lights out, and lock the doors."

Rose went to the bathroom and had a quick wash, and then got into bed. After ten minutes, JP hadn't joined her, so she went to see where he was. "What are you doing, my love?"

Without turning JP replied, "Making up the bed, as I was last up."

Rose raised her eyebrow, and walked up behind him. He only had his underpants on. Rose's hands went down the front of them and gently took hold of his manhood, which reacted immediately. "I'd rather you joined me for 'playtime'." JP's hands went behind him and as he touched her body, he realised she was naked. His hand went between her legs, and Rose started kissing his back. Rose moved her hands and pushed his underpants down. JP turned and picking her up carried her into the bedroom. "Sit up, my love." Rose then straddled him, and lowered herself down on to his manhood. As she moved up and down, JP massaged her breasts and sucked her nipples. His arms then went round her and they kissed each other with a passion. JP massaged her buttocks, and then his hand went to her nub, and massaged it, and Rose's climax hit her. JP carefully pushed her down on to her back and Rose locked her legs round his waist. JP thrusts came hard and fast, and soon both of them went over the edge into oblivion. In the morning, JP loved Rose tenderly, and then he was away to the palace.

Rose got up later and had some breakfast, and then drove over to Ruby's. Ruby and Antoine looked shattered. "Not getting much rest then?" she asked.

Ruby replied, "We try, but the minute we nod off, those little monkeys wake up."

"What time is the nurse due?" Antoine replied she was due soon. "Right, when she arrives, I will help her with the twins, and you two can get some sleep."

Antoine replied, "That sounds great. Thanks Rose."

The nurse arrived and Ruby introduced Rose to her. The nurse asked Ruby when the twins had last been fed.

"About an hour and a half ago."

The nurse looked at Rose and said, "You ready to bathe these two gorgeous babies?" Rose smiled and nodded. Ruby and Antoine went to get some rest, whilst the nurse and Rose bathed the twins, and dressed them. The twins were as good as gold, and Rose loved them.

About an hour later Ruby walked into the room. "Having fun, Godmother?" she asked, smiling. Rose nodded.

The nurse said, "Ruby, have you thought about formula feeding the twins? That way Antoine will be able to feed them as well." The three of them sat and discussed the idea, and both Ruby and Rose agreed it would be a good idea, especially when Antoine went back to work. Ruby told the nurse that she already had the steriliser and bottles that had been given as a present. The nurse replied that she would pick up some formula the following morning, and show her and Antoine what to do. The nurse left, and Ruby fed the twins. Once they were asleep, Rose told Ruby to go back to bed. Ruby had put the twins in their cradles and Rose gently rocked both of them. Rose was so relaxed, she nearly fell asleep herself.

"Everything alright, Rose?"

Rose jumped slightly as she hadn't heard Antoine come in. "Absolutely fine, Antoine. How are you feeling being a papa?"

Antoine replied, "Incredible. Just holding them in my hands, makes my heart melt, but also completes my world. I saw the pain Ruby went through, but we both agreed, it was worth it. I do worry though how Ruby will cope when I'm back at work."

"That's five weeks away yet, and I'm sure you'll both be fine. I wish I wasn't working, as I could be with her every day, but alas…"

Antoine kissed her cheek and replied, "As the boss said, you're only a phone call away!"

A voice behind them said, "Well you two look cosy. He doesn't want a big, fat maman now Rose."

Antoine took Ruby in his arms and said, "I will always love you whatever size you are, but your figure is slowly coming back." Ruby kissed him tenderly.

Rose decided it was time for her to leave, and hugged and kissed them both, and then the twins. Driving back home, her thoughts wandered to how JP and herself would have been as parents, and then dashed it away. No point in wondering what if.

CHAPTER 41

The month of January flew by, and it was now February. Rose, Séra and Mía were off to the fashion shows. Antoine had returned to work, and they had been lucky enough to get a lady to help Ruby with the twins. JP was busy sorting out the President's itineraries and who would be going with him. At least it wasn't as hectic as the year before. The last weekend of March, when JP was home, Rose and JP invited their family round. It was the first time they had all been together since the middle of the last year, and the first time Hugh and Chantelle had seen all the babies. Gabrielle, Céleste and Emilie's babies were now nine months old, and the twins were three months old.

Rose said, " I can't believe how the babies have grown. It's just amazing." Rose took photos of them all, and then JP was told to sit in the middle of the settee, and the five babies were put round him. JP had his arms round them all. Never had he looked so proud. Then Gabrielle made Rose change places with JP and she took the photo. The other children were playing games. Paulette, Michelle were now eight years old, and the baby was called Donatien – Céleste's; Aimée was eight, Lydie was seven, Ouén was four and a half and the baby was called Pierre – Emilie's; Dulé was eight, and the baby was called Andre – Gabrielle's.

JP had made his Boeuf Bourguignon for the adults, and macaroni cheese for the children. The three baby boys were on solid foods, and the twins on formula.

"At this rate, boss, you are going to need a lot bigger table," said Antoine.

JP replied, "Not a problem. Now all of you help yourselves and enjoy."

Pierre said, "I have so missed our meals together, perhaps now we can do it more often?"

They all raised their glasses to that. The next time they did it was JP's birthday, before Rose and himself went off for their two weeks' holiday in Montpellier. In September it was fashion show time again. That Christmas, along with Rose's thirty-second birthday, and New Year's Eve, they all celebrated together at Gérard's. In March of the following year it was time for George and Monica to retire from the hospital. Neither of them were sure what they were going to do, but the hospital staff gave them a great send-off. Ruby had decided that now the twins were fifteen months old, she wanted to return to work. Mathieu said he would be delighted to have her back, and so Monica suggested that she and George looked after the twins during the day. Ruby was so happy, Antoine wasn't so sure, but came round in the end. Chantelle had also decided to quit work, as she wanted to spend more time with Hugh. Rose, Séra and Mía all attended the March fashion shows in London, Milan and Paris. JP's thirty-seventh birthday was celebrated at the farmhouse with all the family, and then Rose and himself were off to their usual holiday destination.

In September it was time for the fashion shows again. This time, however, new designers were showing off their creations, and it made it more interesting. The show in London was at the normal venue, and Rose knew exactly where to get the best photos. In Milan this time though, it was outside the city, in the countryside, and the hotel was huge, and was surrounded by large beautiful gardens. The first four days the show was outside in the grounds. A new designer had all her outfits in black and white stripes. Long flowing black skirts with black and white blouses, with matching hats/scarves. Another new designer had all her eveningwear in sparkling reds and golds, and most of the gowns were strapless. From the other designers came big bold colours, along with Hawaiian swimwear, shirts and shorts. Large floppy hats and bright sandals complemented the outfits. There was even a section full of wedding and bridesmaid dresses. The last four days, due to the weather not being kind, the show was inside. Séra, Rose and Mía were impressed with a lot of the outfits.

On the last day, as always with the end of each show, everyone relaxed and enjoyed a huge buffet, and discussed all the designs. Séra, Rose and Mía had found a table and were eating and drinking champagne. "I have some wonderful ideas for the magazine," said Séra. Rose had a bag full of films ready to be developed by Jules, which she had left in her room. Mía had also done lots of sketches, and shown them how to make certain changes. Séra was impressed. They spent a couple of hours together and then Séra said, "I must go and see some friends of mine over there, and so I'll see you both later. If not, in the morning at breakfast," and she left.

At that moment, a voice came over a microphone. "Designers, ladies, gentlemen, models, and everyone else. May I take this opportunity to thank each and every one of you for making this such a wonderful event. I know this year we have all seen creations beyond our wildest dreams, which can be recreated for the markets. With regards to next year's venue, we have a surprise for you all. We are honoured to say it will be held…" Those were the last words everyone in the room heard.

***

Back at the palace, JP was sorting out the rotas, hopefully, up to the end of the year. His men had just finished surveillance, and other duties, and were heading back to the house for a meal. They had just sat down when another bodyguard came in and said, "Antoine, Ruby's on the phone and she sounds extremely distressed."

Antoine rushed to the phone. "Ruby, what's wrong? Is it the twins?" Ruby told him, and then he rushed back to the dining room.

"Antoine, what's wrong?" asked Andre.

Antoine switched on the television. The news was on and then the announcer said, "Now back to our leading story. Reports are still coming in of a huge explosion at the hotel hosting the Milan fashion show. We have a live link to our reporter." The screen showed a huge building on fire, with some of the roof caved in. The reporter said, "As you can see, nearly half of this beautiful hotel has been completely destroyed. People have been killed, and others seriously injured, and all emergency services are on high alert, along with every hospital. We have no idea at the moment what has happened, but some survivors said it was like a bomb going off. The hotel was hosting the Milan fashion show, and top designers and their models were there, along with invited guests." There was a huge rumble as more of the roof collapsed and the live link went down. The announcer said they would try and get the link back quickly.

Andre looked at Antoine, who was pale and then realised why. "Oh bloody hell," he said, "Rose is there." Andre ran out of the house and into the palace. He had to get to JP. His men just looked at each other totally stunned and then ran as well.

"Andre, why are you running like a mad man along the corridor?"

"Apologies Monsieur le President," and he told him. Both of them ran to JP's office.

JP looked up and stood up when he saw the President. "What's happened?" he asked, concerned. The President made him sit down again, whilst Andre turned on the television. JP watched as live pictures of the hotel were shown, and paled significantly. "Rose, oh my god, Rose. I need to do something. I have to find out is she's alright."

The President put his hand on JP's shoulder, and said, "JP, calm down and drink this," and handed him a brandy. "Now I will go and contact the Milan authorities and find out the situation. Andre, with me. You men, look after JP."

The President and Andre left. JP was looking through his cabinet for something.

"Boss, can we help?" asked Antoine.

JP told them he was looking for a map of Milan. Pierre found it. JP said, "I can land the helicopter here, away from the hotel grounds."

Donatien said, "Boss, we have to wait for the President before we decide anything."

"Don't you understand? Rose is my life. I'm nothing without her," JP snapped and then collapsed in his chair. "Sorry, Donatien."

Donatien replied, "Don't be, boss. We are all worried about her, and if we can, we want to come with you."

JP looked at them through his tears and said quietly, "Thank you."

About an hour later the President returned with Andre. "The reports are grim," he said. "They think there were just under a thousand people there, and until the fires are under control, it's too dangerous for them to attempt rescues. Everyone possible is there trying to help. Rows of ambulances are taking the walking wounded to the hospitals. The good news, if you can call it that, was that it wasn't a bomb. It was a gas explosion, which originated in the kitchens, which were located behind the room they were all in. One of the kitchen porters saw it happen."

JP looked at the President and said, "I need to get there, Monsieur le President. May I ask if I can borrow one of the helicopters?"

The President smiled and replied, "Already sorted, JP, but you won't leave until the morning. I'm sorry, men, but I can only let one of you go with JP. Who goes, is up to you. Now I must get back to my office for any more news. JP, I will keep you informed."

JP thanked the President. Before any of them could say anything JP said, "Don't ask me to choose, because I can't. Now if you don't mind, I need time on my own." His men all gave him a man hug and left. JP shut his office door and slumped down into his chair and watched the reports, totally distraught for Rose. His phone rang and it was Hugh.

"JP, have you heard anything?" he asked, full of concern. JP told him what he knew. "I'm coming with you, JP."

JP replied, "I don't know if you can, Hugh. The President is giving us special permission to go, but I will ask."

Hugh was not at all happy with that reply and said, annoyed, "She's my niece, JP, although I look on her as more of a daughter. If I can't come with you, I'll book my own flight down. I'm determined to be there when they find her."

JP's head was spinning and he replied, "I totally understand, Hugh. Can you give me time to talk to the President, please?"

Hugh apologised and said he was concerned, and JP told him he understood.

JP went to see the President about Hugh. "I think it's a good idea. God forbid the worst should happen, but if it does, you will need each other. I will give my permission and tell Hugh to be here for 8am in the morning." JP thanked the President and went back to his office and phoned Hugh. Hugh was so relieved. He couldn't sit at home and do nothing. JP had just put the phone down when it rang again. It was Monica and George. JP filled them in, and promised he would ring them as soon as he found her. That night JP hardly slept a wink, as he tossed and turned thinking about his beautiful Rose. Was she dead, alive, badly hurt? Now he knew what Rose had gone through when he had been in the plane crash.

In the morning Hugh arrived just before 8am and went to JP's office. They both shook hands and hugged each other. A little later, Raoul turned up. "JP, I'm so sorry to hear the news, as is all of the village. The President has asked me to fly you to the accident site. Ready to go whenever you are."

"Thank you, Raoul. Just get my bag and I understand one of my men is coming with me, along with Hugh."

"Which one?"

"No idea. Let's go find out." It was Pierre. "Drew the short straw, did you?" asked JP, but he smiled.

***

Rose and Mía had decided to mingle, and talked to a lot of the models and some of the designers. The designers had now got to know Rose, and two of them tried to persuade her to work with them, but Rose apologised and declined their offers. A little later on, Mía left Rose to go to the ladies'. As Rose went to make her way over to Séra, suddenly there was an enormous bang and the next thing Rose knew was that she was flying through the air, and her back and head hit a wall and she slumped down unconscious. When she opened her eyes, and looked round, the only way it could be described was a war zone. Bodies were scattered everywhere, people were shouting and screaming. She could see half the roof had collapsed down onto the people. There was rubble, broken beams, dust and small fires everywhere. Rose put her hand to the back of her head and then saw it was covered in blood. Slowly she managed to stand up, but felt dizzy and grabbed onto a beam sticking up from the ground in front of her. She remembered Mía had been with her, but she couldn't see her. Rose staggered around trying to find Mía. She stepped over dead bodies, and saw blown-off limbs and blood everywhere, and at one point threw up. She really didn't know where she was in the room. She thought she saw Mía across from her, and walked towards her, when she heard an almighty rumble. As Rose looked up, the rest of the roof collapsed down on her, and she screamed.

***

JP, Hugh, Raoul and Pierre went to see the President. "The latest is that the fire department have worked through the night, and most of the fires are now out. The reports are saying lots of people have survived but are seriously injured, but there are also a lot who have not survived. There were thirty designers with their models, photographers, guests and other people. A rough total of over a thousand people. Might even be higher, nobody knows. JP, take this letter as it confirms who you all are and gives you permission to search for Rose. I understand Séra and Mía were also with Rose, so let's hope all three of them are survivors. Keep me informed as much as you can. Pierre, your job is to look after your boss and Hugh. Do you understand?" Pierre bowed and replied he did.

JP knew that the President meant that if Rose was dead, he and Hugh would need someone to lean on. "Raoul, I was going to ask you to return, but now I want you to stay. Should the ladies need to be returned to our hospital you can fly them back." Raoul nodded in understanding. "Teams of our rescuers are being assembled and will also be flown down tomorrow. Now gentlemen, go and bring the ladies home."

The four of them bowed and left. Andre, Antoine and Donatien went to the airport, and saw them off. JP didn't have the words in him, so he just thanked them. Once JP, Hugh, Pierre and Raoul had flown off, Andre said, "I hope they find Rose alive. I don't even want to contemplate the other." They drove back to the palace, all totally downhearted.

CHAPTER 42

Once in the helicopter, JP asked Pierre how he had been chosen. Pierre replied, "Andre had to stay to be with the President, and Antoine had to stay because of Ruby and the twins. Antoine said Monica and George have moved in to keep Ruby company. That left Donatien and me. Donatien said I should go as I work well under pressure." JP raised his eyebrow at that.

Just over two hours later, they were in Milan airspace. Raoul contacted air traffic control, and they advised they had been waiting for them, and gave them permission to land where they had been advised. Raoul thanked them. Soon they were down on the ground. A car arrived, and after the helicopter had been moved into a hangar, they were driven to the scene. What met them was absolute devastation. Where a large hotel once stood, it now had two ends and the middle completely destroyed. Hundreds of emergency service people, who were masked, and in green overalls were frantically searching for survivors. JP shuddered but it wasn't because he was cold. It was the stench of burnt flesh, and he gagged trying to keep the bile down. Hugh, Pierre and Raoul felt the same. An official-looking man came up to them and said, "Sorry, this area is off limits. You need to leave." JP produced the letter. The man apologised and took them to one side of the hotel. "Both sides of the hotel have been cleared and this is where all the rescuers are getting some rest, when they can, along with meals being brought in. Sorry I can't give you a room." JP replied that it wasn't a problem.

He then took them over to a makeshift tent, where they were

given the green overalls and masks. The man gave them a special badge to put on. "Gives you access to all areas. It's not a pretty sight in there. Dead bodies all over the place, and some of the bodies are in pieces. Over there are eight makeshift morgues. Four for men and four for the women. Have you checked out the hospitals?"

JP replied, "No we just arrived. Do you think that's where we should start?"

The man replied, "It's difficult to say. The hospitals are inundated with casualties. You must excuse me, as I am needed."

JP thanked him and after putting on their masks and overalls they decided to go to the morgues first. Luckily Raoul had met Séra and Mía, so he knew what they looked like. They took one morgue each, and each one of them was devastated. The bodies were laid out in neat lines, but most of the faces weren't covered. A photographer was taking photos for relatives to claim their loved ones. About an hour later Pierre called to JP. "It's not Rose," said Pierre quickly. When JP saw who it was he gasped. It was Séra.

***

Rose opened her eyes very slowly, but couldn't see anything as it was pitch black, and it was deadly silent. She tried to move but she couldn't, as something was pinning her down. She managed to move her left arm slowly and felt a huge beam across her. She could also feel what was rubble, and it was warm. Rose couldn't feel her legs or her right arm. She tried to move one of her legs, but a pain shot through her that sent her back into unconsciousness. Rose drifted in and out of consciousness, for how long she had no idea. The next time she woke, she assumed it must be night time as it was still dark. Surely she should be able to hear something, but it was all silent. She shouted, "Help, somebody please help me!" Nothing. Rose frowned and thought how strange that was, as she had shouted but didn't hear herself. This time she didn't try and move, but tried to remember what had happened. Her mind was fuzzy, but she did remember she was trying to find Mía, and where was Séra? One minute they were talking, the next minute there had been a huge bang. She felt something dripping on her chest, and slowly brought her left arm up and touched it. It was wet, but when she looked at her hand, she saw nothing, only the dark. Rose suddenly realised what was wrong. Her eyes were open, but she saw nothing. She was blind. She couldn't hear her voice shouting because she was deaf. Could she speak? She had no idea. Tears came to her eyes. Was this her death bed? The darkness was getting darker and she felt like she was falling down a long, long tunnel. Her breathing was getting laboured, and she knew she would never see JP, her uncle or her family again. She could feel her organs slowly shutting down one by one. Her heart was now beating so slowly, and the darkness was darker than she'd ever known. Rose closed her eyes, and took her last breath.

***

Three days had passed since JP, Hugh, Pierre and Raoul had arrived, and they were exhausted. They had checked the women's morgue every day, and had visited all the hospitals, but there was no sign of Rose or Mía. JP had phoned the President to advise him of Séra's death. The President told him he had been informed Mathieu was away on a secret story, and his office had no way of contacting him. On day four, eight more teams of rescuers arrived, but this time there were four rescue dogs. The man in charge called everyone to attention. "First of all, I must say a huge thank you to all of you being here. Last night the coordinators and myself came up with another plan. We are now going to split the site up into four parts. Also with the extra help, we can now split the shifts, so we are all more refreshed. The shifts will be midnight until 6am, then 6am until midday, midday until 6pm, and lastly 6pm until midnight. Your coordinators will advise you. As you have no doubt noticed we have two teams with rescue dogs. For the dogs to operate they must have complete silence. They will not take part until later on, as they need to be rested. We now have a rough idea of how many people were here. It's just over a thousand. The death toll at the moment is a two hundred and three. A quick count from the hospitals is roughly four hundred and twenty. A lot of those were walking wounded, who I'm glad to say are being sent home. Other guests, who were lucky enough to walk away is roughly two hundred and fifty. As it stands we are looking for another hundred, hundred and thirty people. The worst area left is where there was a double collapse of the roof. We have now got volunteers filling up wheelbarrows, trolleys, whatever, removing the rubble. I am going to be extremely blunt here and say, anyone under that double collapse is more than likely to have died, so be prepared. Thank you, everyone."

As JP, Hugh, Pierre and Raoul turned away, they saw two friendly faces walking towards them. It was Doctor Michel and Doctor Pátrinne, with their medical teams. They all hugged each other. "Anything, JP?" JP shook his head. "We are here to help, but the minute you find Rose, come and get us, as she will then be our priority." JP thanked them.

The searches continued, until about 4pm, when a siren went off. Everyone went silent, as the four rescue dogs were put on the site. They watched as the dogs went over different areas, sometimes barking, but nothing. Suddenly two of the dogs were barking loudly, all the time wagging their tails. Their handlers calmed them, and then people started carefully removing the rubble. A voice shouted, "Medical team, we've got someone!"

JP went to dash over, but Pierre stopped him. "Give them a minute, boss, we'll soon know." JP's heart dropped when it wasn't Rose. It was a man, and he told them there were eight other people under a table, but they were unconscious. He then collapsed. The teams immediately set to work, and the eight survivors were brought out. They were all being stretchered away when Pierre said, "Oh my god, it's Mía." The four of them rushed over to her, but she was unconscious.

Doctor Michel was examining her. "She has a broken arm and leg, but her vitals are good. As soon as she wakes, I'll let you know. Don't give up on Rose yet, JP."

JP went and sat down under one of the trees, and put his head in his hands. Hugh went to go to him, but Pierre stopped him. Pierre and Raoul knew to give JP a bit of privacy, but all of them kept their eyes on him.

A couple of hours later, Doctor Michel came over to them. "JP, Mía is awake, and wants to talk to you. Then we must get her to the hospital as her vitals are slowly dropping due to shock."

JP and the rest followed Doctor Michel. Mía was attached to various machines in the back of an ambulance. When she saw JP she held her good hand out to him. "Have they found Rose and Séra?" she asked. JP couldn't tell her about Séra just yet, so he shook his head. "Séra had gone to talk to friends on the other side of the room," said Mía, "but Rose and I were together, and I had just left her to go to the ladies when there was an awful bang. Someone grabbed my hand and dragged me under the table. A lot later, I thought I saw Rose, but then the rest of the roof collapsed. What happened?"

JP told her it was a gas explosion in the kitchens. Mía paled greatly, and the doctor told JP they had to go. JP gave Mía a hug and kissed her forehead. The ambulance left with its sirens blaring. Nobody else was found that day. Doctor Michel and Doctor Pátrinne put themselves on the same shift as JP, Hugh, Raoul and Pierre, mainly so they could keep an eye on them all. President's orders.

Day five they were awoken by dogs barking. The six of them rushed to the site. "What's happened?" Pierre asked one of the rescuers.

"The dogs heard something and started barking. Believe it or not, they found fifty people huddled together in a cloakroom, all alive and well. Bringing them out now." JP watched as the survivors were guided out to the medical teams. He put his hopes up, but they were soon dashed. Rose wasn't one of them. The five of them watched as JP walked away from the site and kept walking, looking totally heartbroken.

JP needed space, and so he walked and walked. He had no idea where he was going. His every thought was of Rose. There was no way he could carry on life without her. He only thought it though. After about an hour, he returned to the site.

"You alright, boss?" asked Pierre.

JP nodded. "Found any others?" he asked.

Pierre said they had, but they were dead, and none of them were Rose.

"Where is she, Pierre? All I can think now is she was blown to—"

Pierre put his hand on JP's shoulder and said, "Don't."

JP could see tears had welled in Pierre's eyes, and they hugged each other.

Early the following morning, the siren went off. As always an eerie hush fell over the site. One of the handlers was whistling. Only one of his dogs responded. The handler bent down and said something to the other dog, which sniffed his way over the rubble, down some holes, and back up again. Then he vanished for about five minutes. Both dogs appeared away from where the handler had let them go. Both were barking and wagging their tails, and then disappeared again. This time they reappeared where the handler was. The senior coordinator went over to the handler, and spoke to him, with the handler pointing out what looked like a line. "We think we might have found something," he said. "The handler said his dogs are convinced there is someone down there between these two holes. We need to be extremely careful, as this is where most of the double collapse happened. The last thing we need to do is to start any sort of tumble. Extreme care, please."

***

As Rose took her last breath, she felt something nuzzling her hand. Then something was licking her face. Rose thought she was hallucinating, but she felt it again. She very slowly moved the fingers on her left hand. Again they were licked, and then whatever it was, was gone. Unbeknown to Rose, as she couldn't hear, the rescue teams were carefully removing lots of rubble and debris above her. The dogs were barking and the handler let them go. One returned barking, but the other one had stayed by Rose's body, licking her face. This time there was no response from Rose. The dog started whimpering and ran back to the handler, extremely agitated. The handler said, "Whoever is down there is very close to death, or has just died." The dog vanished again, but this time when he was back at Rose's side, he started barking. The siren went and everyone stopped. The handler walked towards where he could hear his dog barking. "Here, he's under here!" shouted the handler. He whistled for the dog to come back, but the dog stayed where he was, barking frantically.

About half an hour later, they had made a small hole downwards. The dog jumped out, dancing round and round. The handler calmed him. One of the rescuers shone a torch down and saw a body. "There's a female down here, but no movement. She's pinned down by a beam. We'll need lifting equipment."

Everyone started carefully removing the rubble again, until the hole was big enough for a doctor to get down. Doctor Michel went down, as he was of a slim build. "Rose, oh my god Rose. Hang in

there, Rose. Don't you dare do anything stupid like die on me."
Doctor Michel shouted up instructions as to what he needed. "Get
Doctor Pátrinne, NOW!" he shouted. JP saw both doctors go to the
area, but just watched.

Soon the medical team were all around the hole, and then JP saw
Doctor Pátrinne walking towards him. "JP, we've found her. It's
Rose, and she's in a very bad way. Doctor Michel is doing all he—"
JP shot off like a bullet, with Hugh, Raoul and Pierre behind him.

JP looked down the hole to see Rose motionless, with an oxygen
mask on and an IV tube set up. Doctor Michel looked up at him and
said, "That rescue dog might just have saved Rose's life. I've barely got
a pulse, JP, but rest assured, Rose is not going to die on my watch."

"What can I do?" asked JP, full of concern. "I haven't got a lot of
room to work, and until this beam is moved, I don't know what
internal damage she has suffered. I can see there is a larger hole to
my left. If the rescuers could work to clear that area, once the beam is
away, we can stretcher her up." JP went and had a word with the
coordinator. New instructions were given. They handed down two
large polythene sheets to Doctor Michel and told him to cover them
both, as lots of dust and debris would fall. It was a long, slow
process. Doctor Michel talked to Rose all the time, not realising Rose
couldn't hear him. Now he had more room to manoeuvre, he tested
all her vital signs. Straight away he noticed that when he lifted her
eyelids, her eyes were glazed, and he knew she was blind, hopefully
only temporary. Then he found the head injury. He noticed her pulse
had increased slightly and that was a good sign. About four hours
later, the tunnel was cleared and the full extent of where Rose was
could be seen.

CHAPTER 43

Rose felt somebody touching her and her eyes flew open. She saw nothing, and then remembered. She started to flinch and Doctor Michel saw her dilemma. She couldn't see who it was, and it was frightening her. Rose was saying something, but she had no voice. Doctor Michel clapped his hands, but Rose didn't respond. He now knew she was blind, deaf and couldn't speak. His heart sank. He could see her right arm was broken and was trying to set it, but Rose was getting more agitated, and had closed her eyes.

"JP, are you there?" he shouted.

"I'm here, Doctor."

"Can you get down here? I need your help." Carefully JP got down next to Rose. "JP, I need to set Rose's arm, but for some reason she's agitated by my touch. I'm hoping she will react to your touch. Try and hold her left hand." JP crouched down and took Rose's in his. Rose snatched it away immediately, but then tentatively searched for it. JP took her hand, and he was overwhelmed when Rose squeezed it. She calmed straight away, but tears rolled down her cheeks. Rose knew JP was with her, and sort of smiled. JP brushed her tears away, and bent over and kissed her lips gently.

"Boss, how's Rose? The lifting gear is here to move the beam."

Doctor Michel replied, "She's not good, Pierre. I will need to put Rose into a coma, so please tell them not to do anything yet. I will need Doctor Pátrinne." Pierre nodded.

Both doctors worked on Rose, with JP holding her hand. Soon

311

Rose was in an induced coma. JP then left her, so the rescuers could get in. It took another two hours for the beam to be removed. Rose's vitals plummeted. The doctors got to work on her, and then saw the extent of her head injury. Very, very carefully, she was put on a stretcher, and lifted out. Everyone applauded, as they were so pleased. As it turned out, Rose was the last person they found alive.

In the ambulance various machines were linked up to Rose. JP, Hugh, Raoul and Pierre followed in a car, as the doctors, and their teams went with her. Halfway there, Rose stopped breathing, and they had to resuscitate her. It was touch and go, but they kept her alive. At the hospital she was rushed down the corridor to the theatre. Usually the surgeons from the hospital would have taken over, but with two exceptional surgeons, with their own medical teams with Rose, they waited in the wings, just in case they were needed. Three hours later Rose was wheeled out of the theatre, and put into a private side room.

Doctor Michel went and phoned the President, and told him the news.

"Does JP know?"

"Not yet, Monsieur le President."

"Can we fly her back here?"

Doctor Michel replied they could, but it would be better to wait a couple of days.

"Can you ask Raoul to fly the helicopter back, along with some of your medical team, and then he's to fly the jet down, so you can all come back together."

Doctor Michel replied he would. Both doctors found JP, Hugh, Raoul and Pierre in a relatives' room. JP knew immediately something was wrong. "How bad is she, Doctors? Am I going to lose her?" asked JP with a lump in his throat.

"I suggest the four of you sit down," said Doctor Michel.

Doctor Pátrinne looked at the four men and said, "I'm sorry to tell you that Rose has suffered severe blunt abdomen trauma, hence why we were so long in surgery. JP, Hugh, she will recover. We had to perform surgery on her liver and bowel to stem the internal bleeding. Her spleen was lacerated because her left lower ribs were fractured. We needed to drain the fluid around her pancreas. Her kidneys survived as they are sort of protected by her ribs. All this was done with the aid of x-rays and CT scans. Both Rose's legs are broken and she has a stress fracture to her right arm, which we thought broken at first. The stress fracture should only take between six and eight weeks to heal, her legs twelve to sixteen weeks. Now to the more worrying aspect. Rose sustained a bad head injury, which we hope is only temporary. At the moment, to be blunt, Rose is blind, deaf, and she can't speak. This has been caused by the tremendous shock and trauma to her body. However, she is sensitive to touch, which is a good sign. Rose did die on the way here, but we got her back. Now, hopefully, in a couple of days we will be flying back to Paris. Rose will be sedated for the journey."

The four of them were totally stunned, but JP was in total shock. "Can I see her?" asked JP quietly.

"Of course, JP. Come with me," said Doctor Pátrinne, but as JP stood up he collapsed. Pierre caught him before he hit the floor.

JP came round and Doctor Pátrinne said, "It's alright, JP, it was the shock. You've been through as much trauma as Rose has, but remember, she is still with us, and hopefully in the coming months, she will recover." JP nodded and they left to see Rose.

"Raoul," said Doctor Michel, "I have a message from the President," and told him. Raoul said he would fly back as soon as his medical team were ready to go. It was agreed they would go the following morning. "How many can go in the jet?" asked Doctor Michel.

Raoul replied, "We can lay either the front or back seats flat for the stretchers to go on. That will leave ten seats, more than enough." The Doctor nodded and then took them to see Rose.

As they entered the room, they saw JP sitting at Rose's bedside holding her hand. Rose was connected to the usual machines to keep her alive. Rose's eyes were open, but blank. For a second Hugh was transported back to Birn hospital, where Rose had been taken after her rape ordeal. Pierre and Raoul really didn't know what to do or say, so Raoul told JP about the President's message, and JP nodded.

"Doctors, do you know if this is where they brought Mía? She might like to see a friendly face," asked Raoul. Doctor Michel made a phone call and told Raoul she was in room 240. Pierre decided to stay with JP and Hugh. To Pierre and the rest of his men, they saw JP not only as a friend, but a strong, resilient, authoritative leader. The man he saw at that moment was totally broken, with tears rolling down his face. Pierre turned away so JP couldn't see his grief. Doctor Pátrinne touched Pierre's shoulder and beckoned him outside.

Once outside Pierre broke down, and Doctor Pátrinne comforted him. "It's alright, Pierre, let your grief out, as JP is going to need you, well, all of you soon. Sounds stupid, I know, but try and look on the bright side. Rose is alive, well just, but she will slowly recover."

Pierre looked at the doctor and said, "But what will happen if she can never see, hear or speak again?"

"We will cross that bridge when we get to it. That's why I need to get Rose back to our hospital. I can then carry out more surgery. I could do it here, but I think JP needs to be with his family."

Pierre took a deep breath, and calmed himself, and then went back to Rose, JP, and Hugh. "Boss, Hugh, do you need anything, a drink, something to eat?" he asked.

JP looked at him and could see the deep concern in his eyes. "I don't want to leave her, Pierre, but I need to go back to the site, to thank everyone, especially the dog handler. Will you come with me?"

"Of course, boss. Raoul has gone to see Mía, as she's here in room 240. I'll go and let him know." Pierre then told JP about the flying arrangements.

JP replied, "Be good to go home. Hugh, Doctor Michel, I will be back as quickly as I can. Look after her for me," and he kissed Rose on her forehead.

The doctor smiled and said, "Rose is asleep at the moment, so go and thank them from us as well." Hugh sat at Rose's bedside.

JP and Pierre both went to see Mía. Raoul was holding her hand, and said, "I've told Mía about Séra and Rose."

Mía had tears streaming down her face, and said, sobbing, "I'm so sorry, JP. If I can help in any way, you only need ask."

For once JP smiled and said, "There is something, Mía, get yourself better. I will make sure you travel back with us. I'll keep you informed." He gave Mía a hug, and kissed her wet cheek. "Raoul, you are more than welcome to stay with Mía until we return." Raoul said he would stay.

Back at the site, JP found the chief coordinator and thanked him for everything they had done in rescuing Rose. JP asked where the dog handlers were. The coordinator said they were in their tent, and pointed it out. JP and Pierre made their way over. The men were relaxing with the dogs at their sides. As they entered the dogs stood up and started wagging their tails. "Apologies for disturbing you, but I wanted to thank the dog who found my wife."

One of the handlers said, "That was my dog, Félix, Monsieur Pascal."

JP raised his eyebrow. "You know me?" asked JP.

The handler smiled and said, "We are based in Paris, and we know you are the President's Chief of Security. When we heard the news, we volunteered to come out to help."

Both JP and Pierre were stunned. "I'm sorry, I didn't know, or I would have—"

The handler put his hand up and stopped JP saying any more. "Not a problem, but more important, how is your wife?" JP told them and they all paled. Félix was whining and his handler told him to go. JP bent down and patted Félix. Félix enjoyed it and his tail wagged even harder.

"How much longer are you staying?" asked Pierre.

"We are probably going to leave the day after tomorrow. Tomorrow the dogs will do four sweeps of the area, section by section, and if we find no one, we will leave." Félix left JP and went and laid down by his handler. Again both JP and Pierre thanked all of them, and left to go back to the hospital.

Once back they stopped at Mía's room. Raoul was still there, reading a paper, but Mía was firm asleep. Raoul quietly tiptoed out and closed the door. Back in Rose's room JP said, "I need to phone the President." Doctor Michel said he had been given permission to use the surgeon's office, and took JP there.

"JP, good to hear from you. How are you both? Silly question, I know."

JP brought the President up to date.

"The jet is ready whenever Raoul is. I have had some of the seats removed, as I understand both Rose and Mía will be on hospital trolleys, not stretchers. JP, I'm not sure how everyone will be with this, but Séra's body will also be on board, discreetly covered."

JP replied, "It's only right that Séra should be with us. Does Mathieu know yet?"

The President said he did and would be at the airport with a car to take Séra home. JP felt a lump in his throat, but swallowed it. They talked for another fifteen minutes and then said their goodbyes.

Back in Rose's room, JP was surprised to see Ruby. "Ruby, what are you doing here?" he asked, giving her a hug, as had Hugh, Pierre and Raoul.

"Covering the story, so the truth gets printed. Rose doesn't know I'm here does she?"

JP shook his head, and went to Rose and kissed her forehead, and sat by her bedside. A nurse arrived with refreshments. "Eat, all of you," said Doctor Michel. "You must keep up your strength." They did as they were told.

JP, Hugh, Raoul and Pierre were talking to Ruby, when Pierre said, "Boss, I think you're needed." JP turned to see Rose was moving her left hand, as though she was trying to grab something. JP took her hand and he saw a smile come to Rose's face. Her eyes were opened staring straight ahead. JP swallowed hard and brushed his tears away.

"JP, I have an idea. Rose is sensitive to touch. Hugh, stand by JP. Now JP, write Hugh's name in Rose's hand." JP looked at him but did what he asked. "Hugh take her hand," and he did. Rose felt his hand and then squeezed it hard.

"She squeezed my hand," said Hugh smiling, with tears in his eyes.

They did the same with Pierre, and Rose responded. Rose put her hand up to her eyes and moved it across them. Nothing. Rose then remembered she was blind and couldn't hear anything. She put her hand out for JP, who took it. She placed it down on the bed, and tried to turn it over. "JP turn your hand palm up," said Doctor Michel.

Rose then wrote "Blind?" and turned her palm upwards.

JP wrote, "Yes."

"Deaf?"

"Yes."

"Speak?"

"No."

Tears started to flow down Rose's face. Then she wrote, "Go."

JP replied, "No." Rose started to get agitated, and slapping her hand down on the bed. Doctor Michel took her hand and she flinched, until he wrote his name. Rose calmed slightly, and the doctor took his hand away, but the minute JP held it, she snatched it away, and waved it away as though telling him to go.

"JP, she needs time for this to sink in. Why don't you go and see Mía and tell her about going back the day after tomorrow? JP, the fact Rose understood what you wrote in the palm of her hand, is an excellent sign. It shows her brain is working properly."

Doctor Pátrinne walked in at that moment, and was absolutely delighted to hear the news. Rose was happy to hold her uncle's hand. JP, Raoul and Pierre went to see Mía, who was pleased she was going home. Alas, she would not be going to the same hospital as Rose, but Raoul said he would visit her often. Pierre raised his eyebrow, and turned to JP with a knowing look. JP actually smiled. Ruby had stayed with Rose and Hugh. She took Rose's hand and wrote Ruby on her palm. Rose grabbed her hand so tightly, and Ruby burst into tears. Doctor Michel comforted her.

When JP, Pierre and Raoul returned to Rose's room, she was firm asleep. "Gentlemen, I have given Rose a sedative to make her sleep, as you can see. Now down the corridor are three rooms 134, 136 and 138. Two of you will have to share, but I suggest you go to the canteen, have a good meal, and even some wine to unwind, and then get a good night's rest. JP, I will come and get you if there is any change in Rose's condition. No 'buts', now go. See you in the morning," said Doctor Pátrinne.

Ruby said her goodbyes and said she would see them in Paris. JP was concerned she was on her own, but Ruby explained she had a photographer with her, who was back at the hotel. Pierre and Raoul shared, so JP and Hugh could have time to themselves. After their meal and wine, they retired for the night. JP was absolutely exhausted, and as soon as his head hit the pillow, he went into a deep sleep.

JP woke about 7am and was annoyed with himself. He should have been with Rose. He quickly washed and dressed and went to her. "How is she, Doctor Michel?"

"About the same, JP. You look a lot more rested now." JP replied he was. He went to take Rose's hand, but she snatched it away. This time JP grabbed it and wrote, "I love you" on her palm. Rose squeezed his hand and didn't let go.

Hugh, Pierre and Raoul turned up about half an hour later.

"JP, I'm leaving now, and Hugh has decided to come back with us," said Raoul, "but I will be back later with the jet. Doctor Michel, just a suggestion. We will be back in Paris by midday. All I have to do is swap aircraft, and I will be back here by say, 2pm. Do you want to leave later this afternoon or still wait until tomorrow?"

"We will wait until tomorrow, Raoul," replied the doctor. "We need to sedate Rose and Mía for the journey back. I also understand that Séra's body won't be at the airport until tomorrow." Raoul nodded. JP and Hugh hugged each other and then Hugh left with Raoul.

CHAPTER 44

Pierre divided his time between Rose and Mía, whilst JP stayed with Rose, just holding her hand. The doctors were also in and out, resting in between times. Rose's vitals stayed stabilised, and they were happy. Like the night before, JP and Pierre went for a meal and then retired. The following morning, all sorts of tests were being done on Rose for the flight back to Paris. Raoul had phoned from the airport, about 9am, to say he had arrived and Séra was already there. Just over an hour later, Rose and Mía were carefully loaded into two ambulances. One doctor and his team went in each ambulance. JP naturally went with Rose, whilst Pierre went with Mía. Both of them had been sedated for the journey. Whilst they were on their way, Raoul had Séra's coffin loaded. It was then covered with a cloth. Raoul had one concern. He wasn't sure if the hospital trolleys would fit through the door. He would just have to wait. He then carried on with the general checks of the jet, even though he had done it all in Paris. Soon he saw the two ambulances approaching the jet. Doctor Pátrinne got out of the first ambulance and Raoul went to him.

"We have a problem."

"What?" asked the doctor. Raoul showed him.

"Good job we put them both on stretchers."

Back at the ambulances the doctor said, "Teams, we need to very carefully lift the patients off the trolleys. The trolleys will need to be folded down and put in the plane sideways. Once in, we can then stretcher them inside."

319

One of the ambulance men said, "Excuse me, but we carry two spare trolleys. Take them, and you can then still wheel the patients to the plane and it's only a short changeover."

Doctor Pátrinne thanked them and that's what they did. An hour later, everyone was settled and on board. The door was closed and Raoul contacted air traffic control for permission to take off. "Permission granted, POF2. We hope the ladies have a speedy recovery." Raoul thanked them and just over two hours later they touched down at Paris airport. Two ambulances were waiting, along with a black hearse, and Mathieu. Andre, Antoine and Donatien were also there, and they helped to unload Rose, Mía and Séra's body. JP went to Mathieu and said how very sorry he was. Mathieu thanked him, but JP could see he was a changed man, and his heart went out to him. As Séra's body was put into the hearse, JP and his men, the doctors and their teams, Raoul and the ambulance men stood with their heads bowed out of respect. Two hours later Rose was settled in at the hospital, and Raoul found out which hospital Mía was going to.

At the hospital, JP and his men all gave each other a man hug, and JP was glad he was back. His men were shocked at the state of Rose. The President had updated them about Rose's condition. It was about 2pm, and Doctor Michel told them to all go back to the palace. Rose would be asleep now until the morning, and Doctor Pátrinne was taking her down to theatre for more x-rays and scans. JP replied he would be back in the evening. The doctor shook his head, but understood.

JP made his way to his office once they arrived back at the palace, and sat in his chair. The silence of the room closed in on him. He closed his eyes, and put his hands over his ears. This was now Rose's world, dark and silent. A tap on his shoulder made him jump.

"Sorry boss, just wanted to know if we could do anything?"

JP replied, "To be honest Andre, there's nothing any of us can do. Rose is alive and at the moment, that's all that matters. You can bring me up to date with what's been happening here."

Andre told him, but it wasn't much.

JP said, "I had better go and see the President."

JP and Andre walked down the corridor and Andre told JP to join them when he could. "Boss, Rose will get better, and if there's anything, any of us can do, you only need to ask."

JP smiled and replied, "I know and I really appreciate it, Andre. I'll see you in the dining room later on." Andre left him to go to the surveillance room.

JP knocked on the door of the President's office. "Entre." The President looked up to see JP, and got up and went and gave him a manly hug, which took JP by surprise. "How is Rose and how are you coping, JP? You may have as much time off as needed. At least all our trips are concluded."

JP bowed and thanked the President. "I would rather be working if that's alright, Monsieur le President. As much as I want to be with Rose, it breaks my heart that she can't see, hear or speak to me. I actually feel useless."

The President felt for JP and said, "Doctor Michel told me Rose reacts to touch. Just you holding her hand will bring immense comfort to her. Still talk and read to her. I know she's deaf at the moment, but it might help. Alas, I'm no doctor, but ask the doctors. My wife is dreadfully upset and would like to see her. Would you mind?"

"Of course not, Monsieur le President. Rose would be extremely honoured."

The President smiled, and then they talked work for about an hour. In the dining room, JP's men were talking.

"Ruby was pleased she saw Rose, but it broke her, and now she's worried sick about her, and I think she's scared of visiting her," said Antoine.

Pierre replied, "There's nothing to be scared of. When I wrote my name in the palm of Rose's hand she squeezed it. She knew who I was, as she did Ruby."

Donatien asked, "Did they say how long Rose will have this problem?"

Again Pierre replied, "The doctors are doing extensive tests, it's the question of 'how long is a piece of string?' but let's hope it's soon."

Andre said, "It doesn't matter how long it takes, we are family, and all of us must support the boss and Rose. Both of them need all of us."

Unbeknown to any of them JP overheard their conservation and it brought tears to his eyes. The love and loyalty from each one of them was overwhelming.

Once he had calmed himself he walked in. "At last the boss is here, and now we can eat," said Pierre jokingly.

JP shook his head and replied, "Heaven forbid, Pierre, I should keep you from your food."

Everyone chuckled, but it broke the tension. They all enjoyed their meal and talked about Rose, Séra and Mía. It actually helped JP.

"I think we might have another romance in the air," said Pierre.

Quickly Andre replied, "Don't tell us, at last Emilie has realised, and found a newer model, and I am joking."

For that remark Pierre gave him a gentle slap on his shoulder. "It's actually Raoul and Mía. I asked him if he was going to come to the palace after he secured the jet. He said he had a hospital visit to go to."

"Good for him," said Donatien.

Afterwards, JP went to the hospital and stayed for an hour, but Rose was asleep. The following morning, Rose was having more tests, and was getting fed up with being poked and prodded. Quite a few times she slapped her hand down on the bed to stop them, but they took no notice. Where was JP? She realised he was probably at work. Then she had another thought and said to herself, *Why would he be here? I can't see, hear or speak to him. Not much fun for him just sitting there. All he can do is hold my hand – wow, big deal. Will be the same for the rest of my family as well. If this is my life now, I'd rather be dead. Wonder how Séra and Mía are. Hopefully they'll come and visit me soon, but again why should they?*

Another voice in her head said, *Rose Pascal, stop being such an ungrateful bitch. You have doctors, nurses, and your family, all deeply concerned and caring for you. Where's your fighting spirit gone? So at the moment you have a few problems. Problems that can be put right so get your act together.* After her "two-way" conversation, she fell asleep.

When she woke, she felt JP holding her hand and squeezed it. JP kissed the palm of her hand, and she smiled. Rose then flinched and grabbed the sheet, and her body stiffened slightly. JP took her palm and wrote a question mark. Rose pointed to her legs and opened and closed her hand. For a couple of minutes JP wasn't sure what she meant, but then he realised and wrote "Pain?" Rose gave him a thumbs up. JP pressed the buzzer and Doctor Pátrinne came in.

"Rose has pain in her legs."

Doctor Pátrinne said, "It's good to see you two communicating. Can you ask Rose out of ten how bad?"

JP thought for a second and then wrote, "Pain, bad?" He then touched each finger. Rose understood and moved her fingers ten times. The doctor upped her pain relief.

Rose turned a small corner about ten days later. Her oxygen mask was gone, as she was now breathing on her own. One evening, the nurse brought JP some sandwiches and coffee in. JP saw Rose sniff. "Doctor, can Rose smell?"

"Not sure yet, JP, why?"

"She just sniffed when the coffee came in."

Doctor Pátrinne put a cup of tea under her nose. Rose shook her hand and pointed towards the smell of the coffee. The doctor then clapped his hands but no response. He checked her eyes and saw a very, very faint flicker in them. "Rose is coming back to us, JP. The fact she can smell, and there is a faint flicker in her eyes, is excellent progress."

JP squeezed Rose's hand, and then bent and for the first time kissed her lips. Rose's hand came up and she put it on his cheek. Then she traced her fingers over his face, and JP kissed each of her fingers. Rose had got to know, by hand touch, who was visiting her. All her family had visited her, especially Hugh. Monica taught her some hand signs, which everyone else learnt as well. JP had been in touch with Mathieu, who told him the funeral had been delayed, due to booking the church and people making travel arrangements.

Two weeks later, when JP was with Rose, she fell asleep. As he went to leave the room, Rose sat up and let out a terrifying scream. JP froze on the spot, but both Doctor Michel and Pátrinne rushed into the room. Rose was thrashing around in the bed, and both doctors were having trouble calming her. "JP, take Rose's hand please." Rose started to calm.

"What's happening?" asked JP.

Doctor Michel replied, "I'm going to assume Rose is reliving the accident, and the fact she screamed could be a sign her voice is back." Doctor Pátrinne gave Rose an injection, which relaxed her. He raised her eyelids and shone the torch across them. Rose blinked. He clapped his hands and Rose flinched. "I don't want to get your hopes up, JP, but fingers crossed, Rose is back with us again. She will sleep soon, and tomorrow I'll do some tests and let you know." JP wasn't going to put his hopes up, but he did feel slightly relieved.

The following day, Doctor Pátrinne turned up at the palace, and went straight to JP's office. The President had seen him arrive, and knew where he was heading, so he too went to JP's office. JP was surprised to see the doctor, followed about a minute by the President.

"This has to be bad news?" said JP, as he bowed to the President.

"On the contrary, JP," said the doctor. "I just had to come and give you the news personally. Rose is sitting up, talking, listening and watching everything going on. She can only do small sessions, but as the days go on, she will get stronger." JP felt the relief sweep through him and grabbed the corner of his desk. "JP, sit down," said the President, "and drink this." Whatever the news was, the President knew they would need a brandy. Both men stayed with JP for about half an hour, and then JP phoned Andre and asked for him and his men to attend his office.

When they got there, they saw five tumblers of brandy poured out. His men frowned and waited for what their boss was going to tell them. JP told them, they downed the brandy and then had a huge man hug. All of them were ecstatic, and couldn't wait to go and see Rose, and that's what they did.

Rose was sitting up with her eyes closed. "She's asleep. You stay, boss, and we'll come later on."

A quiet voice said, "I want a hug before you all go."

Andre, Pierre, Antoine and Donatien, all hugged her and kissed her cheeks. JP kissed her lips gently. They talked for about an hour, and then JP said to his men that they really should get back to the palace. They all hugged and kissed Rose before they left.

"Antoine, where's Ruby? Is she alright?"

Antoine told her Ruby had been busy with the story and the twins, but she would no doubt be in the following day. JP sat at the side of Rose on the bed, and took her in his arms and kissed her so tenderly. "Hello you," said Rose. "I've missed you so much."

JP replied, "As I have you, môn amour, and welcome back."

Rose went quiet for a minute and then asked the question JP had been dreading. "Did Séra and Mía survive? As obviously, I've heard nothing."

JP pressed her buzzer and Doctor Michel came in. "Rose was asking about Séra and Mía?"

Doctor Michel nodded and said, "Mía is in another hospital and has a broken leg and arm, but I understand she is doing well. As to Séra…"

Rose looked at both of them and said, "She didn't make it, did she?"

JP held her close as the tears rolled down Rose's face. One of the machines started beeping. It was her blood pressure. "Calm, Rose, calm," said Doctor Michel.

About ten minutes later, the machine stopped bleeping.

"I'm so sorry, môn amour."

"Have I missed her funeral?" JP told her she hadn't, and it was in three days' time. "I want to go, JP, as she wasn't just my boss, she was also my friend." JP looked at Doctor Michel who said Rose should be alright but she would have to go in a wheelchair.

The next day, Ruby came bounding into Rose's room, so happy. She hugged and kissed her and held her hand. "Tell me the story, Ruby. I think they've all been mollycoddling me."

Ruby told her what she had learnt, even about the dog finding her. Twelve of the designers had died, along with a lot of the models. The death toll was, at the moment, four hundred and ninety-six. It was the worst disaster, in history, that Milan had suffered. Once the site was cleared, there had been three days of mourning. Later, they talked about the antics the twins were up to. Rose laughed but it made her stomach hurt. Ruby stayed for two hours, and then Rose fell asleep. Ruby had worn her out.

CHAPTER 45

When JP arrived he saw Rose was asleep, but she looked pale. Doctor Michel came in to check her vitals, and told JP that Ruby had been with her for two hours, and she was just tired. Rose opened her eyes and smiled. "Sorry my love, did I fall asleep?"

JP raised his eyebrow and said, "Apparently Ruby wore you out?"

"She did rather, but it was lovely to see her. She told me all about the accident. JP, if I tell you something, promise me you won't think I'm mad?"

JP replied, "Why would I think that?"

Rose told him about the long dark tunnel she was falling down, towards the end of her life. "I knew I was taking my last breath, when I felt something nudging my hand, and then something licked my face, and then it went, but it made me take another breath and another."

JP took her hand in his and told her about Félix, the dog who found her. "The team is based here in Paris. Perhaps when you're better we could go see him?" Rose liked that idea. "Now môn amour, you need to rest, and I will see you tomorrow." JP wrapped his arms around her and kissed her tenderly. Rose fell asleep in his arms.

As JP left, Doctor Michel called him into his office. "JP, tomorrow we will need to get Rose use to a wheelchair. It would be good if you were here to help her. Any chance?"

JP replied the President understood, and he would be there.

"She will need some clothes, especially for the funeral, and she must be warm. Rose is going to find it hard that she can't stand yet, and the funeral is going to be very emotional for her. Luckily both Doctor Pátrinne and myself will be there, if she needs us."

JP thanked him and said he would see him in the morning. When he got back to the palace, he phoned Ruby. Monica answered, "How's Rose?"

JP replied, "She was asleep when I left her. I think Ruby wore her out, but Rose was delighted to see her. I assume you know Séra's funeral is the day after tomorrow? I was wondering if Ruby had time, could she come with me and pick out some clothes for Rose?"

"Oh I can do that, JP, and I have a spare key to get in. I'll go in the morning and take them to the hospital. Will you be there?" JP told her about the wheelchair. "Rose is going to find that hard, but with you by her side, she'll cope. I'll see you tomorrow, JP." JP then phoned Hugh and Chantelle, to let them know about Rose and the funeral. Hugh said they would be there, and asked the name of the church, which JP gave him.

When Rose woke in the morning, the nurse washed her as usual. "Who's that for?" asked Rose, pointing to the wheelchair. The nurse replied that it was for her, so she could get about until her legs were fully healed. "What!! You are joking?"

The nurse said gently, "Rose, you won't be able to use crutches as you need both arms, and again your right arm isn't healed yet."

At that moment JP and Doctor Michel walked in. "Morning, môn amour," said JP, giving her a kiss. Rose looked annoyed. "Môn amour, what's wrong?"

Rose looked at him and said, "If you think I'm going to Séra's funeral in that, then I'm NOT. Everyone will pity me, and it's Séra's day. Somehow I have to walk." Both JP and Doctor Michel looked at each other and knew they had a problem on their hands.

Monica arrived at the hospital and saw Rose was upset. JP explained. "Gentlemen, why don't you go and grab a coffee?" And she gave them both a knowing look. Once they'd gone, Monica sat at the side of Rose on the bed, and took hold of her hand. "Sweetheart, why are you so against the wheelchair? You know very well, that at the moment you can't walk. Mía is still in a wheelchair, and is enjoying being pushed around by Raoul. She is also staying with Raoul at the pub, and all the villagers are making such a fuss. Your uncle and Chantelle have taken her round the village, and had her stay for the day, to give Raoul a rest. Won't you just give it a go, for me, please?"

Rose sighed and said, "Alright Mum, I'll give it a go."

"That's my girl," said Monica, smiling and hugging Rose.

Monica brought the wheelchair right up to the side of the bed, and pressed the button. Doctor Pátrinne and a nurse came in and Monica explained. Between them, they very carefully lifted Rose out of the bed, and into the wheelchair. Doctor Pátrinne made sure her legs were straight on the elevated leg rests. Both of Rose's legs were encased in a light plaster, until her broken bones had healed. He then opened the door. Wrapping blankets round Rose to make sure she didn't get cold, Monica pushed the wheelchair down the corridor. She took Rose to the lift, pressed the button, wheeled her in backwards and went down to the canteen.

JP and Doctor Michel were just about to leave, when they saw Monica and Rose. Both of them smiled, and JP said, "Would my beautiful Rose like a coffee?" Rose nodded. Looking round she saw lots of other people in wheelchairs and relaxed. It felt weird to her, but she decided there and then, she would be walking again soon, and this was the best way to get around. Maybe she could go home. "Coffee, Madame." Rose smiled at JP, but the coffee was horrible, and she only had a few sips.

"Doctor Michel, when can I go home?"

The doctor replied hopefully in a couple of days. He didn't tell her they had kept her in hospital a bit longer than usual, as they were concerned about the repercussions of the accident, when she remembered what had happened. It also depended on the outcome of the funeral as well.

JP wheeled Rose back, and the doctors showed him how to lift Rose in and out of the wheelchair. "Nice to have you back in my arms, môn amour," and quickly kissed her neck. Rose blushed slightly.

Monica asked Rose if what she brought for the funeral was alright, if not she would go and get something else. Rose said it was fine.

When everyone had gone Rose said quietly to JP, "My love, how am I going to get my briefs on tomorrow? They won't go over my casts, and I can't go with none on. I can't wear a bra because of my arm, but that's not a problem."

JP replied, "What do I ask for in the lingerie shop and I will go and get you some."

"Just explain, my love," said Rose, giggling.

JP could see Rose was tiring, so he wrapped his arms around her and kissed her passionately. "Sleep well, mon amour, and soon we will be sleeping together again." Rose kissed him back and said she couldn't wait.

The following morning, JP arrived to find Rose wasn't in her room. "Don't panic, JP, the nurse has wheeled Rose down to the bathroom, so she can wash her hair," said Doctor Pátrinne.

JP sighed a sigh of relief, and then said, "What signs should I look for today?"

"Difficult to tell, JP. Rose is already upset, and seeing Séra's coffin is going to bring it all back to her. She could have a panic attack, pass out, or go into deep shock. We will be sitting behind you, so just let us know."

At that moment Rose and the nurse returned, and Doctor Pátrinne left. JP went and kissed her. Her long hair was now shining and she smelled of coconuts. "JP, I will help you dress Rose, as you won't be able to do it on your own. Is that alright, Rose?" asked the nurse. Rose nodded.

"Did you get me some briefs?" asked Rose, looking at JP.

"Sort of," he replied, and gave her the bag.

"Good grief, JP, are they big enough?"

The nurse smiled and said, "JP has got you the right thing. These will come up to your waist and protect your surgery scars." Rose held them out and all three of them laughed. An hour later Rose was dressed. Monica had brought Rose some thick wide-legged trousers to keep her warm. There were black ankle socks and shoes. Her top was a black and white striped jumper, and she had her warm black coat on.

"Ready, môn amour?" Rose nodded.

JP wheeled her down to the front entrance. A large black limousine was there, along with JP's men. They all hugged and kissed Rose. "How on earth do you expect me to get in the car?"

JP smiled and replied, "Let's just say it's been adapted." Pierre pressed something and a small ramp appeared. JP turned the wheelchair round and pulled her into the limousine backwards. Andre was driving, and Donatien was in the passenger seat. JP sat by Rose holding her hand, and Pierre and Antoine sat side by side, next to JP. They made small talk as they drove along. Half an hour later, they arrived at the church. Lots of people were stood outside.

"I don't think I can do this, JP."

"Andre, can you drive round the back please?"

"Sure, boss."

The back of the church was quiet. "Môn amour, we can go in through these doors, and we are sitting just to the left of where Séra will be." Rose smiled and nodded. His men helped JP with the wheelchair, and soon Rose was in the church. Ruby, Céleste, Emilie, Gabrielle, Hugh, Chantelle, Monica and George were already there, and greeted Rose. Doctor Pátrinne and Doctor Michel were also there. Raoul then wheeled Mía in, who was also greeted by everyone. The pew in the front had the middle seats removed, and so Rose and Mía were put there. JP sat at the side of Rose, and Raoul sat the other side of Mía. Both Rose and Mía held hands. The rest of their family then sat in the two pews behind them.

The church slowly filled up around them. Rose noticed the front row of the middle pews was left empty. Suddenly the church fell silent and everybody stood up. The organ started playing. JP felt Rose stiffen and gently caressed her hand, and whispered, "I'm here, môn amour." Rose sort of smiled at him. Rose watched as Séra's coffin was placed on the bier, and then saw Mathieu and Marcus, followed by Katriane and Isabella, and two men, who stood in the first pew. Other people then filled up the next four rows, some she recognised, as they were Séra's publishing team. Mía had turned around and told Rose the church was packed. The service began, with Mathieu giving a speech amongst others. Rose's mind wandered to the last day she had spent with Séra and Mía. The tears slowly fell down her cheeks, and she started to shake. JP noticed immediately, and tried to calm her. JP wrapped his arm around Rose's shoulder and held her close, but careful of her right arm. Rose was now reliving the explosion and saw Séra flying through the air. The next minute Séra's body exploded. Her breathing was getting erratic, and JP was getting concerned, and looked round for the doctors. Doctor Pátrinne was sat on the end of the pew behind him, and slowly and not making a commotion, they changed places.

"Rose, concentrate on your breathing, take some deep breaths," said the doctor quietly.

Rose's head was swimming, and she was feeling faint. Doctor Pátrinne looked at Doctor Michel, who gave him a needle, in a sealed bag. "It will calm her," whispered Doctor Michel to JP. A couple of minutes later, Rose had relaxed considerably.

The service lasted just over an hour, and then Séra's body was taken out to go for a private burial. Everyone had been invited back to the château to celebrate Séra's life. Rose, Mía and the rest of the family, left after everyone else had left the church. Mathieu had waited for them. He went to Rose and hugged her so tight. Rose said, "I'm so, so sorry, Mathieu."

"Don't be, Rose, as Séra died doing the job she loved. Are you well enough to come to the château?" Rose nodded. Mathieu went to Mía and hugged her, and then left in a car following the hearse to Séra's final resting place.

"Môn amour, are you sure you're up to going?"

"I will be fine, my love, and I would like to see the team."

Andre tapped JP on the shoulder and said, "Boss, we have to get back to the palace, and our wives need to get home. Porte has brought another car for us, as our wives have our cars, so Porte will now be your driver." JP understood, and they all hugged and kissed Rose and Mía, and promised to meet up soon. George and Monica had shared a car with Hugh and Chantelle, Mía was with Raoul, Ruby had her car, and the doctors had also arrived together. JP was pleased to have some private time with Rose. They chatted all the way to the château.

Once inside they noticed a lot of the mourners had not attended. Séra's team saw Rose and Mía and went to them. They all comforted each other. JP stood back, as did Raoul. Two tables had been reserved for Rose and Mía, because of their wheelchairs. Monica, Chantelle and Ruby went and got some food and drinks and placed it on the table. A little while later, Mathieu along with Marcus, Katriane and Isabella and the two men arrived, who turned out to be their husbands. Mathieu made a small speech and then everyone toasted Séra's life. Marcus made his way over to Rose and gave her a tight hug and kissed her cheek.

"I'm so glad you came, Marcus," said Rose.

Marcus replied, "My brother needed me and since your wedding, we have stayed in touch. We are brothers again." Rose was delighted at that news, and then they caught up with other news.

About an hour later, Mathieu asked JP if he could kindly take Rose to the study. "Please JP, I would like you to stay, if you don't mind. I think Rose will probably need you." JP raised his eyebrow, but replied he would stay.

Katriane, Isabella, and their husbands arrived, along with another gentleman, and some of Séra's publishing team. They all sat round a large table that had coffee and water on it. JP poured some coffee for Rose. "Ladies and gentlemen, I am Monsieur Lebreuvre and am… was Séra's solicitor. The reason you are here is due to Séra's wishes. First of all I would like give my sincere condolences to you all. To business now, and I will read Séra's Will."

I want to say a huge thank you to you all being a part of the wonderful life I've had, and these are my final wishes.

To my sister Katriane, I leave one hundred thousand francs.

To my niece Isabella I leave the same amount, and both of you should be grateful that I left you anything at all, after the way you disgraced the family name.

As to the château and everything in it, I leave to the love of my life, Mathieu Cheffins. You made me so happy Mathieu. Should you wish to sell the château, you have my blessing, but do not sell it to my sister or niece. Should you decide to live here, I hope you will keep my loyal and trustworthy staff.

As to the magazine, I would like it to continue, with the team that I already have, with one exception. Your new editor will be Rose Pascal. Rose, I have so much to thank you for. Not only were you an excellent member of my team, you were also a very special friend.

I also request that the models, the clothing manufacturers, Madame Cherrillé and Mía, all carry on as normal.

The rest of my finances, after all debts have been paid, I leave to Mathieu Cheffins.

There is one surprise, but I will let Mathieu tell you, as I know for a fact, my sister is going to be rather annoyed.

Séra

CHAPTER 46

"This is an absolute outrage. I will contest this Will. The fact she has left everything to you, Mathieu, and the magazine to that tramp is beyond belief. It's not like you were married to my sister," said a very furious Katriane. "All of this and the magazine should have been left to myself and Isabella. After all we are her next of kin."

Very calmly Mathieu replied, "Actually Katriane, you're not. I was Séra's next of kin, as she was my wife. We married about six months ago."

The whole room went deathly quiet, but then apart from Katriane and Isabella, everyone smiled. Mathieu looked at Rose and winked. Rose was still in shock about Séra making her editor.

"I don't believe you," snapped Katriane. The solicitor handed Katriane a copy of the marriage certificate. Katriane, Isabella and their husbands stood up. "I hope you rot in hell, Séra," said Katriane and with that the four of them left.

"Môn amour, are you alright?"

Rose replied, "I'm stunned, but I'm not good enough to be editor. It should go to one of her publishing team."

Mathieu clinked a glass. "People, time for a quick board meeting. The most important thing I need to know is, do any of you disagree with Séra's decision about Rose?"

Rose replied, "Mathieu, as honoured as I am by Séra's request, I have no idea how to be an editor. Would it not be better to give the position to one of the qualified team?"

Jules replied, "Rose, you have worked your way up the ladder, and Séra saw the potential in you, as we did. I will speak for myself and say I think you will be a great editor. Let's face it, you know how to work the models to their potential. You and Séra have spent hours bringing the magazine together. Mathieu, I think we should take an honest vote. All those in favour raise your hand." Rose was stunned when all the team voted for her.

JP whispered in her ear, "Congratulations, môn amour."

Mathieu said, "Now Katriane and Isabella have gone, I can tell you I have decided not to sell the château. This is where Séra started the magazine, and it will continue. Rose, obviously when you've fully recovered, and not before, I will introduce you to some of her clients. The studio here will still be used, but as to the layouts etc., that will be up to you, Rose. Alas, I will release you from doing the wedding photos for Gilmac News. Maybe Suzette might be interested?"

Rose said she would ask her. JP noticed Rose was starting to look tired. "Mathieu, I don't mean to be rude, but it's been a long day for Rose, and I think it's time she rested."

All the team hugged and congratulated Rose, including Mathieu, and then JP wheeled her out. They went back to the table, where Rose told them the news. All of them were delighted for her, especially Mía. JP beckoned to Porte, who went and got the car. All of them left at the same time. When JP and Rose got back to the hospital, Rose was firm asleep. JP took Rose to her room, where carefully the nurse and himself undressed her, and put her to bed. JP kissed her lips gently and whispered, "Je t'aime, môn amour."

Very sleepily Rose replied, "Love you too, my love."

Four days later, after a previous consultation with JP, the doctors told Rose she could go home. Doctor Pátrinne had done more x-rays and told Rose that they could now put a lighter plaster on her legs, which would make it a lot easier for JP to lift her. Her right arm would also stay in plaster. Rose was just delighted she was going home.

Before Rose knew, JP had gone round to see Monica and George. "I need to ask a huge favour of you both," he said. "Rose is coming home in four days' time. Is there any chance…?"

Monica replied, "Of course we will move in and look after her. You must attend the palace, JP."

JP smiled and replied, "It will only be for three weeks. I'm going to get a bed settee so Rose can sleep in the sitting room. Raoul is getting a load of logs delivered to the farmhouse, so the fires can be kept lit all the time. Rose won't have her casts off for another six weeks, which means it will be after the New Year. As always, the President is going away, so I will be home from the 22nd December until the 4th January. I thought all the family, if they can make it, could come round for either Christmas Day, Boxing Day, or New Year's Day, What do you think?"

Monica replied, "To me Boxing Day seems the best, as I expect everyone will want to celebrate Christmas Day and New Year's Day with their families." JP nodded and said he would ask his men and Hugh. Everyone agreed on Boxing Day. JP had another thought for Christmas Eve.

JP arrived at the hospital to take Rose home. It was a Saturday and he had the weekend off. Rose thanked all the doctors and nurses, and said she would see them in six weeks' time. Doctor Michel told JP that if any problems arose, to contact him immediately and he would drive over. JP thanked him. At the entrance was a smaller limousine, with a ramp and JP wheeled Rose inside. This time the back seats had been taken out, and JP strapped the wheelchair in place. Then he kissed Rose, and said, "Home, môn amour?"

Rose smiled and replied, "Oh yes please."

JP drove carefully, as he didn't want Rose jolting over some of the rough roads. Soon they were at the farmhouse. "Looks like some of my family have turned up," said Rose as she saw the cars. JP pulled up right by the front door. Ruby opened the door and waved to Rose. Rose smiled and waved back. JP wheeled her into the farmhouse and into the sitting room. "Welcome Home" banners were hung up and apart from JP's men and the children, everyone else was there. Rose was so overwhelmed that tears sprang to her eyes. Everyone hugged and kissed her. Rose noticed there was another settee and asked JP why. JP said she would see later on. Ruby and Monica came in from the kitchen carrying trays of tea, coffee and macarons. JP put Rose at the end of one of the settees and within minutes everyone was talking away about all sorts of things. JP noticed the smile never left Rose's face. She was where she wanted to be – home.

A little bit later Raoul arrived with Mía. He had pushed the wheelchair up the hill. He placed Mía at the side of Rose, and then both of them joined the conversations. Rose hadn't realised JP had gone missing. As she looked around Hugh said, "JP's cooking a meal, Rose."

At that moment JP poked his head round the door and said, "Monica, Ruby, could you kindly give me a hand?" Both of them went out and about ten minutes later, told everyone to go to the dining room. George wheeled Rose and Raoul wheeled Mía.

Monica said, "Rose you are seated here, and Mía you are seated at the other end. JP will sit opposite Rose and Raoul you next to Mía. The rest of us can sit where we like." George wheeled Rose up to the table and then pushed the chair more or less up to the table, and Raoul did the same. That way nobody couple knock their legs. Ruby came in and put bowls in front of them, which had all of them looking at each other. Monica put French bread out in the baskets. JP then brought one large dish in, which was covered, and then brought the second one in.

"I hope you don't mind, but due to Rose's and Mía's injured arms, I have made us all a beef stew, which needs no cutting up, along with mashed potatoes. Enjoy." JP took Rose's bowl and filled it up with the stew and potatoes. Raoul did the same for Mía.

"Oh JP, this is wonderful," said Gabrielle, and everyone else agreed. JP smiled.

Rose ate the whole lot and JP smiled at her. "My love, can I have some bread please?" JP handed her the basket and Rose took two slices. JP then watched in amusement as Rose pushed the bread round her bowl to mop up the juices.

All the stew and potatoes were eaten. For a dessert he had made a favourite of Rose's – rice pudding. Afterwards without thinking Rose said, "That was wonderful, my love, so much better than hospital food. Now, I'll go and make the teas and coffees." Then her face fell when she realised she couldn't.

JP took her hand and said, "You will be doing it soon, môn amour." Rose smiled and nodded. Monica made the teas and coffees and they sat for another hour round the dining table, chatting. Rose just happened to look down the table and JP saw her expression changed. He looked down to see Raoul giving Mía a quick kiss on her lips.

Rose looked at JP and mouthed, "How long?"

JP mouthed back, "Since the accident."

Rose them smiled and announced, "Dad, Uncle and Raoul, I'm sure you won't mind helping JP clean up, as us girls need a private chat." JP and Raoul wheeled Rose and Mía back into the sitting room. "George, can I ask you to bring in some more logs please? They're in the—"

George replied he knew where they were, and came back with a box full. He put two on the fire, and put the fireguard round it. The logs crackled and spitted as they caught fire and soon the fire was roaring, giving out a lovely smell of pine. Once the men had gone, Rose looked at Mía and said gently, "I think there's something you need to tell us?"

Mía blushed and replied, "It's only just happened."

"What's happened?" asked Gabrielle, Emilie and Céleste, all at the same time.

Mía replied, "Rose is asking about myself and Raoul."

"Ooh do tell," said Monica, all excited.

"When they found you, Rose, I was in the same hospital they brought you to. I heard a knock at my door and looked up to see Raoul. I knew who he was as I had met him a couple of times. Anyway he kindly asked how I was and did I need anything, I asked about you and Séra and he told me. I was totally stunned and started crying. He held me in his arms until I had calmed a little bit. JP and Pierre then turned up and Raoul told them he had told me the news. Both of them were going back to the site, but Raoul stayed with me. We talked about this and that, and then I must have fallen asleep, because when I opened my eyes he had gone. The following day all three of them came to see me to tell me about coming home. I was delighted. The next day Raoul came in to tell me he was leaving and would be back the following day. He also told me that Séra would be with us, and I was pleased. As he went to kiss my cheek, I moved and his lips brushed against mine. It took both of us by surprise. Once we landed in Paris, he found out which hospital I was in and came to see me. After a couple of days, the staff said I had a decision to make. Go home, or go to a care home. Where I live is a block of flats with four levels. I live on the third, but there is no lift. Raoul didn't like the idea of me going to a care home, and suggested I move into the pub with him. I didn't want to be a burden, and declined his offer. Raoul looked so rejected, so I changed my mind.

"He picked me up in a car that had been adapted for a wheelchair. Once at the pub, all the villagers welcomed me. It was so lovely. Then your uncle and Chantelle walked in. It was so good to see them, and we've had some good times together, haven't we Chantelle?" Chantelle smiled and nodded. "The only trouble was the bedrooms were upstairs. He tried putting a wooden ramp up the stairs, but it was too dangerous, so he just picked me up, and took me to the spare bedroom. The other problem I had was going to the bathroom. I sort of managed the first night, but the next day Raoul put bars up for me to hold on to. Raoul carries me in and carefully helps me to stand up, then leaves. I use my good arm to pull my briefs down, and then my good leg helps me to sit down. Takes time, but I get there eventually. I've got into quite a routine now. Two nights ago, I told Raoul that when I was better, I would go home. Raoul took me in his arms and said, 'I need to tell you what you mean to me,' and he kissed me tenderly. I had started to have feelings for him, and so we talked. In a nutshell, I'm giving up my flat and moving in with Raoul. He is such a kind, caring, loving person, but we can't get married, as he's still married to his wife who ran away years ago."

Monica said, "You do realise that after seven years, he can get a divorce on grounds of desertion."

"Really?" said Mía. "I must tell Raoul."

Meanwhile in the kitchen Raoul had been telling his side of the story to JP, Hugh and George. George told him exactly what Monica had said to Mía. Raoul' s face lit up and he said, "I will look into it. Thank you, George. JP, how much longer before we can join the ladies?"

JP said he would go and find out. "Excuse me, ladies, just wondering how much…"

Rose smiled and said, "We're done, my love, so come and join us." The men returned.

"I've got something to tell you," said Mía to Raoul.

"As I have you, Mía." The next minute they were hugging each other. Everyone clapped and cheered.

Ruby had noticed Rose was tiring and said, "As much as I hate to break up the party, I think we need to give JP and Rose some time on their own."

George and Monica said they would ring on Sunday, about Monday. Hugh said they would be up to see her nearly every day, as did Raoul and Mía. Céleste, Emilie and Gabrielle said they would telephone Rose and be over to visit when they could. Soon JP and Rose were on their own.

"Come, môn amour, let me lay you on the settee, as I'm sure you'll be more comfortable."

Rose smiled and replied, "You were going to tell me what the other settee was for?" JP pushed one of the other settees out of the way, and put the new one in its place. Then he pulled the back seats forward. "It's a bed settee," said Rose. "I don't understand, why can't you carry me up to our bed?"

JP replied, "The doctors suggested the bed settee because if you're in our normal bed, you could accidentally roll out, or without thinking try and go the bathroom. This settee is different. Watch." JP then pulled the left arm out and getting smaller in height, it elongated to halfway down the bed. "You can either sleep on your left side or on your back, but you won't fall out."

Rose smiled and said, "Let's make it up and try it out."

JP kissed her tenderly and said, "I can't wait to sleep with you by my side again. It's been such a long time, môn amour."

CHAPTER 47

JP pushed the arm back first. Then he put a duvet on the bottom with a sheet on the top of it. "To make it more comfortable for you." Then he placed the pillows so Rose could sit up, and then put another duvet on the top. "You're bed awaits, môn amour." He picked Rose up and put her on the bed sitting up.

"Oh this feels wonderful, my love. Come and join me." JP got on the bed at the side of her. He wrapped his arms around her and kissed her gently, then let his kisses trail down her neck. "Umm, I have missed you so much, my love," said Rose, "and I wish I could love you."

JP replied, "That will come later, môn amour, you need to be fully recovered first."

"Boring," replied Rose, and they both laughed.

They watched a film on the television for a couple of hours and Rose was getting sleepy. "Môn amour, I think it's time we settled down for the night. Please don't be embarrassed when I ask if you need the bathroom?" Rose said she did. JP ran up the stairs and came back down with their dressing gowns. JP undressed Rose and then put her dressing gown around her and carried her to the cloakroom, where he helped her to sit on the toilet. He had already put a chair in front of the toilet, so he could put Rose's legs on. "I will give you some privacy," he said. "Just call me when you're ready."

Whilst Rose was in the cloakroom, JP re-arranged the pillows ready for sleep. He also undressed and put his dressing gown on.

"JP," called Rose. JP went to her. "Can I have my toothbrush, toothpaste and a bowl of water?"

JP got her what she needed and put the toothpaste on the brush. Then he held the bowl of water whilst Rose brushed her teeth. JP then picked her up and took her back to the bed. "Môn amour, do you want to sleep in your dressing gown, or should I get you a nightie?"

Rose laughed and said, "Do I have such a thing as a nightie?"

JP took her dressing gown off and then he helped her to lay down in the bed, putting the duvet over her, and then pulled the arm out. He then went to the cloakroom. After turning all the lights out, and putting three more logs on the fire, he got in the bed next to Rose. Propping himself up on his right arm he looked into her beautiful brown eyes. "Je t'aime, môn amour," and kissed her with a passion. As both of them were naked, Rose felt her angel rising to the occasion.

"My angel wants to play."

"Well your angel will just have to wait. Now let me hold you gently and let's get some sleep." Both of them slept soundly through the night.

JP woke as normal at 6am. They had both gone to sleep on their backs, with JP holding Rose's good hand. Carefully he let go of her hand, and rolled onto his side and looked at Rose who was still asleep. Suddenly from nowhere it hit him how close he had been to losing her, and he tried to control his emotions. He took a deep breath and let it out slowly, and wiped the tears from his eyes. Rose had stirred and opened her eyes, and her hand went to JP's face. "Don't be upset, my love. I'm here and I'm getting better." They both looked into each other's eyes, and tears rolled down both their faces, as they gave in to their emotions.

"That wasn't the way I was going to wake you up, môn amour," said JP a short while later.

Rose smiled at him and said, "How were you going to wake me up?" JP brushed away her tears and then gave her a long lingering kiss. "I love you, JP."

"Je t'aime aussi, môn amour."

They both then slept for another couple of hours. When Rose awoke, she could smell breakfast being cooked. JP appeared and said,

"Do you need the bathroom, môn amour?" Rose nodded and so JP carefully picked her up and took her to the cloakroom. Afterwards JP said, "Decision time. Wheelchair, settee or stay in bed?"

Rose replied, "Stay in bed as it's a lot more comfortable than the wheelchair." JP put her back on the bed, so she was sitting up, and then put her dressing gown on to keep her warm, piled the pillows up, and pulled the duvet up. A couple of minutes later JP came in with two trays. "Breakfast is served, môn amour, and I hope you're not embarrassed, as I cut your bacon and sausages up. I thought it would be easier for you."

Rose replied, "Thank you my love, and no, I'm not embarrassed." JP put the tray on her lap and Rose tucked in. After she'd finished, JP then handed her a mug of coffee.

"My love, now we're alone, seriously, what do you think about me being editor of Séra's magazine?"

JP replied, "Seriously, they couldn't have picked a better person. You know how to get the best shots of the models, you got the new screens in the studio, you and Séra have sorted and published the photos in the magazine, and not only that, you know the whole team. Mathieu told me you have been a great asset to the company, and I think he would genuinely have been upset if you had turned it down. That reminds me. The staff at the hotel contacted Mathieu to tell him they had all of Séra's belongings she had left in her room, and together with yours and Mía's, they sent it all to Mathieu. Mía has had hers back, and yours are all upstairs, except the film rolls that Mathieu took to give to Jules."

Rose replied, "I'd not given any of that a thought. Is my camera here?"

"Yes, môn amour. Now let me get rid of these trays and then we can cuddle up and watch a movie."

A lot later JP made them a meal, and again cut up Rose's meat. About 6pm Monica phoned to see what time JP had to leave in the morning. "Suggestion," said JP. "Why don't you and George come tonight, and then we can run through everything?" Monica said they'd be there soon.

Once they arrived, they hugged and kissed Rose. "Sorry to be a nuisance, Mum and Dad."

"Since when have you been a nuisance?" asked George.

"My love, I need the cloakroom," said Rose. JP showed Monica and George how he picked Rose up. Once in the cloakroom, Monica took over. "Mum, can you give me a quick wash, as I didn't like to ask JP."

"Of course, sweetheart." Monica washed Rose's body, except her bad arm and legs. "Have you got any panties to put on?"

Rose blushed slightly and said, "JP bought me some huge briefs, but I don't know what he's done with them."

"Will you be alright if I leave for you a moment?" Rose nodded. Monica then came back with the large panties, and eventually between the two of them, got them on. "JP, we're ready," called Monica. JP came in with George, and he watched as George picked Rose up and put her back on the bed. JP felt better now at leaving Rose in the morning. The four of them sat and chatted until about 10pm. JP let George carry Rose to the cloakroom. JP then showed George how to open and shut the bed settee, along with the arm.

"I have made up the spare bedroom for you and Monica. Rose will be absolutely fine down here."

George shook his head and said, "Thank you JP, but Monica has already said she will sleep on the settee. She won't leave Rose alone." JP nodded in understanding.

"George, we're ready," called Monica.

After George and Monica retired for the night, JP helped Rose out of her dressing gown. JP smiled and said, "You've got your big panties on."

"Mum's idea," replied Rose, and they both laughed.

JP rolled onto his side, and putting one arm around her shoulders, and the other one round her waist, he kissed her gently. "I'll try not to wake you in the morning, môn amour, and I will ring you every night. It will only be just over three weeks and then I will be home for two weeks."

Rose kissed him back and said, "I will be fine, my love, so please don't worry, and wake me up in the morning so I can kiss you before you go." They cuddled up to each other as best they could and slept.

The following morning, JP carefully and quietly got out of bed, had a wash in the cloakroom, and then had his breakfast. "Morning JP," said a quiet voice.

JP jumped and turned to see Monica. "Sorry Monica, did I wake you up?"

"No, it's my body clock. Still thinks I'm working."

"Coffee?"

"No thanks. I'll wait until Rose and George have their breakfast. Is there anything Rose can't eat?"

JP said that as long as the meat was cut up, Rose could eat anything. "She would have a problem with her favourite boiled eggs and soldiers though," he said, grinning. Monica raised her eyebrow. "Time for me to go. I'm taking Rose's car, so if you want to drive the other one to take Rose out anywhere, this is the key. Just tell George to make sure he bolts all four latches down on the wheelchair." Monica nodded.

JP went back to Rose and gently kissed her lips. "JP."

"Hush, môn amour, go back to sleep, it's early. Je t'aime." Rose held her hand out, and he took it, and bent over and gave her a long loving kiss, and then kissed her forehead. Rose closed her eyes and drifted back off to sleep.

Over the following weeks, Monica, George, and Rose got into a routine. Hugh and Chantelle came to visit, as did Raoul and Mía. Ruby and the twins arrived at the weekends, and the wives phoned often. Even Mathieu, Suzette and Gérard telephoned. Naturally, JP phoned every night. Rose missed him greatly. The weather had been horrible, with dreadful storms, and so Monica and George didn't take Rose out. Monica would send George off with a shopping list. Most of the time Rose sat on the settee with her mum, watching romantic films, crying, smiling and laughing through them. One morning Rose said, "Mum, my legs feel funny. It's like pins and needles, but it's different." George went and phoned Doctor Michel.

"Can you bring Rose to the hospital, or shall I send an ambulance?"

George replied, "I think an ambulance would be better."

"It's on the way," said Doctor Michel.

Within an hour Rose was at the hospital, as was JP, as Monica had phoned him. Rose was taken down for x-rays. A short while later Doctor Michel returned. "It's nothing to worry about. Her arm has healed beautifully, and we have removed the cast.

"The fact Rose's legs have been straight for so long, the muscles are complaining, so we have re-done Rose's casts. She now has a cast on the top of her legs, and a cast on the bottom. In other words, she can now bend her knees. I've given her some very gentle exercises to do, and the nurse is going through them with her now. I have also given her arm exercises. As to the wheelchair, the leg rests can be pushed in, so I suggest that sometimes she has her legs down, but if at any time her legs start to feel heavy, pull out the leg rests. All is looking well for two weeks' time to have the casts off totally. Rose will then stay here for a week, and will receive physiotherapy every day. We will not release her until we are satisfied her legs have fully recovered."

Everyone sighed a sigh of relief. The nurse wheeled Rose back to them. "Look everyone, I've got my arm back again," and held both of them out to JP, who wrapped his arms round her and gave her a kiss.

"That's wonderful, môn amour, but do as Doctor Michel told you and be gentle with your arm." Rose replied she would. JP wheeled her down to the ambulance, after they all thanked Doctor Michel, and said he would be home in six days. George and Monica got in the back with her. Rose blew a kiss to JP as the ambulance man closed the door. JP then returned to the palace, to fill the President and his men in with the outcome. Soon Rose, Monica and George were back at the farmhouse, and thanked the ambulance men. That evening Rose had two boiled eggs and soldiers, and slept better now she could bend her knees.

The next six days flew by, and JP was home. He thanked Monica and George for everything they had done for Rose, and they said it had been a delight to spend time with her, and would see them both on Boxing Day. That night, in bed, Rose wrapped her arms round JP and cuddled into him. It felt so good to have Rose back in his arms again. He desperately wanted to love her, but it wouldn't be too long now, before he could. They both fell into a deep contented sleep.

The next day, after breakfast, JP said he had to go shopping. Rose said she wanted to go with him, so JP carried her to the car and placed her in the passenger seat, and put her seatbelt on. The wheelchair he folded up and put in the boot. At the shopping centre, JP wheeled Rose around, and she felt great just to be out, but she did notice how busy it was and worried someone might bump into her. JP assured her he wouldn't let that happen. As it turned out the wheelchair came in handy, as JP could put the bags on the handles. They shopped for about an hour, and then JP drove them home. He lifted Rose onto the settee and went to make some coffee and put the shopping away. "Môn amour do you...?" Rose was firm asleep. Carefully JP put a blanket round her to keep her warm, and he also lit the fire.

Later on, Rose woke to the smell of Boeuf Bourguignon. JP came in and saw she was awake. "Looks like I tired you out, môn amour."

"Come here you, as I want a cuddle."

JP obliged. "Come, môn amour, I have laid the table for us. Now how are your legs feeling?"

Rose replied she needed to put her legs up, so JP put her in the wheelchair, with the leg rests extended. Once at the table, JP brought in their meal. "Umm, this tastes delicious my love, thank you."

"My pleasure, môn amour."

"JP, what are we going to do about a tree and the decorations this year?"

JP smiled and replied, "I can, with your guidance, put up the decorations. Maybe, just this year, we'll forget the tree."

"That sounds good to me," replied Rose.

"As it's Christmas Eve tomorrow, I wondered if you would like to go out for lunch or dinner. Which would you prefer?"

Rose thought for a moment and then said, "I promise I'll rest during the day, and would love to go to dinner."

JP kissed her lovingly and said, "Then that's what we'll do, and tomorrow you can tell me what decorations go where."

After clearing away the dishes, JP carried Rose to the settee, and then pulled out the bed settee, and moved her onto it. Both of them then cuddled up to each other and watched the television, until it was time to snuggle up and sleep.

CHAPTER 48

"My love, the silver tree with the red balls goes over there on that table," said Rose the following morning. JP had got the decorations from the barn, and put them up with Rose's guidance. "Now it looks like Christmas," said Rose with a huge smile on her face. "I think you should have a reward, my love. Come here."

Rose was sat up on the settee, and JP sat at the side of her, facing her. Rose linked her arms round his neck and kissed him with such a passion, that JP felt his manhood go rock hard. Rose only had her dressing gown on, and JP untied it. His kisses went down her neck and then gently he caressed her breasts, and swirled his tongue over her nipples, which went hard. He made his way back up to her lips. "Soon môn amour, we will love each other again."

"Good, I have missed you so much."

JP re-tied her dressing gown and said, "Now I will go and make us a light lunch, and then both of us can sleep, or you will be tired later on." He made cheese omelettes with a salad. Afterwards they cuddled on the settee and fell asleep until roughly 5pm. A couple of hours later, JP had helped Rose to get dressed, and made sure she had her long, thick, warm coat on, as they made their way to the restaurant. Rose realised where she was going and smiled.

"Ahh, my beautiful Rose," said Gérard as he hugged and kissed her. "I am so pleased to see you, and you look so well. Come, I have a special table for you." Gérard took charge of her wheelchair, and took them to their table.

"Gérard the tree looks wonderful, as do you."

Gérard smiled and replied, "Thank you, Rose. Here are your menus."

JP and Rose enjoyed a lovely meal, and towards the end of the evening, Gérard brought out a birthday cake, and a bottle of champagne. As the bells chimed midnight for Christmas Day, everyone in the restaurant sang "Happy Birthday". Rose was overwhelmed and thanked everyone. JP kissed her tenderly. Gérard opened the champagne and poured out two glasses, and Rose cut her cake. A little later Rose whispered to JP that she needed the ladies'. JP called Gérard over and whispered in his ear, so as not to embarrass Rose. Gérard replied quietly, "Give me a moment." Gérard asked one of the waitresses to see if the ladies' were free, and they were. JP helped Rose.

Whilst they were in the ladies', Rose told JP she was getting tired and her legs were hurting, but only slightly. JP made his apologies to Gérard, who understood. Just over an hour later, both of them were cuddled up in their bed.

"Good morning, môn amour, and Happy Birthday again."

Rose wrapped her arms round JP's neck and said, "I need the bathroom." JP kissed her and then scooped her up in his arms. JP made Rose's favourite of boiled eggs and soldiers for her breakfast.

"My love, what can I do to help you for tomorrow?"

"Nothing at the moment, môn amour, as I have a present for you." JP saw Rose look downhearted. "Môn amour, what's wrong?"

Rose replied, "I haven't got you anything. I'm sorry," and tears sprang to her eyes.

JP wiped them away and said, "It's not a problem, and I haven't got you a Christmas present either. This is your birthday present, so dry those tears." JP placed a box on her lap, and Rose unwrapped it.

"Oh JP, it's beautiful. Thank you." She held her arms out to him and kissed him with a passion.

"I thought it would go with your new image as an editor." It was a leather briefcase, with her initials, RP, etched in a corner in gold. Inside were various compartments in the top part for pads, pencils etc, all in leather. The bottom part was empty.

The telephone rang, and it was Hugh wishing them both a Merry Christmas, and Happy Birthday to Rose. Then everyone else phoned, all finishing with "looking forward to tomorrow". The rest of the day, Rose and JP just relaxed, and watched movies. For lunch JP made cheese soufflés, followed by apple tart with cinnamon. For dinner they had sandwiches and fruit and ice cream. Both of them enjoyed being in each other's company. It didn't matter if they didn't talk, they were together and that was all that mattered. Both of them knew they could love each other, but wanted to wait.

Boxing Day arrived, and Rose and JP had croissants and coffee for breakfast. JP had carried Rose into the kitchen and seated her on one of the chairs. "Let me know if your legs start to hurt, môn amour." Rose replied she would. Between them they got all the meal prepared, the meat was in cooking, and then with Rose's guidance, JP laid the table.

"My love, I think it's time we got ready. Can you carry me up to our bedroom so I can choose what to wear?" It was the first time Rose had been upstairs since she returned.

"What would Madame like to wear today?" said JP, smiling.

"Umm, I think I'll put my long black skirt on, with my sparkly blue blouse."

JP grinned as he said, "And would Madame like her big panties?"

If Rose could have got off the chair and hit him she would have done. "You just wait until I'm better, my husband." JP roared with laughter, and then kissed her. Once they were both dressed, and Rose had styled her hair, in long flowing curls, JP carefully carried her down the stairs to the sitting room. He had already lit the fire, which was roaring away. The bed settee was now placed between the three large settees, which gave more room for their family to sit down.

Just over an hour later, their family started arriving, and this year Raoul and Mía joined them. Mía, like Rose, was still in a wheelchair. Altogether there were sixteen adults and eleven children. JP just hoped he had cooked enough.

When all of them were settled in the sitting room Emilie said, "Children, can you come here please?" The six older ones went to her. "I have a huge favour I would like to ask of you. As you know, Aunt Rose and her friend Mía were involved in a bad accident, and you can see they are still in wheelchairs. Could you possibly keep an eye on the young ones to make sure they don't bump or knock into Aunt Rose or Mía as it might hurt them. Do you think you could help?" The older children all replied they would. They returned to the younger ones, who were in a large playpen that JP had set up. Monica and Ruby had made pots of tea and coffee, and the conversation flowed. Rose loved hearing about what antics the children had been up to. Everyone was in fits of laughter. Rose noticed JP, Emilie and Gabrielle had gone. She assumed they were helping him in the kitchen.

Rose was right, as they were in the kitchen.

"So JP, how is Rose doing truthfully?" asked Gabrielle.

JP replied, "She's doing well, but there are times when she gets tired, and her legs hurt, but once she puts them up, the pains go. She can't wait to get the plasters off. I don't know if she remembers, but some nights she cries out as though she's reliving the explosion. Rose hasn't mentioned it, so I haven't either."

Emilie then said, "And how are you bearing up, as it can't be easy?"

JP smiled and said, "I'm fine. I have a lot to thank Monica and George for, as they've looked after Rose during the weeks. I've only had the weekends, and I've just enjoyed being with her, just like I always do. Now we have a meal to serve up."

JP went to the sitting room and told everyone to go into the dining room. He wheeled Rose, and Raoul wheeled Mía. Only when Rose and Mía were comfortably placed, did the rest sit down. The children were left in the playpen, and would be fed afterwards. This year JP had cooked a traditional English Christmas meal. He brought out a chicken, a turkey, and a huge piece of beef. There were roast potatoes, garlic potatoes, and a variety of vegetables, stuffing, Yorkshire puddings, and gravy. As always JP carved. Raoul cut up Mía's meat for her, as her arm was still in plaster. Antoine had his usual job of seeing to the wine. Everyone tucked in and enjoyed a thoroughly delicious meal. Afterwards, JP carried a rather large Christmas pudding in, and poured brandy over it and then lit it.

Everyone cheered and clapped. Emilie put jugs of custard/cream on the table. Once everyone had finished, George, Monica, Hugh and Chantelle helped to clear all the dishes away.

Then it was the turn of the children. The six older ones had a smaller Christmas meal, whilst Gabrielle, Emilie, Céleste, Ruby and Antoine, saw to the younger ones. Rose and Mía were in the sitting room with Andre, Donatien, Raoul, and Pierre, who were telling them Christmas jokes, and had them in tears of laughter. Soon everyone was together in the sitting room, and JP and Monica brought in pots of tea and coffee, along with plates of macarons. JP put the television on for the children. The younger ones had cuddled up and gone to sleep. Rose sat back and totally relaxed. She looked at each of her family and thought how lucky she had been to have them all.

JP put his arm round her shoulder and kissed her forehead. "You alright, môn amour?"

Rose nodded and replied, "I was just thinking how lucky we all are to have each other, and the children all growing up together." JP bent over and gently kissed her lips. Rose could see Mía and Raoul were discussing something.

When there was a pause in the conversation, Raoul said, "Mía and I would like to say a huge 'thank you' for letting us join your family, and we have some news. Out of the blue, I received divorce papers from a solicitor representing my wife. Naturally I signed and returned them straight away. Last week I was officially divorced, and so Mía and I have decided to marry, and would like to invite you all to our wedding. It won't be a big affair, just all of us, and the villagers. I'll let you know the date. The reception will be in the pub."

Everyone clapped and cheered and were delighted. Apart from Rose, they all got up and congratulated the couple. JP then wheeled Rose over, and she hugged and kissed Mía's cheek as best as she could. "Thank heavens we both get all this plaster off in a couple of weeks, and then we can hug each other properly." Mía agreed.

The rest of the day carried on with laughter, jokes and everyone having a great time. JP made sandwiches, and brought in various cakes, and they all toasted Raoul and Mía with champagne. The children had all been very well behaved, even the young ones. Soon everyone had left and JP and Rose were on their own.

"What a fabulous day, my love, and thank you for such a wonderful meal. For a couple of seconds I actually felt homesick, and wondered what my brothers were doing."

JP looked at her and said, "It's never too late to go back and let them know."

"No, it's best this way. I know I'll see them one day, but not in this world."

JP kissed her tenderly, and said, "I know you will. Now I think it's time both of us went to bed," and quickly unfolded the bed settee. Once in bed they kissed and cuddled each other.

Rose felt JP's manhood rise and said, "Not long now, my angel." She kissed her fingers and then put them on his manhood. Her angel twitched in reply. JP was on his side and put one arm round her shoulders, and the other across her chest, and held her close. Soon both of them drifted off into a deep contented sleep.

The rest of the week and New Year's Eve/Day, Rose and JP just relaxed and enjoyed their time together. With no one visiting they just had their dressing gowns on. Both of them stayed in the bed settee.

On the Sunday evening, JP drove Rose to the hospital. At last it was time to have her casts removed. Both doctors were there to greet her, and then showed her to her room. JP kissed her and said, "I will see you in a week, môn amour, when I know you will walk back into my arms."

Rose wrapped her arms round his neck and said, "I'm scared, JP. What will happen if my legs don't respond to treatment?"

"They will, môn amour, they will." JP kissed her and left to go to the palace. The doctors and nurses settled Rose in for the night. The following morning she was taken down to theatre, where her leg casts were cut away.

"Feeling alright, Rose?" asked Doctor Michel.

"I feel like my legs are floating now the casts are off. Is that bad news?"

"No Rose, it's not. You are not going to be able to run before you can walk. The nurse is going to massage some cream into your legs, and will do it every couple of hours, as this will help with the circulation. Tomorrow we will try and get you to stand, but after such a long time, your legs will feel like jelly. Don't worry, Rose, as everything has knitted back beautifully. Believe me, in a week, you'll more or less be back to normal." Rose thanked him.

That week was hard work, but by the Friday, Rose was up and walking round. "Rose, today is your last day, but you have one more test to do. May I introduce Sablon, and he is going to give you a driving lesson." Rose looked perplexed, and the doctor explained. "Before you can drive, we must make sure you can do an emergency stop without it hurting your legs. You must be honest Rose, and if you feel any sensation in your legs you must tell Sablon." Rose nodded and left with Sablon. He drove out of Paris to a quiet road.

"Now Rose, it's your turn. This road is very long, straight, and hardly any traffic these days. As we drive along, I will suddenly shout 'STOP' and you will do an emergency stop. Alright?" Rose nodded and they swapped seats. Rose gave herself time to adjust the mirror, her seat, made sure her feet weren't too near or far away from the pedals. When she was happy she drove off. She kept anticipating Sablon shouting, but he didn't, and so she relaxed. "STOP." Rose jumped out of her skin, but both feet went to the pedals as she stopped. "That was good, and you didn't skid," said Sablon. "How are your legs?"

Rose replied, "Honestly, they seem to shudder a bit, but there was no pain." Sablon nodded and told Rose to carry on driving, until she saw a pull in and then turn around, and drive back until he told her to turn around again.

A couple of hours later on the way back to Paris, Rose screamed as the car spun out of control.

TO BE CONTINUED IN THE FINAL BOOK,

The Life of Rose Brambles – Book 4

Printed in Great Britain
by Amazon

56197414R00206